Praise for Michelle Willingham

"Well written, aptly conveying a strong sense of family among the sisters, the quartet shows great promise."
—4 stars, *RT Book Reviews* on *Undone by the Duke*

"Using lots of emotion, *Seduced by Her Highland Warrior* is sure to touch your heart and soul with the tenderness and love that shines from the pages. Michelle Willingham has penned another winner."
—4.5 stars, *CataRomance.com*

"Michelle Willingham writes characters that feel all too real to me. The tortured soul that is Kieran really pulled at my heartstrings. And Iseult's unfailing search for her lost child made this book a truly emotional read."
—*Publishers Weekly* on *Her Warrior Slave*

"Willingham successfully draws readers into an emotional and atmospheric new tale of the Clan MacKinloch. Allowing a gentle heroine to tame a hero who has lost his ability to speak draws readers into the story and keeps them enthralled to the very end. Well crafted, brimming with historical details and romantic from beginning to end, this is Willingham at her best."
—4 stars, *RT Book Reviews* on *Tempted by the Highland Warrior*

"Two wounded souls find hope and redemption in *Surrender to an Irish Warrior*, a richly detailed and emotionally intense medieval romance."

—*Chicago Tribune*

"Willingham neatly folds equal measures of danger and desire into her latest historical, and the snippets from Emily's cookbook that open each chapter add an extra dash of culinary spice to her well-crafted romance."

—*Booklist* on *The Accidental Countess*

"Memorable characters and exciting plot twists make this one worth hanging on to."

—4.5 stars, *RT Book Reviews* on *To Sin with a Viking*

Undressed by the Earl

Also by Michelle Willingham

SECRETS IN SILK SERIES (REGENCY SCOTLAND)

Undone by the Duke

Unraveled by the Rebel

MACEGAN BROTHERS SERIES (MEDIEVAL IRELAND)

Her Warrior Slave

"The Viking's Forbidden Love-Slave" in the *Pleasurably Undone* anthology

Her Warrior King

Her Irish Warrior

The Warrior's Touch

Taming Her Irish Warrior

"Voyage of an Irish Warrior"

"The Warrior's Forbidden Virgin"

Surrender to an Irish Warrior

"Pleasured by the Viking" in the *Delectably Undone* anthology

"Lionheart's Bride" in the *Royal Weddings Through the Ages* anthology

Warriors in Winter

Undressed by the Earl

A SECRETS IN SILK NOVEL

MICHELLE WILLINGHAM

Montlake
Romance

Published by Montlake Romance, Seattle

www.apub.com

ISBN-13: 9781477819814
ISBN-10: 1477819819

Cover design by Kim Killion
Illustrated by Jim Griffin

Library of Congress Control Number: 2013920369

Printed in the United States of America

For Patricia—Thanks for all of your love and support throughout the years. You knew from the beginning that I was meant to write romance, and you stood by me every step of the way. Thanks for being such a wonderful mom and grandma, even if you do feed my children ice cream at nine a.m.

Chapter One

Amelia Andrews had waited four excruciatingly long years to marry the Viscount Lisford. Although everyone said he was a wicked rake who gambled and took advantage of innocent women, she didn't care. He was, by far, the handsomest man she'd ever seen. His hazel eyes were mysterious, and his golden hair reminded her of a prince. This was going to be the year he finally fell in love with her, even if she had to throw herself at his feet.

Well, she could faint in front of him, anyway. Diving at a man's shoes wasn't exactly what her mother would deem ladylike.

In her mind, she envisioned reforming him, until he fell madly in love with her and—

"Planning your attack, are you?" came a voice from behind her. Amelia suppressed a groan. David Hartford, the Earl of Castledon, was here again. Sir Personality-of-a-Handkerchief, as she'd once nicknamed him.

He never danced and had never courted a single woman in all the years since his wife had died. He was just *there* all the time. Watching, like a wallflower.

"I've never understood why the ladies here are so fascinated by Lord Lisford," he remarked. "Would you care to enlighten me?"

She shouldn't be speaking with Lord Castledon, although they'd had numerous conversations in the past year, with him addressing her back. If she didn't turn around to face him, it seemed less improper.

Besides that, Lord Castledon was safe—a man she would never consider as a suitor. He wasn't so terribly old, but he'd been married and widowed. He wasn't at all dashing or exciting. Honestly, he was perfect for her sister Margaret.

A hard sense of frustration gathered in Amelia's stomach at the thought of her prim and proper older sister. There had been a time when she'd been devastated, for her sister had nearly married the man of Amelia's dreams. The viscount had cried off only days before the wedding, leaving Margaret a spinster and Amelia a shred of hope. She felt sorry for Margaret's humiliation, truly she did, but it had been an impossible situation with both of them wanting the same man.

That had been years ago. Surely her sister would forget all about Viscount Lisford, especially if she had another man to wed. And Amelia strongly believed that sensible people ought to be paired together. *She* was not at all sensible. Impulsive, her mother had called her. Amelia preferred to think of herself as spirited.

"Lord Lisford is quite wicked," she told the earl. "When you dance with him, you sense the danger. It's delicious."

"I'll take your word for it," he said drily.

From behind her, she sensed him stepping closer. Lord Castledon was quite tall, and even without her turning around, his presence evoked a strange sensation, as if he were touching her. The air between them grew warmer, and she grew conscious of him in a way that made her skin prickle.

She stole a quick glance behind her and saw the solemn cast to his face. It didn't seem that he ever smiled, though the earl wasn't unattractive. Aside from being tall, he had black hair and shrewd blue eyes. She'd never seen him wear any color except black. And he rarely spoke to anyone but her. She had no idea why.

"Dangerous men are nothing but trouble," he continued, moving to stand beside her. "You'd be better off choosing a more respectable man."

"That's what my mother says." Amelia opened her fan, adding, "But marriage to a man like Lord Lisford would never be dull."

"Marriage is not meant to be entertaining. It's a union of two people with a mutual respect for one another."

She eyed him with disbelief. "That sounds awful. Surely you don't mean that."

From the serious expression on his face, she realized he did. "Didn't you ever have fun with your wife?" she asked. "I don't mean to pry, but I thought you loved her."

"She was everything to me."

There was a glimpse of grief that flashed over his face before he masked it. And suddenly her curiosity was piqued. This boring man, who all too often lurked near the wallpaper, had enjoyed a love match. Try as she might, she couldn't quite imagine him engaged in a passionate tryst. But perhaps there was more to him beneath the surface.

Amelia's heart softened. "No one will ever compare to her, will they?" She stared at him, trying to imagine a man like the earl in love with anyone.

"No." There was a heaviness in his voice. "But I made a promise to my daughter that this Season, I will find a new mother for her." His features twisted as if it was not a welcome idea.

A thought suddenly sparked within Amelia. There was nothing she loved more than matchmaking. She'd successfully paired her sister Juliette off with her husband, Paul, and here was another chance to find a match for Lord Castledon. Her sister Margaret was nearing five-and-twenty, and after being jilted once, she might be amenable to a man like the earl.

"I have an idea," she told him, unable to keep the excitement from her voice. And oh, it was simply perfect. "We could help one another."

The sidelong look he cast at her was undeniably cynical. "And what could *you* do for me, Miss Andrews?"

"Reconnaissance," she said brightly. "You'll tell me all of your requirements in a wife, and I shall investigate your options. I know all the eligible ladies here, and I'm certain I could find the perfect woman for you."

If Margaret wouldn't suit, there were a few wallflowers who might fit his conditions.

His mouth twisted. "Indeed. And for this 'service,' what do you want from me?"

She hid her face behind her fan. "I want Viscount Lisford. You could speak to him and put in a good word for me."

He crossed his arms, staring across the room. "You're not worthy of a man like him, Miss Andrews."

Amelia felt her cheeks grow hot. "And why not? Is there something wrong with me? I know I talk too much, and most people believe I'm a featherbrain. But surely—"

She didn't finish the sentence, for she suspected what he would say. *You're too young. Too innocent.*

And while that might be true, why couldn't she set her sights on the man she wanted? Why couldn't she marry the handsomest man in London who set her pulse racing? Why should she settle for a titled gentleman with a respectable fortune when she could have so much more?

No. She didn't need Lord Castledon's help. Not in this.

There were ways to capture a man's attention, and she was *certain* that this was her year. To the earl, she remarked, "Thank you, my lord, but I don't need your help after all. Especially if you believe I'm not worthy of the viscount." She marched in the direction of her aunt Charlotte, hoping no one would see her embarrassment.

The Earl of Castledon stared at the young woman as she took long strides away from him. Amelia Andrews was impulsive, spirited, and filled with more joie de vivre than anyone he'd ever met.

"No, you're not worthy of the viscount," he remarked under his breath. "You're worth far more."

⚜

He didn't know if he could do this again.

David Hartford, the Earl of Castledon, stood with his back against the wall. He felt as if a hundred bayonets were pointed at him. God above, he needed a drink to get through this night. Or three.

In his pocket, he had a list of instructions that he'd penned to himself, prior to this ball.

Be introduced to a new lady. Hold a conversation with her that lasts longer than thirty seconds. Ask her to dance.

The last one made him want to shudder. He hadn't danced in six years and likely didn't remember how.

Who was he trying to fool? He didn't want to wed anyone again. Though he was no longer in mourning, he still wore black, out of habit.

Every moment he attended a social gathering of any kind felt like a mockery. His friends in the House of Lords kept sending him invitations during each Season, and he accepted a few from time to time, so as not to offend them. He was here out of courtesy, not because he wanted to make merry or flirt with anyone fanning herself. That wasn't his way.

Truth to tell, he wasn't quite certain *how* he'd won his wife's hand in marriage. They had been wallflowers together, if he remembered correctly. Katherine had smiled at him, and that had given him the courage to venture into conversation. Twelve years ago, he'd been one-and-twenty and an empty-headed fool.

Now he felt as if he were living his life encased within a column of glass. He could see the world and speak to those around him, but an invisible barrier kept him from enjoying the years remaining. It seemed like a betrayal to be happy, though he knew that was illogical. Sometimes at night he reached across to the empty pillow beside him, wishing Katherine was there. The loss of her was a physical ache that hadn't diminished at all in the years since she'd died.

He still had silent conversations with her ghost. If that made him a madman, so be it.

He reached into the pocket of his waistcoat, fingering the list. *You'd be angry with me, I know. I broke my promise to you by not remarrying. I know it's my duty to sire an heir.*

But his only child was a daughter.

Christine was now eleven years old and the very image of Katherine. It hurt to look at her gray eyes, knowing that she would grow up to look like the woman he'd loved more than life itself.

I can't do this, he told her ghost. *No one can replace you.*

As always, Katherine's ghost didn't answer. Nothing would bring her back, and on her deathbed, she'd made him swear to marry again. Even Christine, upon her last birthday, had wished for a new mother.

David stared at the room full of ladies and gentlemen of the ton. He wasn't a man who broke his promises. He'd avoided this for six years, even knowing it was the right thing to do.

This year, he would try. And Christine, the mischievous imp, had warned that if he did not find a suitable new wife, she would find one for him. He already knew she had her eye on her governess, Miss Grant, as a potential candidate. Her desire to be a matchmaker amused him. In many ways, she reminded him of Amelia Andrews.

He'd never met a young woman who talked so much. Even when Miss Andrews had been invisibly chained to her chaperone, her mouth had continued without ceasing. He suspected that if one put a potted plant before her, she would talk it to death.

As he went to get a glass of lemonade, he saw her speaking to a group of young ladies. Her gown was a vivid yellow, like a daffodil. The color suited her, transforming her into a splash of joy amid an otherwise dismal evening.

She was not at all a woman he could marry—far too young at the age of twenty. Or perhaps one-and-twenty, for all he knew. Yet it didn't mean he wasn't entertained by her. Her earlier suggestion, to help him find a proper wife, wasn't a bad idea after all. Amelia Andrews was popular among the young ladies, and she could easily discern who would suit him and who would not. It might be worth paying a call upon Miss Andrews to find out which ladies would be the strongest possibilities.

His requirements were fairly straightforward. He wanted someone of a pleasant personality, someone who liked children and would get along with his daughter. And most of all, someone who would not expect him to love her.

He'd already loved one woman and lost her. Never would he go through that again. This time, he wanted a companion and a friend—nothing more.

Against the far end of the room, David spied Miss Andrews's prey—Charles Newport, the Viscount Lisford. David wasn't alone in his vast dislike of the man. Lisford was a known rake who flirted with anyone wearing skirts. Not a word he spoke could be trusted, and the man desperately needed an heiress to save him from drowning in debt.

Amelia wasn't at all the sort of woman the viscount would marry; he'd already spurned her older sister Margaret. But Lisford wouldn't hesitate to use Amelia if it would further his own causes.

David set down his glass of lemonade and made his way toward the viscount. He wasn't alone when he spied Margaret Andrews moving in the same direction. She paused a moment and nodded to him, for they had been formally introduced in the past.

"Miss Andrews." He bowed in greeting.

"Lord Castledon." Even though she maintained courtesy, he could tell that she was distracted by Amelia.

"Is something the matter?" he inquired. "You look as if you want to murder your younger sister."

"It wouldn't do any good," Margaret said beneath her breath. "She won't listen to me when I tell her that man is up to no good."

David shrugged. "She did say that he was dangerous and . . . what was it? Delicious, I believe she said."

"If she dares to throw herself at Lord Lisford, she'll regret it for the rest of her life." Margaret gripped her hands together, watching Amelia standing near the viscount. "He's nothing but a blackguard." Her face was twisted with more than sisterly worry. There was bitterness, too, of a woman set aside.

"Perhaps you'd rather murder *him*, then," he suggested. "Except that it would leave a lot of blood on Lady Rumford's floor." He knew that the elder Miss Andrews had once been engaged to the viscount. Everyone knew of her humiliation, which was yet another reason to dislike the man.

"I *am* Amelia's chaperone," she added. "Which, I suppose, gives me the right to drag her away, if she won't listen."

"Would you allow me to intervene?" he asked. "I may be able to assist." Though he ought not to get involved, he understood her concern.

Margaret stopped a moment, and her eyes held relief. "Could you? She doesn't understand that I only want to protect her." A flush of embarrassment crossed her face, followed by the hardened determination he recognized.

David bowed and nodded. "Allow me." He wasn't entirely certain *how* he would distract Miss Andrews, but perhaps there was a way.

He continued toward the viscount, noting the man's circle of female admirers. When he approached, Lisford greeted him, "Castledon! Good to see you, my friend." Although his voice was jovial, the man's gaze turned guarded.

David inclined his head, though he didn't repeat the sentiment. Quite frankly, he had little respect for the viscount. Thinking fast, he said, "Forgive me for interrupting, but Miss Amelia Andrews has promised the next dancing set to me."

Amelia turned to face him in startled shock, already shaking her head in refusal. He sent her a warning look, but she was clearly choosing to ignore him.

"I'm afraid you're mistaken, my good man," the viscount insisted. "For she already promised it to me." He took Amelia's hand, and from the blush on her face, she was falling hard beneath his spell. She didn't see the reality of Lisford's intentions, nor did she seem to care. The other women dissipated among the crowd, leaving David to feel like a fool for even trying to draw Amelia away.

She held the devil's hand while the other couples lined up for the dancing. The excitement in her eyes revealed a young woman's dream that the viscount would fall in love and marry her.

Nothing could be further from the truth. A man like Lisford would seduce and ruin her, nothing more.

Go and warn her, his conscience urged. *Join the dancers and use the moment to speak to her again.*

But then, David hated dancing. *Hated* it. He'd learned how as a boy and had endured it only because Katherine had enjoyed it. Now, he would sooner set himself on fire than willingly join a set.

But when he saw the viscount's gaze linger upon Amelia's bosom, his hand sliding down her spine, something snapped within him. This man wanted to use an innocent girl and then cast her aside. Amelia didn't need that sort of heartache.

Margaret walked up beside him, her eyes upon the dancing. "I thought you said you were going to stop her."

"She has a mind of her own," David countered. "But I suppose we can try another approach."

He offered her his arm, and Margaret hesitated. "If I dance with you, I might end up as Lisford's partner."

"It's possible," David agreed. "Likely, even."

Her stern face held the look of a woman who hadn't at all forgiven the man for what he'd done. "I don't want my sister to endure what I did. I know that I'm a spinster now and likely won't ever marry anyone. But I can't stand aside and let him hurt her in that way."

David agreed with Margaret on that point. "Shall we?" She put her arm in his, and they waited to join the next dance. He repressed a groan when he learned it was to be a cotillion. Though it would indeed involve switching partners frequently, it wasn't a dance that he remembered too well. From the moment he and Margaret paired up, he spied a gleam of interest on Amelia's face. He managed to stumble his way through the steps until he finally partnered with her.

"I see you did find someone to dance with," she remarked. "But I don't know what you were thinking, claiming that I promised you a dance. It was Margaret's doing, wasn't it?"

Not entirely, but he didn't say so. "Your sister was worried about you."

Annoyance tightened her expression. "Margaret should worry about finding her own husband instead of interfering with me."

"Perhaps she's trying to spare you from the man who broke her heart."

Amelia sobered, just as they switched partners. He left her to mull it over and saw the guilty expression upon her face when she crossed paths with her sister. David was forced to concentrate on the steps he'd forgotten until once again he was paired with Amelia. "I don't mean to spoil your dreams, but think of me as the older brother looking out for you."

"You're nothing like an older brother," Amelia interjected. When he was about to argue with her, she continued, "An older *uncle*, perhaps."

"I'm not that ancient, Miss Andrews." Even so, he saw the mischief in her eyes.

"You might need a cane, soon enough. Or an ear trumpet."

Insolent wretch. And in spite of himself, he smiled. "Stop trying to change the subject. Men like Lord Lisford, who flirt with every woman, will continue to do so even after they marry. He won't remain faithful." Whomever the viscount ended up marrying would no doubt be humiliated by a string of Lisford's paramours.

"Unless he's besotted with his wife," Amelia pointed out. "The way you were with yours."

They switched partners again, and her remark pushed back at the memories David didn't want to face. He stumbled a moment, thinking of Katherine. He *had* been besotted with her, and the fog of melancholy descended once more. He spoke a little to Margaret, but there wasn't much to say. While he agreed with her assessment of Lord Lisford, Amelia would make her own choices.

When he partnered with her one last time, he squeezed her gloved hand tighter.

"Have a care, Miss Andrews. Lord Lisford is indeed a dangerous man, as you said." He didn't want her believing that she could reform a man who lived a bacchanalian life, seeking pleasure wherever he could find it.

From the dark look in Amelia's green eyes, he could see that he'd offended her. She wanted to believe that Viscount Lisford would care enough about her to put aside his past. "I can take care of myself," she pointed out. "You needn't concern yourself with me."

The dance ended, but the viscount did not return to Amelia. Instead, he stood across from another young woman whose name David couldn't remember. But she wore diamonds around her throat, and that was enough to attract Lisford's eye.

When Amelia was about to leave, David refused to release her hand, forcing her to join him for the next dance. While she didn't appear happy about the idea, neither did she protest. He could have this dance with her and speak freely, since Lisford had been her partner earlier.

But this dance turned out to be a reel, and David despised the quicker dances. He felt awkward spinning about the dance floor. And Amelia appeared gleeful at the trap he was caught in.

"Have you finished chiding me about Viscount Lisford?" she asked, whirling alongside him.

David ignored her taunt. "Perhaps I should form a list of suitable men for you," he suggested, "since you're going to do the same for me."

"I was *not* intending to give you a list of men." She sent him a mischievous look. "Unless that's what you'd rather have."

Wicked girl. He sent her a disparaging look. "No, thank you. But I could advise you on which suitors are your best marital prospects."

"You mean the ones my father would approve of."

"Precisely." David kept her at his side, keeping her arm in his.

"Let me guess. They would be mature men, with good fortunes, who tell their wives what to do and expect nothing but obedience."

He strongly suspected that obedience was not Amelia's better qualities. "Is there any harm in that?"

She cleared her throat. "I would die of boredom within a week."

His arm moved around her waist, and there was a sudden flush upon her cheeks. Though the gesture meant nothing, he grew conscious of her body beneath the silk. His smile faded as he imagined a woman like Amelia with her hair undone, lying upon a bed.

The image sent a dormant surge of desire bolting through him, and he let go of her waist.

"Send a list to me within the week, if you please. I'll do the same for you." He stepped back as the dance ended, needing to move away from her.

"Thank you, but I've already found the gentleman I want," Amelia said softly. "I've no need for a list."

A few days later, Amelia had gathered all her sisters together for a meeting. "We need something more daring," she informed them, but none of them was listening. Her oldest sister, Victoria, the Duchess of Worthingstone, was too busy cuddling her newest addition, another baby boy. Juliette had her own daughter, Grace, upon her knee, while Margaret's attention was focused on a scrap of black silk.

"Perhaps something made of black lace," Amelia suggested. While black was usually a color for mourning, the strong contrast against a woman's skin would draw a man's attention to her bare flesh.

Four years ago, when their family had been nearly destitute, they'd begun a secret business designing sensual corsets and chemises out of silk and satin. Aphrodite's Unmentionables was the name they had chosen, and it had brought in thousands of pounds to help them survive the mountain of debts their uncle had left them.

Victoria had designed and sewn the first few garments, while Juliette had kept the accounts. Their lingerie was scandalous and, thankfully, most of the wealthy ladies in London had gone to Madame Benedict's shop demanding more of it. It had changed not only their lives, but the lives of the Scottish women who helped sew the garments.

But now that Victoria and Juliette were married with children of their own, they had less time to devote to the business. Her eldest sister was a duchess, while Juliette was married to Paul Fraser, a Scottish viscount and a physician. Juliette and her husband were visiting London during the Season because Dr. Fraser was conferring with other physicians about a treatise he was writing.

Margaret held out the black silk. "They aren't listening to us, Amelia. They're too busy playing with their children."

"*I* was listening," Juliette protested, kissing her three-year-old daughter's hair and snuggling her close. "But we've done black lace before. And white and red."

"I overheard Madame Benedict saying to her assistant that the garments are not selling as well as before," Amelia informed them. "Some of the ladies have complained that the silk makes it too difficult to wash. Should we try cotton or linen?"

"I think we should stop selling it altogether," Margaret interrupted. "It's been over four years. We've made tens of thousands of pounds in profit. There's more than enough for your dowry."

"And yours," Amelia pointed out, but Margaret's expression remained somber, as if she didn't believe she would ever need a dowry. Despite her debut and all the previous Seasons, Margaret had only received one offer in those four years. When her engagement to Lord Lisford had ended badly, her sister had soured toward the idea of marriage.

"We don't need to sell anything," Margaret insisted. "Besides that, it's dangerous. What if someone found out that Her Grace, the Duchess of Worthingstone, was selling naughty unmentionables? It would make the duke a laughingstock."

Amelia shrugged. "We could deny it. No one would believe it anyway."

But her sister was already shaking her head. "It's gone on too long. It's too easy for someone to accidentally learn the truth."

Juliette frowned, setting her daughter down to play. "If it only involved us, I would have stopped years ago. The problem is the crofters' wives. This is their livelihood. Even if they return to farming and raising sheep, they wouldn't earn nearly as much."

Amelia knew that her sister Juliette still visited Scotland often, for their parents owned an estate nearby at Ballaloch, and Paul's mother dwelled among the crofters. And what she'd said was true— if they ended the sewing business, the women would be reliant upon the wool profits and crops to survive the winter. None of them had forgotten the years before, when so many had been starving or freezing to death.

Victoria let out a breath of air. "Juliette is right. We should look toward letting someone else manage the business. What about Cain Sinclair?" The Highlander had helped them over the years, delivering finished garments and acting as a liaison between Madame Benedict and themselves.

Amelia thought that was a good idea, but Margaret was already shaking her head. "Mr. Sinclair couldn't. He wouldn't know the first thing about how to manage a business about ladies' unmentionables."

"I suspect he knows how to take them off," Amelia said slyly, watching Margaret's embarrassment grow. "He does seem to have a number of women, doesn't he?"

"I do not wish to talk about that man." Margaret picked up the filmy black silk again. "I don't trust him at all."

But the flush on her sister's cheeks suggested there was more she wasn't saying. Amelia felt certain that the Highlander had kissed her sister at one point, though Margaret had denied any involvement.

"We could see if any of the MacKinloch women would like to take our places," Victoria said. "Perhaps if they manage it themselves . . ."

It was possible, but Amelia still didn't think it was practical. Someone needed to remain in London, and it wasn't going to be her. She knew that Viscount Lisford's lands lay to the east, and by this time next year, she hoped to be his wife.

Out of the corner of her eye, she noticed Margaret moving toward the door silently. Her sister was quite upset, but gave no indication of why. Victoria and Juliette were busy with their children, and Amelia followed Margaret into the hall. Her sister was walking quickly toward her own bedroom, and Amelia had to hurry to catch up.

The door closed before she could reach her. Amelia pressed her hand to the wood and asked gently, "Is something the matter, Margaret?"

"Go away and leave me alone."

Amelia strongly suspected her sister was crying. "Let me in, and we'll talk about whatever it is."

"I don't want to talk."

Of course she didn't. But Amelia had a feeling she knew what this was about. Margaret was the second born of the four sisters, and now that she was five-and-twenty—almost six—she was confronted with a very strong possibility of spinsterhood. For a woman who had been planning her wedding since the age of ten, this wasn't good.

"Let me in or I'll keep questioning you through the door," she said. "The servants will hear about it, and so will Juliette and Victoria." When her sister didn't move, Amelia added, "You might as well give in. I'm going to find out anyway."

The door jerked open, and it was immediately clear that Margaret had been crying. Her eyes were wet, and she demanded, "Why can't you stop being such a busybody?"

"Because I'm your sister." Amelia stepped inside and closed the door, locking it behind her. "Now tell me everything."

Margaret walked over to the window, staring outside at the street. "I feel as if I'm going to be a spinster for the rest of my life. I'm never going to have children of my own, and there won't be anyone for me." She crossed her arms around her waist as if trying to hold back the tears. "It's so hard to see Victoria and Juliette with their babies."

The heartbreak in her sister's voice was wrenching. Amelia knew how much it meant to Margaret to have a family of her own. Season after Season, she'd tried her best to find a suitable gentleman. But after Lord Lisford had spurned her, most men had kept their distance. Although her sister wasn't truly ruined, Margaret had been publicly humiliated. And her sharp tongue hadn't made matters any easier in the forthcoming years.

Amelia's eyes welled up as she went to stand beside her sister. "I'm certain there's someone for you. We'll find him."

And she truly did mean that. She wanted Margaret to be happy and have a softhearted husband she could manage. Possibly the earl, if she could arrange it. The man *did* have a daughter already. Margaret could be a wife and a stepmother in one day, if Lord Castledon suited her.

"No one wants me anymore," her sister said, wiping her eyes. "It's been too long."

"The viscount wanted you a few years ago," Amelia pointed out. "He *did* ask you to marry him." The twinge in her conscience poked again, that the man of her dreams was the man who had destroyed Margaret's hopes.

"He said it was a wager," her sister whispered. "He offered to wed me because a friend dared him to ask. For one hundred pounds, he pretended he wanted my hand in marriage, when the truth was, he never cared a whit for me."

Amelia had never known about any sort of wager, and it bothered her to hear it. Was that true? Or had Lord Lisford simply made up the story as a way of crying off? This was treacherous ground, splitting sides between her sister and the man she cared about.

"I don't think the two of you were suited," she said slowly. "It was probably for the best."

"But you believe *you* are meant for him?" Her sister looked incredulous. "He plays on women's feelings, Amelia. He knows what to say and how to say it, to get what he wants. I don't want the same thing to happen to you."

A tingling sensation caught at the back of her neck, but Amelia refused to believe that the viscount could be lying. She'd seen the warmth in his eyes, and he'd never failed to make her smile. "I don't want this to come between us," she said to Margaret. "I want you to find the right man."

"A boring man, you mean," Margaret countered. "An old man who doesn't care who he weds, so long as she will lie still beneath him and bear him a son."

She'd never heard her sister speak of such things, and it shocked her that Margaret had even thought about what went on between a husband and a wife. "You deserve better than that."

"What man will have me now?" Margaret wept. "I'm old." She fumbled for a handkerchief and faced Amelia. "Do you know how it feels to have followed all the society rules? I never once did anything I shouldn't. I never went anywhere unchaperoned, I never gossiped or did anything to embarrass our parents. And what did it get me? Nothing but spinsterhood."

The wild look in Margaret's eyes was making Amelia uneasy. Her sister looked desperate, as if she were about to do something rash.

"Why don't you make a new list?" Amelia suggested. "You used to do that when you were thinking about husband possibilities."

"What good is a list when none of the men are interested in anything but my dowry?" Margaret took her handkerchief and blew her nose. "I've heard them talking behind my back, Amelia. I know what they say about how priggish I am."

"You're not. You're just . . . very proper."

Her sister leaned against the window. "I thought if I obeyed all the rules, I would find the best husband. But I was wrong."

"There *was* one man who was interested in you," Amelia reminded her, thinking of Cain Sinclair. "But you never wanted him."

Margaret turned sober. "He wasn't appropriate. He's not a nobleman."

"No, but Mr. Sinclair liked you. You were different around him. Not quite so proper."

Margaret stared off into the distance. "It doesn't matter. That was years ago, and I told him that I could never marry a man like him. He hasn't spoken to me since."

"He asked you to *marry him*?" Now here was a bit of delicious news she'd never heard before. Her sister . . . and a Scot? Her mind started to put them together, but it wouldn't fit. Mr. Sinclair might have been ruggedly handsome and wicked, but he was also a man who couldn't care less about society rules. Not to mention, he lived in utter poverty.

But when Margaret had been hurt a few years ago, Sinclair had carried her home. Even the mention of it made her sister blush, making Amelia wonder exactly what had happened that day.

"No, he didn't ask me to marry him. Not exactly," Margaret admitted. "It was more of a demand. He was trying to stop me from marrying the viscount. I . . . said some things I shouldn't have."

Amelia let out a heavy sigh. It was rather romantic to think that the Highlander had tried to stop the wedding. Perhaps he wanted Margaret for himself. But then again, a man like Mr. Sinclair wasn't appropriate to marry. Even *she* knew that, no matter how interesting the idea was. "What about the Earl of Castledon?" she suggested. "You were dancing with him earlier."

"No, he's not for me. I've thought about it, but Lord Castledon isn't over his wife's death. You can see it in his eyes."

"He still wants to remarry," Amelia said. "I'm going to help him find someone."

"Amelia," Margaret warned, but she wasn't listening to her older sister's warning. If she wanted to help Lord Castledon, then that's exactly what she would do.

"I really think you ought to consider him. He's not so bad." The longer she was around Lord Castledon, the more attractive he was. He might be far too serious for her, but there was something about his mysterious demeanor that drew her in.

It was his eyes, Amelia decided. They were such an honest deep blue, a woman could lose herself in them. And since he'd never openly pursued any young miss, it only added to the enigma.

She had to be cautious, however. If she continued to insist upon the match between Castledon and Margaret, her sister might protest all the more. Better to arrange things on her own. Subtlety was best when plotting to bring two people together.

"Well, if you don't want to marry him, I can at least help him find someone," Amelia said, pretending that she'd given up on the idea. "What about Lavinia Harrow? She made her debut last year."

Margaret began to set forth arguments of why Amelia shouldn't get involved, but she ignored her sister's comments. She saw no harm at all in playing matchmaker. The earl clearly needed help, and she didn't mind assisting him—especially if she brought him together with Margaret. Even so, she had to come up with other possibilities so it wouldn't be too obvious.

She wrote Lavinia's name down and a few others. As she thought of young women who might suit the earl, once again she thought of his brooding good looks. He needed someone tall, like himself. Someone who could breathe life into his melancholy and give him a bit of happiness again.

A soft tingle pressed down on the back of her neck as she remembered the way his hands had held her waist during the dancing. He was stronger than he appeared, and she suppressed a sigh, remembering those eyes. She could almost imagine him staring at her, before his mouth came down upon hers.

She shook away the thought. Where had *that* come from? The earl wasn't that sort of man at all. He lurked on the edges of ballrooms and likely didn't know how to kiss a woman. A few years ago, she'd made the teasing remark to her sisters that he had the personality of a handkerchief.

But that wasn't true. Not really. Though he might seem boring on the surface, she couldn't shake the thought that there was more beneath it all. Lord Castledon had come to speak with her on several occasions over the years, and his dry wit had made her laugh.

A wall hedge, he'd called himself a few years ago, instead of a wall-flower.

"Amelia, haven't you been listening?" Margaret demanded.

She set down her pen and shook away the daydreams. "I'm sorry, what was that?"

"I said that you have a fitting with Madame Benedict this afternoon. Would you like me to go with you?"

The so-called fitting wasn't at all for a gown. Unbeknownst to her sisters, Amelia had begun working with the modiste to help bring in more sales for Aphrodite's Unmentionables. She often pretended to be there for a fitting while singing the praises of the undergarments. In return, Madame Benedict gave her a significant reduction in price on anything Amelia wanted. It amused her to help with the sales, though it was highly improper.

But then, perhaps there *was* something she could do while she was there. Margaret could benefit from a new gown, one that would help her catch the eye of the unmarried gentlemen. Something with a very daring cut, just above the bosom—one that would make her feel young again. Though Margaret covered herself up too often, Amelia often thought that a good bosom was an excellent way to catch a man's attention.

She smiled at Margaret. "Yes, I would like you to come with me."

Sarah Carlisle crumpled the letter and tossed it into the hearth. Inwardly, her panic was rising so fast, she didn't know what to do now. Her brother Brandon, the Earl of Strathland, had gone mad a few years ago, and a commission of lunacy had been issued, declaring him incompetent. All of his assets and entailed estates had gone under the control of their second cousin, a man whom

Sarah despised. Lewis Barnabas had cut her pin money down to almost nothing, and beyond the basic necessities, she had little to call her own.

It wouldn't have been so bad if she had a husband to rely on. But the one man she'd wanted, the Earl of Castledon, hadn't cast her a second glance. Even her efforts to be alone with him had backfired, and idle gossip had labeled her as a desperate woman.

Her chances of finding a husband were next to nothing, but it was her only way of escaping Mr. Barnabas. Her skin crawled at the thought of that man. He was older, and on the single occasion she'd met him when he'd come to London, his eyes had rarely traveled past her bosom. She'd locked her door and slid the dresser in front of it to keep him out.

According to his letter, he intended to return within the month. Only this time, he planned to live here—which meant she had to find another place. He might allow her to live upon one of the other estates, but she had to find a means to escape him.

A husband was the only way.

She was honest enough to know that her age and lack of beauty made it difficult. But it was her brother Brandon's deeds that had earned him powerful enemies, particularly the Duke of Worthingstone. The man had all but destroyed them, by way of vengeance, after Brandon had arranged for the duchess to be kidnapped a few years ago.

It wasn't fair. Her brother's rash behavior had tainted her own name, though Sarah had done nothing wrong. She wanted to flee London and never look back, she lacked the funds to do so. She had to find a way to save herself, no matter what the means.

Sarah walked across the room to the single pane of glass overlooking the hazy London streets. *I can't do this alone.* There was no one in their family whom she could turn to. She pressed her cheek to the cold glass, praying to a god who had never before answered her prayers.

Why would he start now? she thought bitterly.

If only there was a way to earn money on her own, she would be reliant upon no man. But she was the daughter of an earl, and no one would consider hiring her as a companion or a governess.

She had to find a way toward her own freedom, no matter what the cost. Being kind and ladylike had earned her nothing at all. Perhaps it was time to become ruthless, like Brandon.

A sudden idea crystallized within her mind. There was a secret she'd overheard a few months ago. A secret that she hadn't been meant to overhear, one that would ruin the women involved.

A secret that surely was worth the price of her silence.

Chapter Two

The day with Margaret had been more successful than Amelia had expected. Madame Benedict had chosen a stunning violet silk embroidered with gold for Margaret. Her sister had been so touched by the purchase, she'd hugged Amelia.

"You didn't have to do this," Margaret said.

Oh, but she did. She wanted her sister to feel good about herself again, to know that the years hadn't diminished her beauty. And if Margaret finally found a husband and a happy life, it would be easier on both of them when Amelia eventually married.

"Shopping always makes me feel better," she said. "And when you wear this, you'll catch every gentleman's eye." Particularly the Earl of Castledon's, if she could manage it. Already, she'd sent her initial list to him, by way of a footman. There was no need for a letter of explanation—the simple numbered list of unmarried ladies was answer enough. Amelia had put Margaret as lady number three, among the other six contenders. Seven was a reasonable number of women.

She had deliberately selected the quiet women, the wallflowers who had few options. The wealthy heiresses and the more vibrant women could have their pick of suitors. If the earl hadn't already chosen one of them, it was clear that he had no interest in women of that nature. He was a stoic man, and she suspected that the chattering sort wouldn't appeal.

She, herself, was a prime example of a woman who talked too much. Amelia was well aware of it, and it didn't bother her at all. If she had something to say, she said it. Which was why she felt comfortable making a match for the earl. He had no interest in a woman like her, and she'd been friends with him long enough to recognize that there was no harm in trying to help him. All of the women on the list were nice young ladies who would leap at the chance to marry an earl.

Satisfied with herself, she went to examine a violet corset embroidered with pink roses. "Margaret, this would be lovely with your new gown, don't you think?" She spoke loudly, so that the other women nearby would hear her. "I've never felt such silk. I imagine it would be wonderful against a woman's bare skin."

It was one of the garments that the crofters had sewn for Aphrodite's Unmentionables, and Amelia fully intended to help Madame Benedict sell more of them.

"Perhaps." Margaret reddened, holding out her arms while Madame Benedict took her measurements.

"They're unmentionables fit for a princess," she sighed. "If only Father could afford them."

Her sister frowned, not at all understanding what Amelia was doing. "But he can."

Oh for goodness' sake. Didn't her sister recognize a sales tactic?

Amelia widened her eyes, sending Margaret a silent message to play along with her ruse. "Not this one. It's fifty pounds. An outrageous amount for something so luxurious."

She lowered her voice just a fraction, knowing the ladies were still eavesdropping. "I've heard that only the wealthiest women in the ton are wearing them. Perhaps someday I'll be fortunate enough to own one." Offering a melodramatic sigh, she set down the corset nearer to the young ladies, hoping they would take the bait. Eyeing them with a friendly smile, she saw that the blond girl was intrigued.

"This one would suit you beautifully," Amelia suggested, holding out a chemise in a vivid blue. Conversation with strangers came naturally to her, and she never minded it. Not only that, but since she was of the same social class as the young ladies, they were more willing to listen to her. The young woman studied the silk with the creamy lace and sent a pleading look toward her mother.

"Or perhaps this one?" Amelia held out a virginal white corset trimmed with paste jewels. "It would be lovely for a trousseau."

Now she had the matron's attention. The older woman reached for a night rail that was so sheer, it was hardly more than a scrap of lace. Though she appeared shocked by the garment, Amelia saw the secret glance she sent toward Madame Benedict.

Sold, she thought. Perhaps the woman wanted to add a note of excitement into her own marriage. Amelia felt her cheeks blush at the idea. She was quite curious about what went on between a husband and a wife, but none of her sisters would tell her anything. Victoria and Juliette simply exchanged knowing smiles.

Near the entrance to the shop, she saw a young lady entering. There was something familiar about the woman. *I know her*, Amelia thought, but she couldn't remember the name.

Margaret saw the direction of her gaze. "We have to leave. Now."

"I've seen that woman before," Amelia whispered. "But where?"

"It's the Earl of Strathland's sister, Sarah Carlisle," Margaret murmured in her ear. "You will not speak to her or have anything to do with her. Not after what her brother did to us."

Amelia was fully aware of how Lord Strathland had threatened their family. Four years ago, his men had set their house on fire, trying to force them off their land in Scotland. When that hadn't worked, he'd tried to intimidate her sisters.

Although the man had slipped into madness and was now in an asylum, it wasn't good enough for Amelia. After all that he'd done, he deserved the hangman's noose.

Without really knowing why, she inched closer, just enough to overhear Madame Benedict asking the young woman to leave.

Amelia frowned. Why would Madame Benedict turn an earl's sister away? It made no sense at all. But then, she saw the young woman staring at them as if pleading for help. There was desperation on the girl's face, and she lifted her hand to catch Amelia's attention. It was clear now that Lady Sarah had come to find her. But why?

She didn't know what prompted her to follow, but Amelia ignored Margaret's protests and stepped outside. It had begun to rain, and the young woman was standing there, letting it fall over her without seeking shelter. She appeared utterly lost.

"Do you need help?" Amelia blurted out.

The young woman stiffened and turned to face her. "Yes, I do. And I'm sorry for coming to you in such a public place. But I couldn't pay a call on you at your home. Your family would never consider helping me—not after what my brother did to you."

Her honesty made Amelia feel sorry for her. She now remembered meeting Lady Sarah at a ball, years ago, but no one had paid any attention to the young woman. It seemed that she was still unmarried, and now that her brother was locked away, her options were running out.

"Surely your parents left you some funds?" Amelia questioned.

"They did, but my cousin has cut off a great deal of my pin money. It won't pay for another Season." She shuddered. "And I *cannot* live in his household."

Amelia caught a hint of disgust from the young woman. She didn't ask her to elaborate, but inquired, "Were you hoping to sew for money?" Though it wasn't appropriate for an earl's daughter, perhaps there was a way the young woman could do some work for the modiste, so long as it was in private with no one to see.

"No, I'm terrible at sewing," Lady Sarah admitted. "I thought if I spoke with you here, you might understand my circumstances. I have to find a way out—someone to marry or someone who will take me far away from here. I . . . don't have much time." Her gaze dropped downward, and it was clear that this woman was at the end of her options. "I'm pleading with you for help."

Margaret arrived and stood beside Amelia, holding an umbrella over her head to shield her from the rain. "Amelia, it's time for us to return."

She hesitated. If her family knew she was considering helping Lady Sarah, they would be livid. But neither did she want to step aside and look away when another woman needed help. If she was willing to work, to overcome her brother's sins, then it was only right to give her a chance.

"Come and have tea with me this afternoon," she said. "We can talk, at least."

Her sister looked appalled, but Amelia held her ground. "Wasn't it you who believed a lady should be charitable to those in need?" Without waiting for an answer, she returned inside the shop.

David stared at the list of seven women. Amelia had written the names of several respectable girls—Margaret among them. It didn't surprise him that she wanted to set him up with her sister. They weren't that far apart in age.

Margaret was polite enough, but he strongly doubted if she would consider a man like him. In the past, she'd tended to avoid him, choosing men who were younger and more conversational. Which was understandable, given his lack of interest in socializing.

He crossed off two others from the list because they had dark hair like his wife. Perhaps that was foolish, but he didn't want another reminder of Katherine. He wanted someone as opposite from her as a rain cloud to a rainbow. Someone quiet and calm, who would teach an eleven-year-old girl how to become a respectable, well-behaved young woman.

Christine had begun asking questions he had no desire to answer. Questions that made him distinctly uncomfortable. He didn't doubt that a woman like Amelia Andrews would answer every question his daughter posed, likely telling her far more than Christine needed to know. The idea made him wince, as did the thought of his daughter growing up. Thankfully, he wasn't going to wed Amelia. But it did make him think of her earlier proposition, when she'd asked him to put in a good word with the viscount. He had no intention of trying to bring the pair of them together.

David pulled out a piece of paper and began composing his own list. Instead of writing seven names, he divided the paper in half and wrote *Inappropriate Men* and *Appropriate Men*. He might as well be honest with Miss Andrews.

He wrote Lord Lisford's name beneath *Inappropriate Men* and beside it: *a rake and a wastrel*. Beneath him, he listed the names of several fortune hunters. Last, he wrote his own name upon the Inappropriate Men list. Beside it, he wrote: *too old for you*. He was three-and-thirty now. Although there were marriages between old men and young ladies, the true reason was that he'd known Amelia since she was sixteen. It made him feel like a satyr to be intrigued by such a young, fresh-faced girl.

When David started on the Appropriate Men list, he paused. While there were many gentlemen who were responsible and had strong fortunes, none were what Amelia would consider appealing. Even so, he wrote down their names and sealed the note with a bit of wax.

Her open letter seemed to taunt him, and he folded it up. Who was he trying to fool? He hadn't been able to even enter his wife's room within this town house since she'd died so long ago. Presumably the servants had gone inside to clean it.

He had to stop living like a recluse and face the truth. This had gone on long enough.

David left the study and climbed the staircase leading to the bed-chambers. His wife's room was beside his, but he'd kept the adjoining door securely locked. This time, he stood in front of her door, in the hallway. The knob was cool beneath his fingers, but it turned easily.

Inside, the room was shadowed and dark from the closed shut-ters. David crossed over to the window and opened it, letting the sunlight stream over the dusty furnishings. Katherine hadn't come to London often, but sometimes he'd cajoled her into a visit.

Her bed had the same rose coverlet he'd teased her about—a little girl's covers, not those of a grown woman. The chair closest to the hearth was where she'd spent hours reading. Upon the floor rested a familiar stack of books. He picked up the first title, remembering the way she had loved to curl up with a blanket and read late at night.

She'd been reading *The Life and Surprising Adventures of Robinson Crusoe*. A folded piece of paper marked the place where she'd left off. David opened it, and saw the shaky handwriting of Christine. His daughter had written: *I LUV MAMA* in large block print letters. Below it, she'd drawn a picture of herself with an enormous head and a body that resembled a potato.

The rush of emotion caught him low in the gut. His daughter had lived the past six years without a mother. She likely had very few memories of Katherine. David fingered the childish drawing and let out a deep breath.

"What should I do, Katherine?" he murmured. "Christine needs a new mother."

The thought of replacing his wife was impossible to consider. He tried to imagine what sensible Katherine would say.

Think of our daughter, not yourself.

He set the book down on the stack and folded the drawing to put in his waistcoat pocket. *You can do this,* he told himself. *Just choose a name from the list of women. Pick someone who would be good for Christine.*

His own needs didn't matter.

In that light, he returned to the list Amelia had sent. Surely some of them would fit his requirements for a mother for Christine. As for himself, he had a prosperous estate and a title. Wasn't that enough to win the heart of one of them?

He walked to the door and glanced back at Katherine's chair. For a time he studied it, trying to imagine her sitting with a book. But the image of her face was blurred from the years that had passed. It was harder to conjure the memory without a miniature before him.

"No one will replace you in my life," he promised her ghost. "I swear it."

When Amelia and Margaret arrived at their aunt Charlotte's town house later that morning, Amelia was troubled by what she'd learned of Lady Sarah. Though Margaret had insisted that Amelia should not worry about their enemy's sister, she didn't like the thought of a young woman being blamed for her brother's actions.

Lord Strathland had indeed caused their family nightmares, but Lady Sarah had nothing to do with that.

The footman took their pelisses, and the butler greeted them. To Amelia, he said, "Miss Andrews, these arrived for you." He held out two sealed notes and a small posy of lilies.

"Thank you," she said, accepting the notes and flowers. The bundle of lilies held a heady aroma, and she opened the first note, feeling a rush of excitement when she saw that the flowers were from Lord Lisford. She was careful to keep the name hidden from her sister, and then she unfolded the second note. When she saw it was a list of appropriate and inappropriate men, she bit back a laugh. So the earl *did* have a sense of humor, in spite of his melancholy nature.

"Who are the flowers from?" Margaret asked as they continued walking up the stairs.

Amelia waved the note at her. "I'll show you when we're alone." She wanted to avoid any discussion regarding the earl until they reached their shared bedroom.

Once they were inside, she handed Lord Castledon's note to Margaret. "See for yourself." While her sister was busy reading through the names of appropriate and inappropriate men, Amelia saw that Viscount Lisford had also invited her to accompany him driving through the park in the morning.

She hid her smile, resisting the urge to spin around like a giddy adolescent. If she told Margaret about the second invitation, her sister would undoubtedly forbid it.

"Why would the Earl of Castledon recommend the names of gentlemen to you?" Margaret queried.

"Because I've agreed to help him find a suitable wife. He thought it would be amusing to send me a list of names in return."

Margaret handed back the note and shrugged. "I suppose. But what was the other note?"

Amelia felt the color rise into her cheeks as she tried to act as if it were nothing. "Oh, it was an invitation to go out for a morning drive."

Really, she had to learn how to hide her feelings. For she suspected Margaret could read the anticipation on her face, though she had only spoken the truth.

"From *whom*?" Her sister's gaze narrowed, as if she already suspected the answer.

Amelia didn't want to lie, but she didn't want to tell the truth, either. Her stomach tightened. Why did this have to be so difficult? If only Margaret hadn't been engaged to Lord Lisford, she could share her excitement without fear of hurting her sister's feelings. Instead, she had to choose her words carefully, as if stepping around shards of glass.

She stared at the note and offered, "The earl wants to discuss the ladies I've chosen for him."

Which might be true, though it had nothing to do with the morning drive. It was the best she could manage.

"If the earl wrote both notes, then he would have written his invitation inside the same letter." The narrowed gaze suggested that Margaret was well aware of the lie.

It was at times like these that Amelia wished she were better at hiding the truth. Instead, she shrugged and pretended as if it didn't matter. "How should I know why there were two notes?"

"I think I should come along as your chaperone," Margaret suggested. *Because you're lying to me*, her gaze seemed to say.

There was only one way to avoid her sister's interference, and Amelia seized it. "You *could*. Except, we're probably going to discuss *you*, since I put your name down on the list for him. And that might be awkward."

Her sister was aghast at the idea. "You had no right to put my name on any sort of list, Amelia. It's humiliating, and I don't need you to play matchmaker."

And now Margaret would have little desire to chaperone. Although it was exactly what she wanted, Amelia couldn't hold back the guilt at lying to her sister. She much preferred a straightforward approach. But if she admitted that she wanted to get better acquainted with the viscount, Margaret wouldn't hesitate to tell their parents.

It made her feel sixteen years old, all over again.

She took a deep breath, wanting to soothe her sister's wounded feelings. "You're unhappy," Amelia said, softening her voice. "I know you want to be married and have a family of your own. Why not the earl?"

Margaret shook her head. "Lord Castledon is a kind man, but he's not interested in me."

"He could be, if you'd only try." Amelia guided her to sit down. She studied Margaret's severe updo and reached out to loosen several strands around her sister's face. "You may be older, but so is he. He doesn't want a young girl out of the schoolroom. He wants a woman."

"I don't know about that." Her sister stared at the opposite wall. "He never looked at me before."

"Only because you never gave him a chance. He's a kind man, even if he is a bit too boring for my tastes."

Liar, her conscience chided. *You didn't find him at all boring on the night when you danced with him.*

She could never have imagined the strange response that his simple touch had awakened. If she could feel that way with a man who didn't interest her, what would it be like to kiss a man she was in love with?

Heaven, she was certain. It would be Heaven with a capital *H* and angels singing.

"The earl would suit you perfectly," Amelia said. "I believe that. And I'll find out everything I can about him."

Or, at least, she would when she spoke with him next. The less Margaret knew about this drive, the better.

"Take your maid along as a chaperone, and that will suffice," her sister suggested.

Amelia nodded, inwardly relieved that the secret meeting could go on as planned. This was her best chance to see Lord Lisford without him paying a call upon her here. The broken engagement made that impossible, and she didn't want to cause a rift between herself and Margaret.

She wanted to believe that the viscount hadn't been right for her sister and that, in time, Margaret would come to accept it, if Amelia married him.

But then her sister's warnings came rushing back. That the viscount had only been using Margaret as part of a wager. That he'd said everything she'd wanted to hear.

Amelia walked toward the window, wondering if she was betraying Margaret by allowing Viscount Lisford to take her out driving. But then, what if this man was meant to be the love of her life? Should she turn her back on that, for Margaret's sake?

She didn't know what to think. It bothered her to be torn between her own desires and loyalty to her sister. *I adored Lord Lisford first*, her heart reminded her. *Before Margaret even noticed him.* Surely that meant something.

A knock sounded on their door, and when Margaret called for the visitor to enter, Aunt Charlotte came inside. "I have news to share with the both of you," she said. "Your parents have returned to London. You'll be moving back in with them tomorrow."

"But—so soon?" Amelia blurted out. Although her father, Lord Lanfordshire, had returned from fighting in Spain several years ago, she had never expected this. The baron loathed society, and he'd seemed perfectly content to dwell in Scotland, aside from his visits to assume his duties in the House of Lords. She and Margaret had resided with their aunt and uncle, more often than not.

"I received a note from Beatrice today. Your mother is eager to see both of you and has asked you to join her tomorrow at breakfast."

"Why not this evening?" Amelia asked. "We could all dine together as a family." But when she cast a glance at Margaret, her sister shook her head discreetly. Best to tread carefully then.

"I invited her, but after the long journey from Ballaloch, she wanted to rest." Aunt Charlotte's face grew strained. "I think that she and your father need some time to—" Her words broke off, as if she'd suddenly changed her mind about what she'd been about to say. "Never mind. Tomorrow, I'll have the servants help you pack and move back to your family's town house."

Though Amelia kept her expression neutral, it was as if Fate were dashing her plans into pieces. Her suspicions were aroused by Charlotte's insinuation that something wasn't right between her parents. And why wouldn't they want to see their daughters immediately?

Amelia murmured her agreement, but she had already decided to send a note to Lord Lisford, asking him if they could meet earlier. As long as she returned before breakfast, surely that would not interfere with their family's plans.

The voice inside her head warned that it wasn't right to meet with a gentleman so early. If anyone saw them together, there would be gossip.

But then, she *wanted* to wed this man. If they were seen together—even if nothing had happened—surely it would only lead to what she wanted most.

Sarah's heart was pounding when she entered the house. The butler's face revealed nothing as a maid took her bonnet and pelisse. It was clear that he believed she had no reason to be here. Even so, he would not disobey Amelia's wishes.

"Follow me," he said.

She did, and with each step, her guilt increased. Miss Andrews had been kind enough to invite her here. Likely she would offer her assistance, though Sarah knew she deserved nothing.

The bitter secret was like a venom that she wanted to be rid of. She knew the power it held, and yet, she was afraid to voice it.

When she reached the drawing room, Amelia Andrews was waiting. The young woman was seated upon a creamy settee trimmed with a crimson stripe. As soon as she saw Sarah, she stood and greeted her. "I'm so glad you came to tea. Sit down, and we can talk about what's happened."

Inwardly, Sarah steeled herself, trying not to break into tears. Kindness was nearly impossible to bear. She'd had to be strong over these years, and she could not let down her guard now.

"Thank you," she murmured. Amelia poured her a cup of tea and smiled warmly, waiting for her to speak.

There were a thousand ways to begin, and not one of them seemed right. "I need help," she admitted. She poured out the horrors of the past four years, of Brandon's misdeeds and her struggle to find a husband.

"I know I am not the most attractive of women," she admitted, feeling the rise of heat to her cheeks. Horse-faced, Brandon had called her. And perhaps that was so, but face powder could not cover up the features she'd been born with. She swallowed hard, mustering up the courage she needed. "But I still want to marry. I *need* to marry, for it's the only way I can escape the scandal of my family. I thought you might know of a gentleman who would not be particular about the woman he marries."

Amelia had grown quiet for a time, as if thinking to herself. The longer her silence continued, the more Sarah longed to fill it. "I—I hoped you could get me an invitation to a ball where I—where I could meet someone."

This had to be the most humiliating moment of her life, but she took a sip of the hot tea to hide her embarrassment.

"I'm not sure I can," Amelia admitted. "After all that your brother did, most of the families want no connection with Lord Strathland."

"It's not my fault," Sarah blurted out. A rise of frustration took hold, of all the years of being a spinster. She didn't deserve this life, and she wanted a way out. The longer she remained in this trap, the more likely it was that her cousin, Lewis Barnabas, would find a way to hurt her.

A shudder came over her at the thought. No, she would never let herself be with a man like him.

"I know it's not your fault," Amelia agreed. "But it's a delicate situation. Perhaps it would be better if you attended an outing instead of an assembly or a ball. A smaller group might be best." She sipped at her own tea and offered Sarah a plate of sandwiches.

She took one, but her pulse quickened. Amelia Andrews needed to fully understand the necessity of her finding a husband.

"I want a husband," Sarah repeated slowly. "A respectable gentleman with a decent income, few debts, and a willingness to overlook my brother's deeds."

"I can try to help you, but I don't know if it's possible."

Now was the moment to lay her cards upon the table. Though her conscience cried out, she forced out the words, "I know about Aphrodite's Unmentionables."

Amelia blanched for the briefest moment before she smiled. "What about them? Most of the women in London are wearing the undergarments." The false brightness in her voice told Sarah that she'd guessed correctly.

"I know that you and your sisters are responsible for them," Sarah said. Though it was like a blade shredding her principles, she saw no other choice. "And I know how terrible it would be if the ton learned of your involvement—especially your sister, Her Grace, the Duchess of Worthingstone."

"I want you to leave," Amelia said, rising to her feet. Fury brewed in her eyes, and she pointed to the door. "Your accusations are unfounded, and you'll get no help from me in your quest for a husband."

It burned her, but Sarah nodded. "Very well. Then you'll understand if I spread the news to everyone."

The silence from Amelia Andrews was deafening. For a long moment, Sarah wondered if she'd made the right decision to reveal what she knew.

"You're more like your brother than I'd guessed," she said softly.

"No, I'm not. But as I told you, I have no other options available. If you'll help me find a husband, I'll never reveal your secret. You have my word."

"And what is that worth?" Amelia countered.

"It's worth the price of your reputation." Sarah stood from the settee, her mood somber. She'd never wanted to stoop to this, but there was no other choice. "Or if you cannot help me with a husband, then you can provide me with a house of my own and an income to live on. Perhaps a portion of your profits from Aphrodite's Unmentionables."

"Blackmail is a criminal offense," Amelia countered. "I could have you arrested."

"You've no proof of it." Sarah walked to the doorway and turned back. "I'll expect to hear from you in the next few days."

The next morning, Amelia awoke at dawn. Her stomach was still twisted in knots over what she'd learned from Lady Sarah. Though she suspected she should simply ignore the woman, the risk was there. If a breath of this scandal got out, it would affect all of them.

Margaret was still asleep in their shared room, and Amelia took her clothes into a nearby bedroom so her maid could dress her. She'd chosen a light fawn morning gown, trimmed with velvet ribbon. Though it wasn't a color most women liked, Amelia knew that it set off her hair and drew a man's attention to her face.

She was grateful for Lord Lisford's invitation this morning, for she desperately needed a way to take her mind off yesterday's events. There had to be a way of silencing Lady Sarah and protecting her family's secrets.

The morning was misty and cool as she traveled with her maid toward the eastern bank of the Serpentine, where she'd promised to meet Lord Lisford. *Charles*, she reminded herself, testing out the name. One day she would call him that.

Amelia was impatient to see him and was grateful when she spied the viscount waiting near his phaeton. So he *had* received her note asking him to meet earlier. She was glad of it and motioned for her maid to stand back at a slight distance.

"Good morning, Miss Andrews." He bowed, smiling warmly.

"Good morning, my lord." She returned the smile, and he helped her inside, while her maid took a seat on the rumble behind.

"Forgive me for not paying a formal call upon you," he apologized.

"I didn't want you to feel uncomfortable, after what happened with your older sister."

She had no desire to talk about Margaret and wished he hadn't brought it up. Already she was feeling guilty about this secret meeting. If it had been any other man who had broken her sister's heart, Amelia would never have looked twice at him. But even years ago, she'd begged Margaret to leave the viscount alone. She'd pined for him, wanting so badly for him to look at her and see the young woman who adored him.

But he'd wanted Margaret then, and it had shattered her sixteen-year-old heart. Now that she was older and wiser, Amelia wanted to believe that there could be a chance for them.

"It *is* awkward," she admitted. "It hurt Margaret's feelings a great deal when you broke the engagement."

"How could I keep it," he murmured, "when I was losing my heart to someone else?"

His hazel eyes held an intensity that made her catch her breath. It was just as Margaret had said—he was speaking all the words she wanted to hear. It made Amelia uncomfortable, wondering if there was any truth to them. *Be careful*, her mind warned.

"I was very young then," she said lightly. "You couldn't have noticed me."

Although, to be fair, she'd made a point to be near him at every opportunity. Aside from flinging herself at his feet, she'd done everything possible to gain his attention.

"How could I fail to see what was before me?" Lord Lisford tucked her hand into the crook of his arm as he flicked the reins and began taking the horses in a leisurely drive along the banks of the Serpentine. "You are as beautiful now as you were then. Only now, you've grown into a woman."

His smooth tone of voice heightened her wariness, though Amelia was glad to be beside him. She said nothing, fully aware that his compliments were meaningless.

"I had to keep my distance for a time," the viscount confessed. "Even now, I feel as if I cannot see you without hurting your sister."

Amelia relaxed a little, for that much was true. "It *is* difficult," she admitted. "And now that my parents have returned to London, we will be moving back into our own home."

Which wouldn't make their circumstances any easier. She didn't like sneaking around, but what other choice was there?

"Perhaps I should speak with your father, Lord Lanfordshire, and discuss matters with him."

That wouldn't do any good at all. Her father was furious with the viscount and would as soon throw Lord Lisford out before he'd allow him to pay any calls.

"I don't know that it would do any good," Amelia said. "He's very angry about what happened." Even now, she didn't know how to ease the way. "I could try to talk to Papa, but I know he doesn't want you involved with our family."

"Surely you must know how deeply I care for you," Lord Lisford said, and his tone sounded so sincere, she almost might have believed it. She *wanted* it to be the truth. Except for the fact that this was the first time they'd had a conversation longer than two minutes.

Her common sense remained wary while her wayward heart rejoiced. Amelia forced herself to think clearly. "This is the first time we've spent together. Though I'm flattered, don't you think it's a little early for you to care deeply about me?"

"Four years," he said, reaching to take her hand in his. "I've been watching you for a long time. Waiting for you."

Perhaps he meant it to be a compliment, but Amelia found it disturbing. He had courted Margaret only three years ago. Did he believe she was so naïve that she would believe he was already in love with her? Or did he speak this way to all women?

Her sister's warnings could not be ignored. "I don't want you to speak words of flattery to me," Amelia began, deciding that truth was the best approach. "You may like me a great deal, but we hardly know each other." She wanted to be acquainted with the *real* Lord Lisford, not the dashing viscount who spoke compliments at every turn.

He was so taken aback by her reply, the smoldering mask dropped for an instant. "But—I thought—"

"If it is your wish to court me, by all means do so, but don't treat me as if I haven't a brain in my head. I know when a man is talking with wool in his mouth."

His confusion was replaced by an honest smile. "You aren't like any other women, are you?"

"Of course not. I believe a woman should speak her mind instead of pretending to be something she isn't." Amelia sent him an open smile, hoping he wasn't disappointed by her candor. Honestly, though, she saw no reason to play games.

This time, she saw a hint of candor in his answering smile. "I really do like you, you know."

"Of course you do. I'm quite likable." Amelia's heart twisted with elation when he dropped the façade and spoke the truth. Even so, she needed him to understand the woman she was. "I'm not as empty-headed as the sheep that flock to your side at every ball."

He blinked at that. "No, I don't suppose you are." Brushing a lock of hair back, he added, "This isn't at all the way I envisioned our drive. I somehow thought you liked me better."

Oh, she did—there was no doubt of that. But pretty words meant nothing.

She straightened her shoulders and offered a compliment to soothe him. "You are quite handsome. Anyone can see that. But I think we need time to get acquainted before you speak with my father, don't you?"

"You're right," Lord Lisford admitted. "And forgive me for speaking so boldly. It was just . . . I thought that's what you wanted to hear."

Amelia let out a sigh. "Perhaps the sheep enjoy that, but I would prefer the truth, above all else."

"You are *nothing* like your older sister," he remarked.

"Of course not. Margaret obeys every rule, down to the last punctuation mark. I, however, believe that certain rules may be bent under the right circumstances."

The smoldering look was back, and Amelia forced her attention back to the clear waters of the Serpentine. Charles Newport was a devastatingly handsome man with a great deal of experience wooing women. And she *did* want to be wooed, but only after she knew this man. She didn't want empty words.

"May I kiss your hand?" he asked softly.

Yes, her impulsive side wanted to cry out. *Your mouth upon my bare skin without gloves.*

But she sensed that if she gave this man a single liberty, Lord Lisford would take matters further. She would become like the string of women he'd wooed and rejected. This was a man who loved the hunt. He wanted a woman who couldn't be caught. The more she held him at a distance, the stronger his interest would be.

He was already reaching for her palm when Amelia shook her head. "Not yet."

"Are you afraid of me?" His voice was kinder now, as if he were trying to be gentle.

Amelia shook her head. *I'm afraid of myself.* She already knew she was very different from her sisters—impulsive and eager to charge into the fray for anything she wanted.

She believed in seizing every last moment of joy from life. Sensory experiences were a craving she couldn't deny, whether it involved scent, taste, or most of all, touch. Her body was incredibly sensitive, and she wore corsets and chemises from Aphrodite's Unmentionables that would utterly shock Margaret. But she loved the feeling of silk and satin against her skin. She sensed that when she shared a man's bed for the first time, she would love it.

And that was too dangerous to imagine. She couldn't even risk a passionate kiss for fear that her instinctive urges would lead her down a path to ruin. Amelia wanted this man to love her. She didn't want to be yet another nameless woman out of the dozens he'd courted in the past.

"Tell me something about yourself that no one else knows," she said, trying to change the subject—and her imagination—away from kissing.

He frowned, urging the horses to continue. For a long moment, he thought about it, and finally he said, "Only if you do the same."

"All right." She steeled herself and said, "I'm afraid of heights. I can't bear to be on a balcony."

He inclined his head to show that he'd heard her, and at last he admitted, "I need to marry an heiress."

"What man doesn't?" She shrugged and added, "My father is only a baron, and we've struggled a bit over the past few years, but—"

He interrupted, "I know. But your family is far more settled, now that your eldest sister is wedded to a duke."

She didn't know what he meant by "settled," but she resisted the desire to correct him. Their wealth had nothing to do with her father's income and everything to do with selling naughty undergarments to ladies of the ton, though she didn't say so. Over the years, they had amassed quite a lot of money from Aphrodite's Unmentionables, and now she didn't worry about their family's funds. But maintaining that secrecy was critical.

She swallowed hard at the thought of yesterday's conversation with Lady Sarah. Something had to be done, but what? Clearly the woman needed help and was desperate enough to resort to blackmail. Her mood darkened with fear over what Lady Sarah might say or do. It could threaten all of them.

"I've made some mistakes," Lord Lisford admitted. "I've gambled more than I should have."

Now here was a rare glimpse at honesty. He knew his vices and was willing to be open about them. "Then stop playing cards," she urged him. "Don't even go into White's."

"You don't understand. It's expected of me."

"Appearances are more important to you than protecting your family's assets?" she inquired. Though it might be expected of a gentleman, she had the sense that his debts were growing steadily.

Lord Lisford let out a heavy sigh. "Appearances are necessary for maintaining a standard to which others aspire."

In other words, he wanted to look good in front of his friends and was willing to bury himself in debt for the sake of it.

Amelia took his arm again and said, "If you wish to marry an heiress, then you'll have to give up such nonsense. Why would she want to let you control her money, if you've been whittling it away?" She didn't give him an opportunity to answer, but continued, "Prove yourself responsible, and more doors will open to you."

"And what of you? Would you marry a reformed wastrel?"

Amelia sent him a sidelong smile. "Only if he earned my heart."

Lord Lisford's expression turned somber as he turned the corner. The phaeton moved smoothly as they continued down the opposite banks of the river. "I am sorry about what happened with your sister, you know. That was wrong of me. But it would have been worse to marry her."

"It was a dreadful thing to do," Amelia said. "And you should make amends for it."

His mouth twisted. "There's nothing I could say that would bring about her forgiveness. My actions were reprehensible."

"Once she is wedded to another man, she'll put it behind her," Amelia predicted. "And I know just the earl who would suit Margaret perfectly. You could help me make a match for her."

Lord Lisford listened to her plan, and by the time they had finished their drive, she was smiling. Before long, both the Earl of Castledon and Margaret would have their happily-ever-after.

Amelia would see to it personally.

Henry Andrews rose at half past eight, staring at the empty place beside him in bed. Though he knew it was fashionable for wives to have their own adjoining bedchambers, he rather missed Beatrice sleeping beside him. They had been married for nearly twenty-eight years now, but somehow in the past few summers, she'd become more distant.

Part of it was because he'd been away at war for so long. Beatrice had been forced to fend for herself, making the decisions about their estates and the girls' lives. It was to be expected that she would gain a stronger sense of independence.

Yet after he'd returned, he'd thought their lives would resume as if he'd never left, like pieces of a puzzle snapped together. Instead, the edges wouldn't quite fit. Beatrice was no longer the quiet, obedient wife. They'd had a terrible fight over the scandalous sewing business his girls had started. He'd demanded that they cease at once, and to his shock, Beatrice had refused.

"You left us on our own," she'd told him. *"And you have no right to criticize what our girls did to survive it."*

Even now, the thought of his daughters selling unmentionables—seductive ones at that—was enough to make Henry reach for the brandy. He'd believed they would end Aphrodite's Unmentionables immediately. Instead, his defiant wife had continued her role overseeing the crofters' creations, as if she were unaware of the social consequences of being discovered.

She was a baroness—not a courtesan. But no matter how he argued with Beatrice, she refused to discuss it.

Worse, she'd stopped sleeping beside him, and although she'd continued to follow her duties as Lady Lanfordshire, something had changed between them. There was an intangible distance that he couldn't grasp or understand . . . almost as if she'd fallen out of love with him. They existed together, but her heart no longer belonged to him. And damn it all, he hadn't the faintest idea how to change that.

He rather wondered if anyone had written an instructional guide to reviving one's marriage. For his was certainly on its deathbed.

After his valet finished helping him to dress, Henry went to the adjoining door of his wife's bedroom. He pressed his ear against the door and heard the faint sounds of conversation. Good. That meant Beatrice was awake.

Henry knocked upon the door, and momentarily her maid answered it. Glancing behind her, she said, "Forgive me, Lord

Lanfordshire, but my lady is still abed. Was there something you needed?"

Yes. He needed to speak with his wife without a door between them.

"She is not still abed," he remarked. "I overheard her talking with you."

The maid blushed, but added, "That is true, but she is not ready to receive you. She bid me to say that she will see you at breakfast."

For God's sake, this was his *wife*. It was his right to push the door open and talk with Beatrice whenever he damn well pleased. But he sensed that barging in would only cool her demeanor toward him, and that wasn't what he wanted.

He grasped the door handle and closed the door in the maid's face. This situation had grown more ridiculous with each passing day. For twenty years, he'd slept in his wife's bed. On the journey here from Scotland, she'd wanted separate rooms. Separate! As if she couldn't bear to breathe the same air as him.

His temples were beginning to throb with a headache, and he went to sit at his writing desk. During the war, he'd been an officer. As a colonel, he'd presented quite a few battle strategies to the generals, and he was no stranger to warfare.

He took out paper and a quill and realized that this situation was no different. There had to be a correlation between a battle and a marriage. Both required peace terms, and it was clear that Beatrice believed she had the upper hand.

Not so.

Henry's quill began to move over the paper, outlining the various methods of attack. In warfare, the troops needed to scout the enemy's whereabouts and understand their actions. It seemed a reasonable course of action to shadow his wife. He hadn't the faintest notion of what she did all day, but perhaps he could spy on

Beatrice and thereby understand her better. With women, actions spoke far louder than words.

Satisfied with the results, Henry decided that today he would make a concerted effort to rediscover his wife. He had mistakenly believed that all was well between them, when, in fact, it was not.

But here, in London, they could make a fresh start. And Henry fully intended to enlist the help of his daughters.

Chapter Three

David stepped inside the foyer of the Andrews residence and gave his gloves and hat to the footman. The butler, Mr. Culpepper, was a portly man with a gray mustache and a beard. His expression was grave as he led David inside. "Miss Amelia Andrews and her mother are expecting you."

He followed the butler toward a small parlor and was surprised to see Lord Lanfordshire standing in the hallway. The man appeared to be eavesdropping for some odd reason.

"My lord." David greeted the baron, but Amelia's father only shook his head and waved him onward. Why in the world the older man was lurking about instead of joining them was uncertain. The butler only lifted a finger to his lips and beckoned for David to join the ladies inside.

The parlor was a cozy room with creamy wallpaper and long green drapes to frame the large windows. He bowed to the ladies, greeting Lady Lanfordshire first. "I trust you had a good journey from Scotland?"

"It was wretched, as always." She smiled, gesturing for him to sit. "Thank you for coming to tea with Amelia and me."

He took a seat across from them and saw the gleam of strategy in the young woman's face. Amelia was clearly plotting something, and he wasn't certain what that was. "It was my pleasure."

Lady Lanfordshire began with a banal conversation about the weather and travel conditions, but all of his concentration was on Amelia. She was wearing a deep blue gown, and her blond hair was pulled back into a chignon, though several strands were artfully arranged about her face.

There was no denying her beauty. Her green eyes held mischief, as if she knew a secret he didn't.

Too young, his brain warned. Even so, he couldn't take his eyes off her. David forced himself to reply to Lady Lanfordshire's questions, but Amelia withdrew a scrap of paper from behind a cushion, letting him silently know that she'd received his list. Her eyes shone with amusement, and he raised an eyebrow at her.

Do you really think I'll pay any heed to this list? her eyes seemed to say.

It's for your own good, he responded silently.

When Lady Lanfordshire offered him a piece of cake, he declined politely, keeping to his tea. Amelia, however, closed her eyes when she took a bite, savoring the taste. She appeared lost in a moment of reverence, while she enjoyed the moist cake with currants.

He'd seen that look on a woman's face before, and it reminded him of how many years it had been since he'd shared his wife's bed. It was unnerving to find himself so intrigued by Amelia's response.

"If I may, Mother," Amelia began, "I wanted you to meet Lord Castledon because I believe he would make an excellent husband for Margaret."

Lady Lanfordshire nearly spewed her tea across the saucer. Instead, she coughed, raising a handkerchief to her lips. "Goodness,

Amelia, you needn't be so forward. Lord Castledon certainly has no need of your matchmaking."

Miss Andrews ignored her mother. "He is five-and-thirty, and—"

"Three-and-thirty," he corrected. He didn't need her adding years to his age.

"Yes, well, he's not too old for her yet. He's a nice gentleman, and I believe they would get on quite well."

Lady Lanfordshire closed her eyes as if seeking patience from a higher power. "Amelia, dearest, this is not the way a young woman should behave in front of an earl." She sent him an embarrassed smile. "I understand you have a daughter, am I right, Lord Castledon?"

It was a blatant tactic to change the conversation topic.

"I do." Clearly Lady Lanfordshire had no idea that he and Amelia had already conversed about potential wives. Steering the conversation back, he added, "And it is Christine's fondest wish that I remarry and give her a mother."

The matron's expression softened. "How old is your daughter?"

"Eleven years old," he admitted. "I should have remarried long before now, since I do need an heir. And yet, I couldn't quite bring myself to do so." He saw the sympathetic dismay on Lady Lanfordshire's face. "Miss Andrews offered to help me find some suitable candidates."

The older woman sighed. "Amelia ought to mind her own affairs instead of meddling with others."

"I'm very good at meddling," Amelia interjected. "And I do get results."

That she did. David raised an eyebrow at her, and she sent back a secretive smile. He reached for his teacup. "Shall I assume that this was the reason you invited me here?"

"Actually, it was because I wanted to introduce you to my mother so that she'll side with me about your being a good match with Margaret."

Before the baroness could reply, David pulled out the list Amelia had sent and handed it to her. "And what do you think of these young ladies, Lady Lanfordshire?"

The matron accepted the list, sending a warning look toward Amelia. "All of them come from good families. But I'm not certain how well they would do as a stepmother to your daughter." She began going down each name, listing the attributes of each. Amelia took a sip of her tea, presumably feigning obedience.

He hardly heard a word Lady Lanfordshire said. He was watching the way Amelia's hands moved over the cup, and how her lips touched the porcelain rim. She sent him an impish smile when she caught him staring, and it was like a bullet to his brain.

Stop looking at her. She's not for you.

He wanted an older woman, someone who could help him rear Christine and teach her to be a young lady. Not someone who would train his daughter how to be rebellious.

"In summary, I believe that either Miss Harrow or Miss Pearson would be an excellent choice for you," Lady Lanfordshire finished.

"Not your own daughter?" he prompted, stealing another look at Amelia.

"Margaret has expressed a reluctance to marry," she admitted. "After what that horrid Lord Lisford did to her, it's no wonder."

"He's not a blackguard," Amelia argued. "He simply made wrong choices."

David finished his tea and replaced the cup, giving Lady Lanfordshire his full attention. "I must agree with you, Lady Lanfordshire. The man is indeed a rake, and I should hate to see any of your daughters associated with the likes of him."

All of the humor disappeared from Amelia's face, and she sent him a furious glare. David met her gaze coolly. Was she honestly expecting him to take her side in this? He knew Charles Newport well enough. The man was irresponsible and had a reputation for draining money from his family. He'd sooner see Amelia wedded to a wolf than a man like the viscount.

"I quite agree," her mother echoed.

But the tight look on Amelia's face held more than anger. Her fists were clenched against the cushions, and she looked ready to tell him to go to the devil.

He sent her a smile, but in her eyes, he saw war brewing.

Amelia stood inside the ballroom, fuming inwardly. She knew that she ought not to say anything to Lord Castledon. A proper lady like Margaret would never dream of it. But even three days later, she was still angry with him for insinuating to her mother that Lord Lisford was a bad marital choice. True, the viscount had made countless mistakes. But she had caught a glimpse of a good man on their drive the other morning. Beneath his practiced words and suave manner was a man in great need of a woman's love.

Amelia believed, in her heart, that she could help Charles Newport. He could be redeemed, even after all that he'd done.

Her sister Victoria, the Duchess of Worthingstone, was hosting tonight's soirée, and Amelia had managed an invitation for Lady Sarah, though she hadn't told Toria why. If somehow Lady Sarah met the gentleman of her dreams, it would solve everything. Assuming the woman didn't resort to blackmail.

Logic told her to inform the Duke of Worthingstone. He could have Lady Sarah brought up on charges of blackmail, if needed. But, as the woman had said, there was no tangible proof.

Once again, Amelia dug deep with her instincts, trying to determine the woman's character. Lady Sarah didn't seem to be the sort of person who would resort to criminal behavior—more of a woman trying to escape a fate she didn't want.

Please let this end, Amelia prayed. Having a conversation with her sisters about a possible scandal that would drag all of their names into ruin was the very last thing she needed. She wanted to handle it herself, and perhaps if Lady Sarah won her freedom, all would be well.

It was early, and the dancing had not yet begun. Many of the guests mingled in the ballroom, while others were enjoying the unseasonably warm weather out of doors. Thus far, she hadn't seen Lady Sarah, but that didn't mean the woman wasn't already here.

Amelia crossed the stone terrace and spied Lord Castledon. He was standing on the bottom step of the terrace that led out to a walled garden. As always, he wore black. She doubted if the man had a single color in his wardrobe. As soon as he saw her, he gave a slight bow. "Miss Andrews."

Amelia beckoned for him to walk with her, not wanting to cause a scene. When they were a short distance away from the other guests, she asked, "Why did you side with my mother against Lord Lisford?"

"Do we really have to have this conversation now?" he countered. "It's a lovely evening, and your sister was gracious enough to invite me to her home. Perhaps you should consult the list I gave you and speak to one of those gentlemen."

Amelia tried to gather her patience, but she was so frustrated, she couldn't bear to be patronized. "I gave *you* a list of young ladies in good faith. Any one of them would be perfect to serve as a wife and mother to your daughter. I tried to help you, but you—"

"I helped you as well." He cut her off, offering her his arm. "I simply added a few names by way of warning."

She took a deep breath, realizing that he was completely unaware of how he'd sabotaged her during their tea. Or possibly, he was indifferent to the damage he'd done.

"I have been in love with Charles Newport for the past four years," she informed him. Though "love" was probably too strong of a word, it sounded better than to admit she had pined for him in the corner. "I know the sort of man he is, and I believe he can change his ways," she finished.

"No. You don't love him." His tone suddenly went dark, and his expression turned cold in a way she'd never seen before. Amelia stopped walking. She'd never seen him angry before, and his affable manner had vanished. "You don't know the meaning of love."

She was about to argue, but he wouldn't allow her to speak. "You believe love is about silly words and compliments."

"No, I don't—"

"You know nothing of what it is." Now there was more in his voice than anger. It was a bleakness, a sense that he'd locked away years of grief. Never before had she caught a glimpse of the man behind his mask of loss. Lord Castledon had always been a brooding sort, but this was different.

In his piercing blue eyes, she saw a man who was furious with the world and with her. He looked nothing like a man with the personality of a handkerchief or a man who remained on the outskirts, like a wall hedge. He took a step forward, staring down at her as if he resented the ground she walked upon.

"Love is holding the hand of the woman you worship, praying to God that the next breath won't be her last. It's watching her waste away, unable to eat or drink, and praying for a miracle that doesn't happen." His mouth was tight with such desolation, she wondered how many years he'd held it all inside. "It's wondering how you'll ever manage a single minute without her . . . and knowing that you'll have to, for the sake of the child she gave you."

Her throat closed up, and there were no words that would ease him. Amelia felt the edge of tears threatening, and she finally managed to say, "I'm sorry for what happened. But do you think this is the life Lady Castledon would have wanted for you and your daughter? Hiding away from the world?"

The rigid tension in his jaw never softened. "I never wanted this life at all. I still don't want another wife. Katherine can't be replaced by anyone."

"I'm certain the ladies on that list will be glad to hear of it," she said quietly. "Knowing that they will forever be confined to the ground while the memory of your first wife rests on a pedestal."

It was cruel, but after he'd struck out at her own dreams, she couldn't stop herself.

"You're too young to understand," he countered. "Go on, then. Make a fool of yourself in front of a man who hasn't a responsible bone in his body."

"I don't know why you're even bothering to make pretenses." Amelia crossed her arms and regarded him. "If you don't want another wife, then don't marry. Send your daughter to live with an aunt or someone who will show her how to be a young lady." Softening her tone, she suggested, "Margaret could teach her every last rule of society. But you needn't wed her for that."

His expression didn't change. "I thought your sister's name was on the list of candidates."

Amelia sighed. "Not if you won't even give her the chance to have a happy marriage. She doesn't deserve a life where you're

59

comparing her to Saint Katherine, the Wife Who Could Do No Wrong."

The earl raked a hand through his dark hair, impatience flaring upon his mouth. "You should learn to temper your words, Miss Andrews."

"Since I have no intention of being with a man like you, it hardly matters what I say. I only ask that you leave me to make my own choices." Amelia took a breath, trying to hold back her anger. "I've done what I could to help you. You should do the same for me."

"He's no good for you," Lord Castledon warned. He leaned one hand against the stone wall, and Amelia suddenly realized that she was standing entirely too close to this man. The scent of sandalwood emanated from his skin, and she found herself intrigued by it. Her gaze fixated upon his mouth, and a sudden flush came over her cheeks. This was an experienced man, one who had knowledge of kissing and what went on behind closed bedroom doors.

His body was solid, and she suspected that beneath the tailored coat and shirt was a muscled man. In her mind, she tried to compare him to Lord Lisford. But while the viscount was amiable and teasing, the earl was quiet and tense. She ought to be irritated by Castledon . . . but instead, she found his sudden outburst captivating.

The flare of anger still lingered in his blue eyes, and she suddenly realized how badly she'd misjudged him. This man did have a hidden passionate side . . . but he would never show it to any woman. He was completely unattainable, like a man formed of ice.

She blinked, wondering what had prompted her to think of him in such a way. Lord Castledon wasn't a man she wanted at all. But she couldn't deny that when she was so near to him, she grew aware of the hard cast of his jaw and his hidden strength. He was broad-shouldered and so tall she had to tilt her head back. Right now, he was eyeing her as if he wanted to take her apart.

"I'll be the judge of which man is good for me," she replied. Then she turned back from him, wondering why her heart was pounding so fiercely.

David stood against the far wall, inwardly furious. Amelia's insistence that he leave her alone to make her own choices was akin to watching her throw herself off a mountain. She was too trusting in others, too eager to see the good in people.

He didn't want her to be hurt the way her sister Margaret had been. Viscount Lisford took too many risks and seemed to relish the danger. The man had made many enemies among the ton, but it only seemed to make him more attractive to the women.

He shouldn't care. What did it matter if Amelia Andrews chose to throw herself at a man who would only use her dowry to fund his gambling habits? It was her life, wasn't it?

But when he watched her enter the ballroom, her face flaming, he saw in her a spirit that should not be dimmed. She needed to be protected, even if she was unaware of the danger.

In his waistcoat pocket, he touched the folded letter his daughter had written to her mother, so many years ago. It was a physical reminder that he had to try again, though he didn't want to.

One of the ladies on Amelia's list, Miss Georgina Pearson, was standing with her mother nearby. This was it, then. Time to take his first steps toward leaving behind his widower existence and learning to find someone else.

At first glance, Miss Pearson was fair enough. She had green eyes and long brown hair that was pinned up with a few curls about her face.

Just go and speak with her, he urged himself.

He made it halfway across the room before another gentleman stepped in and invited Miss Pearson to dance. She beamed and accepted, fanning herself as she followed the young man to line up across from him in a country dance.

"Would you like my help in making introductions?" a female voice spoke from behind him. David turned and saw Lady Lanfordshire smiling at him. He bowed and greeted her. "I would be grateful for it."

There was no sign of her husband, Lord Lanfordshire, but Margaret stood at her mother's side. "I believe you have met my daughter Margaret, of course," the matron said.

He bowed to her. "Miss Andrews, how are you?"

Margaret murmured a response, but she appeared more distracted than usual. Her gaze remained upon her younger sister, and David saw that Lord Lisford was already talking with Amelia.

"Would you like me to introduce you to Miss Harrow?" Lady Lanfordshire said, when David didn't ask Margaret to dance. He supposed he should have, but Miss Andrews had already excused herself to go to the ladies' retiring room.

He agreed, but it was difficult to take his gaze off Amelia. As he walked alongside Lady Lanfordshire, she sent him a knowing look. "My youngest daughter has always been a girl who wants to help others, whether they want her assistance or not."

"Lord Lisford is definitely a man in need of assistance from a large dowry." He decided there was little point in mincing words. Amelia's mother was well aware of the viscount's debts.

"The more I try to tell Amelia what she shouldn't do, the more she runs headlong into danger," Lady Lanfordshire insisted. "She has an impulsive, meddling nature."

"Then how do you protect her?"

"Once she's put her mind to it, stopping Amelia is like trying to capture a thunderstorm. I fear she's destined to have her heart broken one day." The matron sent him a rueful gaze. "As a parent yourself, I'm certain you've encountered willfulness."

He had, for Christine had inherited his own stubborn nature. "My daughter has spent many hours staring at the wall after she was defiant," he admitted.

"But how do you punish a young woman who only wants to help others? Amelia hasn't a cruel bone in her body. She genuinely believes there is good in the man. Am I to punish her for trying to help someone?"

David could make no argument with that, and he said, "I suppose not." Soon enough, he found himself in front of Miss Harrow. Lady Lanfordshire introduced them, and he greeted the young lady.

Miss Harrow was a sturdy sort, with a plain face and hair the color of straw. Although she wasn't at all what most men would consider attractive, she had a pleasant way about her. She could not be more different from Katherine, which made it even easier.

"Are you enjoying yourself this evening, Miss Harrow?" he asked.

The woman shrugged and offered a light smile. "I believe I've earned the title of Queen of the Wallflowers. But I'm accustomed to it."

"Sometimes wallflowers have the most interesting conversation. They see everything that happens at a gathering." He offered her his arm. "Would you care to dance and tell me your observations?"

The young woman smiled at him with a blend of joy and surprise. "I would be delighted, my lord." It was as if no one had asked her before, and when Miss Harrow took his arm, she appeared to be bursting with excitement.

The country dance involved intricate steps that David could hardly remember for the life of him. "I fear I may tread upon your toes, Miss Harrow," he apologized, when they lined up across from one another.

She sent him a warning look. "You may have to be mindful of your own toes, Lord Castledon. Sadly, I will likely stumble. Every last dancing lesson has fled my brain at the moment, I'm afraid."

Whatever grace Miss Harrow lacked, she made up for with enthusiasm, and he found himself enjoying the dance. She had a hearty laugh, and he liked her a great deal. True to their apologies, both of them stepped on each other's toes, but he appreciated her blunt humor and the way she laughed at her mistakes.

It was clear that her marital prospects were bleak, but more and more, he was beginning to see the woman as a viable option. So long as she was willing to be a mother to his daughter, she was pleasant enough. He could give her a splendid house, leaving her to run it as she chose.

When they began changing partners, he was startled to find himself paired briefly with Lady Sarah Carlisle. Her face flushed, and she nodded to him but looked as if she wanted the floor to swallow her up.

"My lord, I want to apologize for what happened a few years ago. I—I was wrong to try to ensnare you into marriage when you were hardly out of mourning. I hope you can forgive me."

He tensed, remembering the night when he'd been caught alone in the library with Lady Sarah. She had intruded upon his moment of solitude, and before he knew what was happening, matrons were trying to arrange a wedding. He'd protested vehemently, and though the young woman had been embarrassed, there was nothing to be done for it.

"As I recall, neither of us did anything wrong except to be at the wrong place at the same time," he said. "But I accept your apology, and I'll admit that it hasn't crossed my memory until I saw you just now."

She ventured a painful smile, and he turned her in a circle. "Are you enjoying your evening, Lady Sarah?"

Her smile faded. "Not really. It seems that the ton hasn't forgiven me for my mistakes or for my brother's."

He didn't know how to respond to that, but managed, "I hope you find a gentleman who suits you."

"Finding him isn't my difficulty," she admitted. Her eyes met his, and she held his gaze for a moment. "It's finding someone who doesn't care about my past scandals, who will see that I'll be a good wife to him."

There was a trace of longing there, and it made him uncomfortable to see it. "I'll bid you good hunting, then."

He was paired back with Miss Harrow, and then at last, he was Amelia's partner. She touched her palm to his and said, "I see you listened to me and gave Miss Harrow a chance." The look on her face was smug, as if to say, *I told you so.*

"I did. She is a kind person," he admitted.

There was a softness that came over Amelia, and she nodded. "Few men take the time to know Lavinia Harrow. But she deserves a gentleman who can see her for the woman she is."

He walked in a circle with Amelia, her words sinking into his consciousness. In the past five years that he'd known her, he *had* seen the woman emerging from the enthusiastic girl. He knew the woman Amelia had become, faults and all.

"I also spoke briefly to Lady Sarah Carlisle," he told her. "I wasn't aware that she was still seeking a husband."

A flash of tension stiffened Amelia's smile. "I suppose she is. And I hope, for her sake, that she finds one."

He couldn't understand why Lady Sarah would upset her so— though he remembered how the woman's brother, the Earl of Strathland, had threatened Amelia's family. "I'm certain she will marry eventually."

With a chagrined smile, Amelia squared her shoulders. "I've been thinking, Lord Castledon. We should call a truce between us."

"I wasn't aware we were at war." But he offered his hand, and she squeezed it.

Teasing mischief brimmed in her eyes, but it didn't seem she was holding a grudge. "Only if you continue to disrupt my efforts to win Lord Lisford."

David could give no answer, as they switched partners. He continued the set with Miss Harrow, and before the dance ended, Amelia approached him. In a low voice she murmured, "Come and pay a call upon us Saturday next. My aunt Charlotte is hosting a birthday party for her son Matthew, and all of us will be there. It will be a good chance for you to see Margaret and try another name on the list."

She smiled and returned to her sister. Although it was a reasonable invitation, he wondered at the wisdom of accepting. He doubted if Margaret would seriously entertain the idea of courtship after she'd been jilted once before.

Miss Harrow was a leading candidate for marriage, not only due to her kind nature, but also because he was not attracted to her beyond friendship. There was no danger of falling in love with a woman like her.

He should decline the invitation to the birthday party. Not on Margaret's behalf, but because every time he was in Amelia's presence, he found himself watching her. She had always caught his eye, even when she was too young to join in the soirées and the dancing.

She was the danger, not her sister. She might be a meddling sort, with the genuine intent to help others . . . but he sensed an invisible thread pulling him toward her. Earlier, in the garden, Amelia had caught him unawares when she'd claimed to be in love with the viscount. Her naïveté would bring her into ruin if she wasn't careful.

But then he'd revealed too much to her. She'd looked upon him with the eyes of a woman who sympathized with him. Although David hadn't wanted her pity, it was the sudden pulse of awareness that caught him off guard. Her green eyes had shone with unshed tears while she'd lifted her face to his. If he'd dared to lower his defenses, she might have rested her cheek against his beating heart, offering the comfort of an embrace.

And God above, it had been so long.

So many times, he'd awakened in the night, reaching for the empty pillow beside him. Sometimes he imagined the scent of Katherine's hair lingering. And the ache of loneliness kept him up for the remaining hours until dawn.

"Are you all right, my lord?" The voice of Miss Harrow broke through his dreaming, and he pushed back the memory.

"Yes, of course." He escorted the young woman back to her chaperone, but it wasn't long before he spied Amelia laughing with Lisford. The man was gawking at her, as if he worshipped the ground she walked upon. The more he stared, the more Amelia blushed.

David's hands curled into fists. It wasn't his concern, nor should he care what happened between the young woman and the viscount. But seeing the notorious rake flirting with her made him want to snatch her out of harm's way. Amelia deserved better. She couldn't see that it was all a game to Lisford.

And damn it all, he didn't want her to lose her heart to a man who would only destroy it. Not when he could save her.

"Margaret will be delighted to see you." Amelia greeted Lord Castledon after the footman escorted him inside the parlor. She hadn't known if the earl would attend the party or not, but she was glad he'd come. He had also brought a gift for Matthew, and from the shape of it, Amelia already knew what it was—a hobbyhorse.

It was wrapped in brown paper with a bright ribbon. The footman accepted it from the earl and took it over to the table of gifts.

Secretly, Amelia believed that she could conjure a true love match between Lord Castledon and her sister. Margaret and he had both had their hearts broken. Wasn't it logical that they could get on with their lives together? She was convinced of it.

The earl stood at the edge of the room, as if not wanting to intrude. Once again, he was wearing black. Though it had been many years since his wife had died, it seemed that he'd never bothered to change out of mourning garb. That would have to change if he intended to seek a new wife.

"Do you own anything other than black?" Amelia whispered beneath her breath while standing beside him.

His mouth tilted at one corner. Leaning in, he kept his voice low. "No."

"You really ought to visit a tailor," she murmured. "Your clothes are gloomy. It will be far easier to catch a woman's attention when you don't resemble an undertaker."

"But I never have any difficulty finding attire that matches," he pointed out. "I'm told that black suits my features very well."

"If you intend to remain in mourning, yes." She let out a sigh and added, "Buy a dark green waistcoat. It would make a good start."

"And here I thought you'd ask me to wear orange." His sardonic look caught her unawares, and she suddenly felt small beside him.

Her skin tingled with awareness of how he'd whispered in her ear. Goodness, but he was tall. She smiled up at him, but it was a way of hiding the sudden rush of nerves. It made little sense at all, why she would feel anxious around this man. But when he stared back, her imagination shocked her as she wondered what it would be like to kiss this man.

Amelia had never been kissed, though she'd seen her sisters kissing their spouses when they thought she wasn't looking. Her heartbeat quickened at the thought of Lord Castledon's mouth upon hers.

No. Absolutely not. Clearly she hadn't eaten enough breakfast, and it was addling her brain.

If there was any man's lips she ought to be imagining, it should be Lord Lisford's. She shut her eyes a moment, clearing the thought away. She'd already chosen her potential husband, and it would never be a man who was still besotted with his dead wife.

"Next month, you can try orange." With that, she led the earl over to her aunt Charlotte, who was watching over her five-year-old son, Matthew. The boy was nearly bouncing with excitement, and he chattered unceasingly with his aunts and uncles.

"You've met my aunt, Lady Arnsbury, I know." Amelia stood back while the earl dutifully greeted her aunt Charlotte. His eyes passed over the other guests, who were all family members. Her parents were there, along with her sisters. The Duke of Worthingstone stood behind his wife, Victoria. Their three-year-old son, Christopher, was eyeing the table of gifts as if he believed they were for him.

It was blatantly obvious that Lord Castledon was the only person there who was not family, and he sent her a pointed look. Amelia refused to feel guilty about it. Here, among family, Margaret would be less worried about what other people would think. She might be more willing to loosen up some of her rigid rules and show the softer side of herself.

Besides that, their family knew how to have fun. And fun was something that Sir Personality-of-a-Handkerchief had not enjoyed in a long time.

"Why don't you go and play *The House of Virtues* with Margaret?" Amelia suggested. Her sister sat at a nearby table with the linen game board and tin pieces. She'd been trying to teach Matthew how to play, but he'd abandoned it after five minutes.

"I haven't played that game since I was a child," he countered. "I think I'd rather stand back and watch."

Of course he would. Amelia sighed, for this was going to be a greater challenge than she'd suspected.

"You are not here to be a wall hedge," Amelia reminded him. "That's not the reason you were invited."

He sent her a sidelong glance. "And here I thought I was meant to enjoy myself?"

She stopped, realizing that in her quest to bring her sister and the earl together, her meddling was transforming her into a shrew. Which wasn't her intent at all.

Amelia forced herself to soften her tone. "Of course, I want you to enjoy yourself and get to know my family." She smiled, trying to make him see. "But I don't want you to feel left out, either." The more he remained outside the others, the less likely it was that she could engage in matchmaking between Margaret and him.

His blue eyes locked upon hers, as if he were trying to see past her carefully laid plans. At last, he nodded. "Only if you come with me."

She let out a sigh. "I don't think you need a chaperone in a room full of people, Lord Castledon."

"Either you play with us, or I don't play at all." He crossed his arms and regarded her like a man who had nothing to lose. She didn't know why he was forcing the issue, but he was leaving her with no choice.

"We play for wagers," Amelia cautioned him. "And we cheat all the time. You've been warned."

He offered her his arm as they walked toward Margaret. "I thought your family was honorable."

"Not when it comes to children's games. Prepare to be beaten soundly." He was going to regret cornering her like this. Amelia brightened at the thought, but the earl's hand moved to the base of her spine when they reached her sister. *It means nothing*, she told herself. But the fleeting touch was enough to scatter her thoughts.

"Margaret, we're going to teach Lord Castledon how *The House of Virtues* is truly played," she began, taking a seat across from her sister and thereby forcing the earl to sit between them.

"Are you *trying* to frighten him off, Amelia?" Margaret sent her a dismayed look. "I'm certain he has little interest in a children's game." To the earl, she added, "There's no need for you to endure it, my lord."

Her sister was not helping. Didn't she realize that this was their way of getting to know one another? Amelia sent her a dark look, but Margaret ignored it.

"I am intrigued by the promise of rampant cheating," the earl said. "Rest assured, Miss Andrews, I am quite capable of keeping up with the pair of you." The earl sat down and reached for the teetotum. "Shall we spin to see who will go first?"

"No, the youngest goes first," Amelia said, snatching it out of his hands. She spun the teetotum, and when it landed on a one, she promptly rotated it to a four.

"That was a one," the earl pointed out. "I saw it."

She sent him a brilliant smile of innocence and was rewarded by a faint look of discomfort in his eyes. "It looked like a four to me." Then she passed it to Margaret, who spun a six.

The earl's teetotum landed on a two, but he didn't adjust the number. Instead, he rested his palms on the table, studying the board the way he would an enemy. His piercing blue eyes narrowed upon the embroidered linen game board, as if forming his strategy.

Amelia held out a handful of tin tokens. "Which would you rather be? The knight, the dog, or the maiden?"

He raised an eyebrow at her. "Not the maiden."

"The dog it is!" She beamed at him, just as he stole the knight from her hands.

"A valiant effort, Miss Andrews. But the game has only begun." The sensual tone of his voice made her mood shift. There was a hint of a smile on his face, and she wondered if he was talking about more than this children's game. Sometimes the earl could be deceiving, revealing only what he chose to convey. His clothing was impeccably neat, and his dark hair was combed back so that it contrasted against his skin. Amelia found herself wondering what it would be like to rumple that hair. She suspected that behind his polished exterior was a wilder man, one who *didn't* obey rules.

Or perhaps that was only her imagination. So often, he hung back from everyone else, content to be alone.

Margaret handed the tin dog to Amelia, and the game began. But with each move, Amelia sensed that the pair was plotting against her. Every once in a while, her sister would exchange a look with the earl, one that suggested she knew something Amelia didn't. There seemed to be an unspoken conversation happening between them.

Although the pair of them likely intended to cheat in order to win the game, Amelia didn't mind. If it meant losing this match to make her sister smile again, it would be worth it.

But when Amelia made her next move, she saw the earl's eyes upon her. A shiver rose up over her skin, and she couldn't stop her pulse from quickening.

He was staring at her, and she shifted her piece forward too many squares.

"I saw that," he remarked.

"No, you didn't. I've heard that men often need spectacles as they get older."

Margaret let out a sigh. "You mustn't let her bother you, Lord Castledon. She's *always* like this, and I have to live with her."

Amelia steepled her fingers and flashed the earl a bright smile. *Not for long, if I get my way.*

David couldn't remember the last time he'd played a game with so much cheating. Amelia had openly moved her tin piece too many squares forward, and when he'd corrected her, Margaret had subtly moved her own piece.

They were like wolves, taking turns attacking their prey.

Amelia's face was flushed, and she bit one edge of her lip while she slipped a glance at him.

"Don't," he warned.

Her foot brushed against his as she put her game piece back where it had been. The gentle nudge was meant to be playful, but he froze at the touch.

Now he was beginning to wonder why he'd come here at all. Margaret Andrews might be the woman he was meant to get acquainted with, but it was her sister who was provoking stronger reactions.

He didn't need or want Amelia Andrews in his life. David pushed back his chair, creating a physical distance between them, and he decided it was time to end the game.

Margaret and Amelia had begun writing down wagers on a scrap of paper, pretending to keep score.

"What exactly are we wagering?" he murmured beneath his breath. It was bad enough that they were playing a children's game. Gambling was even more inappropriate.

"Oh, anything." Amelia shrugged. "Sometimes we wager for favors."

He wasn't certain that was a good idea. Even more disturbing was that his mind was conjuring the vision of favors from Amelia, not Margaret. A light flush came over her cheeks, as if she'd read his wayward thoughts. "What sort of favors?" he asked.

"Not *that* kind," Margaret chided him.

"Sometimes we wager for confections," Amelia said. "If I lose, I'll buy Margaret a sugared plum. Or if she loses, she'll loan me one of her gowns."

"What if I win?" he suggested.

Margaret set down the teetotum, her expression worried. "I suppose we could buy you a sugared plum, if you wish it, Lord Castledon." From the tension in her posture, he sensed that she was wary of the direction of their conversation.

"I don't care for sweets," he said.

"You don't like sweets?" Amelia was aghast. "What sort of a man *are* you?"

He gave no explanation, but kept his expression neutral. "You could buy a doll for my daughter, or a toy, if you'd like."

At that, Margaret relaxed. "Higher stakes, then."

"Indeed." He spun the teetotum, flicking his wrist to ensure that it landed upon a five. It placed him within three squares of winning the game.

"If your daughter is eleven years old, she won't want a doll," Amelia pointed out. "You should buy her dresses more befitting a young woman."

"She's still in the nursery," he felt compelled to answer. "It's too soon for her to be putting up her hair."

"Yes, but neither should you treat her like a child."

"She *is* a child," he interjected. There were years left before

Christine would be old enough to attend a soirée or assembly. He couldn't even conceive of the moment when she would marry.

"Not for long," Amelia answered.

"Margaret, darling, may I see you for a moment?" Lady Lanfordshire touched her daughter's shoulder. "Your aunt and I have something we need to discuss with you."

Margaret nodded and stood from her chair. "I'm going to remember where those pieces are," she warned. "No cheating whilst I'm away."

"Of course," Amelia said, but David suspected she was cheerfully lying.

Once Margaret was out of earshot, Amelia studied the linen game board. Each of the squares was embroidered with a figure, and from some of the stitches, David suspected that the girls had made it when they were learning to sew.

"There's another square with the same figure, two rows down," she whispered, moving Margaret's maiden there.

"She's going to know what you've done."

"Of course she will. But where's the fun in following the rules?" Amelia reached for the teetotum, but he stopped her.

"We'll wait on your sister to return."

She sent him a chagrined smile. "You and Margaret are perfectly suited to one another, do you know that? Both of you prefer to obey the rules."

"I think there's a rebellious streak within your sister even greater than yours," he predicted. "She's not as obedient as she looks."

He'd met a few women who outwardly followed every rule. No one would have ever expected them to rebel as much as they had.

"You're wrong." Amelia moved her tin dog a square forward. "Margaret is excessively obedient, to a fault."

"And I suspect obedience is a fault that you do not possess."

She glanced up at him, and her green eyes sobered. "No, I suppose not. I've always believed in honesty. Too many women hide behind the rules, afraid to speak their minds."

He leaned forward. "I believe that is why I like you, Miss Andrews. You would never retreat from the truth." With her, he was at ease, knowing she didn't voice falsehoods.

Idly, he spun the teetotum, and the hexagonal top whirled before it landed on a one. She stared down at the board, as if he'd made her uncomfortable with the words. It had been merely an observation; yet, he'd seen the flush of embarrassment on her cheeks. Before she could gather a response, he reassured her, "It is good to have an ally and a friend."

Her shoulders visibly lowered, and she let out a breath. "Allies, yes." She glanced back at her sister, but David kept his eyes upon her.

Although he knew it was a mistake, he couldn't stop himself from saying what needed to be said. "As someone who would like to remain your ally and friend, let me offer my advice. Stay away from the viscount, for he'll only bring you down into ruin. The man doesn't know when to stop gambling."

She still wouldn't look at him. "You may be right. But I believe there is a good man in him. He's made many mistakes, but that doesn't mean he's irredeemable."

She was far too naïve in the ways of men. Lord Lisford had chosen his own path to ruin, and he didn't deserve salvation from an innocent like Miss Andrews.

"Some men are better off left alone." He picked up his game piece, toying with it a moment before he set it back down. "And you should know that they don't change. No matter what they say."

"I wish you would stop treating me as if I'm wearing blinders," she sighed. "I *do* see Lord Lisford's faults. But I also believe he has a good heart, beneath it all. And that's worth saving."

"None of us wants to see you hurt."

"I know it." With reluctance, she put Margaret's game piece back where it had been. "But believe me when I say my eyes are open."

"The only person who can change the viscount's behavior is Lord Lisford himself," he said.

"And what of you, Lord Castledon?" she ventured. "When will you change your ways and start living again?"

Never, he wanted to say. Too many years had passed, and he'd grown accustomed to being alone. He toyed with his tin knight again, tilting it left and right. "I have no need to change my ways, Miss Andrews. I have several estates in England and in Wales, all of which are prosperous. I provide well for my daughter, and she has everything a girl could want."

"Except a mother, you mean." Amelia's voice was soft, reminding him of his purpose.

"Yes. And that is why I am here. To find a woman capable of mothering my only child." He suspected Miss Harrow would be the best choice, but it was reasonable to consider other possibilities. "I saw Lady Sarah Carlisle at Lady Rumford's soirée last night."

Before he could ask why she was there, Amelia shook her head. "Absolutely not."

Though he wasn't intending for Lady Sarah to be a matrimonial candidate —especially after what had happened before—it surprised him that Amelia held no sympathy for the young woman's plight. "You're judging her based on her brother's behavior?" He knew that Lord Strathland had been a thorn in the family's side and that he'd hired men to attack their family. The man had been imprisoned in an asylum for the past four years, from what David remembered.

"I will only say this—Lady Sarah needs to find her own husband without my intervention." She toyed with her game piece, staring down at the linen. It was the first time he'd seen her this upset, and he couldn't guess what had happened.

"Let us talk about your matchmaking again," he suggested. "Do you honestly think Margaret would make a good wife for me?"

Her shoulders relaxed, and he saw that she'd moved her piece forward again. "She might. I do know she would make an excellent stepmother for your daughter. But—" She hesitated as if she didn't know how to phrase her reservations.

He moved the game piece back where it belonged. "But what?"

She leaned in, dropping her voice low. "What of your needs? Had you considered that you might learn to love someone again?"

He bit back the urge to blurt out a resounding no. "It's not a requisite for marriage, and I would prefer someone who will content herself with raising a child instead of harboring delusions that I would fall in love with her."

"Delusions?" Amelia sat back in her chair. "Is that what you think love is?"

He folded his arms across his chest. "I've been honest about what I want in a future wife. Love cannot be a part of that arrangement." Once before, he'd had his life ripped asunder because he'd dared to love Katherine. It was better to have a polite companionship instead of a loving marriage. The hole in his life remained, and he doubted if anything could ever fill it.

"Women aren't like that," Amelia protested. "A wife wants to know that her husband cares for her. That she is beloved by her spouse."

"Those are your dreams," he corrected. "I could name half a dozen women who would be delighted with me if I allowed them to spend my money freely and only spoke to them a few times a year."

"But is that the kind of woman you want to raise your daughter?"

David let out a slow breath. "I suppose not." What was best for *him* was not best for Christine. Yet, he didn't want to wed a young woman with expectations of love or more children. Quite frankly, the thought of consummating the marriage caused him even more reluctance. It had been so long since he'd been with Katherine, it would be hard to push her out of his memory. Not only that, but each year of imposed celibacy had wound him up tighter, until he suspected a woman's touch would drive him over the edge.

"I will make a promise to you," Amelia said in a quiet voice, spinning the teetotum. "If you consider courting my sister—or any other woman on the list—I will not wed the viscount until he has paid off every last debt." She let the spinner fall to the board and added, "And by courting, I mean you should find someone whom you might love again. You don't have to love her when you wed her. But there should be *something* there."

"I would rather not wed at all," he admitted. "But I agreed to bring back a mother for Christine. And that I will do. She needs someone to help her as she moves into her adolescent years." Although Miss Grant had certainly helped Christine with her studies, the governess was not at all prepared to help his daughter make her debut into society.

Margaret returned to the game table, and she sat beside him. Her cheeks were flushed, and she appeared out of breath. "I am sorry for being away for so long. Aunt Charlotte wanted me to help the boys in a game of blindman's buff." She picked up the teetotum and spun it, preparing to take her turn.

"Our game was nearly over anyway," David said.

"One of us could still win," Margaret pointed out. "It isn't your turn yet."

"Only if I allow you to cheat." He passed the teetotum to Amelia.

She moved her tin dog three squares ahead and laughed. "There, see! The triumph is mine."

Upon the embroidered square, he saw the words *Advance to the end.*

"That makes no sense at all. You're only halfway around the board."

"It's a very special square. And so, I claim the victory." Her mouth curved in a wide smile. "Tomorrow, you will accompany Margaret and me to the tailor's. You're going to buy waistcoats in several colors. That will be your forfeit."

He had a sudden vision of being outfitted with a yellow waistcoat. Wincing, he turned his attention to Margaret. "Is that the forfeit you desire, Miss Andrews?"

"Not at all," she countered. "Instead, I'd rather save my forfeit and claim it at a time when it's needed."

"A favor, then."

She inclined her head. "There may come a time when I need rescuing from a meddling younger sister."

True enough. Turning back to Amelia, he said, "I will agree to your forfeit. But you must promise to keep your word as well, regarding Viscount Lisford. You may find that he is not the man you thought he was."

"Or I might find that he is a man in grave need of saving," she answered softly.

Chapter Four

Margaret stepped outside the servants' entrance of her family's town house, glancing around to be certain no one saw her. In her palm, she carried the note that she'd received this morning from Cain Sinclair. The Highlander had asked to meet with her, and he claimed that if she did not agree, he would come to the front door and cause a scene.

She fully believed he would, for Sinclair was a man who cared nothing for appearances. When he wanted something, he let nothing stop him.

Margaret tucked a stray strand of hair into her chignon, her cheeks already warming at the thought. For *she* was something he wanted, and he'd made that clear. He'd stolen a few devastating kisses that had made her knees weak. But besides the fact that he was a wild Scotsman with hardly a house to call his own, he was an arrogant man who never listened to a word she said.

Sinclair was waiting for her against the side of the house with his arms crossed. He wore a green-and-brown tartan, while his black hair hung past his shoulders. It gave him the air of a man who only obeyed the law when it suited him.

Squaring her shoulders, she approached him, knowing that he must have a strong reason for coming to see her. The last time she'd seen him, he'd asked—no, *demanded*—that she marry him. He'd never forgiven her for the refusal.

"Good morning, Mr. Sinclair," she greeted him, as if nothing had happened in the past few years. Better to pretend that all was well. "Would you like to step inside the kitchen and have something to eat?" she offered. Courtesy might soften whatever complaint he had to give.

"I don't want anything from you, Miss Andrews. I came because I'll no' be your errand boy any longer."

She didn't understand what he was talking about. "You're not my errand boy."

He closed the distance between them, and Margaret forced herself to remain in place. His blue eyes were the color of steel. "Aye, and who's been delivering all the unmentionables over the years? What will you do when I stop?"

All the blood seemed to drain away from her veins. They relied upon Cain Sinclair to deliver the garments from Scotland to London. Without him, they could no longer keep Aphrodite's Unmentionables. And though she knew it was a scandalous, dangerous game they were playing, he was earning a good wage for the deliveries.

"Why would you stop?" she asked. "You've earned a great deal over the past few years."

"Aye. But it's no' the sort of life I'm wanting. I've a younger brother, Jonah, and he shouldna be left alone so often."

She sobered, for Jonah must be nearly fourteen now. "He's getting into trouble, isn't he?"

The rigid cast to Cain's face told her that she'd guessed correctly. "Aye. And this has gone on long enough. Your family doesna need the money, and the risk of you being discovered is too high. Let it go, lass."

Margaret let out a heavy breath, for it wasn't as easy as he might believe. Victoria had begun the sewing business as a means of helping their family survive. The Scottish crofters had helped her increase the quantities, and they had made a good profit over the years. In the past, she'd pleaded with her sisters to end the business, for fear of being discovered. But now, there was a different reason to keep it.

"What about the MacKinloch women?" she asked. "They and their families depend on the sewing for their livelihood."

He moved beside her, silently asking her to walk with him. Although they remained near the house, she understood the need to avoid eavesdroppers.

"You could sell the business to someone else. Madame Benedict might agree."

"She would hire local seamstresses, not the crofters' wives." Margaret shook her head. "No, it can't be someone in London." She stopped walking near one of the tethered horses. "Are you certain you can't continue? What if you brought Jonah with you?"

"I couldna trust him in London. He's hotheaded and goes off with nary a thought. And he's fallen in with the wrong sort of boys."

She understood his reasons, but her heart sank at the thought of having to find another trusted person to deliver the undergarments from Ballaloch to London. "Whom should we trust, then?" she asked. "It has to be someone who would not compromise our secrecy." Raising her eyes to his, she added, "You were the one person we trusted without question."

A hard edge came over his face. "But you didna trust me for more than that, did you, lass?"

Her heart bruised at his words, and she stiffened. She knew who she was: the daughter of a baron. She'd dreamed all her life of wedding a nobleman and living the life of a lady. She'd been groomed to memorize all the rules of etiquette, and she could easily become a duchess or a marchioness.

Everything about Cain Sinclair was forbidden to her. Not only his social class, but also his devil-may-care behavior. Even more, they were worlds apart. He would never understand the intricate social rules she lived by, and if he ever set foot in a ballroom, he would likely behave like a barbarian.

She couldn't let down her guard for a single second, because he was the sort of man her mother had warned her about—a man who could ruin her. Worse, she was afraid she would like it. He was so passionate, so seductive, it was too easy to let herself fall beneath his spell.

Margaret couldn't look at him when his hand reached out to cup her cheek. The touch of his callused palm gave a stark contrast between a working man's hands and her bare skin. "I did trust you," she whispered. Fumbling for a reason, she added, "You know my family would never allow us to be together."

"Because I'm no' a gentleman."

"No." She lost her breath when he guided her into the shadow of a horse stall. "You're not."

His hand moved down to her throat before tangling in her updo. "And you want a baw-headed cuif who will kiss your hand and bring you posies." Her knees went weak when Cain moved to speak against her mouth. "I'm no' that sort of man, lass. And ne'er will be."

She closed her eyes, wanting to feel his lips upon hers. It had been so long since he'd kissed her last, and she couldn't deny that he unlaced her sense of propriety. He was untamed, a man who could bring nothing but ruin to her reputation.

And there was no reasoning with this man or trying to teach him proper manners. It couldn't be done.

"You want a woman who will keep your house and give you a dozen children," she ventured. "I haven't the faintest idea how to live like that. It's not my way."

"I could teach you how to give me children," he said, nibbling at her jaw. A shudder of arousal coursed through her, and she cursed the wicked side of herself that wanted him to do just that. The warmth of his breath tingled against her skin. If she turned her face to his, she could taste his kiss once more.

You can't, her brain reminded her. And with reluctance, she forced herself to step back.

"We're too different," she managed. "As I've told you before, you must find someone else."

"You're lying to yourself, lass."

Yes, she was. But she couldn't let herself even imagine a life with him. He would order her around, shaping her life in a direction she didn't want. And although she suspected that having a man like Cain in her bed would be breathtaking, it wasn't worth the perilous price of her virtue.

"I understand about Jonah," she told him at last. "You're the only brother he has to look after him. You should go back to Scotland."

He kept his emotions shielded, as if he sensed her rejection. With a nod, he answered, "So be it."

He started to walk away, when it occurred to her that she likely would not see him again. The thought was a startling blow, and she blurted out, "Are you leaving right now?"

"Within the fortnight," he told her. "I've a few things I must do here, and then I'll go."

She shouldn't have been so relieved to hear it, but she couldn't understand the muddled feelings inside her. She didn't want this man—truly, she didn't. Why, then, did he cause such strong reactions in her?

She pushed the thoughts away and straightened her spine. "Thank you for all that you've done for me and my family." Without his help, they never could have come this far. "I'll see to it that you're paid extra for this last delivery. And if you find any of the MacKinlochs who can be trusted, tell them—"

"No." He cut her off. "If you're wanting to find my replacement in Scotland, you'll have to come and visit yourself."

She understood, then, what he was saying. He wanted her to join him there, in the Highlands where there were no ballrooms or palaces. No barriers between them except her own inhibitions.

"I can't," she said softly. And he knew it. She met his gaze for a long moment, uncertain of what else to say.

"I'm no good at all for you," he agreed.

Without warning, he took her face between his hands and captured her mouth in a dark kiss that left her reeling. "And that's why you like me so well."

⚜

"Remind me again why I've agreed to do this?" Lord Castledon inquired.

Amelia hid her smile, for the earl looked as if he'd rather be anywhere except at the tailor's. "Because you promised to pay the forfeit when I won the game." She took his arm as he accepted the brown paper package that contained several waistcoats in different colors.

"I still don't understand how you managed to order all of this on my behalf." He fumbled with the ties on the paper.

She shrugged. "It wasn't difficult. I simply wrote a note, pretending to be you, and I had my footman deliver it to the tailor. I said he should use whatever measurements he already had. They were quite willing to make them for you." She shot him a pointed look. "Somehow I rather thought you'd refuse, if I left it in your hands. And if you are serious about finding a bride, you need to abandon your mourning attire."

Lord Castledon said nothing to that but inspected the contents of the package before handing it over to his footman. With a grimace, he said, "I suppose I should be grateful that you didn't choose orange."

Amelia decided that was his way of admitting the colors weren't bad. She had selected dark blue, forest green, cream, and buff for the various waistcoats. "I could have ordered purple. But I am glad you were willing to try another color besides black."

They were joined by her maid as they continued toward her father's carriage, where Margaret had agreed to join them. Although it might seem that her sister was to be their chaperone, in reality, it was the reverse.

The early summer day was bright and the skies were a bold blue, unlike the dismal rainy days of April. Amelia leaned back, welcoming the sun on her face. "This is the sort of day that makes me want to take off my shoes and stockings and wade into the Serpentine."

The earl looked uneasy at her statement. "Your family would be appalled."

She knew it, and beamed at him. "Which is why it would be great fun." When he sent her a sidelong look, she added, "Oh, don't worry. I may be impulsive, but I'm not *that* foolish."

"I wouldn't put it past you." But he offered her his arm and walked alongside her.

Amelia tried to ignore the strange rush at the feeling of her arm in his. Being this close to him shouldn't be any different from walking alongside a brother. And yet, she couldn't deny that her pulse had quickened, as if he made her nervous.

Which was silly. He was going to marry her sister, if she could manage it.

"I know you and Margaret will get on quite well," she said. "She will make an excellent wife for you."

"But would she make a good stepmother for Christine?" he countered. "That is far more important to me."

"You make it sound as if you want a bride in name only."

The earl's shrug was not reassuring, as if a new marriage wasn't at all important to him. But she felt certain that he could learn to love someone.

"Margaret is very sensible and would make a steady wife, one who would never get into trouble," Amelia informed him. "She'd also take good care of your daughter. I know she wants children."

And you need an heir, she thought.

The earl slowed his pace. "That may be. But does she want to marry, after what happened?"

"She does," Amelia told him. "And I think you're the sort of man she should have wed a long time ago. You seem kind enough, on the surface."

He stopped walking. "You make it sound as if I'm a beast, hiding my true nature."

She stood to regard him. Lord Castledon's blue eyes were like a glacier, hiding every trace of emotion. "I don't think you're a beast. But I do think you're hiding the man you are."

He'd been stoic for so many years, practically a statue within the assemblies and balls. Sometimes she wondered why he'd even attended. Had he always been this way? Amelia struggled to remember if she'd ever seen him with his wife, so many years ago. She didn't think so.

From his demeanor, others likely believed he was a dreadful bore. But the truth was, she'd found his dry wit quite entertaining. For years, when she'd been only sixteen, too young to dance or to be courted, he'd been the shadow behind her.

She wanted him to have a true marriage, not one made of words and no substance. One where he could be happy once more.

The earl was saved from answering when they reached the carriage. He helped Amelia into the landau and greeted Margaret. "Miss Andrews."

"Lord Castledon, thank you for agreeing to accompany us. It was very kind of you." Her sister was wearing a cream gown trimmed with lilac ribbon, and she moved over to make room for them. "Amelia told me that you kept your wager, about choosing waistcoats in different colors," Margaret ventured with an amused smile. "What colors did you select?"

"Your sister chose them," he admitted. "Thankfully, she refrained from pink or purple."

"*This* time, I did." Amelia pasted a smile on her face and sat beside her sister, across from Lord Castledon. She decided it would be best to remain quiet for the rest of the drive, in the hopes that Margaret and the earl would find a topic about which to converse.

They did begin speaking about the weather, but it wasn't at all interesting. She bit her lip and touched the earl's foot with her own, hoping he would take the hint to help things along. Her kick resulted in the earl lightly stepping on her foot.

Lord Castledon continued talking with Margaret, and all the while, Amelia's toes were trapped under his shoe. She glared at him, but the slight smile on his face revealed that he didn't care at all. He was doing this on purpose.

"Did you need something, Miss Amelia?" the earl inquired.

"Yes. I should like my foot back, if it wouldn't trouble you."

"How careless of me," Lord Castledon remarked, but the look he sent her was quite deliberate.

Her matchmaking efforts weren't working at all. The earl and Margaret might have been brother and sister to an onlooker, for there was an utter lack of romantic interest. Something had to be done, and Amelia decided he needed intervention. "Lord Castledon, surely you know of a more interesting conversational topic than the weather?"

Margaret exchanged another amused look with Lord Castledon. "Actually, he is correct. To discuss anything else would be most improper."

Oh, for the love of handkerchiefs. Her sister was *not* helping, and moreover, she didn't appear to care.

"No one is interested in the weather," Amelia insisted. "It's a conversational topic used as a last measure, when you have nothing else to say."

"Then what do you believe we should discuss?"

Amelia sighed. "Perhaps a good book you've read. Or places you've visited."

"I don't read," Lord Castledon said. There was a spark of mischief in his blue eyes, and he added, "It's too taxing upon my brain."

He might as well have thrown down a gauntlet with the way he was mocking her. She knew very well that he could read. "Then what *do* you do with your time?"

"I stare at the wall." His voice was monotone, and Amelia wished that she could throw something at him. He was deliberately fighting against her attempts to match him with her sister.

Margaret was biting her lip hard, to keep from laughing. "I do that sometimes, too. Especially when I'm trying to keep from murdering an interfering younger sister."

It was clear that neither of them had any intention of allowing her to redirect the conversation. Amelia knew when it was time to admit defeat. "You may have a corpse to bury at the end of this outing," she insisted. "For I may die of boredom."

"I'll risk it if you will," Margaret said to the earl.

Lord Castledon let out a genuine laugh, the first Amelia had ever heard. Deep and resonant, the sound warmed her, inviting her to smile. His blue eyes crinkled around the edges, but his stare struck her like a club.

Amelia's skin jolted with gooseflesh, as if he'd physically touched her. She was caught up in the man's eyes, suddenly seeing him in a different way. No, he didn't have strong features like Viscount Lisford, but the earl was undeniably masculine, with a stubborn jaw and a firm mouth.

Her plans were crumbling all around her, making her question every decision she'd made. Here she was, trying to set Margaret up with the earl . . . and it was backfiring on her. Her own heart was softening toward Lord Castledon, and that was not good at all.

"We won't let you die of boredom, Miss Amelia." The earl turned to the driver and directed him to take them to Vauxhall Gardens.

Amelia nodded and forced a smile to her face that she didn't feel. Instead, she stared outside, feeling as if her plans were being pulled apart at the seams. She had chosen the man she wanted to marry, and she intended to reform Viscount Lisford until he was the perfect suitor.

Surely the fluttering in her stomach was only nerves. It could not be anything more than that. But when she glanced back at the earl, she found herself imagining what else lay beneath the surface of this man.

He'd locked away his heart and had chosen a frozen existence, one where he wore black and refused to feel happy. If anyone needed saving, it was this man. He needed someone to bring joy back into his life. Perhaps even another child.

No. Her conscience shut off the thought. It was Margaret's turn for happiness. Her sister had waited years to find the perfect man, and the earl was exactly what she needed.

Lord Castledon helped them both down from the carriage, and when he took Amelia's hand, the casual touch of his palm made her want to hold it.

Stop it, stop it, stop it. If there was a way to throttle her own heart, she needed to do it now. She didn't even understand what was the matter with her.

Amelia stepped to the side to allow Margaret to walk near the earl, keeping near enough to chaperone, but remaining slightly behind them.

But when Lord Castledon turned, he winked at her. And she felt her heart sliding further down a path she didn't want to tread upon.

David kept close by the two young women, fully aware that Amelia was bothered by something. Instead of her usual forthright behavior, she was avoiding eye contact with him. He knew precisely why she had arranged this outing—to try and bring him together with Margaret. Though he hadn't particularly wanted to go, there was no real reason to refuse. He'd promised himself he would make an effort to find the right woman to wed. And that meant leaving his house and forcing himself to go out.

To his surprise, Margaret had the same sense of humor as himself. He immediately recognized that she had no interest in him, but she was delighting in thwarting Amelia's meddling. It had become a silent game, to see what move she would make next, after he and Margaret parried each attempt.

But now, Amelia appeared embarrassed, and he didn't know what he'd said or done. He'd winked at her, meaning to show that he didn't intend any insult, but she'd seemed even more uncomfortable after that. He wasn't certain why. A man could make a fortune if he could write a pamphlet of instructions about how to interpret a woman's feelings.

David led the two women around the gardens, past entertainers and jugglers. Margaret was having a fine time, exclaiming her delight when she saw a hot air balloon in the distance. But Amelia remained strangely silent. He moved to her side after Margaret went to look at some rose blossoms. "Are you unwell?"

She shook her head. "No. I'm merely trying to give you and my sister some time together."

Her gaze remained upon the ground, and David commanded softly, "Look at me, Amelia."

When she did, her green eyes held wariness. Her golden hair was pulled back beneath her bonnet, and her skin was pale—almost as if he made her nervous, for some reason. Never in his life had he seen Amelia Andrews afraid of anything.

"I know you aren't feeling well because you aren't speaking." Before she could deny it, he continued. "I've known you for the past four years, and silent is not a word that describes you. You would talk to wallpaper if you thought it would answer back."

She glared at him, which was a definite improvement. "Wallpaper might have more interesting things to say than *some* people."

Now her spark had returned. He decided to bait her a little further. "I am quite good at conversing. You, of all people, should know that."

"The weather, Lord Castledon? Honestly, you should—"

"Margaret and I were only having a bit of fun. Which was what you wanted, wasn't it?"

She quieted and shrugged. "I suppose."

To change the subject, he pointed toward the hot air balloon. "Would you ever enjoy riding in one of those?"

"I would sooner throw myself into the Thames off the London Bridge." Amelia shuddered. "I despise heights. If a woman were meant to fly, God would have placed wings upon her. The last time I checked, I have no wings."

"I thought you were more adventurous than that." He offered her his arm, and after a moment of hesitation, she took it, before they followed Margaret through the gardens.

"Sometimes."

Her mood seemed to have lightened, and when they reached the end of the path, there seemed to be a commotion ahead. Although David would have taken the women away from the disruption, Margaret had already gone to investigate it.

"What is going on?" Amelia asked.

"I don't know, but your sister should stay back, whatever it is. Wait here and—"

"I am *not* going to stand back out of the way. We will go together," Amelia insisted. Though it wasn't what he wanted, he supposed she was safer at his side than alone.

When they reached the small enclosure, David wanted to curse. A group of men had surrounded Lord Lisford, along with another man, who appeared as if he'd been dragged out of Thieves' Alley. The viscount had discarded his coat and waistcoat, and his nose was bleeding. The two men were boxing, while others were wagering against the fight.

"What are they *doing*?" Amelia was shocked by the sight of the men. "In such a public place? Has the viscount gone mad?"

"I imagine gambling was involved in some way." David stepped forward and spoke to Margaret, trying to guide her away from the fighting.

"I'm not leaving," she insisted. Her face had gone white, and her hands were tightly gripped together. It was clear that Lord Lisford was losing this fight, and the other man was taking him apart. The viscount's head snapped backward as a sound blow caught him in the jaw.

"You shouldn't be here, Miss Andrews," David said.

But Amelia stepped beside her sister, recognition dawning in her eyes. "Oh, no. It's Mr. Sinclair fighting him, isn't it?"

David had no idea who this Mr. Sinclair was, but the man was a damned good fighter. He allowed the viscount to swing a blow and dodged it at the last second, leaving the man to go sprawling.

But Amelia appeared frozen by the sight of the men.

"Do you want me to get him out of this?" Though David personally believed the viscount deserved whatever beating he got, he knew the man was important to her.

"Someone needs to stop the fight," she whispered.

He eyed Margaret, who looked ready to step into the ring herself, with her hands clenched at her sides.

Damn it all, he supposed it was now up to him. He removed his coat, handing it to Amelia. "Stay with your sister, and do *not* let her interfere."

"I'll sit on her if I have to," Amelia answered. Then she touched his shoulder. "Be careful, won't you?"

Amelia didn't know what had started the fight between Mr. Sinclair and the viscount, but she strongly suspected it was about her sister. The Highlander had never liked Lord Lisford, and he'd made no secret of his feelings for Margaret.

Her stomach sank, for she didn't like fighting of any kind, much less with the man she wanted to marry. The earl had nearly reached the pair of them, and it was then that Amelia realized Lord Lisford's nose was broken. Dear God, how badly was he hurt? He clutched his side and staggered to his feet. Although she was supposed to stay with Margaret, Amelia ignored caution and started to run toward the viscount. Before she reached them, the earl caught her hand and pulled her back.

"Don't. This is no place for you."

"He's hurt," she started to protest. Lord Lisford could hardly stand, and he needed a doctor.

"It was his choice to engage in the match. If you go to him now, you'll make him appear weak."

She stilled, not wanting to accept that he was right. And yet she understood that the viscount would not want her to see him like this. Silently, she stepped behind the earl.

Lord Lisford dropped to his knees, blood streaming down to his mouth. "Sinclair should be brought up on charges of assault," he demanded. "He attacked me."

"The fight was your idea," another gentleman said aloud. "You were the one who challenged *him*. He won the wager, and all of us can bear witness to it." The man who spoke seemed well pleased with the outcome, as did several others. Likely he'd won money from the fight.

Amelia's mood grew even more despondent, for it meant that Lord Lisford hadn't listened to her pleas. She'd hoped that she could reform him, helping him to become a better man. Now she was questioning it.

Was this the man you wanted? her conscience taunted.

Of course it was. And yet she didn't like seeing him so defeated. A gentleman should never fight in public—it was a scandal and against the law. She didn't like this side to him, and it was sobering to know that Lord Lisford had ignored common sense for the promise of money.

What stunned her more was the look on Margaret's face. Her prim and proper sister appeared delighted to see the viscount bloodied and broken on the ground. When Margaret met Cain Sinclair's gaze, the Highlander's mouth curved in a smile as if to say, *I did this for you.*

It didn't appear that Mr. Sinclair had expended any effort at all in the boxing match. His arms were crossed, and he stared down at Lord Lisford as if he were as insignificant as dust. In contrast, the viscount's face showed signs of perspiration and fatigue.

"He needs help," Amelia murmured to the earl.

"He'll be all right." Lord Castledon showed no sympathy at all. "We should leave."

"Will you . . . help him?" she murmured. The earl turned back to her, and in his blue eyes, she saw the reluctance. "Please."

He didn't want to; she could see that. But in the end, he gave a nod. "Stay here with your sister."

Lord Castledon walked through the crowd until he reached Lisford's side. He started to guide the man out, but before they went any farther, the viscount lunged for the Highlander.

The earl seized Lisford by the shoulders before he could throw a punch. Amelia was shocked, for Lord Castledon had hardly moved at all. He merely kept a strong grip upon the viscount, immovable as a granite wall.

Now where had that come from? She'd never suspected that the earl had that sort of strength. His face held determination, and when Lord Lisford tried to wrench himself free, Castledon dragged him back. "I think you've had enough."

"He's a bastardly gullion, and I'm going to pull his arse through his rib cage!"

Amelia wanted to clap her hands over her ears. The viscount was half-wild with anger, and she strongly suspected he was foxed. She'd never seen the man like this, and instead of appearing deliciously dangerous . . . he resembled a fool.

Margaret's and the earl's warnings came crashing down on her, and she sobered. This wasn't the sort of husband she wanted. Not if he was going to behave like this.

Slowly, she walked toward Lord Castledon, past the onlookers. The moment the viscount saw her, he reddened with embarrassment.

"Miss Amelia. I—I'm sorry you saw this."

"So am I," she answered quietly. "But you chose a very public place. I can't imagine why."

"It was part of a wager. I was promised a large sum, just for agreeing to the boxing match."

"But why here? Why not host it within a private club?"

The viscount shrugged. "It was arranged to allow a wider audience. More people could come if it was held here."

And more people would witness his humiliation, Amelia realized. Had he really believed he could defeat a man like Cain Sinclair? Or had Cain arranged the match, wanting vengeance for what had happened to Margaret? It had been years ago, and it made no sense why he would do this now.

Amelia offered the viscount her handkerchief, leading him away. "Did you already collect the money for the match?"

He shook his head. "I wagered it again, because I had planned on beating Sinclair."

The dismay in her stomach sank lower. "I thought you had agreed to stop making wagers until you were out of debt."

The Earl of Castledon remained a short distance away, but his gaze was fixed upon the viscount and herself. It was as if he was watching over her, ensuring that Lord Lisford did nothing to harm her.

She swallowed hard, recognizing that there was much more to the earl than she'd ever imagined. Lord Castledon possessed great strength to hold back the viscount in the midst of a fight. He was a man of honor, while Lord Lisford was a man who could not stop gambling.

"I apologize for my conduct, Miss Andrews. I hope it does not mean you have given up on me," the viscount said quietly. "It seems I need more help than I'd thought."

More financial help, Amelia was sure he meant. She sighed. "I wanted to believe that you would try again. That there was more to you than a man who enjoys taking risks."

"There is," he insisted, as he wiped the blood from his mouth. "And we are more alike than you know." He stepped nearer to her, and she couldn't help but notice that he was shorter than the earl. "Both of us want to seize life and enjoy every moment of it. We seek pleasure, you and I."

His voice had grown deeper, as if he were trying to seduce her. And Amelia couldn't help but wonder how many women had succumbed to this man's charms. He seemed to know precisely what to say.

"I cannot wed a man who squanders his money," she said. "If you continue down this path of pleasure seeking, as you call it, it will lead to ruin. If you're not there already."

From the slight discomfort on his face, she guessed that he was.

"I need to return to my sister," Amelia said. In the near distance, she saw Margaret standing by Mr Sinclair. Though she couldn't hear what they were saying, she didn't miss the tension between them. The Highlander was staring at her sister as if he wanted to steal her away. As for Margaret . . . there was both frustration and interest on her face.

"I hope I will see you at a soirée later this week, perhaps?"

She studied him, and in Lord Lisford's hazel eyes, she saw an air of desperation. If she told him no, he might pursue her even more. It was a blow to her pride, knowing that she'd believed in him. Her girlish dreams of wedding the handsome viscount were nothing but air.

"Perhaps," she said. But she had already decided not to see him again.

Chapter Five

"I don't trust the viscount," David said to Margaret as they waited for Amelia to return. "He looks as if he's trying to sell something."

"You have good instincts." She sent him a sidelong glance before frowning. "Viscount Lisford has a silver tongue. There are dozens of women he's romanced and set aside." She said nothing of herself, but he saw the trace of bitterness on her face. "I'll murder him before I'll let him hurt Amelia."

"Then we are in agreement." Even as he spoke, he noticed how her gaze followed Mr. Sinclair. "Who is the Scot?"

"A family friend." Though she kept her voice even, he recognized a shield when he saw one. Not only did Miss Andrews know this man, but he suspected her defensiveness was there for a reason.

"If he is indeed a friend, shall I escort you over to speak with him?"

Her face flooded with color. "N-no. It wouldn't be proper." But her eyes gave a different story. Whether it was a harmless infatuation or a secret kept from her family, it was clear that Sinclair was one of the reasons Miss Andrews had remained unmarried.

Amelia joined them, and she appeared miserable. Before either of them could speak, she held up her hand. "I know you were right about Lord Lisford. But I don't wish to hear 'I told you so.' Not just now."

David offered her his arm, and she took it, but he could see the tears welling up in her eyes. He didn't know what the viscount had said to Amelia, but he was relieved to see that she seemed well aware of the man's character.

"Do you want to see more of the gardens?" he suggested.

"What I want is to crawl into a corner and cry," she admitted. "But I won't."

"I would prefer it if you didn't. I can't say that I enjoy seeing a woman cry." He led the two women toward the roses, but he suspected that it was likely best to take them home again.

Margaret Andrews, however, was glancing toward Mr. Sinclair. She was hanging back, and David suspected she only wanted a reason to slip away. He nodded to her silently and increased the pace, walking with Amelia at his side. Soon enough, Margaret had reached the Highlander.

"What are you doing—where is my sister?" Amelia queried.

"She has gone to speak with Mr. Sinclair. They are having a secret love affair, and no one is supposed to know." He kept his tone dry, as if he were speaking of nothing important. By way of an afterthought, he added, "You see, I *can* talk about topics more interesting than the weather."

Amelia's mouth dropped open. "That's impossible."

David shrugged. "You needn't look so surprised. Anyone with eyes would recognize how she feels about the man."

"Our parents will kill her." Amelia gaped and started forward before David caught her hand and held her back. "She swore she'd marry nothing less than a viscount."

"I don't think she would appreciate your interference just now."

He guided her toward the landau, where their servants stood waiting. "She'll be along in a few moments."

"I cannot believe her hypocrisy! She was lecturing me about how inappropriate Viscount Lisford was, when all the while she was carrying on with Mr. Sinclair."

"Let her be." Miss Andrews's behavior was of little importance, but it had clearly made a strong impression on Amelia. "It doesn't matter."

"But she was supposed to marry *you.*" Amelia allowed him to help her into the landau, and from the dismay on her face, he realized that this was not about Margaret's choices, but rather, about Amelia's decisions.

"I already knew we weren't suited to marry," he told her. Miss Andrews was a decent enough woman, but he couldn't imagine her with Christine. His daughter would torment Margaret if the young woman made any attempt to rein in her spirit.

He realized he was still holding Amelia's gloved hand in his own from when he'd helped her inside. And she wasn't fighting him at all. Instead, she stared at him.

"Give her a chance, my lord. This was just an indiscretion." Her green eyes were pleading with him, and she squeezed his hand.

She's just a girl, his mind insisted. *Far too young.* But the expression on her face held sadness. "Margaret deserves to be happy."

"As do you," he felt compelled to point out.

She released his hand, folding her palms together. "I don't suppose I was suited to marry Lord Lisford."

"You will find someone," he promised. "And you'll be happy."

"So will you," she said. "If you're willing to open your eyes and try."

For a heart-stopping moment, he thought she was talking about the two of them. He had a sudden vision of Amelia Andrews reaching out to embrace him. He suspected she wouldn't know how to kiss a man. Innocent and untouched, he imagined the taste of her soft lips, the touch of her hands.

Desire roared through him, and he was stunned at the dormant needs that had suddenly flared to life. No. Not now, not with an impulsive slip of a girl. He wasn't ready to let go of Katherine. This marriage was meant for Christine, not him.

Before he could speak another word, Amelia added, "If not my sister, then perhaps Miss Harrow or someone else on the list."

He inhaled a sharp breath, thankful that he'd misunderstood her. "Perhaps."

Margaret returned to them, and her face was flushed as if she'd been running. A few strands of hair were loose around her face, and he suspected what that meant. He risked a glance at Amelia, wondering if she knew what her sister had been doing.

"I am sorry," Margaret said quickly. Without explaining her reasons, she said brightly, "What did I miss whilst I was gone?"

David sent a conspiratorial look toward Amelia. "Nothing. We were merely discussing the weather."

Beatrice walked inside her bedroom and was startled to see Henry standing in front of her wardrobe, staring at her gowns.

"Is something the matter?" She couldn't understand why he was here. Although he was her husband and had every right to be in her bedchamber, it seemed as if he'd been searching her belongings. It was almost intrusive.

Henry didn't move from his position, and he touched one of the day dresses. "When was the last time you bought a new gown for yourself?"

"Five years ago," Beatrice admitted. And truthfully, she'd been ashamed to wear it. She'd felt as if she were trying to be one of the debutantes, seeking a husband. When another gentleman had given her his attention, it had unnerved her. She was past forty, well beyond the days when being beautiful meant something.

She resisted the urge to close the wardrobe. "I don't really need new clothes, Henry. Our girls need gowns more than I do." It was embarrassing to see him touching one of her gowns. The muslin had frayed at the hem, and the color had faded over time.

"Were things that bad when I was at war," he asked quietly, "that you felt you couldn't afford new clothing?"

She didn't want to tell him the truth. Yes, it *had* been that bad. They had been living in the Highlands where it was nearly impossible to bring in food and supplies during the winter. She'd given up her own portion of food on several occasions, not wanting the girls to go hungry. They had survived—but barely.

He closed the wardrobe door. "It was, wasn't it?" A moment later, he reached for her wrist, his strong palm touching her bare skin. "I noticed that most of your jewelry is gone. Including the sapphire bracelet I gave you."

A harsh lump closed up her throat, and she willed the tears back. "I sold it to pay for the things we needed."

He said nothing for a long time. The silence hung between them with the weight of a marriage.

"Why didn't you tell me?" he asked at last.

"Because even if I had, you couldn't come home. And your brother controlled the estates at that time." Henry's older brother had spent money on whatever he wanted, so much that when her husband inherited the title upon his death, they had also inherited the debts.

"I would have found a way to help you," he said.

"I didn't want to trouble you with our problems when you were so far away." She traced the outline of the wardrobe, not wanting to look at him. The dark expression on his face was a blend of anger and sadness.

"You're my wife," he said. "I would have done something." His hand slid from her wrist down to her palm.

"We learned to take care of ourselves," Beatrice said. And though it had been so hard, she'd found a strength she hadn't known about. "And I never needed sapphires and diamonds."

I needed a husband, she thought inwardly. *Someone to hold me at night when I was afraid.*

"Where is the bracelet now?"

"I don't know. I sent it to Charlotte and she gave me the money for it. I suppose she sold it to a jeweler."

He released her palm. "We're not destitute, Beatrice. If you want new gowns and jewels, buy whatever you want. I'll take care of the bills."

It was clear to her that Henry didn't understand. No longer was it about appearances in society or demonstrating her family's wealth through diamonds.

She'd gained something more in those harsh years—the knowledge that she didn't need anyone but herself. She had weathered the storm and come out stronger for it.

"I don't want jewels anymore, Henry."

"Then what do you want?"

She shrugged. There was little she needed now. Her girls were grown, and two of them were married with children. Forcing a smile, she said, "A kiss from a grandchild is enough for me."

"And what about a husband?"

The loneliness in his voice struck hard, and she didn't know what to say. Heat flooded her cheeks, but she couldn't imagine stepping into his arms. They had grown so distant over the past few years. He'd criticized her for continuing to help with Aphrodite's Unmentionables and had grown angry any time she'd mentioned it.

Though she knew it wasn't what he wanted, she leaned in and kissed his cheek. "I will see you at dinner," she finished.

And when she left her room, she pushed away the emptiness of her own aching heart.

⚜

"We have a problem," Amelia informed Margaret and Victoria. After the latest note had arrived this morning, she could not delay the meeting with her sisters any longer. "Read this." She held out the paper to Victoria.

> *While I appreciate your efforts at the last ball, it met with no success. It is clear to me now that no man will have me for a wife. They have not forgotten the scandal. Therefore, I have decided that I must take matters a step further.*
>
> *I shall require a house with a small staff of servants to tend me. It can be in the country, as long as I can keep my whereabouts a secret from Lewis Barnabas.*
>
> *You have one month to arrange this, or I shall spread the word to the newspapers regarding Aphrodite's Unmentionables. I am sorry, but I have no choice in this.*

"Who sent it?" Victoria asked.

Amelia took the note back and folded it. "Lady Sarah Carlisle, Lord Strathland's sister. I don't know how she learned of our involvement, but it might have been when we were at Madame Benedict's the other day."

"I knew this would happen," Margaret sighed. "Didn't I tell you? Once the world knows that the four of us have been sewing silken undergarments . . ." She pressed her fingers to her temples, as if a headache were coming on. "We'll be ruined. Victoria, it will be worse for you, especially."

Their sister's expression had gone grim. "My husband knows what I've done in the past, but I've only created some drawings in the recent few months." Even so, they all knew that if society learned of her role, it would reflect poorly upon her husband, the Duke of Worthingstone.

"But no one knows anything yet," Amelia reminded her. "We may be able to figure out a way around this. Lady Sarah paid a call on me last week, wanting my help in finding a husband. She's trying to escape Mr. Barnabas, her cousin, who is controlling Lord Strathland's properties."

"This is evidence of blackmail," Victoria said, pointing to the note. "If Lady Sarah is arrested, the matter will end."

"No, it won't." Margaret let out a sigh. "She'll only tell the courts all about us, and the scandal will be terrible."

Another thought occurred to Amelia. "But what is the harm if they *do* find out? Victoria and Juliette are both happily married. I can deny all involvement, because I was so young when we began."

"And I'm a spinster with no chance of marrying anyone, is that what you were about to say?" Margaret's face grew hard, and she set the note aside. "No. No one can find out about this."

"The right man won't care," Amelia reminded her. She still believed that there was no real harm in it.

"The right man won't even look at me if he believes I was designing scandalous underwear."

Actually, Amelia believed that men might indeed look at Margaret in a new way if they learned of her involvement. But she kept her mouth shut, knowing her sister would not appreciate it.

"The true problem is our parents," Victoria ventured. "It would reflect badly upon them."

"Father was furious when he learned of it. It would be humiliating to him in the House of Lords." Margaret set the letter aside. "We must put a stop to this."

"Is there someone Lady Sarah could marry?" Amelia asked. "Or could we afford a house for her?" It wasn't what she wanted to do, but it was all she could think of.

"If we help her once, she'll only demand more." Margaret shook her head. "No, we can't pay it. It's blackmail, after all. Victoria, I believe you should ask His Grace what he thinks we should do."

"I'm sorry I didn't tell you of this sooner," Amelia admitted. "I was hoping she would give up on the idea."

Margaret let out a slow breath. "I won't let her ruin everything we've worked so hard to create. And if she dares to breathe a word about Aphrodite's Unmentionables, she'll regret it."

It became impossible for Amelia to avoid Viscount Lisford. He'd sent her flowers every day, along with badly written poetry. Worst of all, he shadowed her at every gathering she attended. It seemed that the more she tried to stay away from him, the harder he pursued her.

She needed to open her eyes to the other gentlemen during the Season, but although many were kind and the sort of man her mother would approve of, Amelia found herself comparing them to Lord Castledon.

What is the matter with me? she wondered. *He's meant for Margaret.*

The earl would never consider her for a bride, especially after the way she'd made him a list of other candidates and practically forced him on her sister. In fact, he'd spent a good deal of time with Miss Harrow, and he'd also spoken with a few other women on the list. But each time she saw him with them, a shard of illogical jealousy poked at her. Sometimes she wished she could stomp her wayward feelings into the ground.

"Miss Andrews?"

When she glanced behind her on the patio, she saw Lord Lisford waiting. She was strongly tempted to pretend that she hadn't heard him and to march in the other direction. But years of good manners prevented it.

She nodded in greeting to the viscount, who offered his arm. Amelia hesitated for a long moment, not wanting to encourage him. Before she could refuse, he said, "I haven't gambled in a fortnight now. Ask any man here."

She said nothing, but he came closer. "I promise you. That day in the gardens was the last time. You were right, you know. If I don't make changes in my life, I'll lose everything."

Before she could leave, he took her hand and guided it to his arm. "Walk with me a moment, and let me tell you how you've influenced my life. You were my saving angel."

Amelia's stomach twisted in distaste as she recognized the emptiness of his flowery words. But she responded, "I am glad that you're trying to stop gambling." It was all she could offer him.

He continued leading her down the garden path, and she was now wishing she'd never taken a single step outside the ballroom.

"It's more than that," he said honestly. "I realized how much I need you. Amelia, my love, say that you'll wed me."

The words *Dear God, no* came to her lips, but she was prevented from speaking when he mashed his mouth upon hers. She was taken aback, and the next moment, his tongue tried to slip inside her mouth.

Her hand clenched into a fist, and she struck him hard across the jaw, jerking herself free. "No, I won't marry you." She wiped her hand across her mouth, still shaken by what he'd done. It was the most dreadful experience, and it left her horrified. "Leave me alone, and don't ever come near me again."

A blur of motion distracted her, and the Earl of Castledon emerged from the shadows. "Are you all right, Miss Andrews?"

Amelia knew she ought to be grateful for his interference, but instead, shame flooded through her, that he'd likely seen the viscount kissing her. Her hand also hurt from where she'd struck Lord Lisford. "Yes." It was her pride that was gravely wounded. She should have known better than to accompany the viscount anywhere at all.

"I would suggest that you leave now," the earl informed Lord Lisford. The hard edge to his voice made it evident that he would personally escort the viscount away if the man refused.

"You misunderstood what you saw," the viscount argued. "I asked her to marry me."

"And I believe she said no." The earl started walking, half dragging Lord Lisford by the arm. "If you don't go immediately, I'll see to it that you're carried out bleeding."

Thankfully, the viscount obeyed and hurried out, not looking back. Amelia stood by Lord Castledon, her cheeks burning. She'd never been so humiliated, and right now, she couldn't bear the thought of being near anyone. Her hands clenched against her arms, and she started walking toward the tall hedge, needing a moment to gather her composure.

"Did he hurt you?" came the earl's voice from behind her.

"He kissed me when I didn't want him to." It was such a little thing, really, but confessing it aloud broke apart the shield over her hurt feelings. She couldn't stop the tears from escaping, and she wished she could burrow into the hedgerow.

The earl held out his hand to her, and the act of kindness made her cry even more. He led her away, toward one of the stone walls. Amelia sank back against it, letting out her humiliation. "I shouldn't have walked with him," she wept. "I was trying to be polite, but then he forced me to kiss him. It was terrible!"

Amelia knew it wasn't proper, but she couldn't stop herself from leaning against the earl while she cried. His quiet strength was a balm to her wounded feelings, though she knew she was getting his cravat wet.

"It wasn't supposed to be like that," she whispered.

"What wasn't?" His hand curled around her neck, and the warmth of his hand granted her even more comfort.

"My first kiss." She wiped her mouth again. "It was like a wet fish." She lowered her voice so that no one would hear. "And then he tried to put his tongue in my mouth!" A shudder came over her. "Can you even imagine such a thing?"

The earl let out a cough that sounded as if he were trying to strangle a laugh. "It must have been terrible."

"It was a nightmare," Amelia agreed. "If that is what kissing is like, I shall never kiss a man again."

His mouth curved into a smile. "That's not what it's like."

She didn't know what to believe. "Why would he think I'd want to kiss him?"

The earl's hand remained upon her shoulder, and he murmured, "He wanted to kiss *you*. Any man would."

Her heart stumbled a beat at the low resonance of his voice. She wished that Castledon would hold her closer, taking away this terrible memory. She wanted *his* mouth upon hers, not Lisford's.

"Any man?" she whispered.

His blue eyes caught her meaning. For a fraction of a moment, she held her breath, wondering if he would. He cupped her cheek, and the touch of his hand made her close her eyes. She was so glad he'd been there to stop the viscount from harming her.

But then his hand drew away, and he said, "I'll escort you back before they come looking for us."

Her anticipation deflated as his hand moved down to her spine, guiding her into the open. Any man but him, he'd meant.

Amelia couldn't help but feel a surge of disappointment. She couldn't believe that at one time, she'd thought the Earl of Castledon had the personality of a handkerchief. No, he wasn't a man to dance and engage in lively conversation. But that was because he'd suffered a great loss.

He'd shrouded his life, and behind the shield was a man who wasn't afraid to defend a woman. His solitude was a different kind of strength, and she somehow wished that she could unlock his loneliness and find the man who had loved a woman with all his heart.

She stopped walking when they reached the terrace. "Thank you," she told him softly, "for saving me."

"I imagine Lisford will have a sore jaw tomorrow. Remind me not to make you angry." He kept his tone light and walked alongside her on the pathway.

"Wait a moment," she said quietly. "I don't want to go back just yet."

He was about to argue with her, but she touched his arm. "I'd rather not see anyone for another moment or two."

He acceded but stepped back a pace, as if he didn't want to stand too close to her. The night air was warm, and the light fragrance of rose and lavender mingled from the gardens. She studied the darkening sky. Although it was late, there was a faint hue of orange in the skies as the sun continued its descent.

He looked as if he didn't know what to say to her, but Amelia ordered, "Don't speak at all. Just be for a moment." She closed her eyes, savoring the sensations of sunset against her skin, the blended fragrance of the garden . . . and the man at her side. In her imagination, she pictured him cupping her face between his hands and kissing her gently.

It wouldn't happen, of course. He believed she was too young for him, and moreover, he wanted a straitlaced young woman to be a mother to his daughter.

But sometimes it was nice to dream.

Charles Newport, Viscount Lisford, gathered his composure, inwardly cursing himself for what he'd done. He'd thought he could transform Miss Andrews's opinion of him by kissing her. Instead, she'd struck him, as if he had tried to accost her.

That hadn't been his intention at all. He'd never kissed a woman who hadn't wanted to be kissed. Women usually came to *him*. They hung upon his words, smiling and hoping he would grant them his attentions.

He was utterly bewildered by what had just happened. Now she would undoubtedly believe that he was a debaucher of women. It wasn't that at all. But he'd sensed her impatience with him after he'd lost the fight at Vauxhall Gardens.

He'd needed that money. And how was he to know that his opponent would be a bloody Scot the size of an ox?

Worst of all was seeing Miss Amelia there. She'd been aghast at the sight of him being beaten bloody, and he'd known then that any attraction she'd felt toward him was disappearing. A sense of desperation strung tighter inside him, for he liked Amelia Andrews. She was beautiful, charming, and he enjoyed her honesty. She was so different from her sister, and a thorn of regret pricked at his conscience for what he'd done to Margaret.

This wasn't the sort of man he wanted to be. He'd mistakenly believed that Amelia would forgive him if he kissed her. How was he to know that she would spurn him so quickly?

He owed her an apology, but likely she wouldn't speak to him again. With a heavy sigh, he watched her from the shadows of the terrace. She stood among her sisters, but she didn't appear to be having a good time.

His stupidity had cost him greatly this night, and he had to find a means of atoning for his errors. If he won Amelia's heart, there would be a good dowry. All he had to do was convince her that he loved her. With the right words, she would believe him.

Her sister's husband was the Duke of Worthingstone, and her father was a baron. Between the two of them, he had no doubt that Amelia Andrews was an heiress who would solve every last one of his financial woes.

An inner voice warned that her family would not be amicable to his courtship, after he'd abandoned Margaret Andrews. But then, that couldn't be helped. Miss Andrews would not forgive him after he'd humiliated her, nor would her parents.

There was another way, however. If he could convince Amelia that he was the man of her dreams, she was adventurous enough to consider eloping. He fixated upon the possibility, realizing that this was an excellent idea. Amelia had a romantic heart, and if he gave her everything she desired, he would succeed in marrying her and the dowry would follow.

It would work. He was certain of it. She would come to forgive him, in time.

"I know how you feel," came a female voice from the shadows. Charles turned and saw a plain-faced young woman he didn't recognize. She was wearing a dark rose gown, and when she stepped into the light, he saw that she had dark hair and brown eyes. "I know what it is to want something badly and have it slip from your grasp."

He didn't know what the woman was speaking of, but she sent him a wry smile. "You should try again."

"I intend to." He knew he ought to leave, but something about this woman intrigued him. "Have we met before?"

She shook her head. "I'm not even supposed to be here. But I, too, wished to speak with Amelia Andrews." Answering his unspoken question, she confessed, "I am Lady Sarah Carlisle."

He didn't know the young woman, but he nodded in greeting.

"If you want to marry her, then don't give up," she assured him. "Do whatever you must to win her over." Her face turned pale, and she clutched at the edges of her wrap. "Even if you must resort to desperate means."

He frowned and ventured, "You sound as if you're speaking of yourself. What is it that you wanted so badly?"

"My freedom," she whispered. Her eyes turned distant and she stared back at the ballroom. "I would wed any gentleman inside that room, if it meant escaping my circumstances." She sent him a faint smile. "Even you."

Before he could say a word, she reassured him, "Oh, don't worry. That isn't why I came to speak with you. I simply wanted to encourage you."

He studied her, and though no one could call her pretty, there was a strength in this woman, as if she'd endured a great deal. "I wish you luck in finding your freedom, Lady Sarah."

She nodded, but the bleakness in her expression suggested that she had little hope of achieving it.

"I shall," she admitted. "And like you, I will set my reservations aside and do what must be done."

David sat in his wife's wingback chair, leaning back. In his hands, he held Christine's latest letter. She had informed him that he was her favorite father (which made him wonder what she wanted, since he was her *only* father). Then she had gone on to list the attributes of her governess, Miss Grant, whom she believed would make an excellent new mother.

While Miss Grant was a pleasant young woman, David knew that the governess had no knowledge of London society, nor could she teach Christine what she needed to know. When his daughter came of age, he intended for her to have a Season where she would be introduced to titled young men of good families. Christine needed someone who would instruct her in all the rules and good manners.

Someone like Lavinia Harrow or Margaret Andrews. Someone who was sensible and well-bred.

But God help him, all he could think of was Amelia.

"She's not right for me, Katherine," he told the ghost of his wife. If he concentrated hard enough, he could almost imagine her standing by the hearth. "She's far too young and impetuous."

And yet when Amelia had wept in his arms, he'd wanted to tighten his hold and comfort her. He'd wanted to tilt up her innocent lips and teach her what it was to kiss a man. She'd made him *feel* again, and that wasn't something he wanted.

"She should marry one of the gentlemen with a fortune who can give her children."

You can give her children, too, he imagined Katherine saying.

"I won't." He wasn't going to even consider it. Not because there was anything wrong with Amelia Andrews. But he didn't want a woman who would expect him to be a true husband.

The idea of fathering a child upon a woman like Amelia crept into his mind, tormenting him with images of her young body yielding beneath his. She was a sensual creature, and he suspected that, if properly instructed, she would enjoy sharing his bed. And he would enjoy *her*, which was a betrayal of Katherine's memory.

He set aside Christine's letter, wishing for a moment that he'd been buried with his wife. The wasting sickness had drawn her life away, and when he'd lost her, the physician had informed David that she'd been with child. A son, as it turned out.

Even after all these years, he wondered why she hadn't told him until the very end. Perhaps it was because the unexpected pregnancy had shortened what little time Katherine had left. But there had been peace upon her face when she'd died. The doctor showed him the son she'd miscarried in the last moments, and the child had been barely larger than David's palm.

The aching inside his heart hadn't diminished, not at all. No words or any amount of time would heal the wounds still haunting him.

He reached for another folded paper, the list Amelia had drawn up for him. He'd already crossed out several names. Miss Harrow was still a strong candidate, but she seemed to lack confidence in herself. And David knew a certain eleven-year-old girl who would take advantage of that. More and more, he was beginning to wonder if it was a good idea to marry anyone at all.

You must, for our daughter's sake, he could imagine Katherine saying.

He stared at all the names and realized that Margaret Andrews was the one person on the list who *did* know all the rules of society. She was a walking book of etiquette. And although there was not a single spark of romantic interest, perhaps she was beyond those needs now. He ought to speak frankly with her and ask what she wanted. If she desired a marriage based upon friendship, and if she was willing to become a mother and a role model for Christine, then they could begin arranging a betrothal. Marrying a woman like Margaret would be no betrayal at all to Katherine, for he felt nothing toward her.

But she's in love with someone else, Katherine's ghost warned. He'd witnessed that for himself, when she'd slipped away to meet with Cain Sinclair. Would Margaret betray him, if they were to wed?

He wasn't certain. However, Miss Andrews had few options, since she'd had several seasons and only one marriage offer. If she'd intended to wed the Highlander, undoubtedly, she'd have done so earlier.

A grim satisfaction took root at the memory of how Cain Sinclair had bloodied the viscount's nose. Lisford had deserved it, and David wished he could have been the one to land a punch after the man had tried to kiss Amelia in the garden.

The memory of her tears bothered him deeply. She'd let her innocence lead her astray and had paid the price.

You can't have her, his conscience warned. Amelia was too young and was not at all what he needed in a wife. Better to pursue Margaret and see where that led. The decision made, David stared at the hearth. The vision of Katherine came back to him, but she wasn't smiling.

This isn't what I want for you, her ghost seemed to say. *I want you to live again.*

He silenced the imagined voices, for he knew now what he needed to do. He would make a respectable marriage if Margaret would have him, and give his daughter the mother she needed.

And he refused to think of Amelia again. Better to let her go, so she could love a man worthy of her.

"I'm drowning in flowers." Amelia read the latest apology card from Viscount Lisford while her father, Henry Andrews, looked on with amusement.

"He does seem to be filled with remorse."

"And well he should be," Amelia said, as the butler, Mr. Culpepper, set the newest vase of yellow roses on a nearby table. "I'm not sorry I hit him."

"I am glad that you've come to your senses," Henry said. "He may be . . . theatrical with grand gestures, but the man is far too impulsive and irresponsible."

"I think he sees me as a challenge." Despite her earlier infatuation, she was beginning to realize that the viscount had a very strong sense of self-worth. "He wants me to meet with him again, to beg my forgiveness, so he says."

"But you won't." Her father sent her a warning look.

"I don't know." Amelia stood before him, considering it. "If I continue to refuse him, he may keep sending flowers."

"Tell him to send confections or cakes instead," her father suggested. "At least we could eat those."

She smiled, but inwardly worried that the viscount would not cease his efforts. Thus far, she'd received eight different posies of flowers. She was beginning to believe in his apology, despite his ostentatious efforts. Perhaps he was unaccustomed to a woman not wanting to be kissed.

"You cannot meet with him," her father insisted.

"I don't want to," she agreed, "but what if he continues to pursue me? He seems like a gentleman who finds it a greater challenge when a woman says no."

"Is there another gentleman who has caught your eye?" her father ventured. "Someone who could put an end to the viscount's courtship?" Henry studied her, as if trying to read her thoughts.

Amelia kept her face neutral, but she couldn't stop thinking of Lord Castledon. If she hadn't already struck Viscount Lisford, she believed the earl would have defended her.

When she'd been in his arms, she'd felt safe. No . . . more than that. She'd wanted to embrace him, offering her own comfort. He was a man of inner strength, and never once had he surrendered the tight control he held over his grief.

"What are your thoughts regarding Lord Castledon?" her father asked.

Her cheeks went crimson, as if he'd read her mind. "H-he's a kind man."

"Good. I've met him a time or two. He's asked to pay a call upon Margaret."

He what? She blinked a moment, trying to make sense of it. Last night she'd been in his arms while she'd cried . . . but he hadn't embraced her. He'd merely let her cry, letting her take comfort.

She closed her eyes, feeling frustrated with herself. Clearly, she'd misread him. If he intended to call upon Margaret, he'd made his choice—and it wasn't her. Somehow, he must have changed his mind about courting her sister. Something had made him reconsider, though she couldn't say what it was.

This was what you wanted, her conscience chided. *To bring them together.*

And yet, it was awful to think that she was once again falling in love with a man meant for her sister.

"I wish them well together," she said, trying to feign a brightness she didn't feel.

Her father nodded, satisfied with her answer. He straightened, as if something else was troubling him. "Amelia, I wondered if I might recruit your help in another endeavor."

She waited, curious about what it could be.

"Your mother and I have . . . grown apart during the years I was at war. And even though I've been home these past few years, things are different between us. I don't know—" His face reddened, and he stiffened his posture. "That is, I've been trying to—"

Awareness dawned upon her. "You want to court Mother again."

"Not with flowers or confections," he said hastily.

"No," Amelia agreed. "But you could try being thoughtful. Do nice things for her that she doesn't expect."

Her father thought a moment. "The town house does need a few repairs to the windows. Her room has a draft."

Amelia stared at him in disbelief. "Papa, do you honestly believe that fixing her window is romantic?"

He let out a sigh. "I have no idea what she would consider romantic."

"Anything that involves repairing the house is *not* romantic," she assured him. "Why don't you take her out driving? Or perhaps boating. You could take a short trip together somewhere."

"She might not go," he confessed.

In that moment, he appeared utterly lost. Never before had Amelia seen him this way. Her father had always been a soldier, stern and foreboding in his demeanor. To be frank, she knew her mother, Beatrice, had wedded him because she'd had no other offers. There had never been much in the way of love between them. They took care of each other, but her mother had struggled during the war years.

"Start small," Amelia suggested. "But for Heaven's sake, do *not* fix something or give her doorknobs as a gift." Her father had once given them to her mother when he'd forgotten her birthday. It was little wonder her mother had been frustrated. He'd made matters worse when he'd forbidden Beatrice to help with Aphrodite's Unmentionables. Although her mother didn't sew, she had loved organizing the crofters' wives, managing the orders, and ensuring that the work was completed on time.

"You could take her back to Scotland," she added. "I think she liked having a purpose, helping the women with their sewing."

Henry frowned, as if he didn't want that at all. "But she does have a purpose. She's helping you and Margaret to find husbands."

"But what about *her* life?" Amelia pointed out. "What is it that *she* wants?"

He looked utterly mystified by this, and she wondered if he'd ever taken the time to get acquainted with Beatrice. "I don't even know how to begin." Her father stared across the room in contemplation.

"Just try," Amelia urged. "And if you give her a gift, give her jewels or something extravagant. Something she would never buy for herself."

With a smile, she squeezed her father's hand and left the parlor. Before she reached the staircase, she saw that a ninth bouquet of flowers had arrived. This time it was five purple irises, bound in matching purple ribbon.

The butler, Mr. Culpepper, cleared his throat. "Lord Lisford asked if you would consider speaking to him. He's waiting outside in his landau."

Amelia suppressed a groan. "I don't think so, no."

Mr. Culpepper appeared pained at her refusal. "He warned that he would continue sending flowers until you did."

"And our home will become a hothouse in the meantime." She sighed. "I suppose I could speak to him for a few moments."

The butler shook his head. "He's afraid of your father, Miss Andrews. He asked if you would join him for an outing, perhaps a stroll or a drive."

Which would be utterly foolish after the way he'd behaved the other night. Amelia walked past the butler to the front door. He opened it for her, but asked, "Would you like me to send a footman to accompany you, Miss Andrews?"

"I'm going nowhere," she said. "If Lord Lisford wishes to speak to me, he'll have to march forward on his own two feet."

The carriage was indeed waiting outside. Amelia stepped forward so the viscount would undoubtedly see her. She waited, glaring at the landau. A minute passed, and the viscount did not disembark.

"So be it," she muttered, turning around to leave.

At last, the viscount emerged from the carriage and called out, "Miss Andrews, if you please—"

She paused a moment, and he hurried toward the steps. "Forgive me, but I just wanted a word."

"Whatever you have to say can be said here or not at all. And stop sending flowers," she said firmly.

He looked abashed at her words, and then climbed a few of the steps. "Miss Andrews, I owe you an apology for the other night. I had no right to—" He eyed the butler and cleared his throat, saying, "that is, I beg your forgiveness. What I did was reprehensible, and it will not happen again."

In his hazel eyes, she saw remorse and embarrassment. She narrowed her gaze, trying to discern if there was a trace of slyness or untruth. But no, it appeared that he was genuinely contrite.

"What can I do to gain your forgiveness?" he pleaded. "I really do like you, and . . . I think we would get on well together."

"I think you would get on well with any number of women." She tried to keep her voice gentle but firm.

"In other words, I had my chance, and it's gone now." He grew somber, and for a moment, Amelia felt her resolve slipping. He *did* appear quite sorry for what he'd done.

"I accept your apology," she said at last. She could only hope that he would give up his interest in her.

"Good," he promised. "In the meanwhile, I wanted to ask you something." He climbed the remaining stairs until he stood in front of her. The butler remained near the door, and Amelia motioned for him to step back slightly.

"What is that?" She held her ground, uncertain of what he wanted.

"Do you still dream of a romantic marriage?" There was hope in his voice, as if he wanted to believe there was a chance for them.

Amelia thought of her father and mother. Theirs had been an arrangement, a betrothal formed by friendship, not love. Although they had been good companions, she didn't think they'd had a love match.

Then her thoughts returned to Lord Castledon. By his own admission, he'd loved his wife and had mourned her death, though she'd had trouble imagining him as a romantic sort. And yet, the more she grew acquainted with him, the more she saw that he was a man of steadfast loyalty. When he loved a woman, it was forever. And that appealed to her far more than a man who loved when it suited him.

"Yes, I suppose I do," she answered honestly.

A dangerous smile broke across his face, and she glimpsed the young man who had once made her heart flutter. "Good. I'll make all the necessary arrangements."

And Amelia feared that she'd agreed to something she'd never intended.

Chapter Six

David sat at the long dining room table across from Margaret and Amelia. Lord Lanfordshire was at his left, and Lady Lanfordshire sat on the other side of her husband. He'd already spoken to the baron, prior to the dinner, and now he intended to see if Margaret was willing to pursue a marriage with him.

He'd rehearsed his speech in his head, and everything sounded reasonable. He had several prosperous estates and a title that any lady would welcome. A daughter, whom Margaret could bring up to be a young lady. And although Miss Andrews had been on the shelf for a few years, he suspected that she still wanted a titled gentleman for a husband.

Even so, he could almost imagine Katherine warning him: *No. This isn't the right woman for you.*

Margaret Andrews might not be the right woman, but he believed she was the best choice. She had the knowledge necessary for Christine, and her demeanor suggested that she would keep a strict eye upon his daughter. Miss Harrow would be inclined to let Christine do as she pleased. .

Thus, the decision made, he had to speak with Miss Andrews and gain her acceptance. Yet, he wasn't precisely certain how to go about this. It seemed that he should have spoken to Margaret in private first, but she had avoided all of his attempts.

"The weather has been fine, lately," he ventured. A moment later, he received a light kick on his shins from Amelia.

She'd kicked him? He glanced across the table, but she sent him a warning look as if to say, *Don't discuss the weather.*

Well, what else am I supposed to talk about?

Anything but that! Her eyes glared.

"I am glad you were able to join us this evening, Lord Castledon." Lady Lanfordshire smiled warmly at him.

Another kick under the table. His shin was going to be bruised if she kept this up. "It was my pleasure. I was hoping to speak with Miss Andrews about . . ." He paused a moment, trying to read Margaret's face. The young woman had speared a piece of braised beef and had put it to her lips.

"About marriage," he finished.

Margaret's fork clattered to the plate, and she stared at Amelia. "Marriage?"

Another kick. At this, he nudged her back with his own foot. No, this wasn't at all the best way to broach such a subject, but Margaret had left him with little choice.

"Shouldn't this conversation take place elsewhere?" Amelia said, none too gently.

David supposed now that it was out in the open, it hardly mattered. He decided that the best way to handle the matter was to behave as if it were any other topic of discussion.

Ignoring Amelia's advice, he stated, "I have been a widower for six years, and I have an eleven-year-old daughter who is in need of a mother to guide her. My estates are in Wales and in northern England. I also own a house here in town."

He continued listing several assets, but Margaret's delighted smile was on Amelia.

"Why, that's wonderful! I had no idea that you had an affection for my sister, Lord Castledon." She beamed at Amelia, adding, "It will be an adjustment, of course, but Amelia, you would make a wonderful stepmother."

This wasn't going at all as he'd expected. "Actually, I was referring to you, Miss Andrews," he said to Margaret. "I had hoped to discuss it in private, but there was no earlier opportunity." Because she'd found every excuse in the universe to avoid him. It didn't bode well for an acceptance of the proposal, but he wanted to hope that she would consider it.

"I believe we've become friends," he continued, "and I think perhaps we could build a marriage upon it. If you had any wish for a child, a stepdaughter perhaps—"

Another kick beneath the table. This time, he directed his own glare toward Amelia. He didn't know what she was trying to tell him, but her disapproval wasn't exactly subtle.

Margaret had gone pale, staring at him. "I think you're right. We should discuss this in private."

"I, for one, believe it would make a sound match," Lord Lanfordshire declared. "I would give my blessing upon the marriage, should you agree, Margaret. And after all these years, it's high time."

Her father made it sound as if she had one foot in the grave. Margaret's dismay was palpable, and David offered her an escape. "Would you like to talk now?"

"Please. And Amelia can come along as our chaperone." Margaret stood from her chair, folding her napkin.

Given the dismayed look on Amelia's face, she didn't want to come at all. "One of the maids could act as chaperone," she argued. "Or Mother."

"Oh, no. You are most definitely coming with us." Margaret was adamant and refused to take another step until Amelia followed. She led them both up the stairs to another sitting room. Only when the door was left slightly ajar did she speak. "You took me by surprise, Lord Castledon. I thought it was Amelia who had caught your attention."

She appeared flustered, as if she didn't know what to say or do. Before he could reassure her that it was merely an arrangement, Amelia intervened. "Asking Margaret across the dinner table was not wise. She might have choked."

"I highly doubt that." David remained standing and went to study Margaret. "I'm a forthright sort of man, and I'm in need of a wife and helpmate."

"And what of your daughter? Does she know of this?" Margaret rested her hand against the wall. Her expression made it seem that she was disconcerted by his proposition.

"It was Christine's idea," he admitted. "And I don't think it would surprise you to learn that Amelia also thought you would make a good wife. Your name was on the list she provided."

"You don't love me," Margaret said. It appeared to be yet another reason why she was avoiding the prospect.

Was love so important to her? He'd thought she was a sensible sort, but now he wondered.

"No, I don't love you," he admitted. "But you don't love me, either. Both of us are past our younger days. We're beyond the need for a fierce passion."

That sounded like a reasonable argument. And he really could provide for her in a way that would make her life enjoyable. He had no debts, and his estates were prosperous.

"Shall I go and fetch canes for the pair of you?" Amelia interjected. "You make Margaret sound decrepit. She's not, you know."

"I never said that. But she is not as impulsive as *some women*." He sent her a pointed look.

"She deserves a love match," Amelia said. "Are you prepared to love her the way you should? Or will you continue to pine for Saint Katherine?"

Her words were a lighted match to his temper. "You have no right to speak of my wife." How did she dare to dredge up the past, making him sound like a martyr? He still loved Katherine, yes, but that didn't mean he wouldn't treat a new wife with respect.

"Margaret deserves better than a life where she's constantly compared to someone else." Amelia was hardly more than a hand's distance from his face, and her own anger was palpable. Her cheeks were red, and her green eyes blazed as if she were contemplating striking him across the jaw.

"I'm still here," Margaret reminded them. "And Amelia, though I know you're trying to defend me, I have no need of it." She gently pulled her younger sister away, and Amelia seemed to realize what she was doing. Although she fell silent, her eyes were seething with rage.

"I am prepared to give you several estates to manage, a daughter to raise, and enough money to spend however you choose," David told Margaret. "It's more than most of the other gentlemen could offer."

Margaret regarded him, "And what do you hope to get from me?"

She deserved honesty, and he admitted, "This marriage is for Christine's benefit, not mine. There is nothing I need."

Margaret held his gaze, but then she risked a glance back at Amelia. "I would have to think about it."

"That's all I ask. You can let me know your decision within a few days."

With that settled, some of the tension dissipated. It was a reasonable response, and he hoped Margaret would agree to the marriage.

Amelia sat down upon a settee, while her older sister departed the room. Before he could follow, she blurted out, "That was the worst proposal I've ever heard in my life. She ought to turn you down."

No one could accuse Amelia of veiling her true beliefs. David stopped short and turned back to her. "And how do you think I should have proposed?"

"You should have spoken kind words to her, telling her what a wonderful young woman she is. Every woman wants to believe that a man loves her, even if it isn't true. And some flowers wouldn't have been amiss."

"I think you have enough flowers," he said, eyeing the numerous bouquets around the room.

"Well, offering for her across the table wasn't the best way to get her attention."

He knew that. But neither did he intend to lead Margaret astray, letting her believe there was hope for a love match. This would be an arrangement, nothing more.

"Were you hoping she would refuse?" Amelia asked suddenly. Her tone had gone softer, and though he was about to say no, he wondered if perhaps she was right. He *didn't* want to marry again, though he'd agreed to do so, on Christine's behalf.

"You and I both know the reason for this marriage. It's meant to be a sensible arrangement to benefit both parties. She would get all the freedom and wealth she desires, and my daughter would get a mother."

"And you would withhold yourself, keeping far away from her, would you not?"

"We would be friends," he insisted. Surely they could have a pleasant existence together, particularly if Margaret developed an affection for Christine.

"And what of future children?" she asked.

The moment she spoke of it, he tried to imagine himself sharing Margaret's bed. The image wouldn't fit at all, but his wayward imagination conjured up the vision of Amelia lying upon tangled sheets, her hair covering her naked skin.

Where in God's name had that come from? *Too young, too young, too young*, his mind repeated.

But there was a fire in Amelia, and he didn't doubt that she would be a sensual creature who would love every minute of bed play. Heat flared within him, and he forced the thought away.

"I don't have to answer that," he told her. Just because Amelia was Margaret's sister didn't give her the right to pry. Whether or not he had any more children was his own business, not hers.

"You want to begin a new marriage with my sister, when you don't ever intend to be anything more than the purse strings, is that it?" She glared at him, her frustration evident.

"We'll be friends," he repeated. "It will be more than enough for a good marriage."

"It could be more than that, if you'd try."

But he didn't want to try. She needed to abandon this line of questioning, for it would lead nowhere. David crossed the room and sat beside her. "You're so young, Miss Andrews. You believe that love is about flowers and poetry."

"Just because you don't intend to fall in love again doesn't mean it can't happen," she said, resting her hands in her lap.

"It won't," he corrected her. "When Katherine died, she took everything with her."

"Then you don't plan on making this a true marriage. You plan to sacrifice my sister, using her for your own means, thinking nothing of what she wants." Amelia eyed him as if he were a monster offering for Margaret's hand.

He stood and turned his back. No, he couldn't feel anything again. For there was nothing left of his heart.

"I intend to give her a good marriage, and she'll likely be happier than most of the other women of the ton. That will have to be enough." David stood, keeping his posture stiff as he moved toward the door.

"Then I hope she says no," Amelia replied softly. "For both of your sakes."

Margaret stood near her mother at Lady Rumford's ball, fanning herself lightly. The gathering of people was one of many events of the Season, and yet, she couldn't bring herself to dance or make merry.

She hadn't given Lord Castledon an answer yet, though she was seriously considering it. His honesty was welcome, and she didn't delude herself into thinking it would be a love match. He did possess all the qualities she wanted in a husband, and that ought to be enough for her.

Even so, she questioned whether it was the right thing to do. She'd seen the way Amelia looked at the earl when he wasn't aware of it. A few days ago, when he'd issued the proposal, she'd noted her sister's strong response. Whether or not Amelia knew it, Margaret suspected that her sister would be a better match for Lord Castledon. The pair of them were like oil and fire, and although the earl kept a calm demeanor around everyone else, with Amelia, he was different.

If he indeed wanted to make a match with their family, Margaret knew she wasn't the right young woman for him. It ought to be her sister, she was certain. Perhaps she could guide them toward each other. A sad smile tugged at her mouth, for Amelia was not the only one who could be a matchmaker.

Her own options were gone. Regardless of what anyone thought, Lord Lisford had all but ruined her when he'd ended their betrothal. Even though she'd done nothing wrong, everyone wondered why she hadn't been good enough for him to wed. Something was the matter with her, and no amount of good manners or deportment would change it. There were no gentlemen here who wanted her. Not really. Most of them wanted young, wealthy heiresses with no opinions of their own.

She knew, well enough, that this marriage proposal might be her last. A bitterness clenched her inside, for this was not the way it was meant to be. She'd obeyed the rules of the ton, learning everything a lady ought to know. And it was worth nothing at all.

Amelia was standing across the room, holding a glass of lemonade, while Lord Lisford was gazing at her with longing. Thankfully, her sister had come to her senses and had recognized that the man was nothing more than a rake and a wastrel. Even so, it appeared that the viscount hadn't given up. Amelia remained polite, but it was clear that her sister had little desire to speak with the man.

Margaret was interrupted from her musings when Lord Castledon appeared. He invited her to dance, but it was clear that he, too, had caught sight of Amelia and the viscount. "Someone needs to remind Lord Lisford that there are other women here who would suit him better."

"Rich women who want an ornamental husband, you mean."

Lord Castledon sent her a sardonic smile. "Rich, feather-brained women with deep pockets."

Margaret decided that she liked the earl a great deal. Not as a husband, but more like a brother. "Just so."

She held his gloved hand while turning, and found that she was enjoying herself in the dancing set. Were it not for her sister's interest, she might have said yes to the earl's proposal. He was a good man and a kind one. They could get on well enough.

But when she thought of kissing him, her mind turned back to Cain Sinclair. Reckless and wild, the Highlander was a man she could never be with. But his kiss made her blood rise, and he made her feel alive in a way she'd never felt with any other man. He was her stolen secret, a forbidden attraction that she could never indulge.

Thankfully, the earl hadn't pressed her for an answer to his suit. He'd offered for her and had her parents' approval. All that remained was her response.

They danced the remainder of the set, and Margaret was nearly out of breath at the end. She glanced back to where Amelia had been standing, but there was no sign of her sister. Likely she had gone to speak with other friends. But as she turned slowly to study the ballroom, she couldn't see Amelia anywhere.

A dark thread of worry pulled tightly within her. "Lord Castledon, would you mind helping me search for my sister? I don't trust the viscount, and I don't see either of them. I would feel better, knowing where she is."

The earl's face transformed into seriousness, understanding her concern. "You search the ballroom while I go outside."

"If he's dared to lay a hand on her—" Margaret began.

"He won't *have* a hand when I've finished with him." The earl crossed the room, and she had no doubt at all that if Amelia were in any danger at all, Lord Castledon would protect her.

In the meantime, she had to search the rest of the ballroom. *It's likely nothing at all*, she told herself. Amelia could be in the ladies' retiring room.

But after searching there and speaking with several other women, it became clear that no one had seen Amelia in several minutes.

When the minutes turned into half an hour, her sense of panic heightened. A few years ago, her older sister Victoria had been kidnapped. The viscount wouldn't do the same thing, would he?

If Amelia had gone home, she would have said something to them. Margaret didn't want to cause her mother unnecessary alarm if it turned out to be nothing. But when Lord Castledon returned, his expression was grim.

"She's gone, and so is Lisford."

Dear God, no. Not him. Margaret's stomach sank, for she was afraid of what might have happened. "She never would have gone with him willingly."

"Someone thought she wasn't feeling well. Supposedly, Lisford was escorting her back to your mother."

"Does anyone know where she might be?" Margaret demanded.

"I don't know, but rest assured, I'll find her."

Margaret leaned against the wall, dreading the prospect of telling Mother. The earl was already striding across the room, and she felt slightly better that he was there to help. Even so, she thought of another man whom she could rely on to track down her sister: Cain Sinclair.

Time was of the essence. No longer did she care about propriety or what other people would think. This was about protecting Amelia.

She stopped briefly near her mother. "I can't find Amelia. I'm going home to see if she's there. I think someone said she had a headache." The lie flowed easily, and though Beatrice appeared concerned, her mother gave no protest. "I'll give our apologies to our hostess and join you."

No, that wouldn't do at all. She needed time to speak with Mr. Sinclair.

"It's all right," Margaret assured her mother. "She should have told us where she was going, but I imagine she's fine. I'll look after her."

Her mother didn't appear convinced, and Margaret signaled to her maid to accompany her. She had to move quickly, regardless of her mother's intentions.

When she reached her carriage, she saw Castledon outside. "Have you heard anything?"

His face was hard, like frosted ice. "According to another driver, the viscount took a coach, and he'd packed baggage. I think he may have taken Amelia somewhere."

"We have to stop him."

"He won't get far," Castledon agreed. "I promise you that." There was a steely resolve in his tone, as if he would not stop until she was found. But although she trusted him, she trusted Cain more. The Highlander could find Amelia, no matter where Lisford had taken her.

"I'm going to get someone else to help us," Margaret insisted. "Someone who knows London well and can help track them down."

"Sinclair?" the earl guessed.

Her face flushed, but she offered no denial. "Go after her, and Sinclair will follow. He is a good friend of our family's."

The earl studied her a moment. "You were never going to agree to my proposal, were you?"

Margaret hesitated, wondering whether to reveal the truth. But then, it hardly mattered now. She faced him and admitted, "Not while Amelia is in love with you."

He didn't react at all, but she sensed that her announcement wasn't a complete surprise. So, her instincts had been correct. There *was* something between them, though she didn't know if it was only Amelia who had developed feelings.

Before the earl could say anything, Margaret saw her chance to make a match on her sister's behalf. "If Lord Lisford travels too far, Amelia will be forced to marry him. Her reputation will be compromised, and she'll be ruined."

Lord Castledon held her gaze, as if he knew precisely what she was implying.

"You could help her," Margaret said quietly. "You said yourself, you need a wife and a mother for your daughter."

"That wouldn't be fair to her."

"And would it have been fair to me?" Margaret countered.

She knew that Lord Castledon's offer had nothing to do with love or affection and everything to do with keeping his word to his daughter. At least Amelia had the forthright manner where she dared to confront him. And whether either of them would admit it, Margaret had seen the spark between them. There *could* be something there, if circumstances permitted.

"She needs help, Lord Castledon," Margaret insisted. "Don't let her become a victim to the viscount's schemes."

The earl said nothing at all, but she'd made her point. Without another word, he climbed into his carriage and disappeared into the night.

Amelia awakened, her mouth feeling as if she'd swallowed a mouthful of fleece. Her head ached, and the world seemed to sway. What had happened? Had she fainted? She couldn't recall fainting in all her life.

When she opened her eyes, she saw Viscount Lisford seated across from her. She blinked a moment, trying to clear the dream away, but he remained right where her imagination had conjured him. Clearly, she was having an appalling nightmare.

His expression held a blend of relief and terror. "You're alive. I'm so glad."

"Was I in danger of dying?" she blurted out. Her voice sounded woozy, not at all like herself.

"No. That wasn't my intention at all." He clasped his hands together and glanced outside the window. That was when she realized she was in a carriage.

A carriage that was moving entirely too fast, jostling her against the seat. Which then reminded her that her stomach was also tossing.

"Are you taking me home?" she asked, trying to keep herself from being sick.

He glanced out again, and from his nervousness, she suspected the answer was no.

Her nausea rose up higher, not only from the moving vehicle, but also from fear. "I need you to stop this carriage," she informed him. "Right now."

"I—I can't do that, Miss Andrews."

"You had better stop it, or I'll be sick all over your shoes." Again, her body fought the tossing motion. Had he given her something to make her sleep? Amelia tried to think of when or how.

He had gone white, and as she tried to sit up, the dizziness flowed over her. Her brain was still suffering the effects of whatever illness had struck. "You need to tell me what has happened, Lord Lisford."

He glanced outside. "I shall, I promise. But we must go a little farther."

Farther from where? Her eyes widened, and she realized that he had arranged all of this. "Were you trying to kidnap me?"

He wouldn't meet her gaze, and she realized that yes, that *had* been his intention. "No, not that," he said. "I wanted a grand romantic gesture, something that we could tell our children about. We're eloping together."

If she had believed he was foolish before, now she was convinced that the man had nothing save cotton batting in his skull. He'd gone utterly mad.

"Let me see if I can understand you," she said slowly. In her mind, she replayed the events. He'd come to speak with her, offering a glass of lemonade and apologizing profusely for his behavior when he'd stolen a kiss.

After the lemonade, she'd begun to feel odd. He'd taken her arm, escorting her to the ladies' retiring room, and the next thing she remembered was waking up inside the carriage.

"You gave me something to drink and then brought me here with the intention that we should run away together?"

He looked relieved. "Yes, that's it exactly. I thought we could go to Scotland and spend some time there after we marry."

Scotland? Exactly how long had she been unconscious? Amelia tried to look outside the window, but the motion of the coach made her quickly avert her gaze. "You forgot an important detail, Lord Lisford," she said. He waited for her to continue, and Amelia added, "Normally when a suitor tries a grand romantic gesture like sweeping a woman away to marry her, he *asks her first.*"

Bewilderment crossed his face. "Well, of course, you were going to say yes. I apologized to you, after all."

She straightened and forced her stomach to behave itself. He truly believed that, didn't he? This handsome rake honestly thought that no woman would ever refuse him. How had she ever considered him delicious and the man of her dreams? Right now, he was the man of her nightmares.

"Lord Lisford," she said calmly. "I ask that you please tell your driver to turn around and take me home. I do not wish to go to Scotland."

Confusion clouded his face. "Then how are we to marry?"

She wanted to screech at him that she would sooner marry the coachman than him, but she wasn't entirely certain whether she was safe in his presence. Shouting or making demands might make things worse.

"I believe you, when you say that you wanted a romantic gesture," she said gently. "But my family will be angry with you. They will not approve of this."

"They don't approve of me, I know," he agreed. "But that is why we should go away together. Once we're wed, they will have to accept me as your husband."

She couldn't believe what he was saying. "My father hasn't forgotten what you did to Margaret. He won't allow it to happen a second time."

The viscount appeared uncomfortable. "In time, he will see that we were meant to be together."

She gritted her teeth. Did he honestly believe that was true? Exactly how pompous was his opinion of himself?

"How long have we been traveling?" she asked, willing herself to stay calm. There had to be a way out of this.

"Most of the night. We have much farther to go, before we're safe."

A frigid chill came over her as she realized the gravity of her situation. If she'd been alone with this man for most of the night, he had well and truly cornered her. Even if she cried off and refused to wed him, her reputation would be in tatters.

For the first time, she let the fear gain a foothold. If she told him no, if she refused him now, he might leave her in the middle of nowhere. She couldn't survive alone with no money or protection.

Her family would be searching for her; there was no doubt of it. But even if they found her, the damage would be done. All of London society would know that she'd been taken by the viscount. If they married, most would overlook it. His prediction that it would become a Grand Romantic Gesture could become a reality.

Only she didn't want to be married to a man who sincerely believed he was irresistible. She had to tread carefully and do whatever she could to ensure that she didn't end up stranded.

"You put something in my lemonade, didn't you?" she said.

"Just a sleeping draught." He had the grace to look guilty at that. "I was afraid you'd say no when I asked you to come away with me."

Before she could ask anything else, he continued, "I know I offended you that night in the garden. But I was so overcome by your beauty and charms, I acted without thinking."

The way you did just now, Amelia thought. The man hadn't bothered to consider what she wanted—he'd acted only to serve his own needs.

She had to appeal to his pride and somehow make him understand that he'd made a terrible mistake.

"This isn't the sort of wedding a woman wants," she said. "We should stop for the night somewhere."

Which would give her family the chance to find her.

"Your father would murder me for this," Charles remarked. It was the first sensible thing he'd said.

"And that is why we should turn back now. If you can bring me home before he knows I'm gone—"

"It's too late for that." He appeared glum, and he added, "We'll be married just after we cross the border into Scotland."

Amelia decided it was time to be frank and hope that he would be reasonable. "As I said before, I don't want to marry you anymore, Lord Lisford."

"But you did once," he said. "I was certain of it."

Before I knew who you really were, Amelia thought. "If you force me into marriage, you'll get no dowry," she said. "If you were trying to gain wealth, it will bring you nothing at all." She asserted her final point. "If you bring me back now, I promise you, we can make amends."

But the viscount had gone silent, his gaze fixed on the outside. He ignored her pleas, and Amelia realized that she would have to wait until they stopped.

She closed her eyes, praying that someone would rescue her. In her mind, she envisioned Lord Castledon riding hard, intercepting the coach. He would throw open the door to the carriage and pull her into his strong arms. Her fantasy played out, giving her a thread of hope to cling to.

"Would you like to sit beside me?" the viscount offered. "The night air is cold." She wasn't certain if it was his attempt to be courteous or whether he intended to accost her.

"If I move, I'll likely be sick all over you," Amelia responded. It was partly the truth, but she didn't want Lord Lisford anywhere near her.

He grimaced, and she closed her eyes again. Though she was frightened, she had to keep her wits together and find a way out of this mess. Thankfully, the viscount had not laid a hand upon her—possibly because she'd struck him hard the last time he'd attempted to kiss her.

She believed this was about money, more than all else. It was the move of a desperately foolish man, not a villain. As she leaned against the side of the coach, she wondered if anyone was coming to save her.

If not, she would simply have to rescue herself.

Chapter Seven

D avid hadn't planned on driving in the middle of the night toward Scotland, of all places. After confirming with several sources that the viscount had been traveling north, he'd paid his driver a large sum to follow the main road. Margaret had promised that she and Cain Sinclair would take an alternate path, so that regardless of which way the viscount had gone, one of them would intercept Amelia.

He hoped to God that the viscount hadn't hurt Amelia. After what had happened the last time when she had struck out at Lisford, David questioned whether the man had revenge in mind. The thought of her being a victim made him want to tear Lisford apart.

Amelia was an innocent. Impulsive, talkative, and generous to a fault, she didn't deserve a fate like this—much less being forced into marriage to such a man.

Margaret's suggestion, that *he* marry Amelia, weighed upon his mind. It was a solution, yes, but one he didn't like.

She would brighten your days, he could almost imagine Katherine saying. *Christine would grow to love her.*

But he didn't want a wife like Amelia, someone who would drag him out of his solitary existence. He liked being alone, damn it. He liked sleeping alone, without a woman to interfere with his habits. He wanted a wife who would fade into the background, someone who could make herself happy by mothering Christine. Amelia would never do such a thing. She would badger him mercilessly.

And worst of all, he could easily imagine himself sharing her bed. He could picture her gold hair spilling over bare shoulders, her body lithe and inviting. He strongly suspected Amelia would drive him over the edge, until he could hardly remember the sweetness of Katherine's arms.

She's no good for me, he told his wife's ghost.

She needs you, his conscience reminded him. *Perhaps now more than ever.*

The hours stretched onward, and he tormented himself with thoughts of Amelia weeping. Or worse, being violated.

The rage built up inside him until he longed to kill the viscount. He'd long ago believed that Lisford had straw for brains, but he'd never imagined the man would go this far. Idiocy didn't begin to cover this foolhardy act.

His fists were clenched, and God above, he hoped they would reach Amelia in time. It didn't seem possible that they could have gotten too far.

They stopped to change horses, and David went to sit with his driver. He felt certain that they were close now, and at any moment they would find Amelia and the viscount.

But what will you do when you find her? his brain queried. He didn't know. The right course of action would be to wed her himself. But Amelia had already made it clear that she didn't consider him a good marital candidate for Margaret. Why, then, would Amelia agree to wed him herself, despite her ruined reputation?

Unless the ton believed that she had, in fact, run off with *him* and not the viscount.

Ahead, he spied the dim flare of a lantern in the darkness. There. It had to be them. His pulse quickened, and he ordered his driver, "Move alongside the coach." He needed to see for himself if it was Lisford's vehicle.

They would be nearly off the road, but there was a straight stretch where they could manage it. David waited until they were parallel to the other driver. "Pull to the side," he called out to the man.

When the other driver responded by increasing the pace of the horses, David was certain it had to be Lisford's vehicle. His driver, in turn, sped up until the coaches were both in danger of overturning. David hesitated, judging the speed. If he missed the other coach, he could break his neck in the fall. But then again, if Amelia was inside, she needed him to save her. There was no way to know if Lisford was threatening her, even now. He had no choice but to risk it.

Once the two vehicles were parallel again, he gripped the dashing frame and the seat. The only light gleamed from lanterns hanging on the side of each coach, while below him, the wheels jostled against the ruts in the road. It was madness to jump from a moving coach, for one misstep could mean being crushed beneath the vehicle.

David steeled himself and took a deep breath. Then he braced his hands against the seat and leaped across the space. His hands skidded across the seat irons, and he landed hard against the coachman. The driver lost his balance and barely kept from falling over. Before the man could react, David took command of the reins and forced the coach to stop. The vehicle lurched against the ground, but he brought the horses to a halt.

"Lisford has her, doesn't he?" he demanded of the driver.

"I only did what I was paid to do," the man protested, lifting his hands as if to surrender.

Then that was a yes. "Go now, and wait by my driver," David commanded.

A moment later, the door opened, and he spied Lisford peering out. "Why have we stopped?"

Rage boiled through him at the sight of the man. *Because I'm going to beat you senseless.*

David climbed down and seized the viscount by his cravat, knocking his head against the coach. "Did you think no one would come after her?"

The viscount's face paled with fear. He reached up, struggling to free himself, but David wouldn't release him. Panic laced his voice, and Lisford insisted, "She wanted to marry me!"

Like hell. David followed up with a blow to the man's jaw, and Lisford crumpled to the ground. The viscount didn't even have the strength to give a decent fight, which was disappointing. He'd rather hoped the man would exchange blows, giving David a reason to break a rib or two. Instead, he stepped over the unconscious viscount and opened the coach door wider.

Inside, he saw the relieved face of Amelia. He half expected her to begin talking at a rapid pace, babbling her thanks or sobbing.

Instead, she moved toward him and sat down at the doorway to the coach, as if she didn't trust her legs to move. Not a word did she speak. She was deathly pale, and he didn't know what to say to her other than, "Are you all right?"

She gave a single nod but didn't move. Without asking for permission, David lifted her up and carried her over to his own coach. She climbed inside, and after that, he gave instructions for the viscount's driver to take Lisford to northern Scotland, *without his bride*.

It would take weeks for the viscount to return home, and in the meantime, David intended to take care of Amelia. "I'll let you know when to start our journey back to London," he told his driver. "She needs a moment to collect herself."

He climbed back inside the coach and sat across from Amelia. The only sign of her ordeal was her shaking hands. For a long time, she remained silent, which was the strongest evidence of her fear.

"Do I need to go back and kill him?" he asked.

She shook her head. David waited endless moments for her to speak, but she never did. At last, he went outside and gave the order for the driver to begin their journey back to London. He would return her to her parents, and they would decide what to do after that.

Marry her, the voice of his wife seemed to say. He ignored it, watching Amelia. It took every ounce of his patience not to ask questions, waiting for her to speak.

But after long minutes passed and they traveled in silence, he caught the gleam of tears on her cheeks.

David cursed, afraid of what that meant. "Look at me, Amelia," he demanded, using her name for the first time.

She did, and the misery on her face only strengthened his anger toward the bastard who'd taken her.

"This wasn't your fault."

Her shoulders bowed, and she covered her face, still crying. He didn't know whether to speak words of consolation or reassure her that it would be all right. Instead, he pulled out a handkerchief and offered it to her. She sniffed and took it, staring at the linen for a moment.

"You're supposed to use it," he reminded her. "Not stare at it."

An odd expression came over her face, and she wiped her tears away. From across the coach, she appeared lovely, like an angel struggling to remain strong in the face of danger. It struck him in the gut with no warning at all.

He wanted her, even after all of this. Fate had given him the means to marry her, no matter that it was unfair or wrong.

"I used to call you this," she said quietly. "When I was sixteen." He didn't understand what she meant, and she elaborated, "I told Margaret you had the personality of a handkerchief."

He stiffened at the insult, not knowing what to make of that. "Did you?"

"Oh, don't look so offended. Clearly, I was wrong in my opinion of you." She let out a sigh and folded the handkerchief. "Beneath your shyness, you really *are* a hero."

He was still taken aback by her earlier remark. "I think you should give me my handkerchief back. You don't deserve it anymore, since you likened my personality to linen."

She ventured a smile, and it was like a razor, shredding his good intentions. He wanted to pull her to sit beside him and hold her.

But she handed him back the handkerchief. "You're much more than that, I promise you."

David wasn't so certain. "Tell me what happened with the viscount."

Her smile faded. After she explained what Lisford had done to her lemonade, she admitted, "He thought he was making a grand, romantic gesture. And he believed that's what I wanted."

David wanted to ask her what she wanted now but wisely kept his mouth shut.

"Once, I thought I wanted adventure and a man who was devastatingly handsome," she continued. "I wanted flowers every day and a man who adored me."

David resisted the urge to roll his eyes. "Men don't make grand gestures unless they're after a dowry, Miss Andrews."

"You rode most of the night, trying to find me." Her smile softened. "I'd say that's a grand gesture. And I'm so grateful for it."

He froze, recognizing the danger of an attraction he'd never wanted. A soft curl lay against her throat, and her green eyes held him captive. He wanted to kiss her, to take away the horrors of this night. And that was wrong on so many levels.

"You're certain you're all right?" he asked again.

"Now, I am." She drew her hands together in her lap and said, "I was hoping you would come for me. I didn't know if I would have to rescue myself."

He didn't ask how she would have done so but was relieved to hear that she didn't seem to have been harmed during the journey.

"Could we . . . stop at an inn?" she pleaded. "I'm so tired, I can hardly stand it."

No. He couldn't risk an inn, not now. "Your family will be terribly worried. Once we arrive home, you can sleep for days if you wish."

"What will happen when I get back?" she whispered. "I know what they'll say about me. It won't matter that I was taken against my will. They'll believe I was ruined."

"None of us will let your reputation be harmed," was all he could tell her.

"They'll think that I led him on, that I went with him to elope." She bit her lower lip, and he saw the worry there. "And perhaps it was my fault, a little. A few months ago, before I knew the man he was, I *would* have eloped with the viscount."

"But you came to your senses." He motioned toward the cushioned seat of the coach. "Why don't you lie down and sleep? It will be hours yet before we reach London."

He didn't want her conjuring ideas about what would happen next. Everyone would expect him to wed her, since he'd been the one to rescue her. Even Margaret believed it was the best solution. But he resisted the arrangement, sensing that Amelia would expect far more than he could give.

"I want to thank you," she said to him. "You didn't have to come for me."

It had never crossed his mind to refuse. He liked Amelia too well to leave her at the hands of the idiot viscount. "You're welcome."

"And I'm sorry I called you a handkerchief, a while ago. It was rude of me, and I probably shouldn't have told you about it."

He wondered why she was trying to be so courteous, all of a sudden. But then she stretched out on the seat, tucking her hands beneath her face. When she closed her eyes, although the worry still lurked, she was undeniably beautiful.

If she were his wife, she would look like that, lying beside him. Her hair would tangle against her face, those lips turning soft.

"You're staring at me," she whispered, opening one eye. "Why is that?"

"Go to sleep."

Instead, she propped up her elbow, resting her cheek against one hand. "I think I provoke you, without even meaning to. You seem to be angry right now."

He wasn't angry. It was desire taking command of his senses, pushing back the walls of grief and making him crave her. In this small space, he could smell the floral scent of this woman, and he wanted to close the distance, letting her rest her head against his lap.

He locked down those visions. Amelia deserved so much more than a man like him. She should have a husband who would adore her and children of her own.

"I'm not angry," he said. "But I've been thinking about how to solve this problem. You shouldn't be ruined because of one man's impulsive mistake."

"I will not marry him," she insisted. "No matter what anyone else says I should do."

"No. But if you remain unmarried, the gossip will worsen."

Amelia sat up and regarded him, her face serious. It seemed that she'd suddenly understood what he was implying. "*You* could marry me," she ventured. "No one would say a word against me or my family if the man who rescued me became my husband."

Before he could say anything, she sighed. "But then, I don't suppose I would make a very good mother to your daughter. I tend to break the rules more than I follow them."

"Unfortunately, so does Christine." The change in topic gave him the means to avoid a direct answer. "She has a governess, but Miss Grant cannot teach her how to properly behave in London society."

"I do *know* the rules," Amelia admitted. "Margaret drilled them into me, often enough." She let out a heavy sigh, her green eyes staring at him. "I don't know what we should do, either."

He suspected that was an untruth. The answer was there, but she didn't want to force him into a marriage he didn't want.

"If you *were* to marry me," he began, "we would be friends, nothing more. And I know that isn't what you want."

She thought about it a moment. "You mean that I would have your name and your protection . . . but we would not truly be as man and wife."

It was the honorable way to manage this, offering her a celibate marriage. But the idea of being married to Amelia without touching her was another torment. "Not at first," he said. *Not unless you want to.*

She met his gaze, but he could read the uncertainty there. "I thought you needed an heir."

He did. And he wasn't opposed to Amelia giving him a child, so long as she didn't fall in love with him. "If you are uncomfortable with the idea, we can wait."

She cast her gaze downward a moment, as if the topic embarrassed her. "I would think I could manage *that* duty, if nothing else. It might be a trifle awkward, but if we are friends, I suppose I could endure it."

It took an effort to keep his mouth from dropping open. "Endure it?" She made him sound like he had no idea how to make love to a woman.

"You needn't fear that I'd want or expect you to fall in love with me," Amelia continued. "Your first wife can remain upon that ivory pedestal. But I would think that you could at least give me a wedding night and teach me what I should know about my marital duties. Surely that's not too much to ask."

The idea of teaching her how to be his lover was incredibly arousing. His body stiffened at the thought, and right now, he wanted to press her down against the bench. He wanted to touch her skin, to capture that mouth and pleasure her until she shuddered.

"You don't know what you're saying, Amelia." She had no concept of the intimacy of lovemaking.

"That's true enough. I have no experience with sharing a man's bed. But it can't be *that* difficult. Isn't it a matter of fitting one part into another and that's that?"

He nearly choked at her prediction. "Who told you such a thing?"

"No one. But I did figure it out on my own, when I saw some dogs together," she confessed. "My sisters won't tell me anything, but I suppose it must be the same. Mother promised that on my wedding night she'd explain it."

"It's very different," he said. Within the coach, the atmosphere grew charged, almost as if a rush of heated air filled the interior. Perhaps they *could* enjoy that aspect of marriage, so long as they remained only friends. If it was a means of physical release and creating an heir, was there anything wrong with that?

Amelia sat up, watching him intently. "Will you tell me what lovemaking is like? Every time I ask, my sisters start laughing at me."

He leaned forward, resting his elbows on his knees. She did the same, and her face was hardly more than a hand's width away. For a while, he let her anticipation build before he gave her a resounding, "No. I won't tell you about it."

I'd rather show you.

She let out a sigh. "I've embarrassed you, haven't I? I know it's not proper at all, but you *have* been married before. I thought you could give me a little more detail, especially if we did marry."

"Ask your sisters again." He wasn't about to go down that path.

"I don't want to ask them," she whispered. Her hands moved forward to rest upon his knees, and the fragile touch sent a roaring blaze through him. "I want *you* to tell me."

He didn't want to tell her anything. He wanted to show her, by seizing her impudent mouth and kissing away all the questions. He wanted to silence her, teaching her that some conversations were better without words. He took her hands from his knees, holding them for a moment.

"Are you afraid to marry me?" she asked, reaching out to touch his cheek. Then she leaned in, resting her face against his. "Or am I imagining it?"

She wasn't, but he wouldn't say so.

"Wouldn't you rather have a man who can be a true husband to you?" he asked. "One who will do everything you tell him to?"

"You mean to say that you wouldn't do everything I asked?" she teased. Her mouth was a breath away from his, and the temptation was so strong, he felt his body rising to her siren's call.

Don't, his brain warned. Nothing good could come of it.

"I'm not obedient," he countered. "I would never let you have mastery over me."

Her lips parted, and the invitation in her eyes was undeniable. "Don't kiss me, then."

It was a direct challenge, demanding that he disobey her. He touched her face, staring at her while all the reasons for avoiding her turned into meaningless air. He gave in to the impulse and leaned in to claim her mouth. She tasted like summer raspberries, sweet with a hint of tartness. And God help him, she was kissing him back.

Amelia was hesitant, trying not to be too bold. And her shyness only aroused him more, making him want to show her all the things she didn't know. She yielded to him, but he caught the glimpse of her curiosity. She wanted to know what a real kiss was, and this, he could teach her.

"Are you going to strike my jaw?" he murmured against her mouth.

"Only if you stop kissing me," she answered, drawing his mouth back to hers. This time, he let himself go. All the years of denial, all the hunger for a woman's touch, came flooding through him. He wasn't gentle, and he demanded her response. He could feel her trembling, and when he slid his tongue inside her mouth, her hands dug into his shoulders.

But she wasn't fighting him. She was pulling him closer.

Her tongue met his, and a moment later, she was on his lap while he kissed her hard. His body was rigid, her kiss never ending. He hardly cared that they were in a carriage on a long journey back to London.

She was giving back everything he gave to her. The physical lust raged through him with the need to command and conquer. He'd never been this close to the edge of violence, and when she gave a sudden cry, he realized that she was as aroused as he was.

He broke away, his breathing ragged.

And she knew, without him speaking a single word, that a marriage between them was more than unwise. It was dangerous.

It was late in the morning when they arrived back in London. Neither of them had spoken during the past few hours, and Amelia wasn't certain she was capable of coherent conversation. The kiss she'd shared with the earl had knocked her senseless.

He'd been right. She'd had no idea what there was between a man and a woman, but he'd given her a glimpse of it.

Dear God in Heaven. He'd shattered her girlish beliefs, and the physical hunger he'd awakened had been nothing short of terrifying. The kiss had not been a gentleman's kiss. No, this one was carnal, meant to show her how foolish she was. How young and naïve she'd been to think that they could consummate the marriage and only remain friends.

He'd overwhelmed her, and when she'd sat upon his lap to get closer, she'd been fully aware of his arousal. The hardness of his body had nestled against her, until she'd grown wet, wanting to feel his bare skin against hers.

The wanton desires had flowed through her, and when his tongue had entered her mouth, she'd felt an echoing ache between her legs.

But now they were home, and the previous night seemed surreal.

When he helped her out of the coach, weariness overcame her. Amelia's knees buckled beneath her, and she was hardly aware of anything. There were voices calling out, servants rushing forward to help them, and eventually her mother and father came out to greet her.

The Earl of Castledon remained behind her, an unlikely savior. He held her grounded in the mass of confusion around her. His piercing blue eyes caught hers, and she drank in this last sight of him.

I'm in love with him, she realized. This man, whose heart had been stolen by his first wife, would lead her into nothing but heartache. But beneath his invisible barrier, she suspected that there was a man worth marrying.

She went inside with her mother while her father went to speak privately with the earl. Her head was spinning with fear and confusion. Before long, the servants helped her upstairs and into bed. Only when they were alone did her mother take her hand. "I know you've been through a terrible night, my darling. But I must know, did any harm come to you?"

Amelia shook her head. "I am still untouched."

"Thank God," her mother said, squeezing her palm tightly. "And what of Margaret? Will she be back soon?"

"I never saw Margaret," she said. "It was Lord Castledon who found me."

There was a line of tension across the baroness's face, but Beatrice masked it. "Then she doesn't know that you were rescued?"

Amelia shook her head. "No, I don't think so."

"I suppose she'll return soon enough." Beatrice tried to smile, but Amelia didn't miss the worry there.

"She didn't go alone, did she?" The thought of her sister being out all night, still searching for her, was horrifying. She didn't want to imagine all the harm that could come to Margaret.

Her mother didn't answer. "She'll be back," she repeated. "I believe that."

Amelia closed her eyes, letting herself fall into a desperate sleep. Her thoughts tangled up into troubling dreams, not only of her sister, who was still missing—but she also dreamed of the earl and of the way she'd responded to his devastating kiss. She wanted to wed him, even knowing that he had no intention of feeling anything for her. If she became his wife, he wanted her to look after his daughter. Nothing more.

She knew that. And yet, she wanted to believe that behind his grief lay a man worth fighting for. The opportunity was here. But she didn't know what would happen if she dared to reach for it.

❧

"I cannot tell you how grateful I am that you've brought Amelia home to us," Lord Lanfordshire began.

"I'm glad I found her before any harm was done." David joined the baron in the small library and sat across from Amelia's father. Inwardly, he was on edge, knowing what would come next.

"There is another problem," Lord Lanfordshire admitted. "Margaret has not returned." The man rubbed at his eyes, as if he hadn't slept at all. In that moment, David saw a man like himself— a father who worried about his daughter. If anything ever happened to Christine, he didn't know how he would get over the loss. To have two daughters go missing in one night . . . it was enough to take years off a man's life.

"What about Sinclair?" he asked. "Last night, Margaret went to speak to him. She wanted him to help track Amelia down."

The baron straightened in his chair, his face tight with tension. "Do you think she went with him?"

David hesitated, not knowing whether the baron was aware of

Margaret's interest in the Highlander. But there was no sense in hiding anything.

"Yes," he admitted. "Miss Andrews was terrified for Amelia last night. Though she said something about sending a footman, I strongly believe she went to Sinclair, asking him to go with her."

"Where do you think they are now?" the baron demanded.

David described the route where Margaret had planned to go. Lord Lanfordshire listened intently, and when he'd finished, David offered, "She wasn't certain if Lisford would stay on the main roads or not."

"I don't know why Margaret would take it upon herself to go after Amelia, but I'll send men to begin searching immediately." The baron stood, but before David could depart, the man added, "There is still the matter of Amelia and you. Even though I am immensely grateful for what you did, people will talk."

David didn't deny it. He knew what was coming next, and he prepared himself for the marital demands that would happen.

"I respect you very highly, Lord Castledon, and more so after what you've done this night. To have Amelia back, unharmed . . . it's more than any father could hope for." The baron squared his shoulders and faced him. "I know that I, as well as most of the London ton, would look very highly upon you as a potential husband for Amelia. Particularly after this act of heroism."

Before he could say anything, the baron continued, "She must marry. And she must do so quickly, to silence any further talk. I would—I would feel better knowing that someone like you was looking after her. Especially when I don't know about . . . Margaret." There was a pained expression on his face.

David sobered. If he ever lost Christine, he would be going out of his mind with worry. When he met Lanfordshire's gaze, he saw the mirror of himself in a dozen years.

He didn't know how to tell him that another man would be a better choice for Amelia. Her marriage shouldn't be like this. She deserved so much more than a man like him.

"Would you consider it?" the baron prompted. The man didn't press him, nor did he demand acquiescence.

David thought of Amelia's bright spirit. Undoubtedly, Christine would adore her, once they became acquainted. Amelia was brimming with life and excitement. She embraced adventure, and last night she'd kept her courage in the face of danger.

Amelia was not a young woman who would disappear meekly into the background. Not after the way she'd kissed him back. The memory of her innocent embrace was enough to pull apart common sense.

"If you choose not to wed her, I'll have no alternative but to give her to someone else," the baron said. "And that isn't what I want."

Therein lay the problem. The thought of another man claiming her was enough to draw David's frustration tighter. He wanted no man to touch her, much less to hear her broken sigh when she was well kissed.

He'd watched over her these past years, seeing the warmhearted girl transform into a woman who stole his senses. She was life and breath to his barren existence.

"I'll wed her," he heard himself say. And though the baron smiled with relief, it felt like a terrible thing to do, imprisoning her bright spirit in a world scarred by death.

Henry was relieved that Lord Castledon had agreed to the marriage with his daughter, but Beatrice seemed less enthused about the idea.

"I don't like this." His wife paced across his bedroom, her hands clenched together. "I know the earl seems like a decent fellow. But for Amelia to be forced into marriage makes me want to have that horrid viscount put on a ship bound for New Holland. With no food or water," she added. "Scotland is too good for him."

"Lord Castledon will take care of her," he responded. "And he knows Amelia has a sensitive heart."

His youngest daughter had always held a special place for Henry. When he'd gone off to war, she'd given him a pencil drawing of him and herself holding hands. The limbs had resembled sticks, but the love was there. She never knew how he'd folded that paper inside his shirt, wearing it into battle beneath his uniform.

No, he didn't want Amelia forced into marriage any more than his wife did.

"That may be," Beatrice agreed, "but he's always so serious. I always thought that Lord Castledon was a better match for Margaret."

The mention of his older daughter brought another pang of worry. Henry had sent dozens of men to search for Margaret, but the underlying fear, that they wouldn't find her, hadn't stopped lurking. He pushed the thought from his mind, trying to believe that it would all end well.

"Castledon has agreed to protect Amelia. That's all that matters now."

"But to sentence our daughter to a loveless marriage, because she was a man's victim . . . how is that right?" Beatrice paced to the opposite side of the room. "No woman should endure such a thing."

A jagged blade of ice sank through his heart as he stared at his wife. He could almost hear her unfinished words: *The way I did.*

His wife hadn't truly wanted to marry him; he'd known that. When he'd offered for her nearly thirty years ago, she'd been shy and kind to him. He wasn't much of a catch, being a younger son.

Nor was he dashing or handsome like the other gentlemen. He'd never been good at talking to women, and he'd bumbled his way through a courtship. But no one else had offered for her, and eventually Beatrice had agreed to become his.

He'd thought he'd won her heart over the years. Now Henry wondered if she'd seen herself in Amelia's position—trapped into a marriage she didn't want.

"They might learn to love one another," he offered.

She shook her head. "I don't think so, Henry. He doesn't want to love her. It wouldn't surprise me if he put her on one of his estates and left her there to fend for herself."

Again, he felt the cold chill of awareness, as if she were talking about herself. He'd been an officer, responsible for the lives of so many. War had torn him apart from Beatrice, and he'd ordered her to remain behind, to care for their daughters. After he'd inherited his older brother's title, he was expected to leave the army immediately.

Instead, he'd avoided his wife and daughters for a time, not wanting to be around them. The nightmares of death and blood had haunted him, until he'd thought he was better off dead than to return home. Eventually, he'd been forced to leave, but when he'd come back, the years of separation had driven a harsh wedge between himself and Beatrice.

Amelia's words came back to him: *Just try.*

"What do you want me to do?" he asked suddenly. "Is there anything . . . that would help?"

She stopped pacing a moment and returned to stand before him. "I don't know, Henry. I wanted a better start for her than we had."

Henry straightened. "I never thought our marriage was a bad start *or* a mistake." He didn't know what had prompted him to speak, but perhaps it was time that he voiced a truth. "I was *glad* to marry you."

She flushed suddenly. "I didn't mean that the way it sounded."

He moved in and slid an arm around her waist. "I wanted to marry you, from the first moment I saw you. Even if you didn't want me."

The shock in her eyes made him wonder if he should have said all of this, years earlier.

"I wanted you then, Beatrice," he said in a low voice. "And I still do."

✺

ONE WEEK LATER

"It feels wrong to get married like this," Amelia whispered. "Without Margaret." Her older sisters, Victoria and Juliette, were here, but Margaret was still missing. Although her father had sent men to search, there was no trace of her.

Inside, her emotions were raw. Although the earl had agreed to wed her, he hadn't seen or spoken to her since he'd acquired the special license. Then, too, she'd confined herself indoors, away from the gossip that cloaked the London ton.

Thankfully, Lord Lisford hadn't returned. Supposedly he'd gone to stay at one of his northern estates, remaining out of the public eye. At least that was a blessing, not having to face him.

"I believe Margaret is all right," Juliette said. "If she's with Cain Sinclair, he'd move Heaven and earth to keep her safe."

That much was true. The notorious Highlander didn't play by the rules, and he wouldn't hesitate to defend her against any harm.

"He's in love with her," Victoria added. "For as long as I can remember, he's been there."

Amelia knew it, but despite Margaret's feelings, her sister would never wed a commoner. She had set her sights on a titled lord since she was ten years old. Prim and proper Margaret would never consider marrying anyone whose blood wasn't as blue as the sea.

It should be Margaret marrying the earl. Not her.

Victoria held out a package wrapped in brown paper. "I brought you something. It's a wedding gift for tonight." She exchanged a glance with Juliette, and her sister's mouth curved in a smile. "Madame Benedict would be furious if she knew I held it back from the last delivery. She has dozens of orders, but without Mr. Sinclair to deliver them to the crofters, this may be the last of Aphrodite's Unmentionables."

Although her sister had meant it as a present, the package reminded Amelia of Lady Sarah and the woman's blackmail demands. In the past few weeks, she'd done nothing at all to meet the woman's demands. She worried that Lady Sarah would make good on her threat, but thus far, she had not revealed their secret. Before Amelia took the package, she asked her sisters, "Have either of you heard from Lady Sarah?"

Victoria exchanged a glance with both of them. "No. But I've told my husband about it. Jonathan sent her a note in return, with a warning."

Amelia thought back to the first encounter she'd had with Lady Sarah. Although they could easily have her arrested for blackmail, using the note as evidence, it would still bring out their involvement in Aphrodite's Unmentionables. "Before you do anything, I want to speak with her once more. There may be a way to gain her silence." She wasn't certain of how, but she intended to write to the woman and settle the matter.

"Let me know if you have any difficulties," Victoria urged. Beneath her sister's tone, she caught the warning, and Amelia promised she would.

"I think you should open Victoria's gift," Juliette said, changing the subject. "Go on. Let's see the unmentionables. Are they terribly wicked?" The gleam in her sister's eye suggested that they had to be.

I might not need them, Amelia thought to herself. Lord Castledon had already offered her the chance to wait before consummating their marriage. This marriage would protect her family's name and prevent scandal from touching them. But there would be no love in it, only friendship.

The thought bothered her deeply, for she *wanted* a wedding night.

"There's nothing to be afraid of, when you share his bed," Victoria assured her. "And if you wear this, Lord Castledon won't be able to keep his eyes—or his hands—off you."

"I'm not afraid," Amelia lied. "It's just that all of this was so unexpected."

"Do you want to marry the earl?" Juliette asked, frowning suddenly.

"Yes." She did, though she harbored no illusions about the sort of marriage they would have. "Though I don't think he particularly wants to marry me."

Juliette's face softened. "You're so wrong. I've seen the way he's watched you over the years. He likes you a great deal."

"As a companion, perhaps. Not a wife."

"Men don't know what they want," Victoria pronounced. "Once he sees you in these unmentionables, every last thought will leave his brain."

Amelia wasn't certain. Even after the earl had kissed her, he'd gone silent, as if she'd broken an unspoken rule. And yet . . . she wanted to marry this man. She wanted to see if there was any way of learning who he truly was, when he wasn't grieving for his wife.

"I'll try," she managed, taking the dark blue lacy garment from her sister. When she touched the silk chemise meant to be worn beneath her corset, she tried to imagine what he would say if he did see it. Would he want to kiss her or touch her? Or would he retreat again?

For a moment, she allowed herself to daydream of what it would be like to feel his kiss again, to experience the weight of his body against hers. Hard upon soft, muscled flesh to womanly curves . . .

"You will enjoy your wedding night," Victoria said, but Amelia hardly heard any of her sisters' attempts to cheer her up. Instead, she put on her shoes and braced herself for what lay ahead.

Chapter Eight

David stood before the clergyman, at precisely ten o'clock in the morning, in Lord Lanfordshire's parlor. He had gotten a special license from the archbishop a few days ago. They had decided to invite only family and to have the wedding at the baron's home, in order to avoid gossiping tongues.

Amelia looked terrified, her face a pale contrast against the spray of pink roses in her hair. Her gown was the blue of a summer sky, though she looked ready to flee.

David felt the same way. All last night, he'd questioned whether he was doing the right thing. He'd read his daughter's letter at least a dozen times, wondering if Amelia would make a good mother for her.

Or whether *he* would be a good husband to Amelia. He might be saving her reputation just now, but in turn, he was giving her a life shadowed by loss. Her gaze was downcast, and he caught the telltale trembling of her hands.

This was not the Amelia he knew so well. This was not the young woman who would speak her mind and order him around. She looked utterly miserable, like a daffodil crushed by a windstorm.

David wanted more for her. He wanted to bring back the amusing moments they'd shared when they were cheating at games. He wanted to see her smile, to hear her laugh. To kiss her until her lips were swollen and her eyes held the haze of unfulfilled desire. Though he tried to stifle the buried needs, he couldn't deny the effect she had upon him.

He had a mind to put a stop to this and give her an alternative. She was marrying him for all the wrong reasons. But when he glanced over at her parents, he knew that was impossible. Their daughter Margaret had been abandoned on her wedding day, and David was not about to do the same thing to Amelia. It would be utterly cruel, no matter that it would give her other choices.

Right now, she looked as if she were standing before her execution.

"Wait," he said to the clergyman, before the vows could be spoken. "I need a few minutes alone, to speak with my bride."

The shocked silence that met his declaration made him add, "I don't intend to stop the marriage—but we need to talk."

Amelia gaped at him, but her natural curiosity seemed to stun her out of the cloud of misery and fear. "We could go into the hall," she suggested.

He took her by the hand, and they walked past her family and a few servants, into the narrow corridor. It seemed that his actions had caught her completely by surprise.

David had a feeling that most of the family would be trying to eavesdrop if they stood too close to the parlor, so he took her to the farthest end, near a grandfather clock. Amelia looked uneasy about the conversation.

"You looked distraught at the idea of marrying me," he began. "If this isn't what you want—"

She took a deep breath and met his gaze. "I'm still worried about Margaret. I'm afraid she's been killed or lost or . . ."

He knew it had been a week since her sister had gone missing. Despite the efforts to find her, both Margaret and the Highlander had disappeared. The only sign of either of them had been an over-turned coach blackened from fire, and a bonnet belonging to Margaret. The ruined vehicle had been found on the road leading toward Scotland. There was no way of knowing if Margaret had been inside, but the shattered vehicle was on the road leading toward Scotland. "Could she have run away with Sinclair?" he questioned. "Or would he take her against her will?"

Amelia shook her head. "Cain's in love with Margaret and has been for years. All of us know it. He'd die before hurting her."

"Then you should have faith in that," he assured her.

When she appeared unconvinced, he added, "Would you like me to hire men to help search, even beyond what your father has done?"

"Yes," she agreed. "If I knew she was safe, I would feel better."

"I'll see to it." It was a promise that he supposed was better than any wedding present.

Amelia reached for his hand and squeezed it. "Thank you." He started to walk back with her, but she remained in place. "I never thought I'd get married without all of my sisters here. It seems wrong."

"Would you rather wait until we've found Margaret?" Though it wasn't the best solution, he would delay the wedding if that was what she wanted.

"No. We may as well see it done."

She made it sound as if marriage to him was an awful prospect. "Do you still want to marry me?" He would let her out of the betrothal if she was having doubts.

"Yes," she whispered. "But I wish you wanted to marry me. It's disappointing to feel as if I've trapped you into marriage."

"You haven't trapped me into anything," he said, though it might seem so to her. Amelia wasn't the wife he would have chosen at first, but he wasn't about to let her become Lisford's victim of scandal. If he could protect her with his name, so be it.

A part of him warmed to the idea of spending each day with her. *Because you want her*, his body reminded him. The first taste of her kiss wasn't enough to satiate the craving she'd ignited. And this marriage would bring him directly into the path of temptation.

Amelia's face grew wistful. "I'll admit that this isn't the wedding I was dreaming of, as a little girl."

He leaned up against the wall, watching her. "What *did* you dream of?" In the small space, she glanced behind her, as if worried about her family waiting. "Don't worry about them."

Amelia leaned back against the wall, staring at him. "I dreamed it would be a fairy tale—that I would marry a dashingly handsome man who adored me."

"Am I not dashingly handsome?" he queried.

And there was her smile. The fear dissipated, and the inner light returned to her eyes. "In your own way," she admitted. "For a wall-hedge."

He tipped her chin up and regarded her. "I know I'm not the husband you wanted. But we can be friends."

Amelia reached out to touch his cravat, and he flinched at the contact. Though she did nothing more than rest her hands upon his heart, the simple touch burned through him. "We can," she agreed.

Her green eyes fixed upon him, and he was caught beneath her spell. He was conscious of her slender form and the gentle blush on her cheeks. Her hair was tightly bound up, and he wondered what it would be like to see it down around her shoulders.

"Would you kiss me again?" she murmured. "I want to know if I imagined what happened between us in the coach."

He didn't move, for he was captivated by her full lips. He wanted to taste them again, just as she wanted to kiss him. But if he dared to give rein to those feelings, he sensed that he would lose control of himself.

She stood on tiptoe, rising to meet him. David caught her and threaded his hands through her hair. Before she could touch her mouth to his, he pressed a brief kiss upon her lips. The moment he did, he felt her tension. She'd wanted the kiss of a husband, and he'd given the kiss of a friend.

"You're afraid," she accused, and he said nothing to deny it. It wasn't fear that held him back. It was the sense that if he claimed her with a husband's right, he couldn't turn back. Something about Amelia Andrews tempted him beyond measure.

"Try again," she urged.

And this time, he kissed her deeply, forcing her mouth to open to him. He framed her face with his hands, claiming her lips. He tasted her uncertainty and a hint of longing. Her arms twined around his neck, drawing him closer while she kissed him back. It wasn't the kiss of a reluctant bride; instead, her mouth opened, inviting more. He could give her that.

Drawing her up against the wall, he nipped at her upper lip and felt the answering shudder of yearning. She answered his kiss with her own unbridled passion. And God help him, he was nearing the edge of control.

"I can't think when you kiss me," she whispered against his mouth.

Neither can I. He let his hands slide down her shoulders to her waist. "Was that better?" She nodded with a shaky smile, and he took her hand. There was a trace of unrest in her demeanor, but they walked together back to the parlor.

Amelia paused a moment, and before they stepped through the doorway, she turned to him.

In a low voice, she threw down a gauntlet of her own. "If you marry me now, Lord Castledon, I want to be treated like a wife. Not a companion."

It was clear that she had no intention of fading into the background as a mother to Christine. She wanted to be his in every way, not only in name. He reached out to touch her cheek. "Perhaps."

It wasn't the answer she wanted, but he could make no promises. He hardly trusted himself around Amelia. Her kiss pushed him past the edge of reason, beckoning him toward a new addiction. If he did share a physical marriage with her, he suspected it would only awaken a hunger that could never be sated.

The wedding was over so quickly, Amelia could scarcely remember the troth she'd pledged. The earl had touched his mouth to hers, and once she'd become his wife, she couldn't quite grasp the reality. She was now the Countess of Castledon, stepmother to a young girl she'd never met.

They enjoyed cakes and light refreshments after the wedding, but owing to Margaret's absence, it wasn't much of a celebration. "This seems so strange," Amelia confessed. "Almost as if it happened to someone else."

The earl nodded, appearing more than a little distracted. She wondered if there was anything she could say to reassure him. Or better, she could ask about her new stepdaughter.

"When will I meet Christine?" she asked.

At the mention of his daughter, Lord Castledon relaxed a little.

"I could send you on to Castledon in the morning," he offered. "Parliament will be out of session soon enough."

The idea of arriving at his house alone was not a welcome one. "I'd rather wait," she admitted. It would be awkward enough to become part of an unfamiliar household. Without the earl there to introduce her, she'd feel even more out of place.

"We won't have to stay in London very long," he said. "I hope you can find a way to amuse yourself."

She nodded, but inwardly, her thoughts were still with Margaret. "Will you keep your promise to send men after my sister?"

"I said I would." He reached for her hand and squeezed it. "I know how close you are."

A sudden thought occurred to Amelia, that she knew very little about the earl. She had no idea about the rest of his family. "What of you?" she asked. "Do you have any brothers or sisters?"

He shook his head. "My sister died when she was ten, of scarlet fever."

"And your parents?"

He lifted his shoulders in a shrug. "I'm the only one left, I'm afraid. They both died shortly after Katherine did. First my father, then my mother."

She'd never realized that he was all but an orphan. "That's terrible. No wonder you were so glum all those years."

"I'd rather not speak of it, if you don't mind."

"No, I don't suppose it's a very pleasant wedding conversation," she agreed. But it made her realize how very difficult those years must have been. It was a wonder he'd attended any society events at all, and it certainly explained why he'd worn black all the time.

But when she peered closer at his coat, she saw that his waistcoat was dark green. Leaning forward, she touched the brocade, and for some reason, it made her smile. "You're not wearing black anymore."

"Not today."

But it made her imagine that perhaps he would come to accept her as his wife. She took his arm, and a flutter of happiness settled within her heart. In spite of Margaret's absence, there were so many reasons to be thankful. She was now married to a handsome man who truly *was* a hero, though he'd hidden his true nature for so many years. He was wonderful at kissing, and she found herself dreaming of what it would be like if he consummated their marriage tonight. He hadn't said no, and it gave her a reason to hope. This was a new beginning for both of them, and nothing would diminish it.

They said their farewells to her parents and sisters, and the earl escorted her back to his carriage. Amelia let him help her inside, and they began the short drive to his town house.

For a time, he appeared to be bothered by something. She wanted to ask him what it was, but decided he would tell her when he was ready. Within minutes, they were arriving at his house. "When we go inside, I'll introduce you to our staff. They should provide you with everything you need."

Then the earl met her gaze and revealed the reason for his discomfort. "I would ask that you . . . not change the way the rooms are decorated. Katherine made them as they are, and it would bother Christine greatly to see them altered when she comes to visit again."

"I understand," Amelia said softly, but she strongly suspected that this was about his own desire for the rooms not to be altered, not his daughter's. She prayed they weren't decorated in black or a garish gold that would give her nightmares.

The footman opened the door, and the earl disembarked first, helping Amelia down. At first glance, his home was like any other.

The town house had a white façade with large windows, and decorative balustrades rested beneath each one. Two tall Corinthian columns framed a stairway leading up to the front door.

A flutter of nerves took residence in her stomach, but she put on a brave face and tried to behave older than twenty. *Behave as if you know what you're doing,* she told herself. *Be stronger than you feel.*

When the earl led her inside, he introduced her to many of the servants. The only name she remembered was Gus Haverford, the butler, who smiled warmly and welcomed her to the household. She liked him immediately, but the other names blurred together until she could hardly conjure up any of them.

"I'll leave you to speak with the housekeeper," the earl said.

She probably had met the housekeeper, but honestly, Amelia didn't remember the woman at all. The idea of being abandoned so suddenly was intimidating, to say the least.

"I'd rather you gave me a tour of the house," she suggested. At least, then, she could get her bearings and gather her courage.

He offered her his arm, and when they walked beyond the servants, she whispered, "I know there will be many expectations of me, as your countess. I'll do everything I can to fit in with your life here. But for now, could we just be Amelia and David?"

David's hand tightened over hers. "We *are* friends," he agreed. "That won't change."

Amelia mustered a smile. Was it possible to change his mind and move beyond friendship? Over the past few days, she'd chipped away at the icy emotional armor he wore like a shield. She'd tempted him into kissing her and had found a very different man beneath it all. Passionate and strong, he knew just how to take apart her defenses.

She wanted so much more than he was offering. And tonight was her strongest chance at winning the first battle.

"We could have our supper upstairs," she suggested. Away from prying eyes and anyone who might interrupt.

He guided her toward a small sitting room, and as soon as she entered the space, Amelia grew overwhelmed. Nearly every surface of the room contained curios and trinkets. Some were made of porcelain, while others were miniature marble statues in the Neo-classical style. Upon the opposite wall, she spied a portrait of a dark-haired woman. She could only guess that it must have been Katherine. At her questioning look, the earl nodded.

"She enjoyed her . . . collection," he admitted.

"I can see that." Amelia was now somewhat worried about what her bedchamber would look like. She envisioned more cluttered tabletops and possibly a dressing table that would have a hundred bottles of scent upon it. "If you don't mind, I should like to see my room."

And please let it not have been hers, she thought.

"Of course." He led her up two more flights of stairs until they reached a narrow door near the servants' quarters. "I thought you would be comfortable in here."

A sinking sensation took hold in Amelia's stomach. The room was far away from the other bedrooms, and when he opened it, she saw that it was hardly more than a single bed and a dressing table. Had it belonged to one of the maids?

No. He couldn't mean this, could he? Surely he was mistaken. "I don't think it's at all appropriate for me to stay here," she said quietly.

He shrugged. "The room is small, but it's clean. There's a nice view of London from the window."

Amelia took a breath and closed the door behind him. Did he not see what was wrong with this? Or had he done it deliberately, to keep her at arm's length?

"The room was not being used, so I thought there was no harm in it." He cleared his throat, adding, "I didn't think you would want Katherine's room. This house is small, and there aren't many bedrooms."

Perhaps he thought that by putting her here, she would be far away from him, out of temptation's way. Surely he had another bedroom for guests. And yet, he seemed determined to keep her at a distance. She had to put a stop to it right now.

"No," she said quietly. "I cannot stay in this bedroom. It makes me feel as if I am a servant, isolated from the family." She raised her eyes to his. "Surely there is another room closer to yours."

He stilled, as if he couldn't believe she'd dared to challenge him. But honestly, *why* would he believe she would want to stay here, of all places? She was now the lady of the household, and yet he was treating her like a houseguest instead of a wife.

Amelia moved closer and rested her hands upon his shoulders. "Or, if you have no other rooms, I could always share yours. My parents shared a bedroom when I was growing up."

He could have been a statue, with no expression at all. "It may be small, but it will do, for now."

No, it wouldn't. And if he wouldn't find her something more appropriate, Amelia intended to take the necessary steps to find a room of her own.

"I should . . . see to a few things," the earl remarked. "You can join me in the dining room tonight for supper."

In other words, he was seeking a quick escape. And if she did nothing or said nothing, he would continue to push her away.

"Wait a moment," she whispered. She reached out and took both of his hands in hers. From the moment her gloved palms touched his, she sensed the hesitancy in him. Lord Castledon's blue eyes were guarded, his posture tense. Before he could protest, Amelia embraced him, resting her cheek against his heart. Though he appeared uncertain about what to do, soon enough, his arms came around her shoulders, which was a good sign.

"Don't let's quarrel so soon," she said softly. "We are now husband and wife, and I want us to make a good marriage, in spite of our beginning."

If her sisters and mother had taught her anything, it was that sweet words always got a woman what she wanted. Much more than arguing.

"I want to thank you for what you did. You didn't have to wed me to save my family's good name." And that really was the truth. He'd behaved with honor, helping her out of an impossible situation.

There was a slight relaxation in his grip, and Lord Castledon admitted, "I didn't want you to be a victim of Lord Lisford's exploits, like your sister."

The mention of Margaret dimmed her spirits once more, but she pushed back the fear. "Do you think Lisford will ever return to London?"

He drew back slightly. "I don't really care. Does it matter?"

"No, I don't suppose it does." It was odd to realize that she no longer felt anything for the man, save pity. Once, she'd placed all of her dreams upon the viscount. Thankfully, she'd awakened from what could have turned out to be a nightmare.

He released her and stepped back. "I'll see you this evening."

"Lord Castledon," she interrupted, before he could leave.

"When we're alone, you may call me David," he corrected. "Or Hartford."

She liked the name David, and it suited him. "David, then." Amelia took a breath to fortify her courage. "I won't ever try to take Katherine's place. But neither do I want you to treat me like a stranger or a servant. We're married now, and . . . that should mean something more."

He didn't realize what he was doing, Amelia thought to herself. The man was utterly lost with a second wife. And whatever decisions she made in the next few days would shape her life with him.

He said nothing to that but took her hand and squeezed it. "I will see you later tonight."

Though Amelia was inwardly terrified of her wedding night, neither did she want to spend it in the servants' quarters. Somehow, she had to push past his expectations and make a place for herself.

David avoided Amelia for the rest of the afternoon. He knew she'd spent time talking with the servants and making arrangements for her own lady's maid. Her presence was quiet, but he'd known she was there. In fact, it was impossible to do any work at all.

An ordinary bridegroom would have spent the day with his bride, enjoying her presence. But Amelia set him on edge, reawakening a dormant desire. He hungered for her physically, and though he told himself that time and distance would solve the problem, his body had little interest in listening to his brain.

When he arrived at the dinner table, Haverford was waiting. "My lord, Lady Castledon asked that your supper be served upstairs in your bedchamber." The older man's face held a trace of color, but he continued, "She wanted to surprise you."

Did she? David wasn't certain what to think of that, but his suspicions sharpened. He didn't let the butler know of his discomfort, but he merely nodded and walked up the stairs.

He had no idea what Amelia was planning, but he suspected that it involved seduction. He gripped the banister, gathering his control. He wasn't certain if he would consummate the marriage tonight. It wasn't wise, for he hardly trusted himself right now.

When he reached the door of his room, he opened it and found his wife waiting on the floor. She had spread a blanket there and had drawn the drapes to darken the room. Candles were lit all around, casting an amber glow over the furnishings.

Although she was fully dressed, he saw that she was barefoot. The blue gown set off her skin tone, and his eyes were drawn to the pearl necklace around her throat. He'd left the pearls for her as a wedding gift and was glad she'd found them.

"I thought we could have an indoor picnic," she said. "Victoria told me about one she had with the duke, and it sounded terribly romantic."

The soft anticipation on her face brought up his defenses. He had to put a stop to these ideas of romance before he broke her heart. "Amelia, you shouldn't—"

"No." She held up her hand. "This is our wedding day and our wedding night. At least let me fulfill one dream, to have a romantic evening with my new husband."

David didn't know what to say to that. When she pointed to a place across from her, he noticed a plate and silverware.

"Well, you have to eat, don't you?" She sat down, tucking her bare feet beneath her skirts. "It might as well be with me." When she uncovered a silver platter, he saw a spread of cheeses, bread, and thinly sliced meats.

He felt like the fly being invited to dinner by the spider. Though Amelia was untouched by any man, she was also far too naïve about his control. Didn't she realize how long it had been since he'd lain with a woman? Or did she not know how badly he wanted her?

With reluctance, he sat down, and Amelia picked up his plate. She began choosing food for him, and when she bent forward, her gown gaped slightly, revealing a dark blue chemise. The glimpse of lace made him imagine her bare skin covered only by the sheer material.

A jolt of desire went straight to his groin. But when he stared at her, she behaved as if nothing were amiss. When she handed him the plate, he caught a full view of generous curves and a darker nipple peeking through the swath of silk and lace.

"Jesus Christ," he muttered beneath his breath. She was going to be the death of him.

Amelia glanced at him sharply. "What was that?"

He hadn't meant to voice that aloud. Thinking fast, he blurted out, "I said some cheese would be nice."

Amelia didn't look entirely as if she believed him, but she gave him a selection of white cheese. "Which would you prefer? Hard or soft?"

God above.

He nearly choked at her words and said, "Either is fine."

Wine. He needed a great deal of wine to make it through this meal.

"I prefer hard, myself," she said cheerfully, and it was all he could do not to spew the wine across the tablecloth. But again, there was no sly look of innuendo—only the bright eagerness of a newly married bride.

When she handed him the plate, the gown slid down one shoulder, baring her skin. What on earth was happening to her clothing? The soft curve of her shoulder made him want to taste that skin, to watch gooseflesh break over her bare flesh.

"Your sleeve is down," he pointed out, draining his cup.

"I know." Amelia took it from him and refilled the wine. "I asked my maid to loosen my gown and corset so I wouldn't need her help any more tonight." Though she spoke the words calmly, he didn't believe for a moment that it was a coincidence.

His new wife had planned this, and it seemed that she was making every effort to seduce him. The wicked side to him was more than willing, and his groin was aching at the sight of her.

David tried to distract himself with food, but he was acutely conscious of her bare shoulders and the rope of pearls nestled against the hollow of her throat. He imagined taking down the pearls, rolling them across her nipples, sliding the beads over her skin.

Amelia reached for her own glass of wine, and again, the gown slipped farther down, revealing the top of the chemise. It was every bit as daring as he'd seen earlier—some frothy bit of lace and silk that showed far too much. When he gave his full attention to his food, he inwardly wondered what Katherine would have thought of this.

Don't spend the rest of your life grieving over me, she'd made him swear. And he hadn't expected to. But neither was he ready for this, much as his body insisted upon it.

David drained his wine and poured himself a third cup. He was well on his way to becoming drunk at this pace, and frankly, he didn't care. Amelia was talking about the servants, something about maids and God only knew what.

He'd finished eating, and she pushed her plate aside. "You're not interested in any of this, are you?"

He was about to disagree, but she stood up and turned to walk toward the closed drapes. When her back was to him, he saw the unfastened buttons and the corset that hung open. She was silent for so long, he didn't know what to think.

He stood up from the floor, and each step brought him closer to her. Her hands rested on the back of a chair, and from this distance, he could see the naked skin peeking through the lacy chemise.

She was a nervous bride, completely unfamiliar with any of this.

"I'm sorry," she whispered, still not looking at him. "I thought perhaps you could show me what it's like to be a wife, even if there was never any love between us."

He knew what she wanted and stopped just behind her. If he stretched out his hands, he would be touching her.

"When you kissed me, I felt—" Her words broke off when he moved his hands to the back of her gown. Beneath his palms, her skin was cool.

He eased back the sleeves and revealed more of her chemise and corset. The garment was daring enough for a wedding night, designed to tease a man's interest. Her corset was bound tightly beneath her breasts, and when he lowered the dress a little more, he saw that her breasts were exposed, with only a small bit of lace to cover them.

They were larger than he'd imagined, with darker peach nipples beneath the blue lace. They were puckered from the cool air, and his erection grew tight at the sight of her. All he had to do was strip away the gown and corset, and her body would be his. He could lay her down upon his bed and claim the sweet flesh that tempted him. He could feel her velvet sheath around him, clenching him until . . .

David silenced the visions by drawing her mouth to his, kissing her hard. She ignited his lust, making him want so much more. Her mouth tasted of wine and fervor.

He pulled the pins from her hair, freeing the dark blond masses around her shoulders. Her gown slid down to the floor, and he gripped her hair, sliding his tongue into her mouth. It was a kiss meant to punish her, to remind her that *he* was in command of this night. She could wear whatever seductive clothing she wanted, but he would decide when to consummate the marriage.

But the moment her own tongue touched his, it became a new battle. Amelia was eager, seeking his touch. She pulled at his coat, and he let her take it off.

"Slow down," he warned, sitting down in the wingback chair and pulling her onto his lap.

"Why? I like kissing you." She tugged at his shirt, and when it was free from his trousers, her hands moved beneath the shirt to touch his bare skin.

"Because if you don't, your first time with me will be in this chair."

Her palms went still against his ribs, as if suddenly aware of what was happening. "Oh."

He finished unlacing her corset and lifted it away. Amelia flushed when he left the sheer chemise where it was. He drank in the sight of her large breasts and her slender waist. "It's better when you slow down, Amelia. When you savor what's before you." To underscore his words, he drew his knuckles over her erect nipples. She bit her lip, her eyes widening as understanding broke over her.

David continued to kiss her, coaxing her arousal by caressing her nipples through the lace. With her seated upon his lap, she was resting against his hard shaft, only making him more conscious of what he wanted.

"I didn't know," she breathed, and he slipped a finger inside her mouth. Then he used the wet tip to circle her nipple, and her fingers dug into his shoulders.

God above, he wanted this. He wanted her more than anything he'd wanted in the last six years of celibacy. She arched as he teased the nipples with his damp fingertips, and her bottom moved against his erection.

He could imagine her riding him, her thighs on either side as he pumped inside her. Already she'd begun to shudder against him, her breathing growing unsteady. He seized her hips, forcing her to part her legs, kneeling on either side of him in the chair. She was trembling against his rigid flesh, and despite being clothed, he was so close to release, he gritted his teeth.

"Look at me, Amelia," he said, and his voice sounded husky and foreign, completely unlike himself. Her green eyes were glazed over, her lips swollen from his kiss.

She was as aroused as he was, and he couldn't stop himself from leaning forward, closing his mouth over her lace-covered nipples. She jolted from the contact, her fingers moving into his hair.

"That feels so good," she moaned, and he pulled her flush against his hips as he suckled the tips. It wouldn't take much to send her over the edge, and at this moment, that was what he wanted. To give her the release she needed, to make her feel so good she would forget about all else.

He continued to lave at her breasts, while he slipped one hand between her legs. His knuckles brushed against the dark blue silk, and when he stroked her inner thigh, he felt her shiver again. He cupped her intimately, his hands against her damp opening. She was more than ready to accept him inside her.

When he entered her with one finger, she cried out, her breath panting fast. *More*, he thought. He wanted so much more from her. He entered and withdrew with his finger, before adding another. She was shaking hard, begging him, "David, I can't bear it. It's too much."

But if he stopped now, she would feel the fiery ache of being unsatisfied. It was cruel to leave her in this state, and he took her mouth again, murmuring, "Trust me."

He stroked and penetrated with his hand, watching the way she leaned in to him, her body seeking the pleasure he gave.

But she shocked him when she reached for his trousers, stroking his erection through the fabric. The sensation of her fist closing over him was enough to shatter his control. He shoved her hand aside and lowered the chemise to bare her breasts fully, nibbling at one while his hand tormented the other.

She gripped the sides of the chair, and David stroked her hooded flesh until her body began to arch hard, her breathing labored. Abruptly, she let out a keening moan as her own madness swept over her, consuming her with the same forbidden pleasure he'd taken.

"Take me to your bed," Amelia pleaded. "Show me the rest."

Nothing could make him deny her now. He lifted her up and brought her to the mattress, parting her legs. She helped him to undress, and a moment later, guided him to her wet entrance.

His body flared with lust as he slid inside her welcoming sheath, past the barrier of her innocence. She faltered a moment but didn't deny him the union of their flesh. For a moment, he remained inside her, letting her adjust to his size. She was skittish beneath him, and though she tried to veil her fear, it was there.

David withdrew slightly, attempting a slow penetration to make it good for her again. But she tensed, squeezing him tightly as he invaded and withdrew. It made him even harder, the pleasure rippling through him until he gripped the mattress to regain control.

But his wife hadn't let go of her fear.

"Look at me, Amelia," he commanded. "Do you want me to continue?"

She nodded, but the strain was evident on her face.

"Then stop fighting against me and relax." To emphasize his words, he ceased his thrusts and began kissing her again. The distraction was exactly what she needed. She invited him closer, her tongue twining with his. And he could feel it when her inner walls softened, not clenching him quite so hard. Gently, he nudged his hips against hers and was rewarded with a startled sigh.

He kissed a path down her throat to her breasts. He took a swollen nipple into his mouth, and she shuddered, her body responding as he withdrew by a fraction of an inch and her silken depths accepted him once more.

Joining with her like this was better than he'd imagined it would be. Her breathing was hitched, and as he renewed his penetration, she began meeting his thrusts. He gripped her hips with both hands, increasing the pace as he suckled at her breast.

Her fingers gripped his hair, and when she moaned again, he lost his control and emptied his seed within her.

Damn it all.

She went pliant against him, her face tucked against his neck. He was frustrated that he hadn't lasted as long as he'd wanted to. Though he'd brought her to a climax earlier, he'd wanted her to find a second release while he was inside her.

He reached down to touch her, while he remained embedded within her. She shied away the moment he began to stroke. Against his shaft, he felt her body tighten.

"David?" she whispered.

He rested his weight on his arms and met her gaze. With their bodies still joined, he saw the uncertain look in her eyes.

"I've not finished yet," he said. He continued caressing her, and he returned his mouth to her other breast. She appeared confused, but she didn't deny him. Then abruptly, she began to tremble.

"I'm sorry, I don't know what I—"

Her words broke off when he found the swollen nub, arousing her further. He kept the pressure light, never ceasing the rhythm, until she cried out, her body shattering beneath his touch. Her womb clenched his shaft with aftershocks, and the languid expression on her face revealed her pleasure.

Seeing her fulfillment made him want to keep her here, learning her body's needs and watching her find release, over and over.

Like a siren, he would fall beneath her spell, until he lost all sense of reason. He couldn't keep her here, or he would succumb to physical needs. And it wasn't fair to use her like that.

Slowly, he extricated himself and helped her to sit up. "You should return to your room now and sleep. It's been a long day."

Amelia drew her knees up, suddenly shy. "Can't I sleep here with you?"

He shook his head and brought her the fallen clothing from the floor. "You'll be more comfortable alone."

"I won't," she said softly, "though I know why you're sending me away." She tried to dress herself as best she could, but her hands were trembling.

Amelia stared at him for a long moment. He refused to apologize, for this was what she'd wanted. He'd consummated their marriage, hadn't he?

"Nothing has changed," he assured her. "We're still friends."

But Amelia shook her head. "No, David. Everything has changed."

Chapter Nine

Aﬁer a few days of marriage, the day arrived when Amelia had invited Lady Sarah to tea. Although her sister Victoria had offered to have her husband, the Duke of Worthingstone, handle the matter, Amelia felt responsible for the situation. Today, she intended to put the matter to rest, once and for all. It was time to confront the woman about her blackmail note.

When Lady Sarah entered the sitting room, the woman looked as if she hadn't slept in days. Her hair was pulled back in a knot, and a strand hung limply against her face. Her gown was the faded color of smoke, and in spite of herself, Amelia pitied the woman.

Even so, she had to put an end to this.

"The Duke of Worthingstone has enough evidence against you to have you arrested for blackmail," she informed Lady Sarah. "If you continue these demands, it will end badly for you."

The young woman had gone deathly white, but she met Amelia's gaze squarely. "I need help, Lady Castledon. I don't truly wish to harm your family, but I will do what I must. I cannot be anywhere near my cousin." She gripped her arms and stared down at her lap.

"If I arrange to help you disappear, will you let this matter go?" Amelia asked. "I cannot arrange a house and servants, but I can give you a small pension. It would only be enough for you to travel far away and to begin a new life. If you demand anything further, His Grace will have you brought up on charges." She leaned forward, adding, "I convinced them to wait until after I'd spoken with you."

Lady Sarah let out a slow breath. "This isn't the sort of woman I am, you know. I never thought that my life would end up like this." Her brown eyes filled up with unshed tears. "Brandon always said that no man would ever want me as a wife. I suppose he was right."

A pang caught Amelia in her stomach, but she could give the woman no reassurance.

"Help me to leave, and you'll never see me again," Lady Sarah promised.

Amelia passed over the small parcel containing banknotes and a few inexpensive jewels the woman could sell. Although it was a grave risk, giving in to Lady Sarah's demands, she wanted to believe that the woman was telling the truth. "All of this ends, right now. You cannot ask for anything more. If you break this promise, not only will you be arrested for blackmail, but I shall tell them that you stole those jewels from me."

"I won't," Lady Sarah promised, accepting the parcel. Her lips trembled, and she whispered, "Thank you, Lady Castledon."

Brandon Carlisle, the Earl of Strathland, kept his eyes closed, trying to recognize the woman's voice. She was speaking to him, pleading for something. He knew the woman somehow. Knew her name, even. She was familiar, and her words reached down past the forgotten years.

"I know you can't understand my words," she said quietly, "but I came to say good-bye. I'll be leaving England, and I won't return."

Sarah. That was it—his sister, Sarah.

"Our cousin Lewis has claimed Strathland and our other estates," she said. "The courts are going to rule in his favor, since you've been here for so long."

Her words were hardly more than gibberish, but Brandon grasped one word: *claimed*.

Someone had taken what belonged to him. A shattering pain throbbed inside his skull, the memories crashing and tumbling in a mass of broken visions. He didn't know what was real and what was false anymore.

His prison was formed of gray walls, with bars upon the single window. It couldn't have been very long that he'd been here. He didn't remember much except a breakfast that was hardly fit for rats.

Last night, he'd begged them to let him leave. Instead, they'd strapped him down, preventing him from moving or calling out to anyone. Even the taste of water was bitterly laced with laudanum to keep him motionless and silent.

"How long?" His voice was barely audible, and his throat ached with the effort of making sound. *How long have I been trapped here?*

His sister's mouth opened in shock. "Y-you understood what I said?"

He gave a nod, though it wasn't true. She was speaking too fast, the words spilling on top of one another. But in her voice, he caught the fear. From her faded gown and how thin she was, he guessed that Sarah had endured poverty in the past few weeks.

The headache was returning, the immense pressure building inside his skull. But he had to hold fast to sanity, before everything slipped away.

"How long?" he repeated again.

"Four years," she answered. "It's been four years since you've spoken."

No. That wasn't possible. "I've only been here a few days, Sarah. Don't be ridiculous."

But she was shaking her head. "No. No, it's been a very long time. I thought you'd never get well." Tears were streaming down her face. "Thank God. I'm so glad."

Each word was an excruciating effort, but he managed to form the right sentence. "I need to leave this place."

"Yes, yes, of course you do." She wiped at her cheeks with a handkerchief, beaming at him. "I'll start making the arrangements." Touching a hand to her heart, she added, "They will give you a series of tests, Brandon. You must pass them. Promise me that you'll think carefully before you answer."

He lowered his head, trying to keep his thoughts centered. "Let me rest first. I need to sleep."

Sarah remained silent, and he forced himself to look at her. She appeared as if she wanted to argue with him. "Are you going to be all right?"

He inclined his head once. The cloud of pain and confusion threatened to lower over him, but he gritted out one last promise. "I won't let this go, Sarah. What was done to me."

"Hush," she soothed, reaching for his hand. "It's been years now. I'll see to it that you return home to Strathland. The servants will look after you when I'm gone."

Gone? He frowned, uncertain where she believed she was going. "Where?" he managed.

A faint flush colored her cheeks. "I haven't decided yet. But it will be far away from Lewis Barnabas—that I can tell you. Perhaps the colonies, if I can arrange passage upon a ship."

Her words were meaningless to him, and he dismissed them as not having any importance. He stared down at his chained hands, and the anger within him surged. He'd been trapped in this place because of Lord and Lady Lanfordshire and their four daughters. Because of Juliette and that Highland rebel, Paul Fraser.

Then there was Cain Sinclair, the Highlander who had left him for dead in the middle of nowhere. Brandon's mouth grew dry at the memory of the intense hunger and thirst.

The madness lingered, threatening to drag him down. He'd lost sight of reason and had entered a living death during these past few years.

No longer.

"I will have my own vengeance," he swore. "Even if I have to slit their throats while they sleep."

She paled at that. "No, you can't. Truly, Brandon, if you tell anyone about this, they'll never let you out."

His headache was vicious now, and he closed his eyes against the pain. "I want them dead. All of them." Not only the women who had refused to wed him, but also Paul Fraser and Cain Sinclair, who had left him for dead. Because of them, he'd been locked away in this asylum.

"Brandon, promise me you won't do anything rash," Sarah urged, but in her voice, he heard the fear.

He smiled at that. For she ought to be afraid.

TWO WEEKS LATER

"How are you?" Victoria asked. "Have you settled in to your married life?" Her sister sent a warm smile, but Amelia found it difficult to return it. She was trying hard not to think of Margaret and Mr. Sinclair, who were still missing.

"I'm well enough," she managed to say with false brightness. The truth was, the earl had buried himself in work. He'd hardly spoken to her in the past few weeks, and it seemed that he was doing everything in his power to avoid her. Not once had he shared her bed since their wedding night.

It made little sense. He had given her a precious gift, and the feeling of being joined together was wonderful. His touch had awakened a part of her that she'd never known existed. *Now* she understood the secret smiles Juliette and Victoria had shared when they had spoken about their husbands.

But she didn't know if David had enjoyed their night. Although he had found his own release, he'd asked her to leave. She'd felt so vulnerable, wondering if she'd done something to displease him. And since that night, he'd all but abandoned her.

He certainly wasn't aware that she'd moved her belongings into a small bedroom, two doors down from his. Amelia wasn't foolish enough to take his wife's former bedchamber—that would have been too much. But neither did she want him placing her in the servants' quarters. She knew that he was attempting to distance himself from her, but she would no longer retreat.

Now she was left to wonder what she should do next. In the morning, they were leaving for Castledon, his estate near Yorkshire, to meet his daughter. The very thought made Amelia's courage falter. She knew nothing about children and was uncertain of this role. While she was capable of training the girl in proper etiquette, everything about her marriage had turned out wrong, thus far. It was impossible to win the heart of a man who was hardly there during the day.

"What have you decided to do about Aphrodite's Unmentionables, now that the deliveries have stopped?" Amelia asked.

Victoria shook her head, as if she didn't know the answer. "I thought we would simply discontinue the undergarments. Now, the demand is so great, Madame Benedict has put a terribly high price upon them." She eyed Amelia, adding, "I am torn about what to do. If we stop making the garments, the MacKinloch crofters will lose their income. But there is too much risk of discovery."

Amelia knew that. And yet, she didn't want to stop their business. "Lady Sarah is gone, so we needn't worry about her any longer." In the past few weeks, there had been no sign of the young woman.

"I hope that is true, though I don't think you should have given her anything," Victoria said.

"I believed her when she said she didn't want to harm our family. She was simply desperate."

"If we discontinue our business," Victoria suggested, "and she breaks her word, at least we can deny the accusations."

Although her sister was right, Amelia didn't want to end Aphrodite's Unmentionables. "Perhaps we could hire one of the MacKinlochs to make the deliveries. Or what about Mother?" she suggested. "Could she take command of the business?"

Victoria shook her head. "Our father would forbid it. He's already angry with her for taking part in it." Her sister sighed and finally voiced her own concerns, "Both of them are also still trying to find Margaret. While I want to hope that she's still alive—" She took a breath to steady herself, blinking back tears.

"I know," Amelia echoed. "It's been too long. They should have been found by now."

"It doesn't make sense." Victoria stood and began pacing. "Mr. Sinclair knows the countryside well. I can't imagine him ever being lost."

A strange thought occurred to Amelia, one she'd not considered before. "What if they aren't lost? What if they ran away together?"

Victoria gaped at her. "But he's a penniless Highlander."

"A Highlander who adores her. Margaret likes him, too, though she'd never admit it." Lowering her voice, Amelia added, "It wouldn't surprise me if our sister"—she paused a moment, choosing her words carefully—"if Margaret had an affair with him."

"She would die first." Victoria shook her head. "No, she would not stay with him willingly."

Even so, Amelia wasn't certain. "It doesn't make sense that they weren't found. Their coach was in an accident, but neither of them was there." If her sister had run away with the Highlander, then that was the only explanation she could think of.

"They were searching for *you*," Victoria reminded her. "Something must have gone terribly wrong."

Amelia nodded, but inwardly, her unrest heightened. She didn't want to imagine Margaret dead, but after this long, the burden of worry wouldn't lift.

"Let's not speak of it any more," her sister continued. "We will keep hoping for the best until we learn what's happened." To change the subject, she asked, "Tell me, does the earl make you happy? Are you glad you married him?"

Amelia didn't know how to answer that. She had been married for over two weeks, and although her husband had shared her bed once, it was like being wedded to a stranger. He had claimed they would remain friends, but it didn't seem he wanted to be with her at all.

She had purchased a dozen romantic novels, hoping to find a solution. Yet in all of the stories, the women pined for their lovers and did nothing. Or they died from heartbreak. Neither sounded like a particularly good way to win a husband's affections, in Amelia's opinion.

During their journey north, she intended to spend a great deal of time with Lord Castledon—no, David. It was the perfect opportunity to remind her husband that he wasn't married to a pasteboard wife.

"He's been kind to me. But he's still grieving for his first wife," she admitted.

Victoria sobered. "There may be too many memories right now. In time, he may grow to love you."

"Perhaps." Amelia reached toward several sketches of new undergarments that Victoria had drawn. Though she commented on each of them, her mind was already thinking about her new household and the child she was supposed to mother. She knew nothing whatsoever about being a parent, but her sister had many years of experience.

"Toria," she interrupted. "How am I supposed to be a stepmother to an eleven-year-old girl?" The very idea intimidated her. She was only nine years older than Christine, and the idea of instructing the girl on how to make her debut seemed utterly foreign. Margaret would have known how to manage it.

Her sister thought about it a moment, pushing the drawings aside. "Does she remember her mother?"

"I don't know. I believe she was five years old when the woman died."

"Her father will be very important to her," Victoria said. "If it were me, I'd be careful not to take Lord Castledon away from her. She would resent you for it. Perhaps try to take an outing together or do something that involves the three of you."

Amelia nodded, while she tried to imagine ways to bring them together. She'd spent so little time among children, but her nephew and niece spoke their thoughts with complete honesty and almost no regard for anyone's feelings. She raised her cup of tea to her lips, remembering them.

"What about you?" her sister asked softly. "Could you be expecting a child of your own?"

The tea flew out of Amelia's mouth, and she began coughing. "I don't think so, no." Though she knew it was an honest question, her face flamed with color. Her menses had come and gone already, and there was no chance of it at the moment. "Not yet, anyway."

Victoria went utterly still. "Amelia . . . has he consummated the marriage?"

"Yes." Amelia closed her eyes, feeling mortified. "But only once." This was not at all a conversation she wanted to have.

"That's ridiculous," Victoria shot back. "What is *wrong* with him? You're a perfectly lovely young woman."

"I suppose he's still in love with his first wife. He didn't truly want to marry me." The confession was a bitter fact she found difficult to swallow.

"But he *did* marry you," Victoria pointed out. "He must care."

Her sister's words struck a sore note. Though Amelia wanted to believe that David might one day treat her as a wife instead of a companion, she wasn't going to harbor illusions. Right now, she was his wife in name, but little more than that.

"The most I can hope for is friendship," she admitted. "And aside from our one night together, he's been avoiding me during the day."

The smile that spread over Toria's face surprised her, for her sister appeared quite pleased. "Good. That means he *does* want you. He's afraid he wants you too much."

"Or perhaps I wasn't very good, and he has no desire to be with me again." The words were laden with self-pity, but they were the truth. "What should I do now?" She wanted to believe Toria's words, but the fact remained that the earl had isolated himself.

"When you reach his estate, you should try to spend time with him. Don't let him shut you out."

It was a reasonable suggestion, but Amelia wasn't certain if it would resolve the problem. Lord Castledon seemed intent on separating himself.

"Or find a problem for him to solve," Victoria continued. "Men do like to fix things. Break it yourself if you must."

Amelia had no idea what sort of problem to invent, but her sister hadn't finished yet. "Oh, and one last thing," she interjected. "Visit his bed in the morning, before he's awake."

Amelia's cheeks burned at the idea, but she managed to nod. "Bring him breakfast, you mean?"

Her sister began to laugh. Leaning closer, she whispered in Amelia's ear. At her sister's suggestion, she blurted out, "No, I couldn't!"

"If you want to win his heart, there's no man alive who would turn down a naked woman in his bed, first thing in the morning." Victoria sent her a secretive smile. "You might even convince him to give up his plans for the day while he's with you."

Amelia bit her lip, unsure if she was *that* bold. Though she did like her husband a great deal, she wasn't certain if she was quite ready to seduce him.

"Trust me on this," her sister answered. "He won't turn you down."

"I hope you're right."

The journey towards Castledon was akin to touring the depths of Hell. Never in his life did David remember weather this blistering hot. The closed coach made it even more unbearable. He'd removed his coat, but they had two more hours before they reached the inn for the night.

Amelia had not voiced a single complaint, but he was well aware of her misery. Her hair was damp around her temples, and there was a light sheen of perspiration on her skin and neck. Her high-waisted gown emphasized the curve of her bosom, and he was acutely aware of the tension between them. He'd been avoiding her for weeks, and she knew it. To her credit, she hadn't said anything, for they both knew why.

At last, she broke the silence. "Tell me about your daughter."

He relaxed a little and said, "Christine isn't like other little girls. She'd sooner climb trees than play with dolls."

"Did you tell her I was coming with you?" Amelia's tone was even, but he didn't miss her apprehension.

"Ah, no. Not yet." He looked out the window, choosing his words carefully. "She knew I was searching for a wife, but I thought it would be best if she saw you for herself."

Amelia took her shoes off and tucked her feet on the opposite seat beneath her skirts. She leaned back and tugged at her collar, as if to waft air beneath her gown. "So I'm to be a surprise."

She made it sound as if that wasn't a good thing. David couldn't see why not. Christine had been pestering him for years to find a new wife. "I believe the pair of you will get on quite well."

"You might find both of us climbing trees," she warned with a sly smile. There was a flash of mischief on her face, but instead of enjoying her teasing, he glimpsed a trace of a naughty girl.

A surge of heat took him, and David moved his coat toward his lap. Time and distance, he reminded himself. Once he'd brought Amelia to Christine, he could separate himself from them, and eventually, these feelings would go away. It had been nearly impossible to concentrate during the last few weeks. He had awakened, time and again, dreaming of Amelia. So many times, he'd wanted to go into her room and give in to desires of the flesh. But their marriage was fragile enough. If he dared to touch her more, it might break down the careful walls he'd erected around his life.

He tried not to be fascinated by the bead of perspiration that slid down Amelia's neck beneath that gown. Or to imagine the rest of her bare body, slick with heat.

"I hope you'll make yourself at home when you reach Castledon," he offered.

"Are you going to put me in the servants' quarters again? Or must I disobey you?" Her voice taunted him like a bad girl asking him to spank her bare bottom.

Christ, what the hell was the matter with him? He'd never harbored thoughts like that before.

"No, of course not," he assured her. "You may choose a bedroom and decorate it as you please." Preferably one far away from his.

She untied her bonnet and set it aside. Then she eyed him. "Do you have a spare handkerchief I could use?"

He handed her the linen square without question, but when he saw her dab at her face and throat—even the sheen of skin above her bodice—his mind conjured up too many inappropriate ideas.

He wanted her in a carnal way, right now. Though he understood that this was the result of too many years of celibacy, he didn't want to be this close to Amelia. She tempted him beyond reason, and right now, he wanted to unfasten every last button and expose her golden skin.

"It's beastly hot," she said. "I'll be glad when we reach the inn. I'd like to ask for a cool bath to wash away the travel dust."

Was she doing this on purpose? He gave a nod, as if it meant nothing, but her wish only fueled his body's urges. He imagined her naked body beneath the bath, the cool water puckering her nipples.

"How much longer?" she asked.

"An hour or two, at the most."

She sighed and leaned back against the seat, the pose making her breasts strain against the fabric of her gown.

Katherine had never behaved like this in all her life. His first wife had been genteel, proper, and ever the lady. She would have sat with her back ramrod straight, her feet tucked demurely beneath her gown, without a strand of hair out of place.

Amelia looked ready to remove more layers of clothing. And damned if he didn't want her to.

"I don't like the way you've been avoiding me during the daytime," she said at last. "I want that to change when we reach Castledon." Her honesty caught him off guard, and David didn't know what to say. Thankfully, she continued. "Whatever there is between us has nothing to do with your first marriage."

He wanted to believe it was that easy, that he could simply separate the two women into different boxes. But he didn't like what happened to him whenever he was around Amelia. He lost sight of who he was. The dark pleasure of touching her, and her response, was stronger than it had been with Katherine. The physical release he'd gotten from Amelia was a hunger he couldn't satisfy.

Her very presence was infiltrating his life, making his first marriage appear hollow. It wasn't. He'd loved his wife, and she'd loved him. He was convinced that nothing would ever be better than his life with Katherine, but Amelia was slowly destroying that opinion.

He didn't want to have feelings for her. He wanted to lock away his responses and hold on to the shadow life he'd lived. Maybe then he wouldn't feel the burdening guilt of betrayal. He knew that Katherine would give her blessings upon this match, no matter that it was with a younger woman. But he was troubled by the way Amelia made him feel.

"I was busy with my responsibilities in the House of Lords," he said, dodging the real reason.

Amelia stared at him, and in her green eyes, he saw a woman who knew precisely what he'd been doing. "You're being dishonest with yourself. You wanted me that night. And I suspect you still do. Why, then, are you holding yourself back from being with me again?"

"I wed you to protect your reputation and your family's name," he corrected. "And because I didn't want your life ruined because of Lisford. Nothing more."

She continued to study him. "I am grateful to you for it. But I don't want a marriage where I see my husband once a month, and he confines me to a bedroom far away from his. It feels as if you despise me."

It wasn't that, but at the same time, he didn't want a real marriage with Amelia. "I don't despise you. But you knew, when you married me, that it wouldn't be anything more."

"It's not as if I expect you to fall in love with me." But he heard the slight catch in her voice, as if she were holding back her own feelings. She lifted a lock of hair from her neck and stared out the window. "But I wouldn't mind it if you came to my bed again."

Another unholy image surged through his brain, of what it was like to thrust inside her, feeling her flesh yield beneath his. He gritted his teeth against the rising arousal. "Later, perhaps."

"I'll not be a wallflower in this marriage," she said quietly. "I won't let you set me aside like a forgotten coat." Her face had gone pale, and she ventured softly, "Or is it that you don't want to be with me in that way? Was it that bad?"

He hesitated, for this was a dangerous conversation. Touching Amelia had been deeply arousing, haunting him at every moment. *He* was the one who should have lasted longer, making it better for her. "You did nothing wrong." He beckoned for her to come and sit beside him. When she did, he stroked a lock of her hair back. "I'm having trouble with the idea that I've remarried. It's been a long time."

"You don't feel that you deserve to be happy again, do you?" Her voice was barely above a whisper, but he nodded. Her arms came around his waist, and she rested her cheek against his heart.

It seemed wrong that Katherine had died, while he was left to go on living. Watching her waste away, taking one step closer to death each day, was the worst nightmare he'd ever endured. He kept wondering if he'd found a different doctor or if he'd found some other way to help her, then perhaps he could have saved her from dying.

"It's hard," he said at last.

"Will you try?" She held out her hand to his, and he knew that if he turned her down now, it would sever the fragile friendship between them.

He took her hand in his and was startled when she turned to kiss his cheek. The soft brush of her lips burned through him, and he stopped her from pulling back. Instead, he brought his mouth to hers. Her lips were gentle, accepting him, but the invitation was undeniable. When her hands reached up to his hair, he deepened the kiss, pulling her onto his lap.

He didn't care that she was nestled against his arousal. Her tongue touched his, and a breathless sigh escaped her when he rocked his hips.

He could claim her right now in the coach, lifting her skirts and sinking into her willing flesh. She was trembling against him, her green eyes dark with her own desire.

"I love it when you touch me," she murmured. "Don't stop."

He rewarded her by reaching beneath her gown to touch her leg, moving his hands upward to her inner thigh. Amelia leaned in closer, kissing him hard, and she pressed herself against his arousal.

He knew he shouldn't continue, for they would reach the inn all too soon. But he found himself giving in to the physical pleasure of caressing her. She was so responsive, her lips swollen from his kiss.

It was as if his mind and body were separate, as he brought her closer to the edge.

"Do you want this?" he asked huskily, when he slipped his fingers inside her wetness.

"I want you," she breathed.

He rubbed his thumb against her hooded flesh, watching her face. The need to possess her was overwhelming, but he welcomed the physical frustration. He didn't care that he would be in pain tonight—there was no harm in giving her pleasure.

He would enjoy that, he realized. Watching her come apart was a reward in itself, and there was no need to indulge his own needs.

"Let go," he ordered, thrusting his hand against her. "Or I'll keep tormenting you even more."

She shuddered against him, biting her lower lip, while her eyes remained closed. She was fighting him, and when she reached for his erection, he caught her wrist.

"No. This isn't about me."

He moved his mouth to the neckline of her gown. Though he couldn't free her breasts, he kissed the bared skin. "If I could, I'd take your nipple in my mouth," he told her. "I'd suckle you hard until you screamed."

His words forced her past the brink, and she arched against him, a cry escaping as she surrendered to the release. He held her as she went limp against him. His own heart was pounding, his shaft so hard, it was punishment for what he'd done.

But Amelia smiled as if he'd handed her a priceless jewel.

It was a wonder her knees were still functioning. Amelia held the earl's hand as he led her inside the small room within the inn. After he'd pleasured her in the coach, once again he'd locked away every emotion. It was as if he hadn't touched her at all.

She didn't understand the iron control he seemed to possess. It was as if he were a man of stone, one who isolated himself from the moments they shared.

It should have infuriated her. Instead, Amelia took it as a challenge. He might try to separate himself from her, but she wasn't going to stand back in the shadows. Even if it meant she had to become Eve, tempting him with her body, she would set aside her nerves and bring him the same pleasure he'd given her. She wanted *him* to lose command of his senses, even if it meant surrendering to his needs.

Inside their room, there was only a single bed, and the interior was not particularly clean. For a moment, Amelia wondered if he intended to get a separate room from hers.

When his footman brought in the earl's belongings, she let out the breath she'd been holding. Then he was intending to stay. She was thankful for it and promised herself that this night she would set aside her inhibitions. But when she saw the sheets, she questioned if they'd been changed since the last guests. There were stains on the coverlet, and the linen appeared almost yellow.

"Is this . . . the best they could do?" Though she wanted a romantic night with her husband, this room left a great deal to be desired.

David removed his hat and shrugged. "I suppose so. I did ask them to send up water for washing."

She nodded, suddenly realizing that her earlier wish, to have a bath, was an entirely different matter with a husband present in the room.

When she sat down upon the bed, she heard the terrible creak of the rope bed frame. "I'm not certain this bed will hold both of us." It appeared as if it would snap beneath her own weight.

"We may end up sleeping on the floor," he said. "It's not exactly the best of accommodations."

"And there may be lice in the mattress." She shuddered, imagining tiny insects crawling upon her. "I think I'd rather take the floor than risk this bed."

He seemed to agree with her. "Shall I ask for another room?"

"No. If this is the best they had, I can't imagine what a lesser room would be."

There came a knock at the door, and a servant brought in a light supper and a basin of water. The earl directed the man to put their meal down on the table and the basin on the dressing table. Amelia decided to clean the dust from her face and hands before eating and was grateful that the water appeared clean. She had put her bonnet back on when they'd arrived at the inn, but now removed it once more.

After the servant had gone, the earl came forward to wash his own hands. Amelia handed him a linen cloth to dry them, and he stood over her while she dipped her palms in the water and lifted them to her face.

The cool water was welcome, and she closed her eyes, never minding that some of it slid beneath her gown. David passed her the cloth, and she wiped her face and hands.

He remained behind her, and she was conscious of his body heat. Slowly, she pulled the pins from her hair, letting it spill over her shoulders. A moment later, the earl touched her shoulder, pulling his hand through the strands.

"Come and eat with me," he bade her. Amelia started to follow, but the earl stood where he was for a moment. In his blue eyes, she saw a glimpse of longing, and her body softened with anticipation. She wanted to spend this night in his arms, even if it was on the floor. If it meant giving him the same physical release that he'd granted her, it would be worth it.

The food was bland and the meat a mysterious gray color, but Amelia was so hungry, she hardly cared. Her nerves heightened with every moment, for tonight she would sleep beside her husband.

She drank her wine entirely too fast, and her brain felt fuzzy as a result. But she needed the courage, for what was to come. After the last time, she'd been a little sore, but she wanted to please him. A hundred questions tangled in her mind as she pondered how he would like to be touched.

"I believe that may have been the worst food I've ever eaten," David remarked, pushing it aside with a grimace.

Amelia couldn't quite form a response, for she was trying to decide what to do now. Should she ask for her maid to come and undress her? Or should she let him do that?

"You're looking pale," he remarked. "Are you well enough?"

"Do you think we could get this over with?" she asked. "The more I think about it, the more nervous I am."

"Get what over with?" he inquired. "Dinner, you mean? I agree. It was awful."

She swallowed hard, pouring herself a second cup of wine. "No, the part where we"—she glanced back at the narrow bed—"you know."

"The part where we sleep in a bed where the sheets haven't been cleaned and the bed is likely infested with vermin?"

He was making fun of her, and she decided that bluntness was best. "No, the part where we make love a second time."

His eyes narrowed at her, and from the doubtful expression on his face, it was clear he didn't want to. "Not in that bed," he said. "We'd be covered in flea bites, and I doubt you'd enjoy it."

Her cheeks burned with mortification, but she tried again. "On the floor then?"

David took the wineglass from her and shook his head. "Too uncomfortable. Your back would hurt in the morning." But there was a hint of wickedness in his voice, as if he were teasing her.

She lifted her hair off the back of her neck, closing her eyes for a moment. "You're avoiding me again, aren't you?"

"In this instance, yes." He glanced around the small bedchamber. "Admit it—this is not exactly the best location for a tryst."

She had to agree on that point. "Then how shall we pass the time?"

"Counting fleas?"

She grimaced at the idea and went over to see if the bed was that terrible. Although she'd been seated in a coach for most of the day, her body ached with exhaustion. The idea of falling into a dreamless sleep was a welcome one.

But when she reached out to touch the coverlet, the mattress squirmed.

Amelia let out a shriek and backed away. "It moved!" She didn't know what was beneath that coverlet, but she knew that bedding was *not* supposed to do that. If there was a mouse or a rat in the bedding—

She seized a stool and smashed it against the coverlet.

"Most women would be screaming and standing on the table by now," the earl pointed out.

Amelia glared at him. "Aren't you supposed to be helping me? While I don't relish killing a mouse, neither do I want to sleep with him."

"This *is* rather entertaining," he said, leaning back with a gleam in his eye. "I think you should strike it again."

When she hit the coverlet again, there was a groaning sound, and the center of the mattress sank down.

"I think you killed the bed." The amusement on his face irritated her. Wasn't he supposed to be her savior, protecting her from whatever creeping animals were living in the mattress?

"I don't think either of us should sleep here," she pronounced. "It's not clean, and there's likely a dead rodent inside the straw mattress." In fact, she wished they could leave the inn entirely. Nothing about this place made her comfortable. "I'd rather sleep in the coach," she told him. "At least there are no lice or animals inside."

He shrugged. "Or we could ask for a different room."

She rubbed her arms, uncertain of what to do. But the earl ordered, "Come with me, and we'll see if I can find something else."

Amelia took his arm, still uneasy about their accommodations. But this time, the earl spoke sharply with the innkeeper and made it clear he was displeased by the room. She stepped back, leaving them to argue about it, and in the meantime, she saw that her husband was growing even angrier with the man.

In disgust, he gave the innkeeper a guinea and took her hand. "We're leaving. I'd rather drive the rest of the night than stay here."

Amelia wasn't certain he should have paid the man at all, but she decided not to argue. While their servants gathered up their belongings, the earl led her back outside. They waited within the coach for the driver to hitch up the horses, and he said, "I'm sorry for that. I didn't think it would be this bad."

She sent him a wary smile. "At least we had our supper. And we didn't become the rodent's supper."

The earl didn't smile in return. Instead, his face was taut with tension as he sat across from her. The interior of the coach reminded her of the endless hours of discomfort they had already endured.

"Would you like to lie down?" she suggested. "Perhaps get some sleep?"

He shook his head. "You are welcome to sleep, if you want. I'll wait until our journey has started again."

Amelia eyed him for a moment, and said at last, "When I was younger, I used to rest my head in my mother's lap when I slept on a long journey."

He said nothing, but moved to the side in wordless invitation. Amelia sat beside him and laid her head down upon the earl's lap. His hand rested in her hair, and he stroked her temple lightly. It felt good to feel the warmth of his fingers against her skin.

The horses pulled forward, and as the coach continued, the rhythm of the horses was soothing.

And somehow it didn't matter that she had no bed to rest upon. Castledon was here to keep her safe and to watch over her.

Amelia turned over to look up at David. "Will you kiss me good night?" she asked.

He didn't answer her at first, and she reached up to his cravat. "Nothing more than a kiss, I promise you."

Unless you want more, she thought.

He put his arm around her nape, lifting her up to meet his lips. This time, she wrapped her arms around his neck, opening to him. She offered herself to him in the kiss.

And his mouth opened upon hers, hot and inviting. Dear God, he tasted of sin and unfulfilled longings. Amelia kissed him back, and he nipped at her lips, coaxing her into more.

The swift heat clenched her, pouring over her body until she wanted to touch him. She needed to feel his skin upon hers, his weight pressing her back.

But he withdrew at last, tilting her head away. "Good night, Amelia."

Her body was already aroused, wanting more than just a kiss. But she acquiesced, focusing her attention on the opposite seat. It gave her the chance to think about how to go about this, how to break down the walls of ice that were shutting her out.

But when she adjusted her head back upon his lap, she grew aware that her husband was not at all immune to the kiss.

His body was tense, his fists clenched as he stared out the window. It was as if she'd upset him somehow, and she wasn't certain if it was the prospect of driving through the night . . . or a physical frustration.

To test her theory, she adjusted her head against his lap, and he let out a slight hiss of air. From the blunt thickness of his erection, he still wanted her.

Amelia tilted her face up to look at him. It was dark, and only the faint flare of the oil lantern outside let her glimpse his face.

"You're hurting," she whispered. "And I don't know why."

He remained quiet for a while. "It's nothing you should worry about."

Her hand moved to touch his rigid flesh. "Is it because we didn't—"

"Yes." He took her hand away from his lap and muttered, "Now go to sleep."

That was impossible. Though she knew almost nothing about joining with a man, she thought again about Toria's advice. Frowning in the darkness, she thought about the challenge of what to do. Her mind conjured up the forbidden image of the night when she'd sat atop him in the chair. Though he'd only touched her, it was possible to do more in that position.

Her imagination went wild, and at the thought of taking command, she started to grow moist between her legs. She thought of his hands touching her breasts, and without asking, she took his palm in hers and brought it to one erect nipple.

David obeyed her unspoken request, stroking her breast and lightly pinching the nipple with his fingers. An echoing ache clenched deep inside, and she longed for so much more.

He was tempting her, arousing her so much, she lifted her head from his lap. What she was about to do was brazen, unthinkable for a lady. But she was past the point of obeying the rules. She wanted her husband inside her, and there were hours before they would arrive anywhere.

"Don't speak," she ordered, kissing him deeply. She reached for his trousers and began to unfasten the buttons, one by one. It took only seconds to unfasten his drawers and free his hot length from the small clothes. Somehow, in the darkness, it was easier to be bold. Though she was still intimidated by this, the thought of him being in pain was worse. Especially when she could do something about it.

She straddled his lap, hitching her skirts up. Her heart was pounding fiercely, but she wrapped her hand around his thick length, stroking from the base to the tip.

He caught his breath, and it encouraged her to try it again. Her hand grew slick with his heat, and she guided the head of him into her wet entrance.

The earl shocked her when he pressed his hips upward, holding her bottom. "Feeling impatient, are you?"

"I don't really know what I'm doing," she confessed. The sensation of being filled so deeply was both thrilling and frightening. "I was afraid you would refuse. But I know you need this."

He held her waist and lifted her slightly before giving a shallow thrust. "I do, yes." His voice was deep, and in the darkness, it was overwhelming to be this intimate with him. "But I wasn't going to bother you."

"It's not a bother," she whispered, gasping as she felt the thickness of him invading and withdrawing once again. "It's my duty, as your wife."

"Like buying me waistcoats?" he said, while his shaft was embedded within her. The coach rumbled along the road, and the motion of the vehicle created subtle vibrations. She could feel her breathing transforming, growing more shallow. His hands moved up to her breasts, caressing the tips, and she found herself moving against him.

"Yes," she whispered. "Nothing more than that."

It was such a lie, but she didn't want him to think she was falling in love with him. If he believed this meant nothing, then perhaps he would one day see her as a wife instead of a stepmother for his daughter. His heart belonged to someone else, and she didn't know if he would ever let go of Katherine.

She rose up on her knees, sinking down, and was rewarded when he thrust deeply. It was a new sensation, but he kept holding her down, forcing her to endure the tremors of the rocking coach.

A wildness rose up in her blood, and she was hardly able to bear it. She gripped his hair, finding the rhythm she wanted, and he countered by reaching below her skirts to touch the fold of flesh that had brought her such pleasure earlier.

Her body was arching higher, shuddering with the intensity, but he would not let her go. Instead, he pumped against her, forcing her to ride him faster. The explosive force of her release made her cry out, and he drove himself in and out, gripping her hips while he took his own pleasure.

She was drowning in lust, unable to do anything but surrender to him. And then, at last, his breathing shifted, and he let out a harsh breath as he found his own climax.

Her hair was still undone, her body weak. But he didn't force her to get up right away. Instead, he held her close, and she felt the wild beat of his pulse when she rested her fingertips against his throat.

Henry Andrews was at a loss for what to do. His wife had hardly emerged from her room in the past two weeks. She'd barely touched her food, and misery lined her face.

Because of Margaret, who was still missing.

Today was Beatrice's birthday, and he wanted to give her something that would make her smile. It had taken help from Charlotte, but he'd learned that she had kept the sapphire bracelet, giving Beatrice money from her own funds.

He'd paid her back, and now the bracelet was in a velvet pouch, tucked in his waistcoat pocket. He wanted to surprise Beatrice with it, to bring a smile back. After knocking on her door, she called out for him to enter.

"Is there any news?" she asked, when he closed the door to her bedroom.

He shook his head. "My men have searched all the major roads, but after they found the wreckage of the coach, there was no sign of them. They must have gone forward on foot."

"I can't believe this happened," Beatrice said, staring out the window. "I don't want to imagine that she's dead. I can't even think of it in my mind, though I know it's possible."

"I sent other men to Scotland, to speak with Sinclair's family. If he took her somewhere—"

"No, he'd have given his own life to protect Margaret." Beatrice shook her head. "He'd never harm a hair on her head."

But the fact remained that his daughter was stranded in northern England with a man who was not her husband.

"She's ruined," he told his wife. "Even if she's found—"

"Do you think I *care* about that anymore, Henry? I don't even care if he's made her pregnant. I just want to know that my daughter is alive."

The tears streamed down her face, and she gripped her hands together. He wished now that he hadn't said anything.

A heaviness centered over his mood, and he offered, "I won't stop searching for her. No matter how long it takes."

He moved forward, trying to guide her into his arms, but Beatrice shook her head. "I don't want to be touched right now, Henry. I just want to be alone."

The sapphire bracelet remained in his pocket, like a guilty conscience. He tried again. "I asked our housekeeper to prepare a cake today. For your birthday."

She didn't smile but stared out the window. "I have no reason to celebrate being another year older. Not when my daughter is missing."

He fingered the velvet pouch, but his throat tightened. This was not the time to give her the gift. She was so tormented by thoughts of Margaret, nothing would break through her grief.

And so, he kept the velvet pouch in his pocket.

"Papa!" A young girl flew into the earl's arms while Amelia walked alongside him, entering the foyer of Castledon. Christine's dark hair was braided and pinned up like a young lady's, although she was far too young to be wearing it in that fashion. She wore a sea-green silk frock that reminded Amelia of something a mermaid might wear.

David embraced his daughter warmly, and in that fleeting moment, Amelia saw that he truly did love the girl. There was a different air about him, as if a part of his heart were filled up, just by being home again. "I've brought you the mother you requested." He stepped back and led Amelia forward to meet her. "This is Amelia, the new Lady Castledon."

Christine frowned, but dutifully curtseyed. Amelia kept a smile upon her face, though she saw the wariness in the girl's eyes. It seemed that her new stepdaughter wasn't at all pleased to see her, despite her good manners.

"I'm glad to meet you," Amelia said, pretending as if she didn't notice Christine's reaction. But inwardly she knew this was not going to be easy for either of them.

"Christine, how would you like to take your new mother on a tour of the house, while I have our belongings sent upstairs?"

His daughter hesitated, as if she didn't want to. But she responded, "Yes, Papa."

"I would like that very much," Amelia said. "It will give us the chance to become better acquainted. And your father can join us in a few moments."

It was a subtle means of asking the earl to save them both, in case the first meeting didn't go well. Amelia wasn't at all optimistic, given the girl's reluctance.

"Follow me," Christine offered, and Amelia accompanied the girl upstairs. She led her a little farther, until they were out of the earl's earshot. Immediately, she said, "My father wasn't supposed to marry you."

This wasn't exactly news to Amelia, but she decided to tread carefully. "What do you mean by that?"

"He was supposed to marry my governess, Miss Grant. I had it all arranged."

And you spoiled everything, her eyes seemed to say.

Amelia knew she had to choose her words carefully. "I'm sorry to have disrupted your plans. You must be very close to your governess." Or perhaps the woman had allowed the girl to do anything she pleased.

"I was." The young girl's face went sullen. "But Miss Grant left to marry someone else a few weeks ago. She wasn't supposed to—I wanted her to marry my father."

Amelia said nothing, knowing that silence was her best ally at the moment.

"My father is not going to love you," Christine insisted. "You might as well understand that."

The girl's dramatic proclamation wasn't unexpected. Even so, it was dismaying that Christine had already decided that Amelia was unworthy to be her stepmother after they had known each other only two minutes.

Amelia took a steady breath and kept her voice calm. "Whether or not the earl loves me doesn't matter. I am his wife, and that won't change. As for you and I, we will come to our own understanding."

"You won't tell me what to do," Christine warned. "I can promise you that." In the girl's eyes was the promise of trouble with a capital *T*.

Amelia had no desire to be enemies, but at the same time, she would not let herself be bullied by an eleven-year-old. "I think we should have a talk and draw up an agreement between us." A truce, as it were.

Christine's expression appeared wary, as if she had no desire to come to any sort of compromise. It didn't bode well for either of them. Fortunately, Amelia was spared any further conversation when Lord Castledon joined them.

His daughter immediately linked her arm in his, drawing him forward so that Amelia was left behind. The message was quite clear: *You aren't wanted.*

Amelia imagined she was supposed to be heartbroken by this. Perhaps the girl wanted her to cajole or coax her, spoiling her in the hopes of gaining her love. Not so. Amelia had earned the title of Unruly Daughter at an early age and was well acquainted with manipulating others to get what she wanted. Lady Christine would not be granted her every desire simply because she wanted it so.

Her new stepdaughter's machinations were quite obvious, and whether or not Lord Castledon believed them didn't matter a whit.

When Amelia turned the corner, she found them waiting for her. Her husband offered his other arm. "I lost you for a moment there."

"I thought you might want a little time with Christine," she said, ignoring the girl's glare while she took the earl's opposite arm. "You haven't seen her in a while."

"*Lady* Christine," the girl corrected, as if trying to behave like a princess.

"Your stepmother can call you whatever she wishes," the earl intervened. "And I'm certain you will like one another a great deal."

When cats swim underwater, Amelia thought. No, this was going to take more time than she'd expected.

With one hand, Lord Castledon reached up and touched the top of his daughter's head as if measuring her height. Then he squeezed Christine in a light hug. "You've grown so tall in the past few months," he admitted.

"I missed you, Papa." The wistful longing on the child's face reminded Amelia of herself as a girl, when her father had gone off to war. Henry Andrews had been away for so many years, she'd felt all but abandoned.

"Soon enough, you'll have to learn how to be a lady. Amelia can help you with that." He smiled at her, but Christine's answering smile was strained.

"Papa, will you come and eat supper with me in the nursery this evening?" Christine pleaded.

"I think it would be better if you dined with us downstairs," her father said. "You're old enough to begin learning proper behavior and manners among adults." He continued down the hallway and opened a door.

Inside, the air smelled musty, like a grandmother's trunk. It was clear that the bedroom hadn't been used in many years. "I'll have our housekeeper, Mrs. Menford, prepare this room for you." He sent Amelia a slight smile, as if to apologize for the room he'd given her in London.

"Is your room at the far end of the hall?" She wondered if he was intending to continue their physical separation at night or whether he was willing to attempt a true marriage.

"No. It's not far from yours," he admitted. The sudden flare in his eyes gave her a reason to hope, and it was a small victory.

After the stolen moment in the coach last night, he hadn't spoken a word. But the way he was looking at her now suggested that he *did* intend to share her bed again.

Something deep inside Amelia stirred, for it meant he was giving them a chance. Maybe, just maybe, she might have the happy ending she wanted.

Chapter Ten

"I would like to arrange a special supper for tonight," Amelia said to the housekeeper, Mrs. Menford.

The older woman's hair was pulled back in a severe chignon, and streaks of gray lined the edges. Her dress was a dark navy blue, and she wore a starched cap. The housekeeper appeared beleaguered by the request, as if she was not in any way inclined to obey.

"My lady, I need more than a few hours to prepare a special meal," Mrs. Menford said. The tone in her voice was patronizing, as if Amelia weren't aware of the necessary arrangements.

"His Lordship did not send word of his impending arrival, nor yours. We are all at sixes and sevens already. A special meal would simply be too much to ask of my kitchen maids."

Amelia thought back to her own housekeeper, Mrs. Larson. The Scotswoman loved nothing more than to put together a spontaneous gathering. She'd been able to conjure a large meal out of very little and had never hesitated to produce a feast out of a famine.

"We can have the meal a little later tonight, if you need to send the servants out for more food." It was more than reasonable, Amelia thought. "But I do think we should try to make a celebration, if we can."

After all, it wasn't every day that the lord of the household got married. She couldn't imagine why the woman was so unwilling to prepare a good meal.

But the housekeeper only sighed and shook her head. "Forgive me, my lady, but I know that you are new to this household and cannot understand how things are done here at Castledon."

A sliver of anger threaded down Amelia's spine. The woman was behaving as if she had no inkling of how to manage an earl's household. Wasn't she the daughter of a baron? Her mother and sisters had taught her the necessities, ever since she was a young girl. The woman's remarks were completely inappropriate.

"While I appreciate your suggestion," the housekeeper continued, "I must admit that—"

"Do you wish to keep your position as housekeeper at Castledon?" Amelia interrupted. Although she kept her fury in check, inwardly she was on the verge of losing her temper. Yes, she was young. Yes, this was her first household to manage. But she also knew that the housekeeper had no right to question her wishes—it was her duty to carry them out without argument. Mrs. Larson would never dare to go against Beatrice's orders. It was unheard of. For this woman to question her orders on the very first day was not a good sign.

"I—well, of course, my lady." The older woman's face paled as if she'd never expected such a response.

Amelia kept her face emotionless. "My husband and I have been traveling for several days. Asking you to arrange a good meal for our family is not beyond your abilities, I should hope. If you find it an unnecessary burden, then perhaps you should find employment elsewhere."

"I will speak with the cook, my lady." The woman's mouth tightened, but at least she had backed down. The rigid cast to her face suggested that she was holding back anger of her own.

"Very good. And please have her prepare a dessert of some kind. A tart or a cake, if you would," Amelia said. Though she knew Lord Castledon disliked sweets, likely his daughter would enjoy it.

The housekeeper looked as if she wanted to argue, but this time she held her tongue. "As you wish."

Amelia thanked her and left, feeling her cheeks redden with embarrassment. Although it was unwise to make enemies among the servants this early, there was nothing to be done about it. Margaret would likely have dismissed Mrs. Menford on the spot. Perhaps she should have done the same, but Lord Castledon had asked her not to make too many changes. Firing the housekeeper certainly fell into that category.

Amelia's stomach twisted over what she'd done, and she decided to seek out her husband for advice. Or at least he might be able to tell her if the housekeeper was ordinarily so contemptuous.

After asking several footmen, she found the earl in the conservatory. He was standing in front of a pianoforte, idly tracing the edge of the wood.

"May I speak with you a moment?" she asked quietly, closing the door behind her.

He glanced up, but his expression spoke of a man distracted. His hair was rumpled as if he'd run his hands through it a moment earlier. "Of course. Is something wrong with Christine?"

Amelia shook her head. "No, I haven't seen her since earlier today." It wouldn't surprise her if the girl was plotting with Mrs. Menford on how to overthrow her.

"I thought the two of you would spend time getting acquainted." He frowned, as if he'd anticipated that they would become immediate best friends. Amelia wasn't certain if he was aware of Christine's animosity and decided not to mention it.

"There will be time enough for that later," she assured him. "I needed to meet the household staff and make arrangements for our meal tonight."

His shoulders lowered, and he appeared no longer concerned. "Mrs. Menford has everything well in hand. You don't have to trouble yourself about anything. She's run the household ever since I was a small boy."

Terrorized the household, more likely, Amelia thought, but didn't say so. "That's what I wanted to talk to you about. She's already questioning my orders, treating me like a little girl who doesn't know how to manage an estate. It concerns me, and I'd like for you to support me in this."

The earl moved forward and shrugged. "Give her some time to adjust to your wishes. I'm certain it will all turn out well, for she never had any trouble with Katherine. The pair of them got along with no trouble at all, and so will you."

In other words, *Amelia* was the problem, and the earl saw no reason to interfere. For a moment, she was so dismayed by his lack of a response that she hardly knew what to say.

"I asked her to have the cook prepare a special meal for all of us tonight, to celebrate your homecoming and for Christine. She acted as if it was a great inconvenience and out of the question."

"We *did* arrive with no warning," he admitted. "In a day or two, I imagine everything will settle down." He reached out and touched the back of her neck. "Don't let it bother you, Amelia." Then he lowered his mouth to her throat, sending a spiral of desire through her. The gesture of affection caught her off guard, but then she realized he was trying to sweeten her up.

It didn't seem to concern him at all that the servants weren't listening to her. Did he not realize that housekeepers were not supposed to behave like army generals?

She leaned forward to rest her cheek against his shirt. "I know my duties, Lord Castledon. My mother saw to it that all of us were prepared to run a household." And she knew that a housekeeper who disobeyed orders on the first day could not remain here long.

His hand touched her spine. "Everything will be fine," was all he said. Dismay filled her, for he seemed unaware of the true problem. She straightened, realizing that this issue was hers to solve.

Pulling away from him, she bid him a good afternoon. "I will see you tonight."

"Tell Christine I expect her to be kind to you." He smiled, and Amelia didn't correct his assumption. She wasn't about to seek out a second person who didn't like her.

If she did that, she'd start to doubt every decision she made. It was time to retreat, to make plans, and find all the reasons to be thankful. She would *not* weep or behave as if the world had dealt her a bad hand of cards. She simply had to reevaluate her circumstances and make the most of them.

Even if no one really wanted her here.

"You married the wrong woman, Papa."

Christine closed the door behind her, and David was startled by his daughter's proclamation. "You've only just met her," he responded. Although Amelia was young and inexperienced, she needed more than a day to get adjusted to life as a countess.

"Why would you say I married the wrong woman?" he asked, opening his arms to his daughter. "You said you wanted a new mother."

Christine came to sit upon his knee, and her gray eyes remained quite serious. "I wanted one much older. Someone like Miss Grant, someone who understands me."

David had no interest in marrying her governess and had never even considered it. Although Miss Grant was a decent enough woman, she'd given Christine too much freedom.

"Miss Grant resigned her post as your governess several weeks ago. The last I heard, she was going to marry someone else."

"But she could change her mind," Christine insisted. "If you would ask her, she'd say no to that other man."

"I'm not going to ask Miss Grant to marry me," he told her firmly. "I've already married Amelia Andrews, and she will do well enough as your stepmother."

His daughter looked as if she'd swallowed a lemon. "You're wrong, Papa."

"I think you should give Amelia a chance. She's a lovely young woman. Quite amusing, actually."

Though he told his daughter stories about the board game he'd played with Amelia and her sister, his thoughts turned to another type of amusement. She'd startled him last night in the coach by seducing him. That encounter had only awakened his hunger more, making him crave her body.

She was dangerous to his life, like a siren who wove her spell around him. Sharing her bed once in a while was acceptable, but not every night. He preferred to keep their marriage as an amiable friendship, one that never dared to trespass beyond that boundary.

"You should have consulted me before you wed her," Christine said. "She looks like the sort of stepmother who would lock me in my room."

David bit back a laugh. "She isn't that bad."

"She *is*," Christine insisted, keeping her voice in a whisper. "I overheard her telling one of the maids that she planned to get rid of me as soon as you're gone." Her face held all the drama of an actress on the stage. "You won't let her do that, will you? Please say you'll send her away."

"You're making up stories about someone you don't even know," David chided. "Give her a chance, Christine."

His daughter shook her head. "I can't, Papa. When I returned from my walk in the gardens earlier, I saw Lady Castledon leaving my room. Why would she have been in my room?"

"Enough of this. You're being ridiculous, and I'm certain Amelia had a good reason. She likely was looking for you so the pair of you could get to know one another."

"She was searching through my belongings," his daughter insisted. "I believe that."

"Well, I don't." He eased her off his lap and took her by the hand. "Now go and change for supper. I expect you to be there, and you will be on your best behavior."

A sullen expression came over her face. "Why can't it just be us? I haven't seen you in months."

God save him from petulant daughters. "Go on. I will see you later." Without waiting for her to reply, he closed the door. After waiting long enough to be sure that she'd gone, he left the conservatory in search of Amelia.

None of the servants had seen her anywhere, or if they had, they'd refused to say so. When he couldn't find her, he went to her room, hoping to see her there.

Already he could see that she'd taken down the old brown drapes and let more light into the room. She'd chosen a sage green bedcover, and she'd put away many of the trinkets Katherine had been fond of. The room appeared clean and inviting, though more Spartan than it had once been.

He walked over to her writing desk, where he spied dozens of scraps of paper with lists. Most of them were incomprehensible notes like: *Shutters? Green drapes or rose?* Likely these were her ideas about redecorating the room, which he'd given her leave to change.

When he walked to Amelia's window, it was then that he spied her outside. She was walking with a basket over one arm, and he realized she'd gone into the gardens, since the basket was overflowing with roses and other blossoms he didn't recognize.

David stepped upon a crumpled piece of paper, and when he picked it up, he saw another list titled *Thankful.*

A place to live
Enough food to eat
A husband who isn't a troll

The last one made him smile. A troll? At least she'd admitted that he wasn't one. But as he read farther down the page, he saw another list titled *Problems.* First on the list, she'd written Mrs. Menford's name. Second was Christine.

The thought was sobering, for he'd wanted his wife and daughter to get along. Christine's earlier complaints were unreasonable, along with her desire for him to wed her governess. Not to mention her overblown ideas about Amelia being cruel. Honestly, did she really believe Amelia would lock her away? The idea was laughable, for his wife was the kindest person he'd met.

But his daughter's resentment was real, and David didn't know how to solve the problem.

He turned the scrap of paper over and was startled to see a sketch of a ladies' undergarment. Amelia had written *purple with lace* beside the drawing.

He thought back to the undergarments she'd worn on their wedding night. Sensual and seductive, he'd reveled in touching the silk against skin. Never before had he seen anything like them, but seeing Amelia bared in such a way had invited him to pleasure her.

He sobered, realizing how different his two wives were. Katherine had enjoyed making love with him, but she'd never been as bold as Amelia. He sensed that his new wife would drive a saint into eternal damnation. She'd tempted him, not only on their wedding night, but also on the journey here.

If he wanted her in his bed, all he had to do was enter her room. He knew that, and yet he was torn by his body's desires and the illogical desire to remain faithful to Katherine.

David sat down and picked up a pen, writing Amelia a note: *I'm glad you don't think I'm a troll.* Then he tucked it among her other papers and stood to leave.

The door swung open and Amelia entered, nearly dropping the basket of flowers when she saw him. "I didn't realize you were here, my lord."

"You don't have to call me that," he said. "David is fine, remember?"

"Did you need something, David?" she asked, her gaze darting toward the desk. It was as if she suspected he'd read her notes and was embarrassed.

He thought about talking to her about Christine's ridiculous accusations but decided that she wouldn't be able to laugh about them yet. Instead, he said, "I wanted to see that you were comfortable in your room. Is everything the way you'd like it?"

She sent him a wry smile. "Not yet. But even so, I don't think the servants would help me to change it. They're quite loyal to the first Lady Castledon and were appalled when I took down the drapes."

He wasn't surprised, for his household staff preferred to leave everything as it was. Still, they did need to allow Amelia to make a few adjustments. "How would you like them to help you now?"

Amelia shrugged and picked up the fallen basket. She picked up a daisy and snapped off the blossom, tucking it behind one ear. The blossom was a white contrast against her darker blond hair. "I want them to do as I ask without informing me that it's not the way the former Lady Castledon decorated the house. It's not a good beginning, David. As Lady of Castledon, they shouldn't be arguing with me at every turn." She rested a hand upon his chair. "If they will not carry out their duties, I will hire staff members who will do as I ask."

Now this made him hesitate. Most of the staff had been at Castledon since he was a young boy. They were as much a part of the estate as anything else, and he couldn't imagine hiring a different housekeeper or butler. "I will speak to them, if you wish."

"I won't allow them to treat me like a brainless miss," she continued. "I may be young, but I am lady of this household. I cannot keep servants who undermine my decisions."

He didn't want her to feel so unwelcome in her own home. "Amelia, you needn't worry. Let me address the situation and trust that the household will run itself, once you're accustomed to everything. In the past, Katherine never had to interfere with any of it. You'll have more freedom to do as you please."

Her eyes narrowed, and she appeared confused. "Do you mean to say that . . . your wife allowed the servants to make all of the decisions about the meals and so on? She never voiced her own wishes?"

"She spoke with Mrs. Menford from time to time, but Katherine never cared about the menus or the household. She let them run it as they did when my mother and father were alive." David had preferred it that way. He saw no sense in changing what wasn't broken. "And I think you'd be happier not having to concern yourself with it."

Amelia had fallen quiet. Whether or not he'd made her feel better, he didn't know. But then she plucked the daisy from her hair and held it out to him. "You should go and change for dinner. Perhaps there will be bread and water if we're lucky."

He took the daisy and twirled the stem. "Amelia, it won't be that bad."

She sent him a pointed look, as if to say, yes, it *was* that bad. David decided to broach the other concern. "And . . . it will get easier with Christine. I know she's not been easy to like, given her behavior. But once she gets better acquainted with you, she'll come to realize that you'll be not only a new mother, but a friend."

Her expression grew strained, as if she didn't believe that at all. He stood and was about to leave, when he saw that she was fighting back tears. Amelia wasn't one to cry, but it seemed that she was on edge.

"What else is bothering you?" he asked quietly.

She took a breath, gathering her composure. Though her eyes still gleamed, she admitted, "From the moment I've stepped into this house, I've felt sixteen years old again. I'm told what I can and cannot do. I'm not permitted to make any changes or do anything that would alter the household. I don't feel like your wife at all."

He was caught by the unhappiness in her voice and he took her hand, drawing her closer. Without words, he guided her arms around his waist, while he framed her face. "Don't you?"

"Not really." Her words were the barest whisper, and he drew his thumb across her cheek and over her mouth.

Without asking her leave, he kissed her. There was a hint of salt upon her lips, revealing earlier tears.

He didn't want her to be unhappy here. But every time he touched Amelia, it was as if the years of grief disappeared for a moment. The light of her presence twined around him, healing the raw edges. Amelia had been right; it was hard to enjoy happiness again, to take pleasure in another wife after so long. His instincts warned that he should tighten his heart against any emotions. Friendship was acceptable. But love was dangerous.

She sighed against his mouth, pulling him closer. The warmth of her arms and the velvet softness of her mouth beckoned him toward another means of forgetting.

He knew he should let go of the past and move forward. But no one had ever told him how hard that first step would be. It was as if she were melting away the hardened ice of grief, easing him with the balm of her touch.

And when she pulled back from the kiss, he found that his hands were shaking.

Amelia sat at the end of a dining room table that could host twelve people. The earl sat on the opposite side, at the head of the table, with his daughter beside him. Christine sent Amelia a triumphant look, as if she'd planned it this way.

No, more likely it was Mrs. Menford, the housekeeper, who had placed the pair of them so far apart, her husband would need an ear trumpet to hear her.

This wouldn't do at all.

Amelia picked up her silver and marched to the end where Lord Castledon sat. She took a place at his right and feigned ignorance. "I hope you don't mind my joining you. It was lonely at the far end with only a pepper pot to speak to."

Fortunately, the earl nodded, not seeming to care where she sat. But Christine kicked Amelia beneath the table, so her father wouldn't see.

"Ouch!" Amelia said, rubbing at her shin. She sent an incredulous look toward the young girl, who was ignoring her.

"Are you all right?" David asked.

She was tempted to tell him what his daughter had done, but that would only make the girl into a stronger enemy. Instead she said, "Yes. I bumped my leg by accident."

Christine appeared confused, as if she'd expected Amelia to rail at her. But Amelia had three sisters and knew that the girl was trying to provoke a fight to gain her father's attention. She stared at her stepdaughter as if to say, *I know what you did, and it won't work with me.*

But David was not oblivious to his daughter's behavior. His gaze narrowed upon Christine. "Did you kick Amelia under the table?"

"I didn't!" she insisted. "I was only stretching my legs. She must have bumped into me." The young girl put on an expression of false innocence. "Papa, I promise you, I would never kick anyone."

He eyed Amelia. "Were you attacked by the table leg?"

She bit her lip. "I can't say for certain. It may have been an imaginary dog who kicked me. Or perhaps a ghost?"

"Or a ghost dog," David said drily. He seemed aware of her tactic and turned back to his daughter. "I don't believe your mother would have approved of lies, Christine."

"I didn't lie," she said weakly. She held her father's gaze without blinking, for nearly a minute. "Don't you believe me?"

Soon, her eyes welled up, and he let out a sigh. "Christine, I know what you did. Apologize to Amelia at once."

The girl glared at her. "I apologize for my leg accidentally hitting yours."

It was no accident at all, but Amelia forced herself to remain serene. "I accept your apology. Accidents do happen." *Though not in this instance.*

The first course arrived, and instead of a rich soup, there was a bowl of salty chicken broth. Amelia took one sip and decided not to risk any more. The earl and his daughter didn't seem to notice. Both finished the broth while talking about a book Christine had read recently.

The rest of the meal was lacking as well. The meat—which Amelia thought was supposed to be beef—was brown and listless. The vegetables were limp, and she could mash them with her fork.

What startled Amelia most of all was how the earl and Christine were utterly unaware of how terrible the food was.

"How is your food?" she asked, wondering if theirs was as bad. The earl shrugged, and Christine nodded as if to say it was fine. Amelia took a sip of wine and tried to think of how she could solve this debacle. Mrs. Larson would die if she saw this mess.

A flash of inspiration caught her, for the housekeeper could undoubtedly transform this household in a matter of days. Mrs. Larson would know which servants were hard workers and which ones needed to be better trained or replaced.

The thought of seeing her mother's housekeeper was a hope that flared inside her, along with a touch of homesickness. She decided to write to Beatrice and ask if Mrs. Larson could pay a visit, spending a few weeks helping her to sort out the household.

When her plate was taken away, she'd hardly touched any of it, but at least now she had a practical solution. Mrs. Larson was brash and bold and wouldn't hesitate to go after anyone who was disobedient.

Now that she had one problem solved, she had another to manage. When she studied Christine, Amelia saw that the girl's sleeves were well above her wrists. Her gown was better suited to a six-year-old than an eleven-year-old.

"Christine, I plan to visit the village in the morning. Would you like to come with me and we could go shopping?" It might give them a chance to be better acquainted without Lord Castledon. And if the girl needed new clothing, she could help choose the fabric.

"I—I planned to spend the day with Papa." There was confusion on her face, as if she hadn't expected to be asked.

"He can come along, if he wants to." Amelia shot him a knowing look. "He might want to pick out a new bonnet for himself."

The earl sent her a pointed look. "I'll let you pick out one for me," he remarked. "With ribbons and lace, if you please. Purple lace."

The sudden look in his eyes reminded Amelia of the sketch she'd drawn, of the purple lace chemise. Had he seen that? From the faint smile on his lips, she suspected he had.

Amelia swallowed hard, forcing her gaze away. "I'll see what I can find."

The young girl appeared unaware of their hidden exchange. "No, I don't want to go with you."

"Christine, it will be good fun, you'll see. If you need any new clothes, we'll have you measured." Amelia tried to make it sound much more interesting, but her stepdaughter's expression didn't change at all.

"Mrs. Menford can take me shopping. I needn't go anywhere with you."

Before the earl could intervene, Amelia stopped him with a hand. "No, it's all right. I'll go on my own, and if Christine changes her mind, she can join me."

Instead of appearing relieved, the girl stared down at her plate.

"No, she's going to go with you." Lord Castledon eyed his daughter with a steely look. "And she's going to make an effort to get better acquainted. You are her stepmother now."

Christine rolled her eyes and let out a heavy breath, as if her father had ordered her to spend all day scrubbing the floors. "Yes, Papa."

Amelia decided that she needed to intervene before this became a punishment instead of a way to mend their differences. "What do you like to do when you're alone, Christine?"

The girl shrugged and said nothing.

"Christine likes to draw," the earl said. "She's also quite good at watercolors."

But the girl grimaced, as if she didn't care for it at all. Earlier, Amelia had gone to ask Christine a question about the gardens, and when she'd gone inside the nursery, she'd spied towers of books and bits of paper with scribbled stories. Whether or not the girl enjoyed writing, Amelia thought of a different surprise the young girl might enjoy—a writing space of her own with an assortment of pens, ink, and paper. Perhaps a space in the attic where she could look out over the grounds.

It was something to think about.

After a time, the earl sent Christine away for bed, leaving them alone. Amelia toyed with her fork, and in time, his leg brushed hers.

"Don't kick me," she said, smiling at him.

"My leg twitched of its own accord." But his wry expression said that he knew exactly what he'd been doing. David stood and offered his arm to lead her from the dining room table.

"Christine craves your attention," Amelia told him. "She's afraid you'll go off and leave her again."

"My duties in the House of Lords *do* require me to be away. And I have to keep a close eye on the estates to ensure that they are cared for."

"Are you planning to leave soon?"

He nodded. "I often travel during the summer, spending a few weeks at each of the estates."

Amelia had a bad feeling about this, particularly since the household staff didn't appear willing to obey her orders. "Will we be going with you?"

"No. There's no reason for you to accompany me. The pair of you can stay here, and I'll return in the autumn."

Her spirits deflated at the thought of being trapped here with a stepdaughter and servants who despised her. "Then you only stay at Castledon during the autumn and winter."

"Yes. The rest of the year, I have to attend my other duties."

No wonder his daughter felt abandoned. If she'd been raised by a governess and servants, then the last thing she'd want was a stranger telling her what to do.

She mulled over an idea, realizing that the best way to recruit Christine as an ally was to work toward a common cause—asking Lord Castledon to remain here or allowing them to go with him.

The earl had grown quiet, and he led her to walk near the window. The trees had turned into black silhouettes against an amber sunset, foretelling the promise of night.

"I would like you to stay a little longer," Amelia said at last. "Until we're settled here, if that's not too much to ask."

"For a time." Keeping his gaze fixed upon the window, he added, "I'm sorry it's been so difficult for you, since you've arrived here. I'm not precisely the dangerous, delicious rake you wanted."

She reached to take his hand in hers. "Sometimes you are," she murmured.

His eyes flared up, and he stared at her with undisguised yearning. She brought both of his hands around her waist, hoping to tempt him. "And you *did* save me from being wedded to a scoundrel. That's rather heroic."

"It might have been a rescue, but I'm not—"

She cut him off by touching a finger to his lips. "You weren't the man I wanted then. But you're the man I want now."

His hands moved up her rib cage. Then he leaned in close and rested his nose against hers. His breath warmed her cheeks, and anticipation filled up inside her. But this time when he touched his mouth to hers, the light kiss was there and gone. Amelia could hardly imagine that it had happened.

"You're not betraying Katherine by touching me," she whispered, holding him close. She wanted another night with him, here in this place where so many ghosts of the past haunted him.

"It *is* a betrayal," he contradicted. "Especially when your kiss is better than those I shared with Katherine."

With that, he left her standing alone.

Chapter Eleven

David walked inside his former wife's room, lighting a candle. It was nearly past midnight, and he couldn't say what had brought him here. It might have been guilt or perhaps the need to let go.

In six years, he'd changed nothing about this room. Nothing, save the linens that she'd slept upon in her last hours. The mattress was bare, the pillows stripped of their coverings.

The entire room was cold, like a graveyard.

He lit another candle, then the lamp beside the bed. The flare of golden light spilled over the barren mattress, and he went to sit upon it. A chill swept over him, as if her ghost had laid a hand upon his spine. He studied the room, and the familiar emptiness closed in.

"I can't keep holding on to the past," he told Katherine. "Amelia doesn't deserve this. She should have a true husband."

His wife's ghost didn't answer. Though he'd often imagined what she'd say, this time, there was silence. He was left to wonder about this new marriage. He'd agreed to wed Amelia because he hadn't wanted her to suffer from a scandal that wasn't her fault.

But she *was* hurting in this marriage. It wasn't at all fair to Amelia, being trapped like this. She was trying to make the best of her situation, but both the servants and Christine were trying her patience.

As for himself, he knew he wasn't much of a husband. Though he knew how to pleasure her in bed, and he enjoyed touching her, he knew she wanted more.

David rose from the bed, the taint of sickness still lingering in the air. A wooden wardrobe stood at the far end of the room, and he opened it. Inside were several of Katherine's gowns. The colors were still bright, though a stale odor lingered.

A choking sensation caught in his throat, and suddenly he couldn't bear to look at them anymore. He spied an empty trunk and dragged it across to the wardrobe. One by one, he started gathering up Katherine's old gowns and bonnets. It burned like acid in his heart as he stuffed them into the trunk, clearing out the space.

But he needed to be rid of the memories.

Through the next hour he worked, emptying the dressers until they, too, were bare. The trunk was stuffed to overflowing, but at least he'd managed to put away her belongings. After six years, it should have been done long ago.

A dull ache centered inside, but he felt good about what he'd done. He needed to stop feeling guilty about the choices he'd made. Katherine wouldn't want him to sacrifice the rest of his life. Not when he still needed an heir.

He left the trunk in the middle of the room and extinguished the lamp and candles, one by one. When he stood in darkness, he paused a moment, as if waiting to hear her voice.

But there was nothing.

He returned to the hallway, closing the door behind him. For a long time he stood there, feeling the weight of Katherine's loss. But instead of the numbing grief, it was almost a sense of relief. She was gone from his life and would not return. Everything was changing, and he had no choice but to let go. He walked toward Amelia's room instinctively, without really knowing why.

She'd wanted him to kiss her. And she wanted to be treated like a wife. All he had to do was open the door and discard his clothing, slipping inside her bed. He could spend the night touching her, taking comfort in her arms. Right now, he needed to embrace her, to hold fast to a bright spirit that he was slowly suffocating in this house.

His hand paused upon the doorknob, while he tried to piece together what he would say. But there were no words to express his needs.

"Papa?" came the voice of a young girl from behind him. "I couldn't sleep."

He pushed back the ball of frustration and turned to face his daughter. Christine was standing barefoot in her nightgown, and she looked as lonely as he felt.

A moment later, she flew to him, hugging him hard. "I'm glad you're home," she whispered. "I missed you so much."

He embraced her in the hallway. "I missed you, too. Now you should go to bed."

"Will you walk back with me? It's very dark," she said.

"Of course." He returned to Katherine's room for a candle and lit it, before joining Christine.

They walked together for a time, his daughter's hand in his. When he glanced at her, he realized that in seven short years, she might be married. The thought was strange to imagine, but he was glad that Amelia was here to help Christine. She *would* make a good stepmother for his daughter.

David opened the door to the nursery and his daughter climbed back into bed. "Go to sleep," he bade her. After he left her room, he went to seek out his wife.

The doorknob turned easily as he entered Amelia's bedchamber.

She was sleeping in a linen nightdress, and the covers were tangled against her warm body. David removed his clothing and slipped in beside her.

"Did you need something?" she whispered sleepily.

"Yes." He needed her. He needed to drown himself in a physical release that would eradicate the memories that kept intruding. He didn't ask permission, but began touching her, using his mouth and hands to arouse her.

⚜

Amelia didn't know what had prompted him to visit her, but she welcomed her husband. The scent of the earl's skin was entrancing, of soap and warm male. Gently, she drew an arm around his torso, pulling him closer.

Although there was a sudden tension in his body, he didn't move or speak. Instead, he touched her hair, holding her against him. She kissed his ribs, moving beneath the covers to embrace him. David pushed up her nightdress, and she helped him pull it off. Her cool skin came into contact with his body, and it was shocking to feel his muscled chest against her breasts.

Her leg touched his, and her husband answered the unspoken question when he traced a path down her bare spine to rest upon her bottom. A shudder rocked through her, a yearning to touch and to be touched. She was afraid to move, uncertain of what to do now.

But David pulled her atop him, and she was taken aback by the sensation of his naked body beneath hers. His hands moved over her hair, down to her bare shoulders.

Gently, he eased her legs apart until she was straddling him. His thick erection pressed against her stomach, and she wondered if he wanted her to take command.

"Kiss me," he ordered.

Amelia raised herself higher, in order to reach his mouth, and the act nestled his erection against her intimate opening.

She was already wet between her legs, and his hands fixed upon her waist, holding her captive. Obeying him, she leaned down to kiss him. Her hair fell across her shoulders, tickling her bare skin.

David's mouth claimed hers, his tongue sliding within. The motion of his tongue entering and withdrawing was echoed below when he pressed her against his hard flesh. Her breathing grew hitched when his hands moved to the curve of her breasts. He teased her nipples, caressing the hard nubs with his thumbs.

The sensation shot a bolt of heat between her legs. As he explored the tips, she found herself moving against the thick pressure nudging at her entrance. She was overwhelmed by all the sensations, hardly able to claim a breath.

And the more he stroked her nipples, rubbing himself against her, the more she needed him. "I want you inside me," she whispered, trying to guide him.

"Not yet." He pressed her onto her back, caressing her hips. Amelia opened her legs wider, waiting for him, but he kissed her bare stomach, cupping her bottom with his hands.

Why was he moving lower? She couldn't understand until she felt the warmth of his breath against her opening.

"David, you don't have to—" Amelia began, but he cut off her words when he kissed her intimately. He explored her folds and crevices with his mouth and tongue, and the sensations overwhelmed her.

Dear God.

She fisted the sheets, her hips arching as he feasted upon her. His wicked tongue stroked her, and she was so close to the edge, she was trembling. It was a storm of reckless need, gathering intensity. She was aching for him, when suddenly, her body seized up with a thousand tremors. It was like a veil of ecstasy shimmering over every part of her skin. Just as the sensations tightened into a climax, he filled her with his shaft.

She gasped as he thrust inside. Over and over he penetrated, while his erection was rigid with need. He tormented her, making love to her while she welcomed his intrusion. His hand moved between them, and when he pressed the fold of flesh above her entrance, the echo of the earlier shimmering sensation returned.

"David," she whispered, unable to believe what she was feeling. Her body was now pliant to his thrusts, and she gripped his hips, trying to increase the speed.

Instead, he slowed down, circling her flesh with his thumb. Amelia found herself pressing back and squeezing him deep inside.

"Do that again," he commanded, and when she did, she heard him inhale audibly. "Yes. Just like that."

She was starting to feel the same delicious response that he'd conjured within her. It was a slow burn, a tidal pull of desire rushing over her. And she started to shake, straining for more of this.

A shudder rocked through her without warning, and she moaned, her nails digging into his backside as he brought her over the edge a second time. In answer to her release, he increased the pace of his thrusting, and she squeezed him harder, her body throbbing with a dark ache.

"I can't last much longer against this," he gritted out, and she wrapped both legs around his waist, trying to draw him closer.

"Do what you will," she whispered, riding out the pulse of a crest that kept building and rising. With every thrust, she embraced him, understanding that this went much deeper than the joining of a man and a woman. It was a giving of herself, pushing back his dark grief and offering the healing solace of her body.

He took and she gave, until at last he ground into her, his breath shuddering as he emptied himself.

Flesh to flesh, heartbeat to heartbeat, they embraced in the darkness. This . . . this was what she wanted from him. Only more than that, she wanted his love.

She wanted him to love her the way he had his first wife. Perhaps more. Her own heart was utterly lost now, but she held back the words. This was a beginning, and he wasn't ready to set aside the past.

"Stay," Amelia urged him.

David dropped a kiss on her mouth and reached for his fallen clothing. "You'll sleep better without me," he said, though it wasn't at all true. He said nothing more but pulled the coverlet over her before he departed.

For long moments, she stared at the wall, feeling abandoned. He didn't want to stay with her, and it hurt to know that. A hollow loneliness stole over her, but Amelia refused to pity herself. She was in love with the earl, and the only solution was to make *him* love her.

No matter how long it took.

David's actions had haunted Amelia for most of the night. She had never imagined he would come to her, but he'd left her feelings bruised. Though she knew it was normal for a husband to visit his wife and share her bed for an hour or two, she'd felt an overwhelming loneliness after he'd gone.

Then, too, his earlier confession that her kiss was better than Katherine's was even more bewildering. She'd never expected him to reveal such a thing. Especially when he hadn't wanted to marry her—not really.

Was he afraid of getting too close to her? Was that why he had abandoned her so swiftly?

Her marriage was a tangled mess, and try as she might, she had no idea how to mend the frayed edges. Thank goodness she had a distraction this morning, to draw her thoughts away from last night.

Amelia clutched her reticule, holding on tightly to the edge of the carriage as she drove to the village with Christine seated across from her. The girl's expression was sullen, and she had I-don't-want-to-be-here written all over her face. She had also come down with a cold and coughed frequently, her handkerchief clutched in one hand.

When they reached the village, the driver pulled the curricle to a stop, and he helped Amelia down first. When she held out a hand to Christine, the girl ignored it.

"We don't have to be enemies, you know," she pointed out.

"I loathe shopping." Her stepdaughter put on a long face and said, "And since we're alone, you needn't pretend to like me. I know you don't."

Amelia shrugged. "I can't say it's easy to like someone who tells me that I'm not wanted, and she'd rather resent me than get to know me."

At that, the girl quieted. Her expression held wariness, and when Amelia stepped forward, at least her stepdaughter followed. Glancing back at Christine, she asked, "Who created the gowns you're wearing?"

Christine gripped her skirts, her face holding wariness. "They were my mother's, from when she was a girl. I have no need of new clothes, since I have everything she wore."

It was now becoming clear that the girl was clinging as hard to the past as her father.

"Do you remember your mother at all? What was she like?" Amelia prompted.

"I was five when she died. I hardly remember her at all," Christine admitted. She sniffed and blew her nose in the handkerchief. "But Papa told me stories about her. And sometimes, if I close my eyes tight enough, I can remember what it felt like to be in her arms. She did love me."

There was a deep hunger for affection in the girl's voice. "So does your father," Amelia offered. "You mean the world to him." She opened the door to the first shop and waited for Christine to follow. "I'm trying to talk him into staying with us over the summer."

"He won't," the girl insisted. "He's too busy traveling. I ask him every year, and he always says no." She sniffled again and sneezed.

Amelia guessed the earl was avoiding the house, and a thought occurred to her. "When did your mother die?"

"Six years ago," Christine answered.

"Was it in the summertime?" Amelia walked over to look at a few bolts of fabric, keeping her voice low.

Her stepdaughter nodded. "In July."

Amelia didn't bother asking if Katherine had died at Castledon. Undoubtedly she had, particularly if the earl was avoiding this place every summer. It likely brought back bad memories.

To change the subject, she held up a bolt of rose muslin. "This is lovely. We could have a new dress made for you, and a ribbon of the same color for your hair."

"I told you, I don't need anything new to wear."

But Amelia didn't miss the way the girl's attention drifted to a bolt of lilac muslin. On impulse, she saw a length of deep violet ribbon and beckoned for the shopkeeper to approach. There was nothing Amelia enjoyed more than bargaining, particularly when it came to shopping. Perhaps it was because her family had endured poverty in the years her father had been fighting in the war. Although Aphrodite's Unmentionables had made it possible for her to buy new gowns and ribbons without worrying about the cost, she still couldn't bring herself to break old habits.

After the shopkeeper offered her the ribbon for one shilling, Amelia shook her head and sighed. "That is not at all the price they would charge for such ribbon in London." To Christine, she added, "Now you must be careful whilst shopping, to ensure that you do not pay more than the ribbon is worth."

"It's quite a fair price, my lady," the shopkeeper protested. The man appeared indignant that she would question him, until Amelia sent him a sly smile.

"For those who do not know better, I am sure you are right." Then she returned to the lilac muslin. "Now, the purple ribbon would make an excellent trim if I were to purchase four yards of this material. Lady Christine will need new gowns, and I know you would not try to ask too high of a price."

His eyes gleamed as he understood the game. "Perhaps if she also requires a new bonnet, we could come to an understanding on the price."

Amelia sent him an answering smile. "There may be some items I will choose for myself. But only as long as we remain in discussion about how you're going to lower the prices for me."

The man now appeared delighted, and he invited them to look around more. "Why don't you find what else is to your liking, and I'm certain we can agree upon a price that satisfies both of us?"

"We don't need any of this," Christine argued, sneezing again. "And why would you ask him to change the prices?"

"Has no one ever taken you shopping before?" she asked. When the girl shook her head, Amelia saw the bewilderment there.

"Well, Lady Christine, you are about to learn one of the joys of being a woman."

They spent the remainder of the day exploring the village, and Amelia purchased several bolts of muslin and lengths of ribbon for the young girl. She also arranged for a dressmaker to come to Castledon the next day to measure Christine for the new clothing. When they had finished for the day, the girl looked as if she was about to fall asleep. She leaned her head against the back of the carriage seat with a heavy sigh.

"Are you feeling all right?" Amelia asked. "You look tired."

"It's nothing," Christine insisted, sniffling again. "But we didn't need most of those things. My father will be very cross with you for buying so much."

"You will need all of it when you accompany us to London next Season," Amelia said. "And once the new gowns are ready, you will love them, I promise you."

"I *like* wearing my mother's clothes," the girl insisted.

"There is nothing wrong with that." Amelia kept her voice gentle, knowing it was Christine's way of holding on to a piece of her mother. "But it's nice to have new things as well."

"If you're trying to get me to like you by buying me things, it won't work," her stepdaughter insisted.

Amelia sighed. "Frankly, Christine, I don't care if you like me or not. Your father asked me to help you prepare for your debut in society, and you have a great deal to learn. I'm helping you out of courtesy to *him*, more than anything else."

The words were harsher than she'd intended, but it was the truth. David had rescued her from a scandal by marrying her. She'd promised to uphold her end of the bargain by taking care of his daughter—a daughter who wanted nothing to do with her.

On the journey back, Amelia drank in the sight of the green countryside with stone walls separating the land. The rolling hills and moors were sprinkled with trees, and the big blue sky seemed to embrace the land with lacy white clouds. Here at Castledon, she could almost imagine the stories of King Arthur and Camelot. It was near Yorkshire, and sometimes, on a clear day, she could see the gray sea, dotted with stones.

"It's beautiful here," she said, shielding her eyes against the sun. "You must love drawing the landscape."

"I don't actually like to draw," Christine admitted, dabbing at her nose. "I learned how because Miss Grant said that all young ladies must learn how to sketch and paint. But I'm not any good at it."

"Your father thinks you are," she said softly.

"He's never here," the girl admitted. "He doesn't know anything about me." Her tone was matter-of-fact, as if she was used to being left alone.

It made Amelia wonder if she'd guessed correctly about the girl's true interests. She had arranged a surprise for Christine—a purchase the girl hadn't known about. The brown paper parcel rested beside her, filled with different colors of ink, new quills, and paper. Amelia thought it might make a strong peace offering.

"When we're home, I want to go up into the attic," she said. "We might find a place for you to enjoy reading books." She shot her a sidelong glance. "Or somewhere you could write your stories."

"Why would I want to write stories in a dusty, hot attic?" Her stepdaughter dismissed the idea as ridiculous, but Amelia wouldn't be deterred. Christine hadn't denied that she liked to write, which made her think that she was on the right path.

"You never know what we might find up there. There might be more of your mother's belongings. Let's go and look."

"I don't want to. And besides—no one is allowed in the attic. Not even the servants."

Now that piqued Amelia's curiosity. "Why? Is your father trying to hide something up there?"

The girl paused a moment. "He says it's not a place for children."

"Oh, come, now. Use your imagination. Your father hasn't gone there in years. He forbids the servants to enter." Amelia lowered her voice in hushed excitement. "Perhaps there's a ghost who haunts the attic at night, keening for—"

"My mother isn't a ghost," Christine snapped.

Amelia stopped at once, for she hadn't been thinking of that at all. "That wasn't what I meant, Christine. I promise you, I would never imply something so cruel."

The girl went silent, staring outside. And now Amelia wished she'd never brought it up. "I was only trying to inspire a story, that's all. I was imagining the ghost of someone who lived here hundreds of years ago."

"The house isn't that old," Christine pointed out.

"Houses are often built on the site of an older dwelling," Amelia said. "I know many castles were built upon the ruins of medieval fortresses." She tried to entertain the girl on the way back with tales of history, but it seemed Christine had no interest in it.

When they were almost home, the girl interrupted her. "Why did you marry my father? Was it for his fortune?"

"No!" Amelia couldn't believe her stepdaughter would believe such a thing. But neither did she want to tell the girl about the viscount's attempt to elope with her. "He . . . needed a wife and a mother for you. And I found him to be a good man." She softened her voice. "He loves you very much."

Christine stared down at her shoes and dabbed at her nose again. "He might love me as his daughter. But he doesn't like me very much." She cast a sidelong glance at Amelia. "He's going to leave in a few weeks, and we won't see him until winter. You'll see."

The bitterness in her voice revealed a lonely girl who'd been hurt time and again. Amelia was beginning to see why she'd wanted her father to marry again. "I'll try to change his mind."

Christine sent her a dark smile. "If I couldn't change his mind, what makes you think you can?"

✣

The restless need to leave pulled at David. He often traveled south during this time of year, to Thornwyck, an estate near Wales. It was quiet, and the income was primarily from sheep and goats. There were no memories of Katherine there, for she'd never visited the property. It was the perfect place to escape, and right now, he needed a few weeks of solitude.

With each day he spent at Amelia's side, he found himself daydreaming about her. She embraced him openly, giving so much of herself, while he felt guilty for not giving enough. Friendship would never be adequate for Amelia. She needed a husband who would love her.

The sanctuary beckoned to him, and David ordered his valet to begin packing his belongings. "At once, my lord," the man agreed.

David stood before Katherine's room, and the silent tread of footsteps approached. Without looking up, he knew who was standing there.

"You're already leaving?" Amelia came up behind him, her face concerned. "I thought you would stay with Christine and me for a little longer."

"It's time that I visited Thornwyck," he told her. "It won't be for long, and then I'll return."

Amelia studied him for a moment, and then her hand closed over the doorknob to Katherine's room. "May I go inside?"

He wanted to refuse, but then, what purpose was there in hiding what was now only an empty bedchamber? "If you want to."

"Will you come with me?" She held out her hand, and he hesitated.

"I should speak with the servants and ensure that the coach is ready for my departure in the morning."

"Please," she said gently.

He took her hand, and when she opened the door, the trunk was still in the middle of the floor where he'd left it. Silk gowns and bonnets overflowed from the lid, but Amelia said nothing about it. Instead, she closed the door behind her.

"Do you want my help?" she asked, after a few minutes had passed. "If you tell me what you want removed from the room, I'll see to it."

"Leave it." This was his task to bear, and he didn't want her to intervene. "There's no need for you to bother her belongings."

Amelia moved forward and wrapped her arms around his waist. He knew he ought to embrace her, but in this room he found it all but impossible. "I bought some new clothes for Christine yesterday. She's outgrown hers, and I heard that she was wearing Katherine's old gowns."

"She can have them if she wants them," he said. "Though I imagine they're too long for her."

"David, if you must go to Thornwyck, take us with you," Amelia pleaded. "Christine feels as if you abandon her all the time."

He said nothing, for in all likelihood it was true. He knew very little about children, and though he loved his daughter, he had no idea what her needs were.

"She has you now," he said. "You'll be there for her when I can't be."

"She despises me," Amelia countered. "She had the idea that you should have wed Miss Grant, her governess."

"Miss Grant was past forty," he countered. "She couldn't have given me an heir for Castledon if she'd wanted to."

"I could," Amelia said softly.

He knew it, and the very mention of giving her a child distracted him with the way her lips were moving and the proximity of her body.

"Do you believe you're expecting a child?" he asked. A slight sense of unrest gripped him at the thought. Pregnancy was always dangerous.

"Not yet." Her voice was hesitant, and she admitted, "But I would like to keep trying. If you want to, that is."

"Every time I'm near you, I want to." He took her mouth, kissing her hard. Ignoring all caution, he pressed his fingers into her hair, pulling her hips to his so she would know what she'd done to him.

She returned the kiss, opening to him. Against his mouth she murmured, "Shall we go to my room?"

His body raged with him to say yes, to take her by the hand and love her for the next few hours. Instead, he broke away, gathering the shreds of his control. He couldn't keep using her like this, as a means of forgetting about Katherine and the past. It wasn't fair to Amelia, and it wasn't right. Not when he could see the yearning on her face.

"Another time," he promised. But when he left her, he didn't miss the regret in her eyes.

BALLALOCH, SCOTLAND

"You can't go on like this."

Beatrice looked up at her husband, who was standing at the doorway to her bedroom. There was still no sign of Margaret, not after all the weeks of searching. They had retraced all the major roads leading to Scotland and had hired runners to investigate. But her daughter had virtually disappeared with Cain Sinclair.

She didn't know whether the man had hurt Margaret or rescued her. And it was the not knowing that tormented her most.

Henry came inside the room and stood beside her at the window. "We won't stop searching. I promise you that. But when was the last time you ate a full meal?"

She shrugged. "I don't feel like eating when my daughter is gone." The days had blurred together in a sea of anguish. At night, the dreams of death plagued her, while during the day, she couldn't bring herself to leave the room.

"I won't let you punish yourself like this," Henry said. He went over to the table where her untouched breakfast tray had been abandoned. "You need to eat."

"I don't want it." Any sort of food would stick to her throat, or worse, cause a rush of nausea. "I can't, Henry."

He took a piece of dry toast and offered it to her. "Please. You must try."

But she shook her head slowly. And Henry's gentleness suddenly vanished. "Dying won't bring her back, Beatrice. You have to go on, whether you want to or not."

"And why should I?" she blurted out. All the words came rushing out, the anger roaring through her. "Margaret only wanted to find Amelia and bring her home. She went off with—with *that man* only because he knew the roads. If she's dead, why would I deserve to go on?"

The words were irrational, she knew, but it was the truth.

"Because of me," Henry demanded. "I've lost a daughter, too. And I'll be damned if I lose my wife." He dropped the toast back on the plate and pulled her into his arms. "I wasn't there for you, all those years I was at war. I know you had to mother our girls by yourself. But I'm here now."

His words broke a small crack in all the feelings she was trying to hold back. Feeling his strong arms around her, knowing that he understood her pain, was enough to provoke the tears she'd buried.

Beatrice started crying then, and he stroked her hair, sharing the burden with her. She hadn't known how much she'd been holding inside. She wept, not only for the loss of Margaret, but for all the years she'd tried to shoulder everything.

"I won't ever leave you," Henry said, and she felt his mouth against her temple. She gripped him hard, and in his quiet presence, she found the support she'd needed for so long. He *did* know how she was suffering, and it felt so good to release it all.

She didn't know how long she'd cried, but in the end, exhaustion overtook her. Henry dried her tears, and then framed her face with his hands. "We're going to get past this, Beatrice. I promise you."

Then he bent and kissed her mouth. The light kiss was familiar, and when she kissed him back, it was as if the seams of a torn hem were coming back together again. Theirs had been a marriage formed of duty and friendship, nothing more. And yet, when he pulled back from the kiss, she found herself wishing that he hadn't stopped. The loneliness she'd carried like a mantle was starting to drift away. And though his dark hair was shot with gray, his green eyes held kindness and a longing that mirrored her own.

A soft ripple flowed through her, and when she embraced him again, she found herself pressing against his body, seeking comfort. It startled her to realize that she desired him. Even after all this time.

She took a shaky breath and reached for the forgotten toast. Before she could lift it to her mouth, he stopped her. "I brought your favorite jam."

Red raspberry. She almost smiled when he spread the toast with the preserves, but didn't. The taste of the sweet jam and the bread heightened her appetite. Henry poured her a cup of cold tea, but when he offered to ring for more, she refused and drank it anyway.

Yes, she did need to live. For so long, she'd shadowed her daughters' lives, watching them grow into women. She'd forgotten herself, letting everything fade into the background until she was hardly more than a ghost of a woman.

Henry touched his finger to the corner of her lip, wiping the jam away, before he stole a taste of it. Color flooded her cheeks, for she suddenly imagined sharing his bed again. It had been so very long . . . but she had enjoyed his touch.

"I brought you a birthday gift a few weeks ago," he said. "Would you like to see it now?"

She nodded, taking a second piece of toast and spreading jam upon it. "As long as it isn't doorknobs." A faint smile touched her lips, as she remembered the terrible time when he'd given her those for her birthday.

"No. It isn't." He went toward her writing desk and pulled open one of the side drawers that had a hidden back. After he pulled away the false opening, he brought out a velvet pouch. "I put it here, shortly after we arrived."

Though she couldn't say why, her heartbeat started to quicken. The flush from her cheeks spread over her skin, giving her goose bumps.

And when he opened the pouch and revealed a sapphire brace-let, her throat choked up with more tears. "Is that—?"

"I know you had to sell it, years ago, to feed our girls. Charlotte bought it herself and never told you. She was glad to sell it back to me." He fastened the clasp around her wrist, and the glitter of diamonds and sapphires caught the morning sunlight. "I only wish you'd never had to use it."

The heavy weight of the gemstones was a contrast to the lightness in her heart. "It's much better than doorknobs," she whispered, and embraced him hard.

Tonight, she decided. Despite all that had happened to them, he'd given her a tangible hope that they could rebuild their marriage. For a long moment, she rested her cheek against his, taking so much comfort from her husband.

The harsh pounding on her bedroom door made her frown, wondering why a servant would be calling out to her. Henry pulled back and opened the door.

"Forgive me, my lord," the footman said. "But your daughter Margaret has returned. She's downstairs."

Nothing could have dimmed Beatrice's joy at that moment.

⚜

David looked up from the letter he'd been writing when the noise of a visitor arriving caught his attention. He'd delayed his trip to Thornwyck after Christine's cold had turned into a coughing sickness, but now she seemed much improved.

Curious as to whom the visitor could be, he set down his pen and moved into the hall.

"Och, my lass, but 'tis good to see you!"

David was startled to see a barrel-waisted woman embracing Amelia in the hallway. He'd never seen the Scotswoman before and had no idea who she was. What on earth was going on?

"And you, Mrs. Larson. I'm so glad you came." Amelia hugged her back, seemingly overjoyed at the woman's arrival.

His wife began talking at a rapid pace, and David hung back, waiting for an introduction. He didn't know if the Scotswoman was a distant family member or why she was here, but he didn't remember Amelia mentioning anything about a visitor.

When he walked closer, Amelia beamed and drew him forward to be introduced. "My lord, this is Mrs. Larson, my mother's housekeeper."

Although he was polite and nodded in greeting, David was unprepared for the woman's enthusiastic curtsy. "Thank ye for inviting me, m'lord. I've known Miss Amelia since she was a wee lass, and when she wrote and asked me to help with this household, I came straightaway." She clasped her hands and looked around. "It's a lovely home ye have here. I'm certain we can get everything sorted out in a matter of days."

Sorted? He hadn't given Amelia permission at all to invite another servant to Castledon. And what did she mean she was here to help with the household? David sent Amelia a warning look, which she completely ignored. "Mrs. Larson, our butler, Mr. Haverford, will be glad to show you to your room. Then I'd like to speak to you about your duties here."

David cleared his throat. "And how long were you planning to stay, Mrs. Larson?"

"Och, long enough to see that my wee lamb has everything well in hand," the Scotswoman declared. "She's given me an earful, she has, about all the changes that need to be made."

The woman propped her fists against her waist. "And don't you be worrying a bit, my lord. When I've finished with this place, you'll be thanking me and begging me to stay. But I must return to Lady Lanfordshire within a fortnight. Not a day longer," she informed him as she turned to follow Mr. Haverford up the stairs.

David took Amelia by the hand and led her back into the drawing room. In a low voice, he demanded, "Exactly what were your intentions with bringing her here, Amelia?"

"I haven't interfered at all with your servants," she said sprightly. "I simply brought in a housekeeper who *would* obey my orders. I haven't sacked anyone, much as they might deserve it."

"I've already spoken with Mrs. Menford and the others," he informed her. "If anyone disobeyed your orders again, you should have told me. There was no need to bring in an outsider."

"Mrs. Larson is family, not an outsider," she corrected. "And we can continue our discussion in private while she gets settled." Without waiting for him to agree, she began striding away.

David followed and saw that she was returning to her room. He hurried to catch up, and when he opened her door, he saw that she was sitting down at her desk.

She picked up her quill and began writing a list of something. Although her manner was composed, he suspected that she was simmering beneath the surface. His own mood was heating up, especially when she'd said nothing about bringing in another housekeeper. It made him wonder what other changes she was contemplating.

"What are you doing, Amelia?" he asked, coming to stand beside the desk. She continued scribbling her list, until he pulled the quill from her hand.

"I am making a list."

He picked up the paper and saw that it was indeed a list of changes. It seemed that she intended to redecorate Katherine's room and give it to Christine.

"Absolutely not." He'd only just managed to pack away his wife's belongings. And now she wanted to force his daughter to live in the same room where Katherine had died?

"She is eleven years old—almost twelve. She's too old to be in the nursery, and she needs a room of her own."

"Not that one," he shot back. "It's highly inappropriate."

Amelia stood up from the desk and regarded him. "She loves her mother a great deal. Why do you think she wears Katherine's old gowns? She wants to be close to her, and if she has the old room, she'll have a part of her mother."

There was sincerity in her voice, like a woman wanting to heal a broken little girl. And then she added, "She'll read books from her mother's shelves, and she'll sit at the hearth where Katherine spent her time."

"She took her last breath in that room," he told his wife. "Don't you think it will bother Christine?"

"She was only five when her mother died. But I will give her that choice," Amelia continued. "If Christine feels uncomfortable, I'll offer her a different room. She can also help pick out the drapes and rearrange the furniture, if she wants to."

He was torn between agreeing with her and arguing against making any changes. This was his estate, his home. And he didn't want her turning it upside down in his absence.

"And what other changes are you planning?" he asked, glancing at the list. "To change our food?"

She folded her arms across her chest, blocking his view of her curves. "Indeed, yes. It's entirely unpalatable. I prefer my dinner to taste good."

The defiance on her face, along with her dry comment, made him want to fluster her mood. "Is that so?" He pulled her hips to his, lowering his mouth to her throat. She shuddered when the warmth of his breath met her skin.

"Y-yes."

"Aren't you afraid of the consequences, if you make too many changes?"

"You won't be here to stop me," she murmured, trying to pull away. He held her trapped, watching the way she was beginning to respond to his touch. "Being a well-behaved young woman hasn't worked well for me thus far, has it?" Her voice was barely above a whisper, but the wickedness in her tone spoke of rebellion.

"Aren't you afraid of being punished?" He drew his thumb over her lips and saw her flush deepen. "I will come back, you know."

"I'm not afraid of you," she responded. "You're all bark and no bite."

Her open provocation made him react on instinct. He seized her roughly and kissed her hard, silencing the insolent words. The moment he did, she clung hard, her fingers gripping his hair. He responded to her, unable to stop himself from moving against her hips. The feeling of her softness yielding against his arousal made him desire her more.

He broke free of the kiss, nipping at her earlobe. Against her sensitive flesh, he whispered, "Oh, but I do bite, Amelia. Especially when someone taunts me."

She was breathing harder, and gooseflesh covered her skin. Her hands moved down from his neck, slipping beneath his shirt. "Perhaps that's what I should have done all along." Her smooth hands caressed his nape, and the sharp fist of desire struck him.

He wanted to lift her up and claim her this very moment, but he forced the urge back. "I'm leaving in the morning," he told her. "When I return, I want nothing to be changed."

"Everything will change," she said. "I'll handle the consequences later." She squeezed his neck and kissed him again. "Sometimes it's necessary to misbehave."

Her insinuation made him imagine all sorts of misbehavior, all of which involved her being naked in his bed. She was tangling him up in knots, making him want her when he had tried to keep his life in order.

"Don't do something you'll regret." He let go of her, stepping away to keep himself from losing command. Right now, he was envisioning undressing her, using his mouth upon her bare skin, and taking her until she arched with delight.

"The only thing I regret is not acting sooner," she answered. With a smile, she led him out of her room. "I intend to be very, very bad."

God help him.

"That woman is the Antichrist," admitted Mrs. Larson the following morning, when Amelia met with the Scotswoman at the top of the attic stairs. She led the housekeeper inside and closed the door to give them more privacy. "Mrs. Menford, I mean," the Scotswoman said. "She terrorizes the puir staff, and if a body says aught against her, she sends them off to work with nary a bite to eat. *She* is the problem."

Which wasn't at all a surprise to Amelia.

"And if I get a new housekeeper?" Amelia asked. "Will the others fall in line?"

"'Twill no' be easy. Many of the servants are her nieces and nephews. Ye'll have to find someone who's no' related to her."

Amelia thought about it for a moment. "I think we should ask her to go on holiday for a few days, and I'll let you run the household during that time. We should see if there's a kitchen maid or an older servant who could take her place."

"I'd wait until His Lordship is away," Mrs. Larson advised. "She willna go easily, and ye'll have better luck when he's no' here to naysay the orders."

Amelia agreed with that assessment. Changing the subject, she asked, "What do you think of this space in the attic? Will Christine like it for writing her stories?"

The housekeeper surveyed the room. Over the past few weeks, Amelia had worked here in secret, clearing out the older furniture and making a space beside the window. From here, the girl could see across the gardens, and there was enough sunlight for writing. She'd also set out the paper, new pens, and ink that she'd purchased on the day they'd gone shopping.

"Aye, that she will," Mrs. Larson said. "But I sense trouble from the lass. She doesna like ye verra much, does she?"

"Christine has made it quite clear that she doesn't want me as her mother. And I can't say that I know what I'm doing, either." Amelia sat down in the chair beside the window, staring out at the rainy summer day. Clouds misted across the horizon, revealing patches of green. "This wasn't what I thought my life would be like, Mrs. Larson."

"It ne'er is, dove. But at least ye have a good husband, and ye'll have children of yer own, soon enough."

Amelia said nothing, for her courses had come and gone twice already. There might not be a child for months yet. And if David was leaving for Thornwyck, there was no chance at all to conceive.

"He *has* done his bit, has he no'?" the housekeeper asked. "If he's needing a charm to help get it up, I suppose I could mix up a potion to put in his tea. There are ways—"

Amelia choked on the woman's mistaken belief. "No. No, that's not the problem. We—we have already consummated the marriage."

Her face was burning with humiliation. "He's simply getting over the loss of his wife."

Mrs. Larson softened at that. "Och, well, then, he's confused. How long has the puir man been alone?"

"Six years," Amelia answered.

"Six?" The housekeeper rolled her eyes. "That's plenty o' time to put the past to rest. And if the man hasna had much of a romp in six years, he's like to burst open."

Amelia's face flushed even hotter. "I've taken matters into my own hands."

The old woman cackled. "Ye should take *him* into yer own hands, lass. I promise it willna take long for him to be coaxed."

"Mrs. Larson!" Amelia was appalled to hear the woman speaking so plainly.

"Ah, but ye're married now, my wee dove. Bed yer husband every night, and all will be right again. And he'll do your bidding when it comes to the servants."

Amelia wasn't so sure about that. The earl had made it quite clear he didn't want her interference. But then, she was far too wary about letting things be the way they were. She was not a shy flower to wilt in the face of adversity. No, she intended to stand up for herself and make all the necessary changes.

"I'll . . . take care of it," she said at last. "And in the meantime, we'll leave a note for Christine that she can now enjoy this place of her own." Amelia had often wished for a retreat from her sisters, a place where she could be alone and dream. The attic space would be perfect for her stepdaughter.

Mrs. Larson opened her arms and offered a warm embrace. "Don't fash yerself about yer husband. He'll love ye, sure enough."

Amelia wanted to believe it, especially after she'd stood up to

Lord Castledon last night. His fierce kisses twined around her imagination, making her long for more. "He's leaving today."

"Then what on earth are ye doing here? Go on now, and interrupt him before he goes." The housekeeper shooed her off, adding, "I'll finish here."

Amelia ventured a quiet smile, though she suspected the earl had other plans.

Chapter Twelve

Sarah was beginning to wonder if she'd done the right thing in delaying her journey. Although Brandon had been released from the asylum after he'd proven that he understood their questions, she sensed a darkness in him. He'd spoken on several occasions about killing everyone in the Andrews family—starting with Paul Fraser and his wife, Juliette.

Her earlier relief at his recovery had now turned to fear. She didn't know her brother anymore, and he appeared emotionless, as if he frankly didn't care about the consequences of his actions. Though she didn't want to believe he would go through with his plans for murder, his calculating demeanor gave her pause.

She'd found a scrap of paper among his belongings, with every Andrews name listed upon it, including the other three sisters, Lady Lanfordshire, and her husband, the baron.

A coldness settled in her bones, for her brother spoke of killing in the same manner as disposing of an irritating insect. Brandon knew exactly how to appear calm and composed, speaking the right words to the authorities, until he'd reestablished his claim upon the title and entailed lands.

If she remained here with him, she could be implicated in whatever crimes he committed. Sarah closed her eyes, trying to think of how she could slip away. She still had the funds and jewels Amelia had given her, but it didn't sit well on her conscience to disappear without warning them. But how? She couldn't very well travel to Scotland. Perhaps it was best if she wrote to them. She could—

"You seem nervous, Sarah," came Brandon's voice.

She took a breath and faced him. With a false smile, she said, "Not at all. But I was thinking we should return to Strathland and see what's happened to the estate there. Our cousin took control while you were . . . away . . . and I don't know what decisions he made in your absence. And there's the estate in the Highlands as well."

"As it happens, I *do* intend to travel to Scotland," he said. "I'll be visiting Edinburgh first."

The blood drained away from her face, for that was not far from where Juliette and Dr. Fraser lived. For many years, her brother had obsessed over Juliette Andrews, but the young woman had run away and married the Scottish doctor. Brandon had never forgotten it.

"Oh?" She tried to act as if it were nothing. "And how long will you be gone?"

"That doesn't matter to you, for you'll be accompanying me."

No. She could play no part in this. "Brandon, I have plans of my own. I'm leaving within the week."

His expression curved into a smirk. "No. You won't." He made a hand motion for someone to enter, and when Sarah turned around, she saw a tall man approaching. He closed in on her, seizing both of her arms until she cried out in pain.

"You're going to pay a call on Juliette, on my behalf."

"Why would I want to?" she gritted out, well aware that the man behind her could easily break her arms.

"Because if you don't, I'll let Richardson have you. You can spend the entire journey to Scotland in a coach with him, and I'll wager he'll enjoy it more than you will."

The man's hot breath made her skin crawl, and Sarah demanded, "Release me."

At a nod from Brandon, he did. But she strongly suspected her brother had hired the man to help him kill the others. She had to run away from both of them, and today would be her only chance.

"I'll go and pack," she informed him. But inwardly, she prayed she could slip away before either of them knew she was missing.

After saying farewell to Christine, David paused at the bottom of the stairs. Though he knew Amelia had been looking for him, he wanted a moment to clear his head. It was necessary to leave, for he *did* need to inspect Thornwyck and his other estates.

The sadness in his daughter's eyes had reminded him of Amelia's accusation, that he abandoned her too often. And he was avoiding his wife, too.

He admitted to himself that he would miss her. Not only the life she'd breathed into him, but her smile and the way she filled the empty spaces. If he didn't leave now, he would come to depend upon her. He would undoubtedly fall in love with Amelia.

And he didn't want to cross that line—not again.

He started to leave the house, and Mrs. Larson interrupted, "Lord Castledon, will you be wanting any food to take with ye on your journey?" She offered to go and fetch him something, but David refused.

"Not now, thank you. But you can see to it that the footmen load my trunks into the coach for departure. I'll be leaving to go north in the next hour or two."

The older woman's face dimmed, but she curtseyed. "Are ye certain I shouldna be packing Lady Castledon's belongings as well? I can speak to her maid, if ye like."

"No. I'll be going alone to Thornwyck." He turned away and ordered a horse from the stables. Before he left, he wanted to ride to the edges of his estate, simply to escape the wayward thoughts in his brain.

When the horse was ready, his groom helped him to mount the gelding, and David urged it onward. Outside the air was ghostly, the grass cloaked in mist. He rode without thinking, directing the animal to go faster.

His mind turned over the image of Amelia, of her smile and the way she stood up to him at every turn. She was so very different from Katherine. The image of his first wife's face haunted him, and he closed his eyes, forcing it back. He'd had enough of this. He had to relinquish the memories, or he'd fall into madness.

I'm letting you go, he told her ghost.

David increased the pace, turning back toward the house. He hardly cared that the landscape was blurring past them at immense speed. The horse stumbled abruptly, and David had no time to grasp the reins before he fell hard. The gelding whinnied and rolled for a moment before getting back up. He breathed a little easier when he saw that the animal appeared uninjured.

He sat up and saw blood running down over his palms. His body ached from the fall, and for long moments, he remained sitting on the ground. A few minutes later, Amelia arrived at his side.

"I saw you fall. Are you all right?" she asked. Her hair was undone around her shoulders, and it appeared that she'd been running hard.

He remained transfixed by the blood on his palms, and he took a steadying breath. "It's nothing."

Amelia knelt down beside him and took his hand. "You could have broken your neck," she said, fear creasing her face. "I was so worried about you." She gave him a handkerchief, and he wiped at the blood. For a moment, he held on to the stained bit of linen.

"Mrs. Larson said you're leaving." Her face was pale with dismay. "I wish you would take us with you."

The urge was there, to tell her yes. And yet, when he looked into her deep green eyes, he saw the face of a woman who was in love with him. If he asked her to go into a searing desert, she would. She reached up to touch his cheek, and he looked past her, stroking the back of her hair. He should have known this might happen. He'd never intended to hurt Amelia—had never wanted to.

But he honestly didn't want to be in love again. He wasn't worthy of such devotion, and it was best to separate himself. He no longer trusted his ability to remain apart from her.

"I can't take you along," he said. "Not this time."

His groom arrived on horseback then, saving him the trouble of saying anything more. The man took one look at them and reddened. "My lord, I am sorry to disturb you, but your coach is ready to depart."

"Thank you." He took Amelia by the hand. "Lady Castledon and I will walk back. Tell my daughter I would like to see her once more before I leave."

After the groom had left, Amelia held back from walking toward the house. Her face appeared shielded, as if she were suppressing her emotions.

"May I speak frankly, Lord Castledon?"

So. They were back to formal terms again. "You always do," he felt compelled to answer.

She gripped her hands together. "I don't want to be the left-behind wife. I want to be at your side, learning what I need to know about all of our properties."

"It's nothing you need to worry about."

"Then what *do* I need to worry over? You don't want me to make any changes in the household, and I'm not allowed to even see the other estates. You make me feel like a paper doll, good for nothing more than decoration." Her eyes were glittering with frustration. "I won't let you brush me aside. Especially not after the way you make me feel when we're together."

He didn't know what to say anymore. She *did* make him feel, more than he had in the past six years. And he didn't want to go through that madness again.

"We agreed that our marriage would be an arrangement," he said, even knowing that the words were cruel. "I have provided for your needs, and in time, we may have an heir of our own. But don't lift up your hopes for more, Amelia." His hands tightened upon her shoulders. "I lost one wife, and it nearly killed me to watch her die. I won't go through that again."

"I have no intention of dying," she said softly. "I'm perfectly healthy."

"So was she. And the sickness came without warning. She was dead within five months." He released her, quickening his pace so she had no choice but to keep up with him. "You are a good woman, Amelia, with a large heart. Give your love to Christine. Not to me, for I can't return it."

"You won't return it," she countered. "You won't let anyone inside that stone heart of yours."

He stopped walking and stared at her. "You want more than I'm capable of giving."

"And what about the nights we've shared?" she demanded. "Were they worth nothing to you?" Her face paled as if afraid of his answer.

Damn it all, he was going to have to hurt her feelings. He didn't want to speak the words to make her hate him, but neither did he want her to love him. "I see nothing wrong with enjoying the physical side to our marriage, if it pleases you."

She stopped walking, gripping her arms tightly. The fury on her face was harsh, of a woman who loathed what he'd said.

"You're lying to me. I can see that you do feel something for me. Even if you don't want to."

He continued walking away, while a tight ache caught in his throat. This was what he hadn't wanted—for her to see the cold-hearted man he'd become.

And when he reached the waiting coach, he saw her standing on the hillside, refusing to come any closer.

ॐ

Amelia left the first clue for Christine on her bed. She knew better than to show the girl the writing space she'd prepared. Christine would only scoff and turn up her nose. But Amelia truly believed that the girl would enjoy the new paper and quills, as well as a special place for writing. And so it was that she'd invented a treasure hunt, with each note leading to another clue.

She pretended not to notice when Christine entered the drawing room, with a note in her hand. "Why would you think I'd be interested in your silly games?" The girl's tone held ridicule, but Amelia noticed that she was wearing the lilac muslin gown they had bought together. It was a small victory, and so she ignored her stepdaughter's rudeness.

"I don't know what you're talking about," Amelia lied, pouring herself a cup of tea. "It's not a game. Your father simply wanted to leave you a gift." If she told the girl it was from David, she might be more willing to accept it. "I thought this would be a more interesting way for you to find it."

Her stepdaughter frowned a moment. "A gift from Papa?"

"Who else?" Amelia pretended as if it didn't matter and reached for a biscuit dusted in sugar.

"But *you* wrote these clues," she said. "I know your handwriting."

"He's the one who purchased it for you. I simply thought it would be a more adventurous way to give the gift." She held out a plate to Christine. "Would you like a biscuit?"

The girl shook her head, confusion reigning over her face. "No." In her hand, she held the last clue Amelia had left. "But you want me to go into the attic. I can't."

The girl's face held dismay, and Amelia offered, "Do you want me to go with you?"

Christine hesitated. "He told me to never go up there."

More likely this had to do with the first Lady Castledon. Perhaps David had stored his wife's belongings in the attic. "You were younger then," she said gently. "He probably thought you might fall down the stairs. They are rather steep."

"He told me not to go up there," Christine repeated. Her hands clenched against the lilac muslin, as if she didn't know how else to protest.

Amelia didn't know what to say to that, but it was clear the girl believed it. "Well, if you don't want to see the gift he left, I won't force you." She stood and walked with Christine back to the doorway. For a moment, her stepdaughter swayed, as if fighting off dizziness. Christine reached out a hand to the wall and caught herself.

"Are you all right?" Amelia wasn't certain if the girl was still weak from her earlier cold.

"I'm fine. I just felt faint for a moment." Christine took several deep breaths and tried to steady herself. "And my toes are tingling. It's strange."

Amelia offered the girl her arm. "Perhaps walking will help. Sometimes my feet feel that way if I've been sitting for a while." She eyed the girl. "Do you want to go into the attic to see the surprise, as long as you don't touch anything?" After all the hard work, Amelia wanted to see her stepdaughter's reaction.

"I suppose my father might not know I was there," Christine amended. "Don't tell him *or* Mrs. Menford. She tells him everything I've done wrong."

It was the peace offering she'd hoped for. "I wouldn't dream of it."

Mrs. Menford had been wise enough to retreat after Mrs. Larson had explained the full extent of her duties and the consequences of disobedience. Though Amelia wasn't entirely eager to keep the disagreeable woman on her staff, it did seem that she had relented.

Amelia smiled and offered Christine her support while they went down the hallway. Although the girl still seemed a little dizzy, she linked her arm in Amelia's.

They walked up to the third floor, and at the top of the stairs, she opened the small doorway leading to the attic. "Go inside and see."

Christine entered, while Amelia stood back to watch. The interior of the space was lit by the sunlight filtering through the windows. A small desk rested right beneath the window, and there was a stack of fresh paper along with different quills and inkwells.

The moment she saw the desk, Christine went still. She spoke not a word, but stood before the desk, staring at it. Amelia waited for her to say something, but her stepdaughter remained quiet.

"Is it . . . not what you wanted?" she ventured.

Christine crossed her arms, clenching her shoulders as she turned to face Amelia. "My father didn't give me this gift. *You* did."

Something in the girl's voice warned Amelia not to argue. And so she simply nodded once. "I thought you might like a place of your own where you can write your stories. We could even build a seat beneath the window and add cushions where you can curl up and read."

The girl let out a breath and touched one of the pieces of paper. "I never told him I like to write. Papa doesn't know."

"Was it meant to be a secret?"

Christine shook her head. "But he never asks me what I like to do. He's kind enough, but for so long, he never seemed to notice me."

Amelia saw the vulnerability the girl was trying to mask. "He abandoned you for too long."

Christine shrugged. "I don't suppose I was very interesting when I was little."

"It's hard to be interesting when your father is always gone." Amelia leaned back against the desk. "I think we should pay him a visit at Thornwyck, don't you?"

"He'll be furious with us."

"Oh, undoubtedly. But don't you think it's time that we became interesting to him?" She picked up a piece of paper. "Why don't you write a story about an earl who abandoned his only daughter, and she was rescued from her tower by a handsome prince?"

A smirk stole over Christine's face. "No prince would come after me."

"Or perhaps the daughter climbed out of the tower and ran off with the prince before her father returned?"

Her stepdaughter's face softened at the story idea. "Perhaps." She went over to the attic window and opened it, letting in the fresh air. "You're not that bad, you know. As a stepmother."

"I might have lured you here to lock you in," Amelia suggested. "I might be worse than you expected."

The girl climbed up on the desk, not responding to her teasing remark. She shielded her eyes against the sun and said, "There's a widow's walk on top of the house. Did you know?"

Amelia's stomach lurched when she saw where Christine was pointing. "I see it."

"I'm going to walk outside and look over the grounds. Do you want to come?"

The idea of standing on the rooftop of the house was not a welcome one. "No, and I don't want you to walk out there, either. You could fall and be killed."

"There's a railing up here," Christine said. "It's perfectly safe." She took one step onto the roof, and Amelia scrambled forward.

"Please come back. Truly, your father wouldn't want you out there. And neither do I."

"It's a lovely view." Christine rested her hands upon the railing, staring out over the landscape. "You should come and join me."

The thought of setting a single foot upon the rooftop terrified Amelia. "I can't." Her heart was pounding so fast, she could only bring herself to call out, "Christine, you must come back."

The girl let out a sigh and said, "All right." She took a few steps back toward the window, then suddenly swayed without warning. Her knees buckled, and she grabbed the edge of the chimney to keep from falling.

A scream caught in Amelia's throat, but she clamped her mouth shut to keep from startling the girl more. "Hold on, Christine. I'm coming." She ignored the shudder of panic rising in her stomach. Her stepdaughter was on her hands and knees, terror in her eyes.

"I'm sorry." The tears started to come, and the girl's knuckles were white against the brick. "All of a sudden, my feet went numb.

I don't know what happened. I couldn't feel anything when I took a step."

Amelia climbed on top of the desk, and when she risked a look down, her fear doubled. Oh, dear God, if she made a single misstep, she would die.

Don't think of that, she warned herself. Instead, she focused her attention on Christine's pale face. The girl was shaking, and Amelia ventured onto the roof, keeping to her hands and knees for balance.

"I'm going to help you get back inside," she said. Her words were calm, belying her own dread. "I want you to try and sit on the walkway."

"I'm afraid," Christine sobbed. "Why can't I feel my legs?"

Amelia didn't answer, but kept all her attention on reaching the girl. "Don't worry about that now. I'm going to help you back inside first."

Silent prayers rose up inside her when she finally was able to touch Christine's hand. "Can you crawl forward?"

"I don't know," she wept. "I might fall. I don't want to die."

"That won't happen," she promised. Though inwardly Amelia wanted to join the girl in her tears, she had to be strong. "I'm going to crawl behind you, and I'll make sure you don't fall when you move back inside." Blood pulsed hard within her veins, but she forced back the fear. "Don't move."

It was awkward, trying to crawl around Christine on the narrow walkway leading to the roof, but she managed. Only when she was seated behind the girl did she coax her to crawl forward.

One of Amelia's legs dangled down the side of the roof, and if she leaned too far to the right, she would tumble to her death.

God help us both, she prayed. Once, Christine's knees swayed, and Amelia grabbed the girl by the waist to steady her. "It's all right," she soothed. "We're almost there."

The last three minutes seemed to become an hour, and Amelia could hardly breathe until Christine reached the window. Only when they were both safely inside did she allow her own tears to fall.

The girl launched herself into Amelia's arms and sobbed out her relief. "I'm so, so sorry for what I did. I should never have walked out alone."

Amelia hugged the girl back, and at the moment, she wasn't certain if she could take a single step of her own. "I think we both should have a cup of chocolate right now. With the biggest slice of cake Mrs. Larson can find for us." She pulled back and wiped her eyes. "Are your legs any better?" It was then that she realized that Christine was still holding on to her for balance.

Her stepdaughter shook her head. "I can't feel my feet or my ankles."

Amelia kept her arm around the girl's waist. "Can you walk at all?"

"I can. But it feels so strange." She leaned against Amelia, her feet shuffling along the floor. "I've never felt like this before."

An awful premonition struck Amelia, and though she put on a brave face for the girl, inwardly she was shaking. It wasn't right for her to be unable to feel anything in her legs, and her stepdaughter needed to see a doctor.

Her sister Juliette's husband, Dr. Paul Fraser, was a skilled physician as well as the Viscount of Falsham. *He* would know what to do, and she trusted him far more than anyone here. She decided to write to him today and ask him to come and look at Christine. Thankfully, Castledon was only a few days' journey from Edinburgh. She felt confident that Dr. Fraser would know what to do if something was wrong.

"I'm going to send for the best doctor I know," Amelia reassured her stepdaughter. "But I don't want you to worry. It might be some lingering problems from your cold. Your body may be overtired."

Christine gripped her harder around the waist as they went down the attic stairs together. "What if it isn't? What if I'm going to die, just as my mother did?"

"I don't think it's as bad as all that," Amelia soothed. "And Dr. Fraser is the best physician I know. He's married to my sister Juliette."

Her stepdaughter said nothing more as they returned downstairs. True to her word, Amelia ordered Mrs. Larson to fetch them a pot of chocolate, as well as cake for their tea. Although Christine was able to walk, she seemed unsteady on her feet. When they reached the parlor, the girl sank gratefully into a chair.

When Mrs. Larson returned with a tray containing a pot of chocolate, sponge cake, and plum preserves, she fussed over the pair of them. "Now, now, my lamb. Ye look as if ye've seen a ghost! Puir child, have some cake to put the roses back in yer cheeks."

Christine brightened a little. After the housekeeper left the room, she leaned in toward Amelia. "She's not at all like Mrs. Menford."

"Thank goodness." Amelia added a nip of sugar to her cup, then took a sip of the creamy chocolate. "Perhaps she might convince your housekeeper to mend her ways."

Christine took a spoonful of plum preserves and cake. From the way she was shifting her feet, Amelia knew the numbness hadn't ceased. "Mrs. Menford has been here for as long as I can remember. Even when my mother was alive." There was a trace of guilt, as if the girl didn't want the housekeeper to leave.

"I will allow her to stay," Amelia said. "But only if she obeys my orders."

Christine picked at her cake and ventured, "I wasn't very kind to you when you arrived. I was angry that my father married you when I'd never seen you before."

"Do you still wish he'd married your governess?" Amelia asked.

"Not anymore. Miss Grant would never have let me eat cake and drink chocolate." She took another bite, then set the plate aside. "I'm sorry, but I'm not feeling very hungry right now."

"Why don't you have a lie-down, and perhaps your feet will feel better?"

The girl nodded, but as she tried to stand up, her balance swayed again. "I'm having trouble walking."

Amelia went to her side. "I'm going to help you back to your room. And once you've rested, I'm certain it will go away. Try not to worry."

But though her words were cheerful, she couldn't stop her own rise of fear. She'd never seen anything like this, and as soon as she reached her own room, she penned a note to Dr. Fraser with orders for it to be delivered with great haste.

Then she wrote to David, asking him to come home immediately.

Chapter Thirteen

ONE WEEK LATER

David wasn't certain what to think of Amelia's note. Her terse command to *Come home now* sounded entirely out of character. He bristled at the idea of returning when she hadn't bothered to give a reason.

He was within a mile of Castledon, but he couldn't help but wonder what was happening and why she was so adamant that he should travel home immediately.

When he arrived at the estate, the coach drew to a halt. David disembarked, only to find a strange silence upon the grounds. A sense of foreboding came over him the moment he walked toward the house. Hastening his pace, he went inside, only to find grim expressions on the faces of his servants.

"What's happened?" he asked Haverford.

The butler shook his head and let out a slow breath. "My lord, I fear it's your daughter. She's unwell, and Lady Castledon has—"

David didn't wait for the man to finish, but ordered, "Send for the doctor if he's not here already."

"But my lord—"

He was already hurrying up the stairs, two at a time. Though he didn't know what was wrong, the mood of the servants was entirely too somber. He could sense the presence of death, and God help him, he couldn't endure this again.

Without knocking, he tore open Christine's door and found Amelia seated at her bedside. The moment her eyes met his, he saw that she'd been weeping. His daughter's skin was the color of snow, and she appeared lifeless.

"Thank God you've come," Amelia said, rising to embrace him. And though he knew he ought to hold her, he couldn't bring himself to return the affection. A coldness had taken root, a numbness of fear that blotted out all else. His daughter was fighting for her life, and all he could pray was, *Dear God, not her, too.*

"Where is the doctor?" he demanded, stepping back.

Amelia's face brightened, but she said, "Dr. Fraser should be arriving today. I thought he might be here yesterday, but I suspect there was a delay."

He wasn't certain who she was talking about, though the name Fraser seemed familiar.

"My sister's husband, the Viscount of Falsham," she reminded him. "He's the best physician I know."

"What of Dr. Greenford?" he asked. The local physician had treated Katherine's wasting sickness, never leaving her side. Even at the end, the man had given her medicine to ease her pain when she was dying. "Why have you not sent for him?"

"She dismissed him," Mrs. Menford said briskly as she entered the room carrying a kettle of hot water. "Lady Castledon told him not to return."

David was aghast at that. Why would she send their only doctor away, to wait for some Scotsman who lived several days' journey from them?

"Dr. Greenford was making her worse," Amelia said. "He was trying to bleed her."

"Bleeding is a respected method of treatment," he argued back. "All the physicians do so, when it is necessary."

"I cannot see any good reason to weaken our daughter further, when she's already so ill."

It was the first time he'd heard Amelia refer to Christine in that way. Before he could wonder what to make of it, his daughter opened her eyes. "Papa, are you here?"

"Yes, sweet, I am here." He reached for her hand and squeezed it. To his shock, her fingers were limp, and she didn't hold his hand in return.

A dismayed smile touched her mouth. "I can't move my hands and feet anymore," she whispered. "The sickness is creeping up my limbs."

Horror filled him at the thought. "What do you mean?"

His daughter let out a shaky breath. "It started a week ago, with my feet. They were tingling, and I couldn't feel them. Then it spread to my legs and my knees until I couldn't walk. Now it's up to my hands."

David turned to Amelia, who was gripping her palms together.

"Papa, I don't want to die. But I'm afraid of it spreading higher."

"We'll find the right medicine for you," he promised. "If we have to hire the best physicians in London."

"They couldn't save Mother," she whispered. "Why would they be able to save me?"

"Because you're young and stronger than she was." He leaned down to kiss her cheek. "Rest for a moment, while I talk to Amelia in private."

David stayed with her a moment, until he was certain she had calmed herself. Then he reached for Amelia's hand and led her outside the room. The fury of helplessness came over him, and as he guided her toward his own bedchamber, she winced. "David, you're hurting me."

When he'd closed the door, he demanded, "Why didn't you hire every doctor in Yorkshire to come and see her? Why would you send our best physician away while you wait for a doctor who might not come? If she dies . . ." He couldn't even grasp the thought for fear that imagining it would make it happen.

A flare of anger caught in Amelia's eyes. "You weren't here when she first got sick. You decided that going alone to one of the estates was more important. I had to make the best decisions I knew how, and I knew Dr. Greenford would kill her if I let him continue his 'treatment.'"

"You don't know anything about medicine," he argued.

"And neither do you! But I know enough to see when a little girl is getting worse instead of getting better. He was heating up glass cups and searing her skin with them!"

Amelia was openly crying now, but he could make no move to comfort her. This was his only daughter. His last living piece of Katherine.

"I'm sending for Dr. Greenford right now," he said.

But Amelia shocked him when she stood in front of the door, blocking his way. "She's my daughter too, now. And I won't let that man hurt her."

"Dr. Greenford has been our family physician for over twenty years," he argued.

"How do you know Katherine didn't die at his hands?" She had her hands on her hips, glaring at him. It was a low blow, but he knew the doctor had done everything in his power to save his wife.

"She was too sick for anyone to cure."

"Was she?" Amelia asked. "Or is that what you tell yourself?" She stepped aside from the door and warned him, "I trust Dr. Fraser to help her. He is one of the best physicians in Edinburgh. After he inherited his uncle's title, the Viscount of Falsham, he's continued to write medical treatises and research the best ways to help his patients. He's traveled through Scotland and England to meet with many doctors. If anyone can save Christine, it's him."

"But he's not here," David gritted out. And he wasn't about to wait for a man who might not come.

"He *will* be." Amelia softened her tone and opened the door. "I don't want to fight with you. Christine shouldn't hear us snap at each other, not when she needs us."

"She needs *me*," he corrected. "Her father."

With that, he left her standing in his bedroom while he returned to Christine's side.

Amelia felt as if she'd taken a blow to her stomach. Did he honestly believe she'd behaved irresponsibly by sending the doctor away? In the past five years, she'd never known Dr. Fraser to be anything but a miracle worker. But her husband was treating her like a recalcitrant child who thought she knew best. It wasn't that at all—she'd agreed to let the doctor examine Christine, but the moment he'd begun his "treatments," she'd stopped him. The last thing her stepdaughter needed was to be weakened by bloodletting or cupping.

For a moment, Amelia leaned against the wall, letting out her heartbreak. No, she wasn't the girl's mother. But she wasn't about to stand around and wring her hands. She needed a trustworthy doctor, not a man who would drain away the remainder of her stepdaughter's strength.

Hearing David accuse her of negligence was like a knife slicing her courage into shreds. She wept harder, knowing that a good cry would give her the means to be cheerful later. Even though the young girl had been a trial to her, they had grown closer in the past few days. She was beginning to think of Christine as her own daughter, and the thought of watching her die was a nightmare she couldn't bear to face.

The girl had slowly lost all feeling in her legs and now her hands. Amelia had never seen anything like it, and unless they found a way to reverse it, Christine would undoubtedly die or be left an invalid.

She wiped her eyes with her handkerchief and forced herself to return to the sickroom. But before she could take another step, she heard the voices of her sister and Dr. Fraser downstairs.

Amelia raced down to them and threw herself into Juliette's arms. Her sister was holding her daughter, Grace, but she hugged her back, even with the child between them. "I suppose you're glad we've come?"

"I pray you can save her." To Dr. Fraser, she explained what had happened, and once Lord Falsham heard the symptoms, he held up a hand.

"I will do what I can, Lady Castledon. But you must ken that this is no' something I've heard of in my studies. It sounds like a rare illness."

Mrs. Larson arrived at that moment and embraced them both. "Go on up and see the wee lass, Dr. Fraser. She'll be needing ye to bide awhile. And Miss Juliette, come inside, and I'll find some food for ye and yer sweet bairn." The housekeeper ushered them inside the parlor while Amelia led Dr. Fraser up the stairs.

The doctor fired questions at her, and she answered as quickly as she could. He was muttering to himself beneath his breath in Gaelic, but the moment he entered the sickroom, a change came over his demeanor.

He walked over to the bed and greeted Christine warmly. "I'll bid you a good morn, lass. I am Dr. Paul Fraser, and I'm also the

Viscount of Falsham. Your stepmother asked me to come and look at you."

Amelia stepped back, but she didn't miss the wariness in her husband's eyes. David was staring at the doctor as if he didn't know what to expect. His eyes seemed to warn her that if Dr. Fraser couldn't cure Christine, he would do whatever was necessary to find a physician who could.

An ache centered inside Amelia, but she forced back the fear. The Scottish doctor felt the girl's pulse and examined her. He paid particular attention to Christine's hands, not only checking her muscles, but also testing her skin with both hot and cold water. "Do you feel that, lass?"

When Christine shook her head, Dr. Fraser looked into her eyes and checked her mouth and throat.

"What do you think this is?" Amelia asked Dr. Fraser when she could bear it no longer.

"I canna say that I've seen it before," he admitted. "But I've brought many of my books with me. If there's a doctor who has written about this illness, I'll be finding out what he's learned. And we'll do what we can to cure it."

Then he asked Christine, "How long has it been since you've moved your legs or hands?"

"About a week," she admitted.

"It's no' good for limbs to remain idle for so long," Dr. Fraser said. To the earl, he ordered, "She needs to have her legs and arms moved several times a day, so the blood can flow to them. You can do it yourselves or have a servant help her. But if the blood doesna flow where it's needing to go, she could lose her ability to walk once she's healed."

"I'll help her," David said. He went to sit at Christine's side, while Amelia took the opposite end.

"I'll be seeing about Juliette and Grace for a moment, and then I'll return with the books," Dr. Fraser promised. He departed the room, leaving Amelia alone with her husband.

The bleakness in David's posture bothered her deeply, for she sensed him shutting her out. After he lowered the bedcovers, Amelia took Christine's left leg, meaning to bend it.

"I'll do it, Amelia," he said. "You can go."

"Both of us can help her," she said. "I can do this leg while you do the other."

"No." There was frost in his voice that bewildered her. "Go and leave us. I will take care of my own daughter."

The way you didn't, she imagined he would say. His words were an invisible blow, and she felt the physical ache of his rejection.

"She can stay, Papa," Christine offered.

"Not this time," he insisted. "Amelia has other duties that require her attention. I will take care of you."

The tightness in her throat held the foreboding of tears, and Amelia stood up. To Christine, she offered, "I'll bring you a pot of chocolate if you like."

The girl ventured a smile, but in her eyes, Amelia saw hopelessness. "Perhaps later."

She squeezed her stepdaughter's hand and stole another look at David. He was moving Christine's right leg, gently bending her knee. Amelia waited for him to say something before she left the room.

But he wouldn't even look at her.

His little girl was dying.

Though David tried to put on a brave face and behave as if she was going to get better, he sensed the truth—that Christine would follow in her mother's footsteps. But God help him, he didn't know how he could face this again.

She was just a girl, hardly more than eleven. Her entire life should have been ahead of her, a pathway leading toward a happy future. Instead, he looked upon her face and saw the dark shadow of death.

"Why did you send Amelia away?" Christine asked, her voice barely above a whisper.

"I thought you weren't getting along with her," he said. He switched to her other leg, gently bending the knee.

"I like her better now," Christine said. "She gave me a desk and some paper and pens for my writing."

"Your writing?" He'd had no idea that she enjoyed writing stories. Christine nodded. "I never told her, but she guessed."

His daughter had never told him, either, David realized. "Amelia does seem to know many things."

"I have my own space in the attic now, and the window looks out over the grounds. There's even a widow's walk on the roof." There was a yearning in her voice, as if she'd guessed that she might never go up there again.

"It sounds nice." He switched to her hand, bending the wrist back and forth. "Can you bend your elbow?"

Christine tried, but she only managed to lift her arm a little. "Not really."

He continued to work with her other wrist and fingers, and she fell silent. He wanted to converse with her, to say something that would lift her spirits and make her feel better. Inside, all he could feel was rage that something like this could happen to a child. He wanted to lash out at the illness that was stealing her away from him. *Please let there be a medicine that will cure her.*

But he was afraid to let himself hope.

When Dr. Fraser returned, his wife and daughter were with him. David's first reaction was to send them away, but he saw that Christine was interested in the three-year-old girl who beamed at her. The child was dressed in pink, with matching ribbons in her plaits, and she held a tiny reticule.

"I brought Grace for a moment," Lady Falsham explained. "She wanted to cheer up your daughter."

David wasn't certain it would work, but he supposed there was no harm in it. "For a little while."

"Do you want to play?" the girl asked, climbing up on the bed beside Christine. "I could play with you."

"I can't play very well," Christine apologized. "I'm sick, and my legs won't move."

"You don't have to move." The little girl held up her reticule. "I'm going to brush your hair."

The wry smile on his daughter's face suggested that she didn't think Grace could do very much, but she allowed it.

In that moment, while the child was happily chattering nonsense to Christine, David froze. Seeing the two of them together was like the memory of when Christine had climbed to her mother's bedside on the day Katherine had died.

Suddenly, he couldn't breathe. "Forgive me," David said, pushing his way out of the sickroom. "I'll be back in a moment."

He needed air, to escape the stifling atmosphere of hopelessness. Outside, the weather had turned cloudy, and he hardly cared. Ignoring the servants, he pushed his way out the front door, heedless of the impending storm.

"David!" He heard Amelia calling out to him, but he didn't turn to face her. Sympathy wasn't what he needed right now. He needed to escape all of it, to be alone where he could regain the rigid control over his emotions.

He kept his pace swift, striding down the gravel driveway and toward the open moors. The wind slashed at his face, but he didn't care. He welcomed the physical punishment, reveling in the prelude to a rainstorm.

Amelia would follow him, he suspected. But when he glanced behind him, he saw that she'd stopped at the front door. Good. The reckless anger coursed inside him, and he would offend anyone who tried to talk with him now.

The rain began to spatter against him, and he kept walking, letting it soak through his clothing. He didn't care about it at all. Right now, he wished he'd never left Castledon. If another doctor had seen Christine sooner, she might not be suffering this badly.

It was irrational to blame Amelia, for she'd sent for two doctors. But he couldn't stop his wayward mind from wondering if she'd done everything possible to help Christine.

Ahead, he spied an abandoned cottage that had once belonged to his gamekeeper. It would offer solitude and a brief shelter from the storm. He went inside, shivering from the cold. A sensible man would start a fire in the hearth, but instead he sat down on a wooden stool and stared at the chimney stones.

He didn't want to go through this again. It had taken years to get over the pain of losing Katherine, and Amelia ought to have a better husband than him. He never should have married her.

Upon a low wooden shelf, he spied a chipped plate. Without thinking, he picked it up, his thumb grazing the edge. Then he threw it against the hearth, watching it shatter like the pieces of his life.

And with that, his thread of sanity broke.

David picked up the stool he'd been sitting on and slammed it against the chimney, watching as it splintered and fell against the stones. The need to destroy, to release all the violent rage, was visceral. He broke every piece of pottery he could find, letting the mindless destruction offer its own peace.

When he turned and saw Amelia standing in the doorway, he didn't care what she thought of him. The tiny one-room cottage was destroyed, full of broken glass and fragments of furniture.

"This is who you married," he told her. "And if I lose my daughter to death, you need to leave me."

She said nothing but took a step forward and closed the door behind her. From beneath her cloak, she withdrew a woolen blanket that she'd taken from the house. He guessed she'd brought it to help warm him from the storm.

But the ice inside of him could not be warmed.

"Stay back," he warned her. "I'm not safe to be around right now."

"You wouldn't hurt me," she whispered. "And I know why you're angry. You've a right to be." She continued walking toward him, and he stood his ground amid the broken pieces.

"I don't need pity right now."

"I didn't come here for that." She reached out and put the blanket around his shoulders. "I came because you need someone right now." Then she rested her face against his heart and put her arms around his waist.

He couldn't move, couldn't breathe. The soft scent of her hair and the touch of her body against his were an offering he didn't want to deny.

"I care about her, too," she said. "And I refuse to believe that she'll die."

He took her hands away from his waist, holding her wrists. "I've seen it happen before, Amelia. And this is exactly what death looks like."

Her green eyes filled with hurt, but she stared back at him. "We can't lose hope."

"I lost hope six years ago."

"Don't push me away, David," she said quietly. "I may not be the woman you wanted. But I love you, and I won't walk away when you need me."

He relaxed his grip, tensing even more at her words. "You don't love me, Amelia."

"I know that your pain is mine. I see what you're enduring, and I need to help you."

"Unless you can stop her from dying, there's nothing you can do."

She startled him when she rose up on tiptoe and drew his mouth down to hers. It wasn't the kiss of a young woman trying to flirt or gain his attention. Instead, it was the desperate touch of a wife hurting from his rejection. He tasted the rain from her mouth, and when she began to remove his sodden jacket, he stopped her. "You didn't come here for this."

But her face held seriousness. "I came to comfort you. In whatever way you need me."

It was a way of forgetting about the horror of his daughter's illness; he understood that. And yet, he couldn't touch her. Not now, not like this.

"Go back home," he told her, lifting the blanket around her shoulders. "I'll follow shortly."

When she returned to the door, he caught a glimpse of the heartache on her face, which made him feel even lower. Before she could venture out into the rain, he caught her hand and drew her in for a soft kiss. "You don't deserve a husband like me, Amelia."

"No," she breathed, wrapping her arms around him, "but know that I am here."

✿

Impatience plagued Brandon Carlisle when his coach arrived at the Falsham estate near Edinburgh. His opportunity was here, after so many years.

He reached inside his coat, feeling the heavy pistol that he'd brought with him. This weapon was already loaded, and he had another in the opposite side. Or, if the occasion required it, he also had a small blade with which he could cut Paul Fraser's throat.

He smiled, imagining the man's sightless eyes.

"You will go now," he told Sarah. "Tell them you've come to pay a call upon Lady Falsham." Juliette would be distracted by his sister, and when Brandon came for Sarah, the servants would not dare turn him away.

His sister was trembling, especially when Richardson came up behind her. Fear, in a woman, was something to be encouraged. Sarah had been given too much freedom over the years, and he didn't want her making decisions.

"Brandon, this will never work. Lady Falsham hardly knows me, but she does know that I am your sister."

"Tell her you've come to warn her," he added. Even better. He liked the idea of instilling fear in Juliette. Because of her and her husband, Brandon had spent the past four years chained in an asylum. His mind had been lost, sedated, and caught in its own silent prison. Now he wanted vengeance for what had been done to him.

He didn't want Juliette anymore. No, he wanted her to watch while he killed the people she loved. First her husband. Then her sisters and parents.

And last, her daughter.

Brandon smiled as he remained within the carriage. He'd waited four years for this, and he relished the idea of making Juliette endure everything he'd suffered.

But his sister returned entirely too soon. There was a blend of relief and anxiety on her face. Even Richardson appeared grim when he allowed her to enter the carriage first.

"They aren't there," she said in a rush. "They left a day ago."

"Where?" he demanded.

"I don't know—" she started, but was cut off by Richardson.

"Castledon." The man met Brandon's gaze. "She went with Lord Falsham to visit her sister Amelia, who lives at Castledon, a few days south of here, near Yorkshire."

"Did she?" It was better than he'd hoped for, for he could then kill her youngest sister.

Sarah paled. "You *are* mad," she whispered. "And you feel no remorse for what you're about to do."

"None whatsoever," he agreed. "They took everything from me. It's time they paid the price for it."

Brandon ordered the driver to travel south, toward Castledon. It didn't matter to him that it would take days to arrive. He wanted vengeance, to kill those who had taken his life from him.

As far as he was concerned, the consequences didn't matter. So long as the Andrews family was dead, he would be satisfied.

⚘

Amelia's gown was soaked from the rain, but the chill she felt had nothing to do with the cool weather. She tried to untie her bonnet, but the ribbons were knotted, and her hands were shaking.

She found her sister waiting for her in the parlor. Juliette stood, her face filled with worry. "Are you—is the earl—all right?"

Amelia nodded but couldn't seem to find the right words.

"Where is he now?" her sister prompted.

"At the gamekeeper's cottage. He n-needed a moment alone."

"And so do you." Juliette took her by the hand. "Show me where your bedchamber is."

Amelia started to walk up the stairs, her tears falling down her cheeks. This day had been the worst of all. Though she'd known David would be devastated, as she was, she wouldn't let herself believe that Christine could die. But he seemed so certain of it.

When they were alone, Juliette pulled her into a hug. "Don't cry, Amelia. Paul will find out what's wrong with Christine, and he'll do everything he can to make her better."

"I do pray that she'll get well," Amelia said, pulling back, "but I'm more worried about David."

"Grace has gone with her nurse for a while, so you can tell me everything." Juliette locked the door and went to sit down.

Amelia couldn't stop herself from spilling it all out and having a good cry. "I used to think my life was going to end like a fairy tale. That I would marry the viscount, reform him, and we'd be wealthy beyond our dreams." She accepted the handkerchief Juliette offered her. "But then I saw the villain he was. Lord Castledon saved me from Viscount Lisford and married me, but I was so naïve to think that there could be more between us. He only married me out of kindness. Not love."

"Are you unhappy being married to him?" Juliette asked in a low voice.

"I thought I was happy," Amelia hedged. "But he's never made a secret of the fact that he only remarried to provide a mother for Christine." She dried her tears and eyed Juliette. "I'm not much of a mother, am I?"

"I'd say you're doing quite well," Juliette corrected. "Christine seems to like you very much."

"I think Lord Castledon blames me for her illness," Amelia confessed. "He was so angry when I told him I sent the first doctor away. But all the man wanted to do was bleed Christine. He would have made her worse." A dull ache caught her heart. "And now, if she dies, my husband will never forgive me."

"It's not your fault," Juliette insisted.

"I know it. But our marriage is already fragile enough. She has to live, or everything will end." Amelia swallowed hard, trying to gather up her courage. "I might remain married to David, but he'll reside on one of the other estates. He'll avoid me, and I can't live like that."

"Then don't," Juliette said. "Paul will do everything possible for Christine. We won't leave until she's well again. And perhaps you should come to Edinburgh with us for a visit."

"But what good would that do?"

"It may bring the earl to his senses, so that he'll see what's before him."

Amelia understood what Juliette was saying, but she didn't want to go. Not now, when her household was in disarray and her step-daughter was fighting for her life. "I can't leave him, Juliette. He may not realize he needs me, but he does."

Her sister squeezed her hand. "Then I'll be here for *you*, when you need me."

"What have you learned?" David asked the doctor.

Dr. Fraser sat beside Christine, who was sleeping lightly. "It's no' a common disease," he began, keeping his voice low. "I've read of only a few accounts. One from Germany, and another from France." The physician handed him a few letters that had been tucked into a medical book. "Due to the war, it's been hard for any correspondence to reach us."

It wasn't encouraging, for David suspected the doctor didn't have a diagnosis yet. "What do you think it is?"

"She had a cough and a sore throat before this, aye?"

David nodded. "But she improved. That was weeks ago."

"Some of the physicians think it's a form of Boulogne sore throat." His eyes met David's, and the graveness of the man's expression spoke the worst.

He'd heard of that illness, and many children had died from it. Still, he didn't want to alarm Christine. "*Is* that what it is?"

"I'm no' certain. She doesna have the swelling or the fever I'd expect to see." He began listing the symptoms he'd noted, the paralysis being the worst of them. David listened to the physician, but he felt a cold fear take command of his courage.

Christine's going to die, his mind insisted. *Everyone you love dies.*

The thought was a jagged blade into his heart. He couldn't bring himself to think of losing her, though he knew it was likely going to happen. "What can we do?"

"We have to stop the paralysis from spreading to her lungs." Again, the doctor sent him a hard look, making it clear that Christine would suffocate if it got that far.

"And you have medicine that can do this?"

The doctor paused. "Some say strychnine is a common treatment. But I say 'twould more likely poison her than be of help. I think we should keep exercising her arms and legs tae keep the blood flowing. There was one account I read where the condition reversed itself after a week. We'll pray for that."

In other words, this was an ailment with no cure. David lowered his head, holding back the frustration building inside. His daughter was fighting for her life, and there was nothing he could do to help.

Amelia came inside the room, and an invisible tension caught him in the shoulders. Never before had he lost control in front of a woman, and it bothered him that she'd seen him resort to violence, when he'd destroyed the cottage.

She took a seat on the opposite side of the bed while Dr. Fraser repeated his suggestions for treatment.

"It sounds reasonable," Amelia pronounced, and then asked, "Has she eaten anything for supper yet?"

The doctor shook his head. "When she awakens, she can have some broth. I'm certain Mrs. Larson has prepared a feast to help her."

"I thought she had already returned to Ballaloch," David said, meeting Amelia's gaze.

His wife ventured a slight smile. "No one could stop her from remaining here while her 'wee lamb' is ill. It would be like trying to stop a thunderstorm."

"And what of Mrs. Menford? Have you dismissed her?"

"No. Mrs. Larson is helping her get accustomed to my methods, and I have every faith that she'll come around." Amelia softened a moment. "She even made a pot of chocolate for Christine when I asked her to."

It sounded as if the housekeeper was starting to accept Amelia, but David hardly cared what happened with the staff anymore. His mind was entirely focused upon his daughter, praying she could survive this illness.

When she opened her eyes, Christine seemed relieved to find both of them at her bedside. "Papa, can you help me to sit up?"

He leaned over, and Amelia helped him to lift her into a seated position. She arranged the pillows around Christine and asked, "How are you feeling, now?"

His daughter let out a sigh. "The same. I can't move my arms or legs." Her face colored, and she admitted, "I feel rather like a baby again."

"It will get better," she reassured the girl. "And I've asked Mrs. Larson to come and bring you a good supper to help you get your strength back."

David said nothing while Amelia chattered at Christine, realizing that she was trying to bring back his daughter's good spirits. Once or twice, he saw his little girl smile, and it struck him in the heart with fear of never seeing her smile again.

But when Mrs. Larson arrived at last, Mrs. Menford was with her. The housekeeper carried a tray of food, while Mrs. Larson held a bucket of water in one hand. The Scotswoman gestured for Mrs. Menford to put the food down upon a table before she strode forward. "Now then, my lamb, I ken the good doctor will do all he can for ye, but I've come to help in my own way."

David wasn't exactly sure this was a good idea. "What you do mean, you plan to 'help?'"

The housekeeper brightened. "Oh, 'tis just a prayer that will help keep the evil spirits away. It's naught but a wee bit of water."

Before he could protest, the housekeeper barreled her way to the bedside and handed him the bucket. She scooped up some water and let it drip over Christine's head. Then she poured two more handfuls of water as she quoted:

"Tri baslaichean na Trianaid Naoimh,
Gu d'dhion 's ga d'shabhaladh
Bho bheum sul."

His wife murmured, "Amen," while Christine blinked at both of them. "What was that for?" she asked the housekeeper.

"'Tis a prayer for you, dear one." She took a towel and dried off the girl's brow. "When a new bairn is washed by her nurse, we give this blessing against the evil eye. 'Twill keep death away."

"Superstitious rot," Mrs. Menford muttered. "You've done nothing but get the girl wet."

"Is that like a baptism?" Amelia countered. "I say, there's no harm in prayer, no matter how it's done." To Mrs. Larson, she said, "Thank you for bringing Christine her supper. You and Mrs. Menford may go now."

But before either of them did, Mrs. Menford stopped a moment. "Lady Castledon, I *am* sorry for the way we started out. You can be certain that I'll do all I can to help you."

Amelia saw that the woman's contrition was genuine, and she nodded. "Thank you."

Once the servants had gone, she turned back to Christine. "Mrs. Larson is most definitely a superstitious woman, but she means well."

A bead of water dripped down the girl's cheek, and a smirk crossed her face. "I'm soaked, and I can't even dry myself off."

Amelia answered the smile, and Christine began to laugh. It was the first time David had heard her laugh in a long time.

He glanced over at his wife, who was biting her lip. "I don't think it was Mrs. Larson's intention to drown you, Christine."

His daughter began to giggle, and a moment later, Amelia joined her in laughing. "She is a strange housekeeper, but I do love her. She used to put nails in my toast to keep the fairies away."

Christine was laughing so hard now, tears were escaping her eyes. "Did you ever eat one by mistake?"

"No, but her toast was as hard as a nail, sometimes. She didn't like waste, and we had to finish the loaf of bread, whether it was stale or not." Amelia pushed back on Christine's arms, trying to move them. "David, why don't you help me with her other arm?"

He complied, but it bothered him to see his daughter's limbs so frail and useless. Amelia continued talking and manipulating her arms, and he caught himself staring at them.

"You look tired," she said. "Why don't you go and have something to eat, and I'll look after Christine. The food may make you feel better."

"I'll bring it back here," David said. He didn't recall seeing Amelia eat, either.

She shrugged and pulled back the coverlet, reaching for Christine's feet. "We'll be just fine, won't we?"

His daughter's laughter had abated, and she lifted her gray eyes to his. "I'm glad Papa married you, Amelia. You're much more interesting than Miss Grant."

"I've an idea," she said. "Since none of us has had our supper, why don't we have a picnic in the gardens before it gets dark?"

Christine's expression turned hopeful, and though he was tempted to refuse, David realized that she'd been confined in this room for nearly a week. For all he knew, these could be her last moments outside.

"Your mother has a moonlight garden, doesn't she?" Amelia said, pulling the covers all the way down. "It's full of white flowers. She has hydrangeas, lilies, and roses, from what I've seen. Have you ever been there at night?"

Christine shook her head. "No."

"Then we'll have to go, won't we?" Amelia glanced at him, and in her green eyes, he saw that she was clinging to hope as hard as he was. "Your father and I will form a chair with our arms and bring you downstairs and outside."

She reached under Christine's knees and behind her shoulders. "David, will you help me?"

He shook his head. "I'll carry her myself." When he lifted Christine into his arms, he realized how very long her legs and arms had grown in the past year. She was nearing the end of childhood, and if she lived, she would be as tall as Amelia one day.

His wife appeared slightly disappointed that he hadn't allowed her to help, but she opened the door and picked up the supper tray Mrs. Larson had left. "I'll tell Mrs. Menford that we'll want our supper in the moonlight garden. Then I'll join the two of you there."

Chapter Fourteen

T he sky was clear and held a golden haze as sunset approached. Amelia walked down the stone steps leading to the gardens. The moonlight garden was one she'd discovered a few nights ago. At first, she hadn't realized what it was and had dismissed it as a colorless collection of flowers. Then, one night, she'd stood outside while the moon cast its rays upon the earth. The blossoms had turned into silver, and she now believed that if any garden held a piece of Katherine's spirit, it was this one.

She found David seated beside a low wall. Mrs. Menford followed them with a tray, while Mrs. Larson carried a tureen of soup. Surprisingly, the two housekeepers appeared almost amiable toward each other.

The footmen had brought a table and chairs for the three of them, while the housekeepers laid out the food. Mrs. Larson lit two tapers, and the candlelight added an aura of magic. There was chicken soup, roasted pheasant, sugared peas, fresh bread and butter, and even a small lemon cake.

"It's beautiful here," Christine said. "I've been to this garden before, but never at night. I didn't realize how different it would look."

Amelia fixed a plate for her stepdaughter and set it before the girl. She smoothed Christine's damp hair back and then raised a forkful of cake to her mouth.

The girl frowned a moment. "Shouldn't I eat my vegetables and pheasant first? Miss Grant says dessert must always come last."

"But then you might not be hungry for it," Amelia said. "Sometimes my sisters and I would eat our cake first and then the rest. Not often, but it made our dinner more fun. Don't you agree, my lord?"

David ignored his cake and took a bite of roasted pheasant. He might as well have been eating dirt, and Amelia suspected his worry over Christine superseded any ability to take joy in food.

"Papa doesn't eat cake or sweets," Christine said. "He never does."

Amelia set down her own fork. Though she'd heard it before, she questioned the reason. "Why is that?"

He cut another bite of the pheasant and shrugged. "I don't like the taste."

"Has it always been that way?" she prompted, raising another bite of lemon cake for Christine to eat.

He stared at her as if to demand, *Stop asking questions.* "No."

His daughter glanced at him. "This is about Mother, isn't it?" Her expression turned serious. "She loved cakes and biscuits, didn't she?"

"She did."

From his clipped tone and the way he kept his attention firmly fixed upon his plate, Amelia guessed that he didn't want to talk about it further. "How do you like the flowers?" she asked Christine.

The girl turned to look at the wild profusion of Queen Anne's lace. "I used to think this garden wasn't much to look at. But it's beautiful at night." Her gray eyes held wonder, and as twilight descended, the candlelight cast a soft glow over her face.

Amelia helped her to finish eating, but Christine had little appetite. Her mood mirrored her father's, and both of them looked as if they were facing an executioner. She'd brought them here to cheer them up, and it wasn't working at all.

"You're going to get well," she told Christine. "You need to believe that."

"It's hard, when I can't move my arms or legs," the girl admitted.

"We should take you back to your room," David interjected. "You must be tired."

"No. Wait a moment." Amelia went over to one of the rose-bushes and snapped off a small bud. She tucked it behind Christine's ear and said, "I want you to think of your mother when you smell this. She'll watch over you."

"I'm afraid to die," her stepdaughter admitted. Her voice was thick, as if she were holding back tears.

"Listen to me." Amelia took the girl's limp hands in hers, then touched one cheek. "We are going to listen to Dr. Fraser and keep the blood flowing through your limbs. We'll move your arms and legs for you, until you can move them yourself."

The fear in her stepdaughter's eyes was mirrored by David. "I keep waking up at night, dreaming that I can't breathe."

"Have you lost the ability to move anything else? Your shoulders?"

Christine paused a moment and turned her shoulders one way and then the other. "No. I can still move them."

"And you haven't lost the feeling in anything else?"

The girl shook her head. "Not yet." Her voice was hardly above a whisper, but she seemed to take comfort from Amelia's observation.

"If it isn't spreading, then that's a good sign," David said. He reached down to lift Christine back into his arms. "Come now, and I'll take you back so you can rest."

His gaze turned back to Amelia for a moment, and in his eyes, she saw the weariness. Like his daughter, he was afraid to hope. And he'd been alone for so long, he refused to rely on anyone but himself.

He was trying to shoulder a burden alone that no father should have to face. "It was a nice picnic," he said to Amelia. "Thank you."

She remained seated there after they'd gone, wondering what to do now. David seemed determined to separate her out of his life. He was hurting deeply and kept up the mask of indifference. Only during his violent outburst had she caught a glimpse of the pain he was hiding.

Slowly, she rose from her chair in the garden. When she reached the door to the house, she overheard low voices speaking in the parlor. Amelia tiptoed nearer and spied her sister Juliette talking with her husband.

"Will she live?" her sister was asking.

"I canna say," Dr. Fraser answered. "If the paralysis doesna spread further, it should recede in the next few days."

"And if it doesn't?"

"Then she'll die tonight or tomorrow. She willna be able to move her lungs."

Amelia leaned back against the wall, feeling as if her knees were about to buckle beneath her. Inwardly, she felt sick to her stomach, and a rise of nausea caught in her throat.

She didn't want to believe it could be true, and before she could hear another word, she began running up the stairs.

Tonight or tomorrow, he'd said. She prayed that it wouldn't happen, that the girl would survive it. But Christine's premonition about being unable to breathe was a tangible threat.

And if the worst happened, she needed to be at David's side.

The night was long, the hours creeping by, one by one. David's shoulders ached, and he'd been unable to leave Christine for even a moment. It was as if he could fight the invisible hand of Death by shielding her.

He'd give up his life for hers, if it were possible. Watching her struggle to breathe, seeing her fight to live, was something he'd never imagined would happen.

Dr. Fraser had come in several times, but there was no change in Christine's condition. David sent the physician away for a few hours, needing the time to be with his daughter. He promised to alert him if she took a turn for the worse.

Amelia, however, had refused to leave. She sat across from him, keeping her own vigil. Her green eyes held exhaustion, and her blond hair tangled against her throat. For a moment, she met his gaze, and he couldn't help but remember what she'd said before, that she loved him.

How could she? She'd seen him lose control of his temper, destroying most of the gamekeeper's cottage. He was hardly her ideal husband, and he'd brought her to this miserable marriage where she wasn't even mistress of her own household.

He'd never seen her look this fragile before. Amelia should have so much more than this bleak existence.

She stood from her place and moved to stand behind him. "If you want to rest for an hour, I'll keep watch over her."

Her hands rested upon his shoulders, but he shook his head. "I'll be fine. But you should go to sleep. There's nothing either of us can do right now."

"I won't leave," she whispered, and her hands pressed against his shoulders, massaging away the stiffness.

Her hands felt so good, and he closed his eyes for the slightest moment, enjoying her touch. David leaned back his head, taking the comfort she offered.

A fleeting second later, he felt her mouth come down on his in a light kiss. There was hesitancy in her lips, as if she were afraid to show any affection to him. But before he could kiss her back, she pulled away.

He said nothing, and her hands moved away from his shoulders. She was waiting for him to say something, he knew. But the silence hung between them, deepening the rift.

Then, out of nowhere, he confessed the truth. "Katherine was going to have another baby when she died."

When he turned to her, Amelia's face held shock. Though she appeared as if she wanted to say something, she waited for him to go on. David didn't know why he'd said it, but once he'd begun telling her, it became impossible to stop. "She had a . . . wasting sickness. A cancer, they told me. One moment she was fine, and then it struck her so fast. She was in such pain, but she tried to hide it from me."

"You were there for her." She took his hand, as if to reassure him. "And I imagine that brought her comfort."

"I never knew she was expecting a child when the sickness hit her. She . . . kept her body under the covers for many months. Even the doctor didn't know. Katherine fought so hard to live, and it was only in her last hour that she told me."

His eyes burned, and it felt like acid was burning the back of his throat. "She—she thought they could cut the baby from her and save it. But I knew she would die if they did. The child couldn't have lived anyway, since she was only a few months into the pregnancy."

Tears were rolling down Amelia's cheeks, and she squeezed his hand tightly. "It wasn't your fault."

"I let both of them die," he said. "She took her last breath in my arms, and when the doctors tried to save the child, in case there was a chance, my son was already dead."

He wanted to grieve, to release the harsh pain that he'd buried deep. But he didn't want Amelia to see the weakness. It had been six years—far too long to think of it now. But his son would have been running around, perhaps learning to ride his own horse.

Amelia drew her arms around him, and she whispered, "You mustn't blame yourself. There was nothing you could do."

He knew it, but it didn't assuage the raw emptiness. It was easier to embrace the silence, to lock away any emotions.

"Sometimes I wish I could have given myself in their place," he said. "If I hadn't given her another child, she might have been strong enough to overcome the sickness."

"You couldn't have known it would happen."

"No. But I blame myself, nonetheless." When Amelia moved back, he admitted, "I never wanted you to endure something like this."

Her face held sorrow, and she added, "Do you regret this marriage?"

He did. But not because he hadn't wanted her to share in his life. It was because he'd reached the end of his strength. He had no love left to give, and if anyone deserved to be loved, it was Amelia.

"I wish I could be a better man for you," was all he could say.

His answer brought a flush to her cheeks, and she looked down at her hands.

Christine began to toss her head in her sleep, and her breathing suddenly turned into gasps. He didn't know what was happening, but he ordered Amelia, "Go and fetch Dr. Fraser. Now!" He shoved her out the door, praying to God that his daughter would live.

Chapter Fifteen

They fought to save her. Amelia's feelings were raw and bruised as the hours went on through the morning. She heard Dr. Fraser barking out orders to the servants and to David. When she asked Juliette if she should return to the sickroom, her sister shook her head.

"Leave Paul to help her. He'll do whatever he can, I promise you."

Her niece Grace was whining to her mother, raising her arms. "Up, Mama."

Amelia lifted the little girl instead, and the moment she did, Grace began playing with her hair. She seemed distracted by the task, and when she went to sit down, Grace remained on her lap, twisting the long strands.

"Sit still," Grace ordered. "I do it."

The young girl continued plaiting and tangling the strands, and Amelia glanced up at her sister. "If Christine dies, I'm going to Edinburgh with you. The earl won't want me here."

Her sister didn't ask questions, but the sympathy in her eyes made Amelia feel even worse. "All right."

She let Grace continue to play with her hair until the little girl lost interest. After a time, Juliette took her daughter away, and

Amelia stood. At last, she ventured up the stairs to find out what had happened to Christine. It had gone quiet, and when she reached the hall, she saw her husband standing outside the room, his head bowed. Both of his hands rested upon the wall, and from his posture, she suspected the worst.

"Is she—" She couldn't bring herself to voice the fearful question.

"She's alive," David answered. "The worst has passed, and she was able to move her upper arm a little while ago." He didn't look at her, but the relief that struck her was so strong, Amelia went to embrace him.

"I'm so glad." She waited for his arms to come around her, for him to share in her joy. But he held himself back.

"I need to go to her. Forgive me." He extricated himself from the embrace, and it was as if her own limbs had turned to ice.

Amelia's heart was aching, but she didn't follow. She needed a few moments to gather her composure. As soon as she entered her room, the tears blinded her. She sat in a chair numbly, so grateful for her stepdaughter's life. But she didn't know how to bridge the distance with David. He continued to shut her out, and she didn't know what to say or do now.

You're overreacting, she told herself. *He was simply hurrying to see Christine.* Though she wanted to believe it, she wasn't quite certain.

Amelia sat for a long while, fighting back the tears, until she had control of herself. When at last she had locked away her emotions, she returned to see her stepdaughter.

Inside, the room was hot and stifling. Christine was awake, while Dr. Fraser was taking her pulse. David was seated beside his daughter, and his eyes were heavy from the sleepless night.

Amelia crossed the room and pulled the white rose bloom from Christine's hair. "You see. Your mother was watching over you."

The young girl slowly lifted her hand to take the blossom from her. "I think so, yes." She managed a smile. "And I had another mother with me, too."

She wasn't prepared for the catch in her heart. Never had she imagined Christine would accept her as a stepmother.

"Yes," she said quietly. "You had me, too." She smoothed back the girl's damp hair. With a teasing smile, she asked, "Has Mrs. Larson been in to douse you with water again?"

"It worked," Christine said. "She can pour water on my head as much as she likes."

Lightly, Amelia kissed the girl's temple. "I'll go now, and let you rest." She didn't speak to David, but crossed the room. Inwardly, she felt brittle, like a piece of cracked porcelain.

"Will you stay a little longer?" she asked Dr. Fraser.

"I'll stay a few days more," he said. "Until I know she'll make a full recovery."

"I am grateful to you for all that you've done," David said to the physician. "There are no words."

Dr. Fraser nodded. "I'm glad the lass has improved. Now, I think you should be getting a bit of rest yourself, Lord Castledon."

The earl nodded. "I think I will." He leaned in and ruffled his daughter's hair. "Sleep well, my dear."

He walked past Amelia, and though he ventured a relieved smile, she sensed the distance between them.

⚜

"Amelia asked to accompany us back to Falsham for a visit," Dr. Fraser informed him, after David stepped out of Christine's bedroom. "If you don't mind her spending time with her sister."

It had been several days since his daughter's illness had abated, and Christine was now able to move all of her limbs, though she'd been weakened severely.

"If she wants to go, she may," he agreed. But it made him realize how he'd neglected Amelia these past few days. He'd been so caught up in helping his daughter to get well, he'd barely given any attention to his wife.

She'd never once left Christine's side, nor his. And though he'd been so consumed by worry, he'd taken comfort from having her there. Her quiet presence had given him strength when he'd reached the end of his reserves. It had felt right to have her there, and he'd been grateful.

David started to continue down the hall, but the doctor stopped him. "If it were me, I wouldna be letting her pay a visit to Falsham just now. The lass has that look in her eyes, of a woman hurting. But 'tis no' a physical wound."

"She's tired," he agreed. "We both are." It had been a grueling week, one he wanted to forget. But the look on the doctor's face suggested that there was more Fraser wasn't telling him. "Why? Has she said something to her sister?"

"Aye. And women are complicated creatures. If it were me, I'd be finding out her reasons for the '*visit*.'"

David wasn't certain he understood what the man was implying by emphasizing the last word. "She is free to travel as she chooses. I have no quarrel with her."

The Highlander sent him a twisted smile. "My God, your head is made of wood, is it no'? Go and seduce your wife, before she leaves you." With that, he moved toward the staircase, leaving David more than a little confused.

Was he implying that Amelia wanted to leave their marriage? Whatever for?

David continued toward his wife's bedchamber, and when he knocked, she called out for him to enter. He turned the door handle and found Amelia seated beside the window. Her belongings were packed in a trunk that suggested she intended to stay with her sister for quite some time. His instincts grew uneasy, for it *did* look as though she intended to leave him.

"How long were you planning to visit with Juliette?" he asked, eyeing the baggage.

"I haven't decided." She kept her gaze averted from him, which wasn't a good sign. Though logically, she had the right to go with her sister whenever she pleased, he sensed that something was very wrong. This wasn't Amelia's way, to run from her problems.

A sense of foreboding caught him in the gut. He didn't want her to go at all, particularly if she was unhappy.

Amelia rose from her chair and walked toward him. "How is Christine today?"

"Each day she improves," he said. His wife nodded, but her attention remained upon the packed trunk.

She's leaving you, unless you stop her, a voice inside taunted him. And perhaps directly addressing the problem would be best.

"Are you planning to return to Castledon?"

She stared at him and let out a slow breath. "Do you want me to?" Before he could say yes, she continued, "You hardly spoke to me when Christine was ill. I tried to be there for you, but you didn't want my presence."

That wasn't true at all.

"I was afraid of losing her," he insisted. "Katherine died, and all I could imagine was having to bury Christine, too. I couldn't think from one moment to the next." He crossed his arms, eyeing her steadily. "But I knew you were there."

He had done a poor job of showing his gratitude, but every time he let himself think of Amelia, confusion knotted inside him. He didn't want her to leave.

"Thank you for staying with both of us, all those days," he continued. "And for all that you did."

She stood without speaking for a long moment. Then at last, she admitted, "I felt like an outsider. As if I wasn't supposed to be there at all."

"No you're wrong," he admitted. Far from it. He'd needed her, more than he could have guessed. "But I didn't know what to say to you, after you saw me lose my temper." He didn't doubt she was shocked by what she'd witnessed. He'd lost control of his rage, and it had felt so good to release the anger within him. "That isn't who I am."

"I wasn't afraid of you on that day," she said. She clenched her hands together and confessed, "But it's too hard for me to be here, knowing that you don't love me." Her eyes filled up with tears, and she continued, "It hurts too much, when I want more than you can give."

He didn't know what to say, especially when it struck him that he *did* care. If she left him now, the house would return to the emptiness that had haunted him for so many years. Amelia had quietly slipped into his life, making him aware of how badly he needed her.

But if he said that now, she wouldn't believe him. Instead, he took her hand in his. "Let's go outside and talk."

It was a means of delaying his answer, for he needed time to come up with all the logical reasons why she shouldn't go. He took her gloved hand, suddenly aware of how nice it was to have her fingers intertwined with his.

But her face remained pale, as if nothing he said would change her mind.

As they walked together toward the gardens, he went over the list in his mind. There were many reasons why she should remain at Castledon, and he fully believed that with the right one, she would agree to stay.

It might not have been the best idea to bring her to the moonlight garden, but at least here, they were away from eavesdroppers.

"I believe that we are well suited to each other," he began. "It might not have been the marriage you dreamed of, but you have a good home, enough money to spend however you like, and all of your freedom."

"I never cared about money," she reminded him. "And I thought that this . . . existence . . . would be enough for me, once. It isn't now."

The flat sincerity in her voice brought another ripple of unease. She sounded as if she truly meant to leave, no matter what he said. Damn it all, he was making a mess of this. He laced his fingers with hers, as if the physical gesture could stop her.

But maybe he could say the words she wanted. He would say anything if it meant keeping her here.

"What if I told you that I *do* love you?" The words felt foreign on his tongue, as if it were another man saying them. But the moment he spoke, they felt right. It was as if the years of ice had cracked apart, filling him with a strange sense of purpose. There was relief in admitting it to her, and the more he thought of it, the more he realized that he wasn't giving her false words.

He *did* love her. His earlier belief, that he was incapable of loving a woman again, was blatantly wrong. His love for Amelia wasn't less than his love for Katherine—it was equal in a different way.

Amelia had given him strength when he'd had nothing left. He'd needed her desperately, and she hadn't shied away from him when he'd been at his worst.

Perhaps logic wasn't the way to a woman's heart at all. Perhaps it was about loving her and telling her so.

"You're just saying that." Amelia let go of his hand, dismissing his declaration as if he'd told her it was going to rain.

But no, this was more. So much more.

"I don't want a husband who pretends I don't exist, whenever problems happen." She started to pace across the garden, and he rather liked the way her hair was falling out of its arrangement, her green eyes filled with fire. She was a beautiful woman, and one who never failed to speak her mind. He'd always liked that about her.

"Well?" she demanded.

David blinked, not realizing he'd been supposed to answer that. He'd been contemplating the best way to show her he cared.

"I wasn't trying to ignore you," he said. "It was a terrible week, and if I was inattentive, it was because I was afraid of losing Christine."

Her expression grew pained. "It wasn't that I needed attention, David. I wanted to ease your pain, to share it between us. Don't you think I worried about her, too?"

He knew she had, for she'd been as exhausted as he was. Every hour that his daughter had fought for her life, he'd looked across the bed, and Amelia had been there. "I'm not explaining myself well."

"No, you're not." But she stopped pacing and waited for him to try again. That, at least, gave him hope. He was reaching the end of his list of arguments, and he decided that Dr. Fraser was right. Women were far too complicated, and words weren't going to get him anywhere at all.

"I've made mistakes," he admitted. "I'll likely make many more in the next few years. But give it time, and our marriage will be just fine."

"I don't want our marriage to be just fine," Amelia countered. "I want it to be wonderful." Her voice was wistful with longing. "I want you to kiss me as if you love me. I want you to smile and enjoy the life we have together. And I want to share your bed at night and awaken with you beside me."

"I can give you that," he said quietly. But Amelia appeared unconvinced.

She let out a sigh and offered, "I suppose, to you, a good wife sits in the corner and embroiders handkerchiefs. That isn't the woman I am."

"I would never expect that of you," he pointed out. "But neither am I a knight, charging up on a white horse, to sweep you away to live in a castle." He didn't want her creating illusions about what their life would be like.

"I'm not a young girl who still believes in those things," she said. "But you did save me from Lord Lisford."

Her reminder gave him a reason to hope. "The man was going to ruin you. You didn't deserve what he did." He glanced around him. "I don't suppose you deserved this, either. But you're trapped here, and that's the end of it."

She wasn't going anywhere. Not if he had to chain her to his side.

"Trapped?" She frowned, and he sat down where they had shared a picnic only a few days earlier.

"Yes. You made the decision to wed me, and I'm not allowing you to leave. Especially if you love me."

Her face was flushed and incredulous that he'd changed his tack. "I could change my mind. I might not really love you."

"But you do." He crooked his finger. "Come here, Amelia."

"No, I won't. I'm leaving with Juliette and Lord Falsham within the hour."

In a sudden move, he stood and caught her around the waist. "You'll be too busy to go with them."

"Doing what?"

He drew her close and murmured against her mouth. "Embroidering handkerchiefs." His hands moved up her spine, and he appreciated the lush curve of her hips, and the way her body fitted to his.

"Have you lost your mind?"

He was beginning to think that he had. It was far better to simply take command of her and do as he pleased than to try and justify it to her. He wanted Amelia to stay with him, and stay she would.

"I hate embroidering," she said.

But then he moved his hands to her breasts and flicked the tips with his thumbs. "No, you don't. You like it quite a lot."

Her mouth dropped open as she suddenly caught his hidden meaning. David seized his opportunity and kissed her hard. He gave her no opportunity to argue with him, not after all that they'd been through together. For so long, he'd mistakenly believed she was little more than a girl, unable to accept the responsibilities of caring for a household. She had proven herself to be a more commanding woman than Katherine, taking charge of what she wanted.

Just as he was doing now.

"Th-that's not embroidery," she stammered as he slid his tongue into her mouth, cutting off further arguments. The thin muslin she wore revealed curves that he wanted to explore intimately.

"It isn't?" He hardly cared that they were in the garden where anyone could happen upon them. "There's a gamekeeper's cottage not far from here," he suggested. "Though I might have destroyed it."

"What are you doing, David?" she murmured against his mouth. Her lips were swollen from his kisses, and she looked utterly desirable.

"Showing you all the attention you should have had when I was otherwise distracted." He nipped at her lips. "I'm not very good with words."

"You're better at actions," Amelia agreed. She leaned in and kissed him softly, and the touch of her mouth was a physical reassurance. He crushed her in his embrace, and the warmth of her arms broke through the ice of his solitude. He wasn't used to her unreserved affection, but his lonely soul reveled in it.

"If you hadn't been there this past week, I would have lost myself," he admitted. Pressing a lock of her hair back, he added, "That's what a real marriage is, Amelia. Loving someone enough that you don't run from the worst moments."

"Why did you keep pushing me away?" she whispered.

"Because I was afraid of how much I've come to love you. I felt like I was dishonoring Katherine by letting myself feel again. I should have known it would be impossible to stay apart from a woman like you."

The need to touch her again was a visceral force, pulling him closer. He hardly cared where they were—he wanted to push away the shadows of death and hold fast to this woman. He lost himself, kissing her hard until their tongues mingled.

"Stay with me," he commanded.

She lifted her green eyes to his. "Convince me."

The glint in her expression only magnified the urge to be wicked. "All right."

He sat and pulled her onto his lap, keeping her legs sideways. He caressed her spine, his hand drifting to the edge of her skirts.

"David, no. I didn't mean *that*. Someone might come and see us." Her face had gone crimson, and he fumbled with her skirts until he could reach beneath them.

"They won't see anything," he swore. "And if they do come, all they'll discover is a wife seated upon her husband's lap."

His words were like a match, flaring a pulse of need within her. Amelia was torn between curiosity and horror that he would indeed make love to her in the garden. Her fears came to fruition when his hand reached beneath her skirts, rearranging them over his lap. He found the seam of her intimate opening, brushing against her curls. She was shocked by the way her wanton flesh responded to his touch.

"David—"

"What?" He caressed her intimately, exploring her sensitive opening with his hands. She was taken aback by the way he was coaxing such a reaction. "It's no different than what you did to me in the coach that night, on our journey here." He invaded her with his fingers, and she suppressed a moan of pleasure. "You offered yourself to me on the day I destroyed the cottage. I'm simply going to accept your invitation now."

Her body was melting against his fingers, achingly wet as he found the nodule above her opening and began to rub it.

"You're being very wicked," she whispered, her hands digging into his trousers.

"But you love me anyway."

Yes. Yes, I do.

With her skirts covering his lap, no one could see what he was doing. They were utterly alone, and the thought of him taking her right here was shocking.

"Do you want me now, Amelia?" To underscore his words, he began entering and withdrawing from her with his fingers.

"Yes." She was drowning in sensation, lost with the way he was touching her. She leaned down to kiss him hard, trying to arouse the same feelings in him.

She did love this man, no matter that he'd isolated himself in the past. At this moment, he was giving her his undivided attention, and she could hardly bear it.

He shifted his hand a moment, and at first, she didn't know what he was doing. Then she realized he'd unbuttoned his trousers and had freed his erection. Against her wet flesh, she felt the hard length of his shaft.

"W—we shouldn't," she breathed. "Anyone could come and see us." But she pressed against the arms of the chair, lifting slightly until he could fit himself inside her. The moment he was buried within, she felt another surge of need.

A shattered breath caught her, and she couldn't resist the urge to squeeze his length. Not only did he pull her hips tightly to him, but he murmured in her ear, "God, I love it when you do that."

He urged her to lift up and sit on him again. The sensation was breathtaking in a position she'd never tried before. Though it took her a moment to find the rhythm, she grasped his shoulders and pressed herself against him.

"I don't think a fairy-tale husband would do this," she said, arching as he began to pump inside her.

"The villain might," he countered with a strong thrust. Her body convulsed against him, and she squeezed him again. "If he's ravishing the woman he wants."

"This is too dangerous," she warned, trying to hold back the storm of desire building. Being here with him, in this garden where anyone could happen upon them, only heightened every sensation. She could feel the thick hardness of him as he entered and withdrew.

"You'd better ride me fast, then," he told her. "Before we're found."

He gripped her waist, urging her to find the right pace, and Amelia sighed while he filled her. The intimacy of being joined with the man she loved evoked an emotion so strong, her eyes stung.

She was losing control, unable to grasp any more thoughts. He kissed her roughly, thrusting against her as she accepted his body into her own. It was fast and hard, a reckless lovemaking that she'd never expected her quiet husband to initiate. Her breathing was coming faster, and his hands suddenly were everywhere. Not only at her hips, but he filled his palms with her breasts, fingering the nipples beneath the muslin. Her chemise was made of a flimsy lace, and she could feel his touch burning her like a brand.

He jerked against her, and in time, her body slipped over the edge in a violent rush. He kissed her to silence the broken cry, and continued lifting her up and down until she provoked his own release.

It was a swift pleasure, one that made her want to go back to the house and do it all over again. Her hair was tangled around her shoulders, her body utterly sated.

"You were right. Someone's coming after all." David buttoned his trousers again and moved her off his lap.

Amelia's knees buckled as she held the chair for balance. "I can't believe what we just did. I never dreamed that a man and a woman would ever risk that."

He stood up, kissing her again and pulling her to his side. "I would risk it with you."

She leaned back, taking his face between her hands. "Do you promise?"

He nodded. Then abruptly his expression shifted as he shoved her down, and the deafening sound of a gunshot interrupted their reverie.

Amelia screamed when she saw a bloodstain widening across David's shirt.

Chapter Sixteen

Fire blazed through his shoulder with an unholy pain. But the moment of agony was overcome by the need to protect his wife. David ignored the wound and moved through the shrubbery until he could see where the gunman was. A man was retreating on horseback, and he could hear the shouting of servants. He tried to make out the assailant's features, but the man was already riding hard through the hills.

Two of his footmen spied him, but David ordered, "Go!" It took only moments for them to seize horses and pursue the man.

Then he turned back to Amelia, who had come up behind him. The bullet wound was so intense, he could hardly breathe. Yet his greater concern was his wife.

"You're bleeding," she whispered in horror. "David, you're covered in blood."

"It's only my shoulder," he admitted, shrugging it off. He didn't know what instinct had made him react. The moment he'd seen the glint of the pistol, he'd thrown himself in front of her, shoving her down.

It didn't matter that he'd been wounded on her behalf. He'd have done it again without question.

"Who did this to you?" she demanded. Then she paled, as if she'd come to the same conclusion he'd realized. Slowly, she reached to touch his bleeding shoulder. "That bullet was meant for me. He shot . . . where I was standing."

David nodded in silent agreement. He didn't know who would ever threaten Amelia, but she was already walking with him back to the house.

"We need Dr. Fraser," Amelia continued. "He'll know how to fix your shoulder." She pressed a handkerchief against the blood, trying to stanch the flow.

"Don't press too hard against it," he warned, grimacing at the pain.

She softened the pressure, and when her worried green eyes met his, she said, "You saved my life."

Despite the fiery ache, he leaned in and kissed her. "I would do it again."

She sent one of the footmen to fetch Dr. Fraser, and it took only moments for him to appear with his wife. Lady Falsham was holding Grace, and the moment Juliette saw David's wound, she handed her daughter to Mrs. Menford. The older housekeeper was startled, but her face softened when she took the young girl.

Amelia started to explain what happened while Dr. Fraser examined David's shoulder. Thankfully, the bullet had gone through, but her husband bit his lip to fight against the pain.

"Who did this to you, Hartford?" the doctor asked.

"I didn't see him clearly. He was older, though, closer to the age of Amelia's father."

They walked back inside the house, and Juliette gave orders for water and bandages. While he wiped the blood away, Fraser kept his voice low. "And you think he was aiming at Amelia?"

"I know he was." He hissed when the doctor blotted the wound again.

"David shoved me away," Amelia admitted. Her hand moved to her throat, and she looked toward her sister. "Could it have been Lord Strathland?"

David had heard stories of the earl who had caused untold problems for Amelia's family. The man had been locked away in a lunatic asylum, but he hardly cared whether or not it was the earl. Regardless of who had tried to shoot his wife, he wouldn't stop until the man was found. He would let no one threaten the woman he loved.

Juliette's gaze moved toward her husband. The fury on the doctor's face spoke of a man who was contemplating murder. "He's the only person with a reason to kill any of us."

Amelia came to stand beside David. "If Lord Strathland *did* come here, his first target would have been Dr. Fraser. Not me." She linked hands with her sister to offer silent support.

"I sent men in pursuit," David told them. "When they return, we'll know who it was."

And he would hunt the man down and bring his own retribution upon him. Suffering wasn't enough—he'd rather see the assailant buried.

"I've no wish to wait that long," the doctor countered. "Have you a fast horse I could borrow?"

He did, but Juliette was already shaking her head. "No. You can't go after Strathland, if it was him." She took her husband's hands in hers. "Paul, it's what he wants. And then he'll come after me and after Grace." Her eyes filled up with unshed tears. "You can't leave us."

"It doesn't make sense," Amelia ventured. "If he came here to kill any of us, why would he come after me? And why would he leave so soon afterwards?"

"He was nearly caught," David responded. "And because he has another target to attack." The answer crystallized in his mind, and he had no doubt what the man intended. "If it was Strathland, then he'll pursue your parents. He won't go swiftly, because he knows you'll follow him. And then he'll have all of you."

Dr. Fraser nodded. "You're right." He finished bandaging the wound and ordered, "You're going to be wanting something tae help you sleep tonight." He withdrew a small vial from his leather bag and said, "Take a few drops in a cup of tea, and it will ease the pain."

"My lord," a footman interrupted, "Forgive me, but this young woman insisted upon seeing you."

It was Sarah Carlisle, the Earl of Strathland's sister. The moment she appeared, the room fell deathly quiet. For there was no longer any doubt that Strathland was behind the attack.

"I'm so terribly sorry, Lord Castledon." Her face burned bright red, and she confessed, "M-my brother was released from the asylum a few weeks ago. But he's . . . still very ill. He's not thinking clearly and never should have been let out."

Her hands were shaking, and she said, "He came here with the intent of killing Dr. Fraser and Lady Castledon, Juliette's sister. H-he wanted Juliette to see them suffer."

"Do you think he's gone northwest, toward Ballaloch?"

She nodded. "Please, my lord. Someone has to stop him. He doesn't care what happens to him. Vengeance is all that matters."

The doctor met David's gaze. "I'm taking your fastest horse and any men who are wanting to come with me."

"No," Juliette insisted. "Don't, Paul."

"Then you want me to hide here while the man goes tae kill your father and mother?" The doctor underscored his harsh words by stroking his wife's cheek. "I don't think you do, *a chridhe*."

Juliette was openly crying now, holding tight to her husband. "I don't like this."

"My brother won't stop," Lady Sarah admitted. "He *is* mad, and if you don't find him, I fear the worst." Her face colored, and she stared at Amelia. "I had to warn you."

Amelia nodded and laced her fingers with David's. There seemed to be an unspoken agreement between them that he didn't understand. But then his wife ordered, "Send whatever men you want to help Dr. Fraser. Juliette will stay with us. *She* is who the earl truly wants. We'll keep her safe here, along with Grace."

David didn't like the idea of staying behind, but he recognized the need to protect the women. He stared at Fraser, who nodded. "So be it."

The doctor reached for his coat and added, "This time, I'm going to finish it, Juliette. Strathland won't come back alive."

He'd missed the shot.

So close, and yet the bullet had caught the earl instead of Amelia Andrews.

With every mile that passed, Brandon was taunted by his failure. It infuriated him, for the pistol wasn't as accurate as he'd thought.

He'd had no time to reload before one of the servants had seen him. There had been only seconds to get away, for if he'd been caught then, he could not have killed the rest of them.

Brandon kicked his horse's flanks and urged the animal faster. He hardly cared about those who would pursue him. Instead of feeling fear, it only heightened his excitement. It was the thrill of a very different chase. One that would end in the way *he* wanted it to.

He rode west until he located the coach that had brought him this far. Richardson was waiting, along with his driver.

Brandon pulled his horse to a stop and stripped off his coat. "Give me your coat," he ordered. "Put on mine."

Richardson appeared confused at the command. "My lord, why?"

"Just do it."

He handed over his coat and accepted the one Brandon gave him. Before the man could ask another question, Brandon shot him in the chest.

Richardson dropped to his knees beside the horse and died within seconds. He'd never had time to take a second breath. Feeling satisfied, Brandon reloaded his pistol.

His pursuers would be searching for a man on horseback, wearing a green coat. They would not guess that he was in a coach. The driver was staring at him with wide eyes, as if he couldn't believe the murder he'd just witnessed.

"I would suggest that you drive me to Ballaloch, as fast as the horses can manage it," Brandon said, climbing inside the coach. "Your life depends on it."

Within minutes, they were continuing on the road, as fast as possible. Undoubtedly, Lord Castledon's men would track him down soon enough, but in the meantime, Richardson's body would delay their progress. A few hours were all he needed.

His sister's escape would pose a problem, but he hoped that his pursuers hadn't had time to speak with Sarah. If they'd struck off immediately, they wouldn't have seen her.

Inside the confines of the coach, he blinked as his head began to hurt again. He fought against the haze that threatened his clarity. His purpose was clear, and he had the weapons he needed to accomplish this task.

He closed his eyes, imagining their screams.

�֎

Days passed, slipping into nights, until Brandon lost track of his bearings. He knew they were in Scotland, but he could not say how far away they were from Ballaloch.

Darkness surrounded him, but on this night, he found it difficult to sleep. He sensed that someone had caught up to him. Although he'd stopped once or twice, it had been for only an hour or two. He hardly cared that his coachman hadn't slept. The man would sleep for an eternity once they arrived.

Abruptly, the coach stopped for no reason. Brandon pounded against the ceiling of the coach, demanding to know why. The silence was ghostly, making him reach for a loaded pistol. Every part of him was alert, waiting for the moment the door would fly open.

Minutes crept onward, and his blood ran cold, waiting. At long last, he could bear it no longer. He opened the door of the coach, staring into the darkness that was only illuminated by the dim lantern light.

He never saw anyone. The night closed over him, making his pulse quicken. His driver lay prone upon the seat, his neck twisted at an unnatural angle.

Brandon kept the pistol pointed forward, waiting for his enemy to emerge from the shadows.

He never saw the face of the man who pulled the trigger, nor did he feel anything more after the bullet entered his brain.

✖

FOUR DAYS LATER

Amelia stood at the window, watching as Sarah Carlisle stood before the coach. Her brother's body had been found in Scotland,

and an investigation of the murder had begun. Thankfully, Dr. Fraser was not a suspect, since Strathland's body had been found before he'd reached the man.

Outside, rain splattered against the cobblestones, but Sarah didn't hurry to leave. She looked desolate and lost, but she risked a glance above, as if she could see Amelia watching.

In silent thanks, she raised a small bundle, which contained the jewels and banknotes Amelia had given her earlier, as part of the blackmail payment. Sarah had tried to return it to her yesterday, but Amelia knew that she would need it more than ever, now that her brother was dead.

David came up behind her and rested his hands on her shoulders. He said nothing, but offered the quiet comfort of his presence. Amelia watched as the coach drove away, feeling as if a burden had been lifted from her. The Earl of Strathland would never trouble her family again.

Turning back to her husband, she asked, "Are you in pain?"

David's shoulder had been bound up in linen after Dr. Fraser had treated the wound. Although it would heal, she worried about the danger of a fever.

"A little." His hands slid down to her waist, and he pressed a kiss against her throat.

"You should be in bed," Amelia reminded him. "You were shot."

"Good idea." He caught her hand, lacing his fingers with hers. "I'll let you take care of me."

She led him back to the bed, and he leaned back against the pillows. "Come and lie beside me so I'll feel better."

Amelia obeyed. For a moment, he lay on his uninjured side, watching her. She grew self-conscious under his gaze. "I'm so sorry this happened to you."

"I would take another bullet for you without question, Amelia." He reached out to touch her face. She heard the truth in his voice and saw the honesty in his eyes.

His palm moved down to join with hers. "And you can't leave me now, can you?"

"No," she whispered. "I won't leave you. I never really wanted to." She raised his hand to her lips, so thankful that he was alive. If anything had happened to David, she didn't know how she could go on.

She understood, now, why he had grieved for his first wife for so long. It would be like ripping her spirit in half.

"And you won't leave me, either, unless you take me along," she insisted.

David threaded one hand in her hair. "I love you, Amelia." The warmth in his voice washed over her, pressing back her fear of losing him. "And even if I'm not the kind of husband you imagined marrying, that will always be true."

She leaned in and touched her mouth to his. "It's true, that you aren't the man I dreamed of." With a smile, she added, "You're so much more."

Epilogue

H old your shoulders back," Amelia instructed Christine. "Curtsy and hold up your hand as we go in a circle."

David stood back, watching his wife and daughter dance together. Christine was wearing a gown that he didn't entirely approve of. While Amelia reassured him that lilac was perfectly acceptable for her to wear, it struck him to see his little girl growing up. It felt as if a dozen more years had slipped away in a single moment.

"When can we go to London, Amelia? Next spring?" Christine's voice held the excitement of a girl eager for her first Season.

"Yes, we will." His wife shot her an amused look. "You must endure the hardships I endured when I had to watch my sisters while they danced and enjoyed themselves. I was escorted away, just as all the fun was beginning."

David couldn't help but smile. "Or you could wait a few more years, Christine. There's no harm in that."

"Margaret would agree with you on that point." Amelia said At the mention of her sister, David didn't miss the relieved look in her eyes. The young woman had returned unharmed, and all of them were grateful for it.

"I had to learn proper manners at a young age," Amelia continued. "Our mother taught us how to walk, how to behave, and how to dance. Just as Christine will learn what she needs to know, to manage an earl of her own."

He reached to take her by the waist, and Amelia tapped him lightly with her fan. "If a rogue tries to accost you, Christine, be sure to strike him with your fan."

He leaned in to her ear. "You like it when I accost you."

"Sometimes." She beamed up at him, and he took her through the steps of the country dance she'd been trying to teach their daughter.

"I've received some news," he said, turning serious. "Cain Sinclair's younger brother was arrested for the murder of Lord Strathland."

Amelia paled. "He's just a boy. I can't believe he could have done such a thing."

"He didn't, so Sinclair claims. Margaret and he are trying to find who really did kill the earl." He spun her in a circle before taking her hand to walk forward.

"I'm glad Strathland is dead," Amelia admitted. "And I'm thankful that your wound is nearly healed."

He leaned in again. "You only say that because you want to accost me later."

"You're right." Amelia stole a swift kiss, and he ended the dance. To his daughter, he signaled for her to go and bring the gift he'd arranged earlier.

"I have something for you," he said. "It's for your birthday."

"But my birthday isn't until December," Amelia teased.

He knew when her birthday was, but he'd invented a reason to give it. "Then it's a very early birthday present."

Amelia rose up on tiptoe to whisper into his ear. "Is it from Aphrodite's Unmentionables? A gift that both of us will enjoy?"

His wife had been more than enthusiastic in bed, and there were times when her inventiveness astounded him. "No, it's not that. But perhaps I'll buy you unmentionables later." He sent her a dark smile, and Christine brought over the paper-wrapped package. "Here it is."

Amelia took the gift and remarked, "It's very light." She opened it and revealed a set of three embroidered handkerchiefs.

"How boring," Christine said, rolling her eyes. "Papa, you should have bought her diamonds. When I have a beau of my own, he ought to know that a girl wants beautiful jewelry that sparkles."

But Amelia's face had softened at the sight of the handkerchiefs, as he'd hoped. She unfolded one and saw their initials embroidered together on each. Then she threw herself into his arms. "I love you, David. And I never should have said you had the personality of a handkerchief before I had the chance to know you."

He breathed in the scent of her hair, so grateful that she'd come to be a part of his life. "Do you like them?"

She pulled back from the embrace, and in her green eyes, he saw love. "Handkerchiefs are something I can't live without. And I never want to." She kissed him deeply, while he overheard his daughter muttering about how his gift made no sense at all.

David ignored her, and as he continued to kiss his wife, he imagined what Katherine would say if she could see the way his life had transformed. He could only believe that she would be happy for him, though Amelia could not be more different. He would never forget Katherine, but the pain of losing her had faded. Perhaps she had sent Amelia to him, knowing that she was the light he needed to overcome the darkness.

"I hope you never have to use these for grief," he said, touching a handkerchief. "Both of us have had enough sadness to endure."

"They would only be for tears of joy," she said, squeezing his hand. "I promise you that." Then she held his palm and walked with him in a circle, as if they were dancing.

He reached down and lifted her into his arms. Amelia let out a shriek of laughter but held on tightly. "David, that isn't part of the country dance."

"It isn't?" He nuzzled her neck, thankful that Christine had already left them alone.

"No." But her laughter stilled while she wrapped her arms around his neck. "But I don't mind."

"I thought you wanted a man who was delicious and dangerous," he reminded her.

"Not anymore." Her eyes softened with love. "All I want is you."

LONDON, 1815

Her sister had gone missing.

Most older sisters would have left such a terrible problem in the hands of their parents. Or possibly alerted the authorities. Margaret Andrews did neither.

For one, she knew exactly who had kidnapped Amelia. Second, she knew that the blackguard intended to force her sister to wed him. And third, Margaret had suffered untold humiliation when that same awful man had abandoned her on their wedding day three years ago. Lord Lisford might have shattered her girlish dreams, humiliating her in the face of society, but Margaret would never let the same thing happen to her baby sister. This was more than a dangerous situation—this was her opportunity for vengeance.

It didn't matter that it was the middle of the night or that she was the daughter of a baron. The man who had wronged her was about to destroy Amelia's life, and Margaret was *not* about to stand aside and let it happen. She'd beg the devil himself, if she thought he could help her.

Cain Sinclair was the next-best thing.

A flutter of nerves caught her stomach as her coach pulled to a stop in front of the inn where he was staying. It was nearly midnight, and she'd left Lady Rumford's ball the moment she'd heard about Amelia's disappearance. She still wore the sage green silk gown with white gloves, for she'd not taken the time to change.

This was a very bad idea. What was she thinking, venturing into a public inn while wearing a ball gown?

But it couldn't be helped. *Please let him be there*, she prayed. The Highlander was a man she'd known for nine years. From the moment she'd laid eyes on him, she'd known that he was the sort of man her mother had warned her about.

Taller than most men, he had broad shoulders and lean muscles. His piercing blue eyes and black hair gave him the look of a fallen angel. He wasn't a gentleman, and he didn't care what anyone thought of him.

Ruthless was the best word to describe him. And when he wanted something, he never stopped until he got it.

Unfortunately, what he wanted was *her*.

She took a deep breath and stepped out of the coach. Her footman eyed the inn and shook his head. "Miss Andrews, I think you should wait inside the carriage. I'll go and find Mr. Sinclair on your behalf."

That was the sensible thing to do. It was what her mother would want. But she knew, without a single doubt, that Sinclair would ignore the footman and do whatever he wanted to.

With every moment she sat in this coach, Lord Lisford was taking her sister farther north, toward Scotland. Time was critical, and what did she care if it was not an establishment a lady would dare to enter? She was already ruined. After five Seasons, Margaret knew what the ton thought of her. They believed she was to blame for the viscount abandoning her on her wedding day.

Instead, she ignored her servant and marched straight toward the door. The haze of tobacco cloaked the room, while the scent of ale filled the space. Men were playing cards in one corner, while others busied themselves with getting drunk as soon as possible.

She stared at each of the men until at last she saw Sinclair. He didn't move, but his mouth tightened when she stepped closer. Her presence was as out of place as a pig in a ballroom, and every male eye fastened upon her.

Her conscience was already screeching at the idea. *Get out of here! Ladies do not associate with men in a public inn. You cannot be here.*

"You don't belong here, lass," Sinclair said. His icy-blue eyes regarded her as if she'd lost her mind. And perhaps she had, since she'd gone to such lengths to seek his help.

"Amelia's been taken. You have to help me find her." Margaret crossed her arms, staring coolly at a drunkard whose attention was fixed upon her bosom.

How did you think these men would react to your presence? her conscience chided. *They're nothing but rogues and vagrants. Any one of them would attack you, and then where would you be?*

Sinclair leaned back in his chair, his long black hair falling past his shoulders. He wore a brown-and-green tartan, and his white shirtsleeves were rolled against his forearms. A faint scar edged his lower arm, a reminder that he'd been in many fights. Somehow, it made her feel somewhat safer, knowing that the Highlander could protect her far better than the elderly footman who had accompanied her.

"Come with me, and I'll tell you more about what happened," Margaret urged. The sooner she left this place, the better she would feel. The question was whether or not he would help her.

"Do your parents know?" he asked softly.

She shrugged. "I didn't tell them. I want to find Amelia before any harm is done."

They would find out soon enough. But more than that, she felt a sense of responsibility. *She* was supposed to chaperone Amelia at the ball. If she'd remained at her sister's side at every moment, this wouldn't have happened.

Her guilt was a hair shirt against her conscience. This was her fault, without question. And she had to atone for it, no matter the cost to her own reputation.

Sinclair took a slow drink of his ale, studying her. She couldn't guess what he was thinking, but he needed to hurry up.

"Why did you come to me, lass, instead of a constable?" His lazy tone held a hint of wickedness, and she faltered.

"Because I—"

Because I know you'll find her. I know you won't let any harm come to her, and I trust you more than any man.

She drew closer and reached for his hand. It felt as if she'd thrown out every shred of decent behavior. A wildness thrummed in her blood as her fingers laced in his.

"Because I need your help," she whispered.

His thumb brushed the edge of her palm in a silent caress that echoed deep inside. His rough hands were callused, but his touch was light enough to set her senses on fire. What did that say about her, that she would be so attracted to a man so inappropriate?

She was a good girl. She obeyed the rules, listened to her parents, and never wore a gown with a daring neckline. All her life, she'd been a model of proper behavior.

And yet, right now, she realized that she was asking this man to come with her. To be alone with her in a carriage for hours on end.

Don't do this, her sense of propriety begged. *You cannot behave in this way. It's not right.*

But she met his gaze steadily and said, "Please."

Author's Note

The mysterious illness that plagues Christine Hartford in *Undressed by the Earl* is a rare illness that we now know by the name Guillain-Barré syndrome. It was not documented until 1859 by Jean Landry, but it certainly mystified many physicians prior to that.

In most cases, it follows a respiratory or digestive ailment. Nerve endings are attacked by the immune system, causing paralysis that slowly spreads throughout the body. It can reverse itself as long as it does not progress to the lungs, which can be fatal.

There still is no cure for this syndrome, but in modern medicine, blood plasma exchange and high doses of immunoglobulin can speed recovery. Dr. Paul Fraser's decision to exercise her limbs was an effort to encourage blood flow and to prevent muscle atrophy.

Special thanks to Dr. Deena Obrokta for her story suggestion.

About the Author

2010 RITA® finalist and bestselling Kindle author Michelle Willingham has written over twenty books and novellas, set in medieval Ireland, Scotland, and Victorian England. Her books have been translated into languages around the world and have been released in audiobook format. She has consistently received four-star reviews from *Romantic Times* magazine, and *Publisher's Weekly* called her stories "A truly emotional read." She has also been nominated for the Booksellers' Best Awards, and she won an Award of Merit from Virginia Romance Writers for historical romance.

She lives in southeastern Virginia with her husband and three children. Her hobbies include baking, reading, and avoiding exercise at all costs. Visit her website at: www.michellewillingham.com for more details.